1

STIR IT UP

The CIA Targets Jamaica, Bob Marley And the Progressive Manley Government

A novel

David Dusty Cupples

www.facebook.com/StirItUpCIAJamaica

Also available as a Kindle ebook on Amazon.com

ACKNOWLEDGMENTS

The author wishes to express his appreciation to all persons who helped further this book toward completion, including those who read and commented either on part of the manuscript—Bruce Bromage, Don Cachat, Bob Carson, Lenny Hall, Eric Pica and Sarah Mosko—or the entire draft— Pat and Court Holdgrafer, Susan and Tom Hopton (my biggest boosters), and Saul Landau. Thanks also to Sam Newman, Neville Garrick, Arnold Bertram, Louis Marriott at the Michael Manley Foundation in Kingston, Prof. Mike Witter at the University of West Indies, the folks at Jamaica House and the archives section at the *Daily Gleaner*, and Tony (rest his soul) and everyone at the wonderful Bob Marley Museum at 56 Hope Road, all who extended invaluable help during the research phase. I am grateful for Sarah Manley's kind assistance with logistics in Kingston and to Beverley Manley for opening her home for a personal interview. I am indebted also to Prof. Noam Chomsky for his patient counsel on several factual matters. Very special thanks to Roger Steffens, who corrected early drafts and was a font of knowledge about reggae and Bob Marley, and to Jim Marshall for his excellent editorial suggestions and tutoring on Rastafari. Lastly, a tip of the hat to James Brooks for designing and creating an outstanding cover for the book. (jlbrooks(at)dslextreme.com -- jaybrooks.carbonmade.com)

This work of fiction is set against a backdrop of true events. Most characters, like Scott Gallagher, are fictional, though his father Matt is (very) loosely inspired by an actual person. Though efforts were made to adhere as much as possible to the historical record, events didn't necessarily happen exactly as portrayed. But they might have. For questions and notes on historicity, see the author's website or Facebook page.

Jamaican Reggae, circa 1976

Tribal War.........................Little Roy
Tribal War.........................Trinity
No Tribal War....................The Prophets
Tribal War Dub...................Yabby You
War Ina Babylon.................Max Romeo (& Upsetters)
War................................Bob Marley (& Wailers)

"I played with Bob Marley. That much I do
remember, like it was yesterday. On the porch
at the House of Dread. It was great hanging
with the guys, strummin' and singin', smoking
herb. After that it gets vague, flashes and shadows,
my life flushed down the memory hole. Waking in
a cold sweat to these weird dreams."

--Scott Gallagher, to Doc M

1

BLOOD WAS WET on his lips and soaked into his T-shirt as he came to. Faces peered down at him with expressions of concern. Had he fallen? He'd been running, he remembered that much.

"Are you all right?" asked the young woman.

He stared up into the sun at the haloed figures floating above like fretting angels. Blood was streaming down his front and there was a helluva pain radiating from his lip to the back of his skull. It seemed he wasn't all right. He'd been at home on a perfectly ordinary Sunday morning listening to reggae on the radio and here he was lying on the ground gushing like a stuck pig and... oh God.

Had he been shot? He coughed and panted in growing panic. Shot in the mouth! It must have been at a glancing angle, otherwise he'd surely be dead. Or *dying*, and how did he know he wasn't? The image of an M14 rifle flashed into mind—and how did he know it was an M14? He didn't know anything about guns.

The young woman kneeled and held his hand.

"Everything is going to be all right," she said in a Spanish accent. "The ambulance is coming now."

Ambulance? "Am I going to die?" he said, peering into her gentle eyes.

"No, you are not going to die," she smiled. "You were jogging and you fell, that's all. Everything will be all right."

Inside the ambulance he wrestled back his fear. People didn't usually get shot jogging at City College. There seemed no injury beyond his torn lip. He must have fallen on his face as the young woman had claimed. He'd been at home listening to tunes and everything had been fine. Then he'd gone out for a run and now everything wasn't fine. As he nervously glanced about this sterile coffin on wheels an overwhelming sense of dread welled up, and fear struck back. As the ambulance arrived at Cottage Hospital he threw a fit for the medical books, kicking, punching, screaming like a madman until he was subdued and sedated.

Aunt Sylvia was by his side when he roused from his drugged stupor. She paid the bill, picked up the meds and drove him home in her red Rabbit with the *RE-ELECT JIMMY CARTER* bumper sticker. Ronald Reagan frightened her to death, she often said. She feared the worst about the upcoming elections.

6

"What happened in the hospital?" Aunt Sylvia asked, the Rabbit's top down and wind ruffling her hair. "What got you so upset?"

He shrugged and the face of his father flashed into mind.

"I wish you'd come stay with me," Sylvia said, at 45 an aging hippie, an Earth Mother type and successful potter who grew her own vegetables and filled her windowsills with plant clippings. The changing times cast a dark shadow over her gentle soul, the love and consciousness of the '60s giving way to the "Me Generation" '70s—and what would the '80s bring? Communists in power in Vietnam, Sandinistas in Nicaragua, the economy in the tank and Americans held hostage at this very moment by Islamic radicals in Iran, only months ago a rock-solid ally under the Shah, now deposed. What havoc would Reagan wreak in such a world?

"Let me take care of you a few days," she said, glad that Scott hadn't hurt anybody or damaged any equipment in his rampage at the hospital.

"I'm fine." He winced. He'd taken seven stitches in his lip from the fall on the athletic field. He hoped the blood would come out of his Bob Marley T-shirt.

"I can cook for you," Aunt Sylvia said. "Miss having you around. We used to have a lot of fun together. You're like a son to me, Scotty."

"Mmmhh."

"Hurts like a bugger doesn't it. Don't talk if it hurts. Just listen to me. Take your medicine if you need it. If your marijuana doesn't do the trick it's okay to take drugs a while. I know you try to live healthy and don't believe in drugs, although technically grass is a drug, and I support you one hundred per cent in that, but you don't have to suffer needlessly when the doctor says it's okay."

"Unnnh."

Navigating quick lefts and rights through the shoddy Westside neighborhood beneath the low mesa leading to City College, she turned into a driveway and rolled back to the rear dwelling, a cheap free-standing, two-bedroom unit with yard. As they got out of the car Aunt Sylvia took her nephew's arm.

"Scotty," she said, the crow's-feet at the corner of her eyes wrinkling, "I want you to talk to someone. Shhh, listen now. The doctors couldn't find anything wrong. They thought it'd be good for you to talk to someone." She'd thought that herself for some time and was glad for this opportunity to get him in for help.

"Everybody needs to talk to someone sometime," she said, noting his obstinate expression. "Didn't Dean Martin say that?"

Scott smirked at the attempt at humor and immediately grimaced in pain.

"Ow, ow," Aunt Sylvia cringed in sympathy, "hurts even to smile doesn't it, poor boy. I'll take care of everything. Uh uh, not another word. If I can't help my favorite nephew what's the point of even being here? I'll call you and let you know, okay? It's settled."

"Wan' come in... smoke spliff?"

"Thanks but I'm going home and having a nervous breakdown about Reagan getting in. God I hope Jimmy wins." Aunt Sylvia kissed his cheek and took off. Scott went inside and put on the latest Bob Marley LP and fired up a spliff. He sat on the threadbare couch and examined the medicine in the little white paper bag. Vicodin. Forget that. Marijuana grew naturally in the earth untainted by men in white coats. *The healing of the nation.* Even the act of smoking hurt, but he puffed away as the events of the last hours floated through his mind in clouds of confusion. He'd been running as he often did, on the beach or at the college, but there'd been something different this time, a desperate blind urgency churning his legs faster and faster until he'd collapsed trembling, convulsing, foaming at the mouth, consumed in angst. Then the chaos of craziness at the hospital. What could have precipitated all this?

He went now to the bedroom and from the top dresser drawer found nestled beneath the clean underwear a photograph of a young woman. Holding it to the lamp, he drank in the vision of loveliness in black and white.

"Marva," he whispered her name, "what happened to us? Why can't I remember? God I miss you."

But that was four years ago during the Lost Time and here the events of just that morning had flown him as well.

Deep in the silence of night he woke with a start, images flashing through his mind. In the darkness of the cramped bedroom it was as if he could see the floating phantoms projected on the ceiling above his bed:

A machete chopping down hard. A stooped-over little black man with a lion-headed walking stick. Black birds suddenly taking flight. White lilies along a fence. The M14, holding it in his hands and squeezing off a burst.

There came just then an otherworldly shriek that sent a chill down his back. Sweat beaded on his brow as he lay deathly still and waited for the whining to stop, but it did not cease. Again and again it came, demonic and haunting. *It's just a cat,* he told himself, but an ordinary tabby could not inspire such fear. Then, as if some force or entity occupied his body, he got up, went to the kitchen pantry and took the five-pound bag of organic brown rice from the cupboard. Walking room to room, he spread grains on the floor like a farmer casting seed, having not the slightest idea why.

8

Two weeks later -- October 5, 1980, Santa Barbara

Running late, he pedaled the Schwinn Cruiser hard across State Street to the Eastside. A rumpled white fleece of cloud hugged San Marcos Pass at the top of the low mountains beyond town but there was little chance of rain in this trade wind West Coast wonderland. Twenty years old and seeing a shrink. The indignity of it. He pictured a stuffy old fart sucking on a pipe and waxing wise, stroking his beard. Would he make him lie down on his couch and dice his mind into little pieces? What demons would be found there among the debris, and could a dissected psyche ever be put back together again?

At Anapamu he jogged right and left again onto Canon Perdido.

At the Santa Barbara Psychiatric and Psychological Services (aka "the Suites at Canon Perdido") Phil Mitchell set his cigarette on the abalone ashtray and went on a bathroom break before his new patient arrived. Out in the corridor he ran into his colleague Stan White, a psychiatrist out of Berkeley and at 56 a walking billboard of physical and psychological health. The man was Jack LaLanne, Dale Carnegie and Norman Vincent Peale all rolled into one, spiced with a dash of Gypsy Boots. Everything *he* wasn't.

"Hi, Mitch," greeted White, his tie-dye Tee and pony tail testimony to his bristling individuality. He didn't dress to impress, or need to. When patients looked in his eyes they saw the real deal.

"Gang's going up to Cold Spring Tavern Friday night. Old stagecoach station up by Red Rock, know the place? Guy up there wails on sax like it was Springsteen and the E Street Band. Couple single gals coming along. Could be just what the doctor ordered."

"Ah, I don't know, Stan." Mitchell wore white bell bottoms and a broad-collared paisley shirt, his hair below his ears. The '70s were over but seems he'd missed the memo.

"Life goes on, friend," White said kindly.

"Life," Phil sighed deeply. "It seems such a farce sometimes. A sadistic joke the fates play on us mortals. Even these patients of ours... do we ever really help any of these poor bastards?"

"Buck up, man," White slapped Phil's shoulder. "Trust your gut. Healing comes from down here," White touching his stomach, "not here," now tapping his head.

"And with those words of wisdom I better go," Mitchell said. "New patient."

"There you go. Another opportunity to touch a life."

Mitchell inwardly cringed. He'd once been driven with the same incorrigible enthusiasm about helping people. A young psychologist fresh out of UCLA, newly-attained Ph. D. in hand, he too had been eager to join the ancient society of soothsayers and shamans that worked the art—not quite science—of healing the human soul. Now the magic was gone and for the life of him he didn't know how to get it back. He took a Valium with a sip of coffee, just to take the edge off. What did patients see when they looked in his eyes?

Back at his desk, he glanced over his notes on his new "opportunity." Scott Gallagher's aunt, an old acquaintance, had called out of the blue asking if Phil wouldn't mind seeing him. He had recently collapsed while jogging but a thorough examination at Cottage Hospital revealed no underlying organic etiology—no anemia, diabetes, epilepsy or a hundred other things that might have been the cause. Sylvia said the doctors didn't have a clue why a healthy young kid twenty years old would suddenly fall on his face exercising on a beautiful sunny day. They suspected he'd blacked out before he fell—had he simply tripped, he seemingly should have been able to break his fall with his arms, which clearly he had not done, judging by the injury to his lip. It conceivably might have been a matter of stress, a sudden strong emotion producing a vasovagal fainting response. The acting-out episode at the hospital, though, hinted at deeper issues.

Sylvia further offered that Scott was very bright and sensitive, a good decent lad, but that his mother had died of cancer (uterine) when he was young and there had been a falling out with his father a few years back, evidently while they were in Jamaica. The father had called long distance asking her to keep the boy and days later Scott had showed up, alone, and nothing had been heard from his father since. It would have been late 1976, December, she thought. Scott had been quiet and withdrawn for a time but there hadn't been any further problems as far as she knew. He'd lived with her in her Goleta home while he completed his junior and senior years in high school and the two years since then he'd been on his own. He never talked about his father or what happened in Jamaica, even when asked, Sylvia said. "Scotty" was "a sweet, wonderful kid" and she hoped very much that Phil could help him.

Mitchell set down the file and sighed. Would this new kid be the one to get him out of this insidious rut and back in the groove like Stan White? He pushed back in his big leather chair, cradling his coffee mug in both hands, and took a sip.

Scott found the Canon Perdido address and rode into the rear lot ten minutes past the appointed hour of ten. The Suites occupied an adobe-style bungalow with red-tile roof in keeping with Santa Barbara's Old Mexico ambience. The Spanish Mission, Fiesta Days, *enchiladas rancheros con arroz y frijoles* and brown-skin laborers picking up the yard. He chained his bike near a cerulean blue Porsche 911S and went inside. The secretary's eyes flared at the sight of this slender youth in jeans with the fuzzy tuft

10

under his chin and hair tucked up under a red, yellow and green tam like a bag of writing snakes atop his head. He liked that his appearance got people's attention.

"You must be Scott," Jasmine smiled. "Come with me."

She led him down the corridor to an office and knocked as Scott examined the nameplate on the door:

Philip Mitchell, Ph. D.
Clinical Psychologist

Mitchell quickly snuffed out his cigarette, fanned the air and set the abalone shell ashtray discretely on the floor beneath his desk.

"Come in," he said and Jasmine cracked the door.

"Scott Gallagher, doctor, your ten o'clock," she announced. "I believe Mr. Gallagher's aunt contacted you?"

"Yes yes, come in." Mitchell rose from his chair to receive his new patient. Scott removed the Rasta tam and shook out blond shoulder-length-and-longer dreadlocks as he strode in boldly, head high, shoulders back. It was the proud king-of-beasts strut of a lion, Rasta-walk, the way Bob Marley laid it down, though much practiced and affected.

"Sit down, please," Mitchell said, gesturing to two comfortable-looking overstuffed chairs in front of the desk. Scott sat in the closer of the two chairs and glanced about the room. There was a leather sofa, a bookcase heavy with volumes, and coffee paraphernalia on a utility table. Framed portraits adorned the wall behind him, across the desk from the doctor's point of reference. A Persian or Turkish rug covered much of the bare wooden floor. In the corner was a golf putter and in the air the smell of cigarettes and coffee. Over the doctor's shoulder a window opened to the back lot and beyond to the foothills of the Santa Barbara Riviera, the natural backlighting casting Mitchell in an otherworldly glow.

"What can I do for you today?" Dr. Mitchell said.

Scott said nothing, stroking the wispy whiskers he styled low on his chin—this too an affectation ala Bob Marley—and avoided the doctor's eyes.

"You were in the hospital recently, is that correct?" Mitchell tried again.

The kid sat in obstinate silence. The portraits on the wall must have been famous people, he thought, and maybe the rug was Navajo or something.

Mitchell yawned nervously. He was off his game and he knew it, living out of a bottle, drinking too much, not eating well. Staying up late watching old movies and waking in the morning with the TV going. Last night it had been *Tarzan and His Mate* with Johnny Weissmuller and

11

Maureen O'Sullivan and that was *after* the Tonight Show. He'd backed the video up numerous times to watch Jane's nude swimming scene over and over again. Karen had possessed that same lithe body and every ounce of Jane's spunk. Perhaps not her devotedness. He'd managed to polish off most of two bottles of Chianti. His world was shrinking, collapsing into itself like a black hole defined by the four walls of his living room and the steep-sided mental box of defeatism and melancholy in which he had become ensconced. Forty-three years old. Used to be a decent tennis player. Now his shoulders drooped pathetically and a cavalier round of golf was as much physical exertion as he could muster (nipping at the flask and trying not to dump the cart in the lake). Forty-three going on sixty-three. This was the downhill slope and he'd been tobogganing down it ever since Karen walked out sixteen months ago.

His patience tried, Mitchell reached for his cigarettes and lighter.

"Can't smoke in here," Scott spoke out. "Sign says." He nodded toward the *No Smoking* sign on the desk. "Or we could both smoke. Do you get high?"

"You do, I take it." Mitchell snapped his lighter shut.

"It isn't about *getting high*, exactly. Most of the world's religions have used psychoactive substances in their search for truth, did you know that?"

"Why were you in the hospital?"

"Took a tumble jogging. Mashed up my lip. No big deal."

"It looks sore. There was some trouble at the hospital?"

"Got a little frustrated. It's all right now."

"What were you frustrated at?"

"Nothing. Everything. I don't know." Scott's eyes darted out the window to the back lot. He sometimes thought someone was following him.

"You were jogging. Did you black out?"

"Nah. I don't know. I'm fine."

"Were you upset about something?"

Scott shrugged. There was something strange about the doctor's eyes, he thought, an oddness in the way he looked at him.

"I ran in the morning too," he said.

"You ran twice that day?"

"Yeah."

"How often does that happen?"

"Only time."

"A break in your pattern. That's significant. Did something happen to make you get out there again?"

"No."

"There must have been something."

"Fine. Why'd you ask?"

12

"Does this have anything to do with your father?"

"Dickhead," Scott's jaw clenching tight. "They said I tried to kill the prick. Came at him with a machete or something. Down on the Rock. Jamaica."

"You came at him with a machete and don't remember?"

"Hey, you're the shrink."

"Suppose your father walked in the room right this very instant."

Scott's eyes flashed to the stiletto-like letter opener on the desk. Doctor Mitchell's gaze followed his and Scott flushed with a sense of power. For an instant he felt an exquisitely grotesque urge to let it rip.

"I hear you like reggae," Mitchell changed course.

"Bob Marley rules!" Scott cried like a high school cheerleader, pulling back his denim overshirt to reveal a Marley tee, Bob with dreadlocks flying. "I sing in a band, you know."

"Mmm-hmmm." (A hint of condescension edging in.)

"What lights your fire, Doc?" Scott fired back. "Don't tell me. Wayne Newton. Olivia Newton-John."

"I like classic rock."

"Well now. Like what? What would be your favorite song?"

When I Was Young, know that one? Eric Burdon and the Animals."

"Mean something to you?"

"Just a song I like."

"Something from your childhood? You can tell me, Doc. We were all young once."

"Are you in touch with your father?" Mitchell sidestepped.

"Not a word in four years. Now you're wondering if he's dead for real."

"Tell me about Jamaica. You and your father spent time there, did you?"

"Let sleeping dogs lie, Doc. Trying to remember messes with my head. The last part is all a blur anyway. Lost Time."

"All the more reason to dig in."

"Got a bad feeling about this, man. Jamaica is a wild place. Eerie. *Eer-rie*. Mystical. Haunted. The Land of Look Behind. More medicinal plants than the Amazon. Juju. Ghosts. Out in the country it's darkest Africa. Sometimes feel like it was all a dream, like Alice through the looking glass, and there is no real place called Jamaica. Not on this planet anyway."

"You can sit here and waste my time if you want. But I'd prefer to work with someone who wants to learn about himself."

"Fuck," Scott sighed.

"Why don't you start at the beginning... when you arrived in Jamaica."

13

Scott shifted in his chair, tugged at his jeans, crossed and uncrossed his legs. Memories crashed and piled up like tree trunks in the swollen streams of consciousness. Were they real or phantoms? Much was clear and much more lost in fog. Especially the last part was shrouded in clouds, a hole in the fabric of his past. The Lost Time. A good portion would be beyond the pale to the uninitiated anyway, too incredible to take literally, like a Marquez novel. *Love in the Time of Ganja,* perhaps.

"We were coming from Argentina. The capital, Buenos Aires. Before that, Chile, Venezuela, Bolivia."

"You really get around," Dr. Mitchell said. "What does your father do?"

Scott stared like he didn't understand the question.

"Did your father work in Jamaica?"

"Uh, yeah, at the, uh, embassy."

"Something about this is disturbing to you?"

"No."

"What about your mother?"

Scott stared at his hands.

"Scott."

"Yeah."

"Your mother."

"She went away," he said.

"You mean she was--"

"—Rasta nah deal wi' dat, mon!" Scott cried, bursting to his feet as if infused with the wrath of God, his voice rough and full of fire. "Rasta deal wit' life, yuh hear? Yes I. Seen? Jah Rastafari, ever living."

Mitchell startled at the intensity of the outburst. He had maybe forty pounds on the kid but such explosive fury would be tough to manage even if he were in good shape. He could imagine what must have gone down at the hospital, the kicking and punching and all that.

Scott grinned apologetically and eased back down in his seat.

"You miss her," Dr. Mitchell said.

Then the most curious thing… patient's left hand came to the base of his throat and worked its way in discrete tell-tale hops down his front to about the level of his navel. Mitchell recognized it as an *automatism* performed without conscious awareness, hinting at unconscious emotions and conflicts.

"Did you see what you did?" Mitchell asked.

"I didn't do anything," Scott said in his normal voice.

' came down your shirt. Like mommy doing your

a break."

speaking in a strange voice."

14

"Patois isn't strange."

"You picked it up in Jamaica, I presume. When were you down there? Give me a time frame."

"Would have been early '76, late '75," Scott said, words coming easier now. "December '75. Dickhead and I were on the Rock, would've been about a year. I was sixteen years old then, wasn't wearing dreads yet. The Prick a Vietnam vet, two Purple Hearts, Silver Star, the whole shot... lost an eye over there. Macho man. Not the egalitarian type. Not the Martin Luther King Award winner for the year. Shit, we weren't even there yet— we were flying into Kingston, I remember it was just as we were coming in over Port Royal and the Harbour—and he's going on about how I should watch out for the evil black man. That kind of bullshit. Like all Jamaicans were shifty bastards out to settle the score for the four hundred years...."

The Jamaica that Scott and his father flew into in winter 1975-76 was a country struggling to find its way in a brave new world. Ninety miles south of Cuba between Hispaniola and the Mexican mainland in the Greater Antilles, Jamaica was barely 100 miles wide and 40 miles north to south, about the size of Connecticut, the third smallest state, and much of that hilly. It occupied a strategic position on the shipping and drug-smuggling lanes and was said to have the most churches per square mile in the world—nicely balanced by having the most rum bars too. Called Xaymaca "land of springs" or "land of wood and water" by the indigenous Arawak Indians, Jamaica was "discovered" by Columbus on his second voyage and brought under Spanish control by his son Diego Colon in 1509; Britain chased the Spaniards out in 1655 and held sway the next three hundred years. Columbus called the magical isle "the fairest land that eyes have beheld," lush with guava, cassava, cashew, cocoa, grapefruit. Coffee arrived from Ethiopia in 1728. Bananas and sugar cane were long the nation's economic lifeblood, backed up later by bauxite and tourism. Jamaica's magnificent white sand beaches along the north shore had seen the island exploited as a vacation destination for winter-weary Americans but the country's image as a tropical paradise belied a harsher truth. After centuries of colonial subjugation, independence from Mother England had come in 1962 but the hope and joy of that great day had not led to prosperity and a better life. If anything times were tougher now, bleaker, more brutal. Poverty, unemployment and the ghastly specter of ragged uneducated children with swollen malnourished bellies plagued the nation. People flooding to Kingston in hopes of better life found crowded slums and more ways to suffer. Gangs ruled the streets as the capital descended into tribal warfare. Violence was a way of life, the toughest ruling as "Top Ranking."

15

"We settle into our new home," Scott said, the events of four years earlier—almost five now—jogging back to mind. "Big house on the hill, maid and everything. I had to go to a private school. Sunridge High, far from the inner city. 'No kid of mine is going to school with blacks off the street, labba labba labba,'" the guttural utterance a caricature of his father's voice.

"Those were your father's words, 'blacks off the street?'"

"You think I'm making this up?"

"We tend to fill in gaps with what we believe to be true."

"Like whether we smoke or not?"

"Touché," Mitchell said.

"First day at school I get in a fight."

"What happened?"

"It was in Miss Williams' class. Cute young thing with a charming English accent. All the students were white or could pass for white, except these two black guys sitting in the back trying their best to fit in while bursting at the seams to tell the whole system to go fuck itself. Teach asked what my father did and one of the black guys gave me shit after school…."

Forty pairs of eyes nervously studied the fearsome-looking foreigner with the dark patch over his eye as he and his son appeared like fairytale creatures in the classroom. Their mothers had warned them about the Blackheart Man, a mythical ogre who lived in gullies and snatched foolish children away never to be seen again. They were old enough to have outgrown such childhood legends but superstition died hard in Jamaica, and just who was this one-eyed white devil anyway? A collective sigh of relief gushed as he left and Miss Williams introduced the new boy to the class.

"All right then, class," Williams said, "shall we all welcome Scott to Sunridge?"

"Welcome, Scott," the students sang in unison as they sat there in their uniforms, brown for the boys and blue with white blouse for the girls. The class was reasonably well behaved—a lash of the cane from the headmaster a powerful disincentive to the mischievous impulses of youth.

"You are coming from the States, is that correct?" Miss Williams asked.

"South America, actually. Argentina."

"Do you speak Spanish?"

"Poco," Scott replied, though like his father he was quite fluent after having spent six years south of the border.

"And your father is with the embassy?"

"Yes, that's right."

16

As school let out that afternoon Scott was walking past the bike racks when Henry, who was as dark as Scott was pale, took it upon himself to welcome the new kid to Kingston properly.

"Oy, white bwoy," Henry called as Scott passed. "CIA in that embassy."

"What? Is not."

"Cha! Yuh daddy CIA an' yuh don't even know it."

"What do you know about anything, *pendejo*?"

Henry, who understood the tone if not the dictionary meaning of Scott's insult, was up fast and in his face. Scott gave a shove, Henry pushed back and they were into it, fists flying. Henry, a stout lad with pounds and muscle on thin Scott, tattooed the white kid with a one-two, bloodying his nose. Scott flew into a rage, swinging wildly, and split the Jamaican boy's lip.

"Don't know what side your bread is buttered on, do you white bwoy?" Henry spewing blood down the front of his school clothes.

"Stupid nig–" Scott caught himself an instant too late. Henry was already up and charging with a fury that drove Scott staggering backwards, defenseless against such a fierce assault. At the last minute Henry's friend Louis stepped in and restrained him.

"C'mon, man," said Louis, leading Henry away while looking back at Scott as if to say he'd saved his worthless life but was none too happy about doing so.

"Didn't mean nothing," Scott muttered feebly, his fighting spirit evaporating. He wiped blood from his nose and wished he could take back his words....

"Hated myself," Scott said, shaking his head as he recounted the incident for Dr. Mitchell. "I never use that word. Like Dickhead was talking through me."

"That's what growing up is all about," Mitchell said. "Separating ourselves from our parents. But in another sense you were standing up for your father against Henry's slander."

"What slander was that?"

"That your father was some nefarious CIA spy."

"Is there any water?"

Mitchell rose and poured a glass of water. Scott drank it down fast.

"Don't think it was slander," he said. "No, definitely not."

"You're saying your father was with the CIA?"

"Yeah."

"And we know this because...."

"Gut feeling."

"Go on."

17

"It was an election year and we had a horse in the race."

"We?"

"Uncle Sam."

"It seems a stretch that the United States would give two hoots about the politics of some tiny Caribbean island."

"That's what I thought too."

"Let's move on. You're settled in to school and—"

"Bauxite," Scott said, as if from a sudden awareness.

"Beg your pardon?"

"Jamaica has bauxite. The ground is red with it. Bauxite makes, uh...."

"Aluminum."

"Aluminum, thank you. Aluminum goes into all kinds of shit. Lot of companies down there mining it. Refining it. American companies."

"You're saying we were meddling in Jamaican affairs over bauxite?"

"Manley nationalized the industry, got the business elite up in arms. Manley, the prime minister."

"Aluminum," Mitchell repeated, as if the idea wouldn't quite sink in.

"Manley was buddying up with Castro. You know we didn't like that."

Leaning forward, Mitchell attempted to make sense of what this colorful and curious young man was saying. He had heard plenty of bizarre stories from patients in his time but the kid's ramblings were drawing him in, the Oedipal fantasy, the paranoid allusion to spies and secret conspiracies. It had been too long since he'd looked in a pair of eyes and known he'd helped a fellow wayfarer on this cold and weary planet make it through difficult times and come out the better for it. Gratification like that could go far toward getting a man back on his game.

"Don't ask me how I know," Scott said, "but the CIA was working out of the Kingston embassy and my dad was head honcho. Doesn't that just frost your balls."

Phillip Mitchell, Ph. D., *cum laude* clinical psychologist out of UCLA, couldn't have put it better himself.

3

December 1975, Kingston, Jamaica

The golden Caribbean sun was already bright in the morning sky as the taxi pulled up in front of the Mutual Life Building on Oxford Road in New Kingston, a recently built-up business and shopping quadrant a skip and holler inland from downtown and the harbour district. He'd had the driver cruise those historic parts down by the wharves and it had been an eye opener. It could have been Miami or New York or a city in darkest

Africa. Women black as night in flimsy faded scarves and bust-up sandals lugging big raggedy sacks of goods to hawk. Men with open collars and cheap gold chains around their necks loitering at the corner. Invariably, a game of dominoes going somewhere, players slapping their pieces down with inexhaustible bravado, *cha!* Streetside crowds waiting a-weary for jam-packed clattertraps of buses that looked good for five more miles. Young bucks surfing traffic on 175cc Suzuki motorcycles. Street-savvy teens hustling a buck and the shirt off your back. Twelve-year-old girls selling box drinks and banana chips at the bus stops. Fruit and vegetable stalls down the way, goats and pigs rooting about in the gutter. Pushcart vendors shouting the virtues of their spicy jerk chicken and Rastas cooking up I-tal fare in colorful backstreet stalls. Dreadlocked entrepreneurs tooling around in slapped-up wooden discos-on-wheels selling 45s and seven-inch EPs. Police looking for heads to bust. The Yards, the tenements of West Kingston, a few short blocks away, the godforsaken abject ghettoes where the rudest of the rudeboys held dominion like a nest of angry hornets no one dared meddle with. All this and more was Kingston, life in the Third World rolling on, *anno domini mille novocento settanta cinque,* coming on five hundred years after Columbus.

Matt Gallagher paid the driver, who wrinkled his nose at the unspectacular tip, and stepped out into this slicker, cleaner uptown Kingston. Weather to put Buenos Aires to shame, shirt-sleeve pleasant in the dead of winter, but he would sing a different tune in the heat of July. He studied the twelve-story Mutual Life building that housed his new place of employment: the United States Embassy, occupying the entire third floor. His latest job would be a big step up—chief of station—but if truth be told he'd rather have been out in the jungle stalking the enemy with black paint under his eyes and a knife clenched between his teeth. Sitting in shirt and tie in an office wasn't his style. He wore a big-handled .45 holstered around his waist like Pat Garrett. His official cover: Attaché.

Gallagher, 38, walked into the building, a slight hitch in his step from having lost a chunk of his calf to VC shrapnel in Nam. He rode the elevator to the third floor, saluted the Marine Corps guard and entered into the 4000-square-foot space of the embassy. Visas and passports were handled over at another branch of the embassy at Cross Roads, sparing the main Oxford Road office the spectacle of throngs of Jamaicans queuing to get their papers "to go a foreign" to the US or UK. Here it was all peace and quiet.

The floor was divided into two sections, one devoted to the embassy proper, including the ambassador's office, while the other was walled off and separate, to which regular embassy personnel were not admitted. A Jamaican secretary sat at a desk outside this walled-off section monitoring who came and went. She flinched as Matt appeared with the black patch over his left eye but she quickly caught herself.

"We've been expecting you, Mr. Gallagher," the attractive black woman said, rising to offer her hand. Her brow danced at Matt's rugged good looks; people said he resembled the actor Robert Conrad with the body of Rocky Marciano. Not quite six feet, the force of his personality made him seem taller than he was. A former Army Ranger in Vietnam, he could kill a man with his bare hands and not think twice about it. No gladiator in the blood-soaked arenas of ancient Rome was ever so fearless. His sacred mission was to defend America and he would do so to his last ounce of strength.

"Right through that door, sir," the secretary said.

Gallagher passed through the indicated door, where he was met by the acting station chief, a rotund bear of a man with a ready grin that could instantly snap into a fierce stare.

"You must be Gallagher," he greeted, thrusting out his hand. "Frank Lake, deputy chief." Lake had been second dog at the Kingston station for four years and taken for granted that he was first in line for the top job. New man coming in out of the blue had been no small disappointment.

"Nice to meet you, Frank."

"How was your flight? Coming in from the States?"

"Buenos Aires."

"Argentina. Had some fun down there, didn't ya?"

"Very successful operation. But Chile was the pearl."

"You there in '73 when all that shit was going down, bombing the presidential palace and all that?"

"Better believe it."

Lake drew Matt over before a large wall map of the world. Frank tapped his pointer finger on Kingston in the southeastern corner of the island between the hills of Mona and the St. Andrew plain.

"Jamaica is the center of the cyclone," Lake said. "Manley's kissing up so close to Castro he pees red. Lookie here."

Lake, holding his finger on Kingston, swung his thumb over to Cuba's capital, Havana. There was no space between finger and thumb.

"That's how close the bastards are," Lake grunted. "The last thing we need, the *quintessential* last straw, is a coalition of commies and socialists spreading the Red Menace in our backyard like they never heard of the Monroe Doctrine… like the fucking Soviet Union was running things around here. Now you've got this goddamn reggae singer stirring things up with revolution and everything else. There's a fire to put out here and fast. Can you handle it?"

"A reggae singer. My, my."

"I'm here to help you in any way I can. Any questions?"

"Just one."

"Fire away."

"What does quintessential mean?"

Lake's jaw dropped and he fumbled for words until the corner of Matt's mouth wrinkled in a wry grin.

"Got me, didn't ya?" Lake grinned.

"Listen, Frank, got a man here you can depend on? Need someone to keep an eye on my son for me."

"I got just the guy. I'll set you up."

The rest of the afternoon Matt spent setting up his office and meeting with Ambassador Gerard.

Two days later Gallagher convened a meeting of his small group—Frank Lake and three other white male case officers. The good news was that HQ in Langley had promised to beef that up and increase funding. Matt was anxious to move forward with the same type of programs that had been so successful in Buenos Aires and Santiago. Deputy Chief Lake had briefed him over the last forty-eight hours on the situation on the ground: The two major political parties, the People's National Party (PNP) and the Jamaica Labor Party (JLP), were at each other's throat—an ideal scenario for implementing the time-honored strategy of divide and rule. Both parties had their own labor unions and entire neighborhoods tended to align with one side or the other as the political bosses rewarded the faithful with jobs and housing schemes. Ghetto gangs attached themselves to the party that fed them; times were tough when your side was out of office.

"Listen up," Matt said as the old-timers huddled around the conference table with mugs of Blue Mountain coffee. "As you know, Jamaica is assuming an ever larger profile in regional politics. Since the twin debacles of the '59 revolution and Kennedy's fuck-up at the Bay of Pigs, Company strategy has been to keep Cuba isolated at all costs. It's the whole goddamn key to Latin America, one might say the entire Western Hemisphere. By aligning with Castro, Manley sets a dangerous precedent that must be, shall we say, *repealed.* So what's the chink in the prick's armor?"

"Chink in the armor is that Jamaicans hate communism," Lake replied. "His Achilles heel is he fancies himself a ladies' man. With those elephant ears, can you imagine? Big scandal a while back—he got involved with his third wife while she was in divorce proceedings from her husband. He's on number four now."

"The cad. Maybe we should bait-up a she-goat and catch this rogue tiger."

"Want HQ to send down a girl?"

21

"Best-looking gal they can find. Tits like Jayne Mansfield. Hell, see what Jayne's doing herself."

"Jayne's dead, Matt."

"What, Jayne Mansfield is dead?"

"Nine, ten years ago. Traffic accident. Lopped her head clean off."

"Christ, is nothing sacred?"

"I'll put in a call to Raquel Welch." Everyone by now tittering.

"What else about the guy?"

"He likes roses."

"Roses. Give me something to work with here."

"Usually goes jogging in the morning."

"Bingo. Have them send us a jogger. Maybe bouncing boobs will give him a heart attack and we can all go to the beach."

More laughter.

"Now listen up. The suits at Langley are supposedly kicking in funds and personnel to help us out. How many and how much we don't know yet, but we aren't going to sit on our thumbs waiting to find out. As I understand it Secretary of State Kissinger is coming in on vacation after Christmas and there is a joint IMF-World Bank conference scheduled for early January. Do I have my facts correct?"

"On the money," Lake nodded.

"We expect a massive influx of international press on the island during this period. A prime opportunity to paint a mustache on Manley's pretty-boy mug. All assets need to be fully engaged. We want those snoopy-ass journalists filing reports to curdle the blood of anybody even thinking about vacationing in Jamaica. I want this city *on fire*. I want blood on the front page and Attila the Hun rolling in his grave. Get the word out to your people. I expect everyone including myself to work thirty-six-hour days while Kissinger and the foreign press are on the island. Make sure your agents are paid up. Keep in close contact with your police and army contacts. See to it that the gunmen are stocked with bullets. I want no stone left unturned. Is that clear as mud and cherry pie?"

"Absolutely," affirmed Lake, as all heads nodded.

"Let's get it done." With that Matt stood and went to his office, leaving his colleagues in awe. This Gallagher was a force of nature. An Alexander who marched his army into battle and burned his ships behind him. No retreat, no surrender. Kingston would no longer be a sleepy rum-and-hammock Caribbean backwater. Great deeds could be accomplished in the cause of freedom. All would give their very best… except perhaps Frank Lake, who had his wounded pride to nurse.

Late December 1975, Kingston

In predawn darkness, Frank Lake and Matt Gallagher hustled aboard the Company helicopter, ducking low under the *whup-whup* of the rotors. Two Jamaicans climbed in after them. Pocket Thunder (known to Lake as Pocket and his spars as "Pockie" and "Thunda") was a diminutive wisp of a man but a savvy street fighter good with a ratchet knife, whereas William the Conqueror had the body of an NFL halfback and relied on his fists in a scuffle. William the C sported a choppy Afro and Thunda wore dreads. The two were assets Lake was developing with an eye to bringing them on as full salaried agents. Ghetto toughs sympathetic to the JLP.

The pilot lifted the bird off from its secret pad and up above the sleeping city, heading for the rugged terrain of the Blue Mountains.

"Where are they coming in?" Matt asked as he studied a topo map under a flashlight. The two Jamaicans sat quietly across from the white men.

"Up in the hills," Frank replied. "A runway carved out of the bush. Back end of a ganja run to Miami. See the X on the map? That little plateau there?"

Matt ran the flashlight over the map. "X marks the spot, eh? Ah, here we are. Coffee country?"

"If you like ganja with your cup. Ready to smoke a spliff, mon?"

"I'll pass."

Lake lit up a tobacco cigarette and offered one to Matt, who waved it off.

"What happened to your eye?" Lake asked. "Or is that a sensitive topic?"

"Nam. Mother-fucker NVA flicked me with his bayonet. Last thing he ever did in this world."

"Pretty tough over there."

"Best days of my life, amigo. Better than sex."

He'd loved it so much that when shrapnel ripped his calf open he finagled his way into staying in Vietnam. When his wife was diagnosed with uterine cancer, he refused compassionate leave to remain with his boys. Deep down he believed the war couldn't be won without him. Deep down he also believed that Linda, Scott's mother, wouldn't have succumbed to the cancer had he been there with her. Such was the nature and extent of his hubris.

Matt scanned the moonlit terrain a thousand feet below while mindlessly scatting an old Beach Boys song. Soon the hillside mansions of Jamaica's elite upper class—the ones that had not fled to Miami—gave way to the coffee plantations and thickets of the higher mountains, rising over 7400 feet at Blue Mountain Peak, from whence on a clear day you might see Cuba to the north and Haiti to the east.

"Whadja do after Nam?" Lake asked.

"Handled some chores down in the Canal Zone," Matt replied. *"La Escuela de las Americas."*

"The squirrel of... huh?"

"The School of the Americas, bonehead. Ft. Gulick, Panama. Fighting leftist assholes south of the border."

After the loss of his eye took him out of the war Matt continued serving his country by teaching at the United States Army School of the Americas in Panama. At SOA, officers from right-wing militaries and paramilitaries throughout Latin American received training in the dark arts of counterinsurgency, surveillance, and interrogation. From SOA Matt was recruited into the CIA, which in its eagerness to get someone of his caliber waived the usual four-year college degree requirement and sent him straight into training in covert operations at "the farm," Camp Peary, Virginia.

The chopper flew on over thick uncharted bush until Frank spotted the flashing light that designated the landing zone.

"Take 'er down, Jose," he said.

Pilot Jose set the bird down on the remote landing strip, a narrow islet of land carved out of the jungle with machetes. The flashing light seen from the sky was a Jamaican swinging a lantern, the landing strip one of many hidden away in the backcountry; ganja smuggling was big business and an important component of the island's economy. Exports were also made via ship through the Bahamas utilizing anything from canoes to luxury yachts to fast boats which could outrun pursuing government vessels.

The men climbed out of the chopper, its engine running, as the Jamaican ground crew came over. Pocket Thunder handled introductions.

"Dis man Johnny Two Teeth," he said, the smell of rum on his breath. "Him dere name Yard Bird and him Marlon Brando."

"Stella!" cried Lake, unable to contain himself. "It was you, Joe."

"Don't mind him," Gallagher said, the Jamaicans averting their eyes in disgust and not shaking hands. "So when's this bird due in?"

"Five-t'irty," said Thunda.

"Five-*t'irty,*" Matt mimed bluntly, drawing cold stares.

There was no love lost here. It wasn't just these whites with their proper diction looking down their noses at islanders with their colorful names and quaint Quashie talk, the patois brought over from Africa by slaves and spiced with Spanish, Creole, English, even Arawak, the tongue of the island's indigenous inhabitants, the gentle Taino, now vanished into the pages of history. Except for the educated upper classes most Jamaicans were bilingual, patois the native tongue acquired in the home and Queen's English practically a foreign language studied in the schools. Let these uppity white devils try their hand with patois. No, it was more the idea of foreigners running around giving orders like they owned the place. They

24

were tolerated only because of a common interest in ridding the country of Michael Manley and his commie ways.

Bloodclot white mon, yuh time gwine come.

Matt glanced at his watch. "Hell, it's five-*t'irty* now."

There came the low hum of a small aircraft. The lantern man swung the glowing orb and the plane circled, lined up with the runway and landed, bouncing like a stone skipping over water and finally scuttling up right to where the men waited. Jumping out with the engine running were the pilot and two crewmen holding AK-47s as if eager to discharge them. The three appeared to be Cuban, their English heavily salted with Spanish accents; in fact the flight had originated in Miami and been stocked by Cuban exiles allied to the Agency. The pilot and crew wandered over and wolfed down some stew the Jamaicans had cooking in a metal bucket. Meanwhile Marlon Brando, Yard Bird and Johnny Two Teeth—who looked like he would soon be Johnny Gums—scrambled into the plane and offloaded nineteen heavy wooden crates. The crates were pried open with crow bars to reveal a treasure trove of M-16s, rifles, handguns, ammunition. Other shipments would come in straight to the JLP-controlled wharves in Kingston Harbour.

"Beautiful," said Matt as the booty was loaded into a VW microbus and several other vehicles. Frank Lake hustled inside the chopper and retrieved a large satchel. Meanwhile Thunda and William the Conqueror stuffed kilogram bricks of marijuana into the empty crates before hefting them back onto the aircraft. If they'd figured a way to stuff a brick or two down their shirts no one was the wiser. Pilot and crew washed down their stew with shots of white rum and got back in the plane. The whole unloading-reloading process took twenty-seven minutes.

"Cuba *libre!*" the pilot shouted as he swung the plane around and took off.

"That bird catches fire the whole Western Hemisphere will be higher than a kite," said Frank.

"I'll take that," said Matt, indicating the satchel. It was crammed to the brim with packets of white powder, a weapon as valuable as any gun for the power it commanded over men, the things it would make them do just to get a snort up their nose. The arms-laden vehicles began winding their way down into Kingston, where they would be met by ghetto Rankings who would divvy the spoils out to their posses. Days later Jamaican TV was filled with images of bloody death in the tenement yards of West Kingston. The finger of blame was pointed at Michael Manley, eliciting high fives all around in the CIA section of the US Embassy.

October 12, 1980, Santa Barbara

The expanding of morning ritual on Mondays to include weekly session with Dr. M meant that Scott, with his tendency to run late for anything not having to do with music, had to watch the clock. He lived by his routine, up at dawn to go jogging, fortified with ganja and a fruit smoothie. Afternoons working at the bike shop out at UCSB, riding his Cruiser along the bike path past Goleta Beach to the university campus. (Saving his pennies for his dream car, a silver-blue BMW Bavaria.) For dinner he would cook I-tal food or as close as he could manage, veggie burritos and brown rice typical fare. Evenings the band didn't have a gig or rehearsal he spent practicing at home into the wee hours. He would put on a Wailers album, grab his guitar and sing and dance along with Bob Marley, imitating his moves and mannerisms, facial expressions, intonations, his manner of playing to the audience, the whole shot. Singing and strutting and whipping his dreadlocks, aping the King of Reggae to every last twitching muscle. In this he was driven. He didn't bother with TV or politics, who shot JR Ewing, the Iran hostage crisis or the Carter-Anderson-Reagan election campaign that had everybody up in arms. He was so intelligent he somehow stayed abreast, but it was all about the music and following the Rasta path, Bob's path.

He arrived at the Suites at ten past, locked his bike and went in. Today's Marley T-shirt featuring the Afro-coiffed image of Bob from the cover of *Natty Dread*. The everpresent denim overshirt so like the one Bob wore up on stage. As he sat he noticed dark circles under Dr. M's eyes and that the NO SMOKING sign was gone from the desk.

"You look out of it today, man," he said, doffing his purple and gold tam.

"Little tired is all," Mitchell sighed. He'd been up late last night with a cheap Cabernet and Basil Rathbone's Sherlock Holmes outsmarting the evil Dr. Moriarty. A nip of Codeine cough syrup, just to help him sleep.

"Do you love your job, Doc?" Scott asked.

Mitchell, taken aback, struggled for a response.

"It's what I've always wanted to do," he said, but perhaps he'd hesitated an instant too long. "Last time we talked about your father being in the CIA."

"You thought I was off my rocker."

"Help me understand."

Scott stretched out his feet and clasped his hands behind his neck. He'd been up late too, serenaded by that demon alleycat, and lately in the twilight state before sleep images had been flooding into mind, disconnected fragments: Marva in a low-cut purple dress. Black birds, white lilies, slashing machetes and that hunchback with his lion-headed staff and piercing eyes. Again the M14, with its handsome wooden stock. *Sniper rifle.* Talking to Doc M was loosening things up. It made him nervous. Leave well enough alone.

He bit his lip and plunged ahead. "The country was descending into tribal war," he said. "Elections coming up. Our horse in the race was the JLP's Edward Seaga. Locals called him C-I-A-ga. Not a drop of black blood in him. Jamaican-born Lebanese. Harvard educated. Right-wing free-market type of guy. Weasely little dweeb, didn't have any of Manley's charisma. Always hammering at him being a communist. Jamaicans hate communism with a passion and Manley lost a lot of them paling around with Castro. I seem to recall a top US official arriving on the island around this time. Wasn't Ford or Carter... started with a K, I think."

"Henry Kissinger?"

"Bingo. Mr. Bad-ass Henry Kissinger. Something to do with Cuba no doubt... maybe about Africa."

"Cuba sent troops to Angola around that time."

"That's it. That has to be it. So we sent down Kissinger to lean on Manley."

"The juices are flowing today."

"This is from early on when we first got to Jamaica. Before the Lost Time. My memory is pretty good about that. I... something...." Scott stroked his forehead as if realizing something for the first time.

"What is it?" Dr. Mitchell asked.

"Damn, I bet they brought my father in for the same reason."

"To deal with Manley."

"Adds up. They'd have needed someone ruthless like him."

"The CIA. Down there in Jamaica."

"Just because it ain't on the front page of the *LA Times* doesn't mean it didn't happen."

"We don't want to fill in gaps with what we assume to be true."

"There you go with your gaps again." He caught again the glint of something strangely familiar in Doc M's eyes.

"Does it seem rational to you," Dr. Mitchell said, "that the United States with all its might would worry about Cuba sending a few soldiers to Africa?"

"Who says Uncle Sam is rational? If it was trivial why would they be bent out of shape over Manley buddying up to Castro in the first place?"

"That was my next question."

"You're fighting me man."

Mitchell sat back and let the air cool a moment.

"They slandered Manley up and down the block," Scott went on. "Graffiti saying he was gay. If there's anything worse than communism in Jamaica it's being a homo. The guy had three or four wives and they said he

27

went to Cuba to blow Castro. How rational is that? The Rastas said it was a stinking pile of CIA propaganda. High grade crapola."

Mitchell edged forward in his big chair behind the desk. He was taking no bets patient wasn't either a pathological liar or the biggest spinner of conspiracy theories that ever came down the pike. Yet the kid's fantasies were drawing him in, leaving him eager to hear more. CIA spies, propaganda wars, international intrigue… and not least of all the simple mystery of what could transform this skinny kid from someone who fought fisticuffs for his father's honor into someone who wanted him dead?

At first light Michael Manley pulled his six-foot-three-inch frame out of bed to begin his morning routine. The bedroom he shared with Beverley in the upstairs living quarters at Jamaica House was lush with green plants and colorful paintings by Caribbean artists. He stood a moment at the window to the rear of the property, thirty acres of fruit orchards, blooming shrubs and rolling lawns, purple and pink bougainvillea and sunburst crimson Poinciana splashing the verdant landscape with a riot of color. Built in 1962, the year of independence, to serve as the prime minister's mansion and offices, Jamaica House (also called Government House) with its stately white façade was a symbol of Jamaica's newly won place in the global community. *Wa-da-da…* a free and autonomous black nation.

Manley turned as lovely dark-skinned Beverley entered barefoot in her nightgown. In her hands was a platter of fresh fruit—papaya, pineapple, mango—and a cup of black coffee, properly served in good china with saucer.

"Morning hun," she smacked him a kiss. Manley's fourth wife, Beverley Anderson was the first full-blooded black among them, from a working class family but perhaps the smartest of the lot. A radio and TV personality with JBC before Michael met her, she was president of the PNP Women's Movement and wore her hair in an Afro in solidarity with the black power/civil rights struggle in America. A more competent woman could hardly be found anywhere in the Caribbean. It had been her idea to invite Bob Marley and other reggae stars to perform on the stump for the PNP during the 1972 campaign because their songs put forth the same message of protest Michael was fighting for.

Michael's father was the illustrious Norman Manley, war hero, Rhodes Scholar, barrister who never lost a capital case and one of Jamaica's seven national heroes. Almost the father of the country, no one having fought harder to bring about Jamaica's emancipation from British rule. Norman Washington Manley, buried alongside memorials to Nanny of the Maroons, Marcus Garvey, Paul Bogle and the other giants in the hallowed

Shrine section of National Heroes Park in the nation's capital. Even the international airport in Kingston was named for him.

"Pardi" had left big shoes to fill, but young Michael rose to the challenge. A graduate of London School of Economics, he cut his political teeth as a union man representing sugar cane workers. It was as if he had been born to it, running up and down with his megaphone rallying the troops, challenging the mighty and powerful. Born to lead, destined to take over for his father. With Beverley campaigning at his side, Manley, tall, fair-skinned and charming, was elected prime minister in 1972 in a landslide.

He and Beverley had promptly gotten down to redressing the lingering inequities of the colonial system. Public works programs were instituted to create jobs. Land lease and agrarian reforms to help small farmers. Free education through university. Community health clinics, a literacy campaign, national minimum wage. A forty-hour week ended the days of working 80 hours on the plantations for $5 take-home. A fair return on bauxite production was negotiated; royalties had not been adjusted for inflation in sixteen years and stood at a paltry $1.50/ton. Fifty-one percent of mining operations was to be nationalized and a quarter million acres of land repatriated (at a fair price). Jamaica's share of revenues from the bauxite industry increased seven-fold from 1973 to 1974, yielding $145 million for critically needed social services. Though awash in profits from bumper years the multinational corporations retaliated, cutting back on production of Jamaican ore. Strike One on Manley.

Yet against all odds things were starting to get better. Kids were attending school, folks were working, wages rising. Infant mortality fell precipitously. Manley's miracle was taking root and people were lifting their chins off their chests and daring to believe the PNP's slogan that "Better Must Come." Then came the second big blow: the oil crisis beginning in 1973.

The days of cheap oil were over. In a single sitting in 1974 OPEC almost *quadrupled* the price of a barrel of oil, threatening to break the backs of poor postcolonial nations like Jamaica. Escalating violence dealt a crippling blow to tourism and its Yankee dollars and capital flight spirited much-needed foreign exchange out of the country as well-off Jamaicans fled to greener pastures in Miami and New York. Fourteen years after independence, Jamaica was teetering on the brink, Michael Manley fighting to keep the dream alive.

"Mmm, love my Blue Mountain coffee," Manley said, sipping in unabashed pleasure. "Gets a man going in the morning."

"Off jogging?" Beverley asked.

"Christmas calories to burn off." Manley grabbed the loose flesh at his midsection. "Overdid it this year with all the rum cake. What say Bev, are you coming with?"

"Better not. Natasha has an upset tummy."

There came the cries of their only child from the next room. Born prematurely, Natasha was a fighter and against all odds had survived, earning her the name of the heroine of *War and Peace*.

"There she is now. Be careful out there, Mike."

"I'm just going for a jog Bev, don't worry so much."

Beverley attended to their daughter and Manley took his coffee out onto the balcony, where his thoughts turned to Henry Kissinger. The United States Secretary of State had flown in the day before, recently married and in the company of his wife and pet dog. He'd ensconced himself in a posh resort on the pristine north shore, with its beaches of fine white sand. With the Jamaican economy in shambles Manley had asked the US for a hundred million dollar line of credit. As it happened, Kissinger was eager to meet with Manley too—for a different reason entirely.

Manley donned his jogging shoes and bounded down the rightmost of the two curved, red-carpeted stairwells to the first floor, passing the portrait of Queen Elizabeth II and Prince Philip on the wall to his right—the Queen of England still the official head of state of Jamaica. Outside he was met by two Cuban-trained bodyguards packing heat who would jog with him. The three walked past the circular fountain in the turnaround and down the long drive to the main gate to warm up. Manley saluted the guards and the small entourage jogged onto Hope Road, turning left away from downtown. It was early but Hope was a major thoroughfare, cars already out and whizzing by, and the bodyguards kept a sharp eye. Fronting the prime minister's mansion as it did, the avenue was well-maintained and without the ruts and craters of many of the city's roads. Passing number 56, Bob Marley's home, Manley looked for any of the crew in the yard playing soccer. Only a Rasta thwacking at the grass with a machete, the Jamaican lawnmower.

After running his guards into the ground on two laps around Mona Reservoir and arriving back at Jamaica House, the prime minister showered and was digging in to a hearty Jamaican breakfast of fried saltfish fritters, calaloo and roast breadfruit when Bev came in with Natasha.

"Here's my girls," he said, standing to kiss his daughter on the forehead and his wife lightly on the lips. "How's that little tummy of yours, Natash?"

"Better than yours with all the fritters you're packing away," said Bev.

"You're the one who got me eating Jamaican food."

"Stop shoveling them into your face, man."

Manley wolfed a final bite and pushed his plate away as if the china itself were at fault for his burgeoning waistline. The Jamaican peasant diet, on the whole, was healthier than the traditional English fare he'd grown up on *and* it was the food of the people. To the fair-skinned prime minister of a nation of blacks, that was important. He was grateful to Bev for bringing it to Jamaica House and his table.

"And now I must change your daughter's diapers," Bev said. "Oh by the way, Henry Kissinger called."

"Kissinger called?" Manley sprang excitedly to his feet.

"Somehow the call came through to me. Here I am on the line and he's on the other end and--"

"For Pete sake Bev, stop beating around the bush. What did the man say?"

"He invited you to visit him at his resort in Ochi."

"Excellent," Manley rubbed his palms and paced in eager anticipation.

"You're *not* going out to Ocho Rios."

"Of course I am."

"Excuse me?"

"Beverley, I need to ask about that line of credit we've been waiting on. Without it all of Jamaica may as well pack up and move to the back hills of Haiti. That credit is crucial to our economic survival."

"So. The American snaps his fingers and you come running. Cocky little strutting rooster crows and Michael Manley lines up at attention. 'Here I am suh, did you call suh, came as fast as I could suh.'"

"Beverley, why are you—"

"Damn it man. The prime minister of Jamaica should sit at the feet of Mr. Big Shot Henry Kissinger? In his own country?"

As if overcome by sudden pains Manley collapsed to his chair and clutched his head in his hands. Beverley came near and laid her hand softly on his shoulder. One of the traits she most admired about her husband was his willingness to stand up against bullying. It was fundamental to his love of democracy, the belief that no powerful person or state should usurp the rights of another person or state just by being bigger and stronger. As a young student threatened with what he considered an unfair caning, he'd challenged the headmaster to give it a go himself and then *resigned* from the school. Later leading a union strike against JBC, he'd lain down in the street and dared traffic to run him over—a stunt that earned him the nickname Joshua.

Joshua lead the sufferah to the Promised Land.

"Never forget who you are," she said, massaging his neck. "Or *what* you are."

"Just who and what am I?"

31

"You are the hope of Jamaica. You are Michael Norman Manley, son of the great Norman Washington Manley and before you are through you will be acclaimed the equal to your illustrious father. You are the people's champion and don't you *ever* forget it."

"You are absolutely right," Manley said, slamming fist to table. "Heck if I'm dragging myself off to Ochi like a houseboy answering the bell. If Mr. K wants to see me he can haul his presumptuous Yankee ass to Kingston, the sonuvabitch."

"Now that's the man I married," Beverley cooed, easing down onto her husband's lap.

Henry Kissinger accepted Manley's invitation and came to Jamaica House for a private lunch. Kissinger, 52, Ph. D. summa cum laude from Harvard, survivor of the disgraced Nixon administration and architect of the secret bombing of Cambodia and Laos which had nearly wiped those nations of peasant farmers off the face of the earth, was received with all the graciousness of traditional Caribbean hospitality.

Manley didn't have to be a psychic to know Cuba was on Mr. K's mind. Ever since the CARICOM nations Barbados, Guyana, Trinidad and Jamaica had recognized Cuba in 1973, it seemed all the Americans could think about was communist plots to take over the Western Hemisphere. When Manley flew with Fidel Castro in a Cuban government jet to Algiers for a summit meeting of the Non-Aligned Movement, and followed that with a state visit to Havana, the Jamaican establishment turned on him and never let up, the North American press playing right along.

Now there was Angola. The African nation had recently won independence from Portugal only to be attacked by forces allied to South Africa and backed by the CIA. The young government turned to Fidel Castro, who shipped off reinforcements that turned back the invading armies. It was an important victory in the liberation war against South Africa and a huge inspiration to African freedom fighters—a black Third World army had defeated the invincible white imperialists. Had Castro not intervened, had South Africa prevailed, strengthening its hand throughout the region, would Nelson Mandela's release from life imprisonment on Robben Island, his presidency and the dismantling of apartheid—would these iconic events of the Twentieth Century have happened as they did?

Like Manley, Kissinger was feeling the pressure. United States' prestige had plummeted as a result of Vietnam, Watergate and House and Senate investigations into dirty dealings of the FBI and CIA. The ignominious helicopter evacuation from the roof of the embassy in Saigon barely seven months gone. Kissinger had remarked upon the need for bold action to demonstrate that the US was still the tough guy on the block. Kick somebody's ass somewhere.

And so the stage was set. Both men at the peak of their powers, very nearly the same age, both graying at the temples, both with heavy agendas. Tall graceful Manley, his sideburns darn near as long as Elvis'. Stocky ebullient Kissinger, so full of himself. The white imperial magistrate and the black philosopher-king from the islands. A mismatch on the order of David vs Goliath... but David, as we know, was a scrapper.

A sumptuous meal was served in the breakfast room at Jamaica House: ackee and saltfish, rice 'n peas, Johnny cakes, fried plantain, steamed bananas—and for a VIP like Kissinger, lobster and a nice French wine.

A cork popped and the Jamaican servant, white napkin across his forearm, approached with a bottle of champagne (not easily come by in a country staggering under a critical lack of foreign exchange).

"Champagne sir?" the young man said in drilled politeness.

"This could get to be a habit," Kissinger said, holding up his glass. "So tell me, Mr. Prime Minister--"

"--Michael, please."

"Tell me Michael... how will Jamaica vote on the Cuba matter when it comes before the UN?"

"Our view, Mr. Secretary—"

"--Henry, please."

"Henry, the Angolans are fighting for their freedom against colonial oppressors and Cuba has every right to come to their aid. The Organization of African Unity stands in unanimous support, even those states opposed to communism. It's simply the right thing to do."

"Cuba is aggressing against the only democracy in southern Africa."

"South Africa is a democracy, Henry?" Manley recoiled, unable to contain his shock.

"Castro is acting as Moscow's proxy."

"Patently false, though you seem to wish me to act as yours."

"Mr. Prime Minister—"

"--Mr. Secretary, I know Fidel Castro. He is his own man. He would no sooner kowtow to the Soviets than you would. In fact, there is reason to believe Moscow didn't approve of Cuba's intervention in Angola. Castro had to dispatch his brother Raul to Russia to explain his decision to the commissars in the Kremlin."

"We are not unaware of your affiliation with Fidel Castro."

"I carry no brief for Fidel Castro. Jamaica is a non-aligned nation as far from communism as the founding fathers of your American revolution. We have always welcomed foreign investment. But surely Henry you don't believe Cuba was better off under Batista? By Cuba I mean the Cuban people, not American business interests."

Kissinger stewed silently a moment, not used to such insolence. Whole nations were meant to bow before him. Weeks before, he and President Ford had flown to Jakarta and given the okay for Suharto to invade East Timor. Indonesia, the most populous Muslim nation in the world, jumped when America said jump. They could have called it off with the snap of their fingers but Operation Komodo was allowed to proceed. Hundreds of thousands would die. This rat's ass Manley didn't know who he was playing with.

"I urge you, sir," Kissinger said finally, dabbing the corner of his mouth, "not to support Cuba at the UN."

"We'll take another look, but I can't make any promises," Manley said.

Servants arrived with coffee and two large bowls of mango cobbler swimming in coconut cream.

"Did you know, Henry," Manley said, "that Winston Churchill was so fond of our Blue Mountain coffee that he ordered it served at the Yalta Conference with Roosevelt and Stalin?"

"I think we're through here," Kissinger said abruptly, after wolfing his dessert and setting down his cup. "Oh, the line of credit you were asking for?"

"Yes, Henry?" Manley's every sense came to attention. Without the line of credit things would look bleak indeed. Manley leaned forward in his eagerness to hear what the American had to say. If ever there were an occasion for Big Brother to the North to prove a friend in time of need, this was it.

"We'll take another look," Kissinger said, "but I can't make any promises."

That night over dinner Beverley sensed the encounter with Kissinger had not gone well. She coaxed Mike into a moonlight stroll around the grounds, leaving Natasha with the nanny. They walked past the circular rose garden and fruit orchards, night-blooming jasmine and gardenia scenting the cooling night air, on to the expansive lawns of the property which had once belonged to King's House, the residence of the colonial governor-general.

"Want to talk about it?" Bev asked.

"About what?"

"Your meeting with Henry Kissinger."

"Bah!" Manley kicked at a clump of grass.

"That bad? What was the hangup?"

"It's all about Cuba and Fidel."

"Because Cuba did the world a service and fought back the bloodsuckers of South Africa? And the line of credit?"

34

"I wouldn't hold your breath."

"For shame. It wouldn't hurt them to lend a helping hand. We've always paid our debts."

"Of course we have. They'd recoup every bloody penny plus interest. Sometimes I get so het up, Bev… it's all a game to these people. People's lives mean nothing. Jamaica is a pawn on their fucking chessboard."

"We'll find a way," Bev tugged at his elbow.

"If we don't I'll end up farming yam in Clarendon."

"City boy like you? You'd go buggy in a week. Might as well start a reggae band."

"Fine with me," Manley grunted.

"Shall I let my dreads grow out?" Bev said.

"The wife of the prime minister in dreadlocks, oh they'll love that!" Manley roared. As he broke into a rolling guffaw, tears of relief streaming down his cheeks, Beverley tittered along and knew she had done her job as a woman who just happened to be the wife of the leader of the country.

Manley did not get the line of credit. In June, 1976, the United States vetoed Angola's admission to the United Nations and the CIA secretly continued to support South Africa's attempts to overthrow the young Angolan government.

6

January 1976, the US Embassy at Oxford Road, Kingston

The CIA section was buzzing with excitement. The new case officers had arrived from the States—*eleven* of them. Even Matt couldn't believe it. Headquarters was going after Jamaica like they'd gone after Chile—full throttle. The new people, nine white males, one black man and one white woman, struggled not to fall all over each other. One would have thought it was a second Bay of Pigs.

The joint International Monetary Fund (IMF)-World Bank conference had been held January 7 to 9 at Kingston's Pegasus Hotel, with World Bank President Robert McNamara attending. Gallagher's ghetto gunmen had unleashed a spectacular burst of violence in welcome, burning large sections of Trench Town and Jones Town to the ground. Hit squads threw Molotov cocktails and sprayed the air with their freshly-arrived M16s, frightening foreign journalists out of their wits. Hiding out in uptown hotels, they wrote horrifying accounts that scared off vacationers and delivered a crippling blow to Jamaica's already hard-hit tourism industry. It was a great success by any measure and a scintillating beginning for Matt Gallagher.

Everybody at the embassy was on razor's edge from the gunning down of two Jamaican police guards stationed outside the building. The two were blown away while on duty, blood everywhere, sirens wailing. Two other policemen had been killed the same morning at a construction site on Marcus Garvey Drive as six gunmen rode in on motorbikes and shot the place up. Matt Gallagher loved it. He wasn't wearing that .45 on his hip for nothing. Many thought the Americans were behind the shootings in the first place.

The secretary had yesterday gone to Courts at Crossroads and bought a large wooden conference table, around which everyone now gathered. Set out on the table were a large map of Kingston and small photocopied maps for the new personnel. Gallager extended his greetings and turned it over to Frank Lake to advise the new case officers what time the cock crowed and which way the wind blew.

"Good morning," Lake said. "On the table in front of you is a large map of Kingston as well as a small one for you to keep. As Matt said, the socialist government of Michael Manley, the PNP or People's National Party, is building a coalition with communist Cuba. The JLP, or Jamaica Labor Party on the other hand is sympathetic to American interests. Your basic good guys and bad guys. We want the PNP out and JLP in, as simple as that."

When intervening in foreign nations—case in point, the so-called "banana republics" of Latin America and the Caribbean—the ultimate goal was to seize control but have the local sheriff run things. The US Marine Corps Small Wars Manual, 1935 edition by Lt. Col. Harold H. Utley, stipulated that after the initial invasion and establishment of order, all efforts were toward installing a puppet government while pointing to "free and fair elections" as proof of a successful democratic transition (as long as the winning candidate was acceptable to the US). Once the favored man was in office, the next step was withdrawal and handing off control to the resident gendarmerie. It was right in the damn manual, step by step by step. With covert action it was just the same, get your man in power and let his people run the show. As long as the regime remained in the good graces of the United States, methods would not be questioned—bloodshed, atrocity and repression rationalized as the price of freedom and "birthpains of democracy." In Jamaica, Washington's man on the beat was to be Edward Seaga.

"As you see on your maps," Lake continued, "the city of Kingston is situated at the southeast corner of the island. The downtown area near Victoria Pier is the historic heart of the city; north of Half Way Tree Square is the newer uptown district where we are right now. To the south are the harbour and Caribbean Sea. To the east the Papine Hills above the University of the West Indies. North, the distant heights of the Blue Mountains. And to the west the tenement yards, the ghettos of Trench Town, Tivoli Gardens, Concrete Jungle and so on. The yards can be dangerous for foreigners with white faces, so enter with caution. Best to avoid them completely and let your agents deal with it. Neighborhoods tend to align with one party or the other, so take your pen and mark the political affiliations of the various districts as I give them to you. You will mark them yourself so you will learn them. First, JLP neighborhoods. That's our guys: Tivoli Gardens... Newport West Harbour... West Kingston... Wareika Hill...."

Everybody busily made their notes.

"Now PNP areas," Lake continued. "Orange Street... Southside... Rockfort... Dunkirk... McGregor Gully... Concrete Jungle... waterfront Central Kingston—"

"—Let me interject a few words here," Gallagher said, stepping up and cutting off a surprised Lake. "We will mount anti-Manley propaganda campaigns, pamphlets, graffiti, anything to get the message across. I want 'Manley is a traitor' and 'Manley is a communist' on every street corner. We will print scathing denunciations of the man in the newspapers. I won't tie your hands asking you to fight fair. You kick and bite and scratch to gain advantage. If you have to hamstring someone's grandmother I expect to see the old gal hopping around like a one-legged chicken. We will spread rumors about Manley's character—lies in service of a greater truth. PNP rallies will be disrupted in a thousand ways, from spreading itching powder to setting off stink bombs to open gunfire. JLP meetings and rallies will also need to be attacked occasionally in ways that cast suspicion upon the PNP. Any questions?"

No one spoke.

"Good. Frank will now tell you about our upcoming charity golf tournament. Excellent PR plus an opportunity to make important contacts in the community so coax, coerce and cajole the wives and hubbies into pitching in. Dance naked for them if you have to."

Nervous chuckles followed from the group. Lake edged forward to resume but Matt wasn't ready to relinquish the floor just yet.

"Those of you who play golf will be expected to participate," Matt went on, "so dust off your clubs and get out there and practice. Go out to Caymanas Country Club and join a foursome. Cultivate relationships. Be charming and witty and make people like you. Be dependable so they will trust you. Talk to anyone and everyone with an eye to what they can do for us. Be alert to possible recruitment of agents. I don't have to tell you how to do your job. Frank."

Lake picked up where he'd left off and Matt quietly slipped into his office. A diplomatic pouch had come in that morning from HQ and he'd been too busy to go through it. There had been no official word yet on the new funding and Matt was hoping this was it. Inside he found an envelope addressed to him from Director of Central Intelligence William Colby, his old friend from Vietnam days and Operation Phoenix.

Matt ripped open the envelope to find a brief memorandum:

TO: Matt Gallagher, Kgn. Stn.
FROM: Wm. Colby, Director
RE: Funding.
Matt,
Ten million dollars US allocated for your needs. Counting on you.
(signed) Bill

Gallagher punched his fist into the air and let out a whoop. The big boys were going after Jamaica hard, pumping as much into this tiny island as they did in all the years hounding Allende in Chile. He went out and relayed the good news to the crew. A hearty round of *hip-hip-hooray* followed.

In the next several days Matt assigned operations to his new case officers (the term "agent" applied only to local hired assets, not regular CIA personnel). There was a lot to do and he would make sure it got done: writing and disseminating anti-Manley literature; bugging and surveillance, especially of the Cuban Embassy, consulates of other leftist states and PNP bigwigs; cultivating assets at the phone company and post office; updating the LYNX list of persons to be detained during any period of instability; planning and organizing labor actions—strikes in major industries like bauxite would deliver heavy blows against the economy; actions in the transportation sector would produce hassles in commuting to work and market for which disgruntled citizens would surely blame Prime Minister Manley. There was the business of smuggling in guns and materiel and ongoing efforts to recruit agents, including turning Cuban assets and intelligence officers, and infiltrating personnel into leftwing conferences and conventions throughout the Caribbean and Latin America. The PNP Youth Organization and Women's Movement were both left wing and needed to be monitored. The new woman, Sandra Welks, would prove invaluable in infiltrating community associations and creating others like the "National Council of Women" and the "Silent Majority" and in getting housewives out on the streets to bang the drum against the socialist government. Matt had never thought the day would come but he was grateful to have a woman in the crew.

Gallagher had acquired his embassy vehicle, a Ford LTD, and after work he and Lake drove out to Port Royal to meet with assistant editor of the *Daily Gleaner*, Oliver White. Approaching the waterfront Matt turned east and picked up the A4 to Harbour View and onto Norman Manley Highway, reversing direction west across the Palisadoes, a reinforced spit of land connecting the mainland to Port Royal, originally an island plopped

38

just at the entrance to the harbour. Squinting into the setting sun, the expanse of the Caribbean Sea on his left, the sequestered harbour off to the right, he pondered developments. Headquarters at Langley had come up with a bait girl who was scheduled to arrive in Jamaica in the next few days. An apartment had been rented for her along Manley's jogging route. If she could get into the PM's bed their pillow talk might yield useful intelligence.

The *Gleaner* was Jamaica's *New York Times*, the newspaper of record and conservative voice of the establishment. Founded in 1834 in the dying days of slavery—full emancipation coming in 1838—the *Gleaner* kept an eye out for the interests of privilege. *No* to black power, Rastas, marijuana smokers and socialists; *yes* to the business elite and good relations with America. It had never championed black leaders like Bogle, Gordon, Garvey and even blamed the 1938 worker riots on communists in Cuba—as if the slave wages the plantations were paying had nothing to do with disgruntled workers rising up and burning the cane fields. Not since the days of Cudjoe, Nanny and Accompong, the great Maroon freedom fighters, had there been such a revolt, which spread like wildfire across the nation to the wharves and warehouses of Kingston.

"Is the *Gleaner* on board with Seaga, Frank?" Matt asked as they passed the international airport.

"Ah, they're all right," Lake said. "They backed Manley in '72 but have since pulled their heads out of their asses and seen the light."

"Good. We'll work with them."

"Rag's owned by one of the twenty-one rich families that control Jamaica. Good white folk mostly. Hector Wynter the editor is former chairman of the JLP. Good man. They'll do anything to get rid of a scumbag like Manley out to take money from business and give it to the goddamn poor."

"Perfect."

"What's the move?"

"We help them do their job."

"How, exactly?"

"Pavlov."

"Pav *who*?"

"Psychology, my dear fellow."

Having a few moments to kill, Matt parked and they walked the ancient streets to Ft. Charles. Lake sniffed out a fish-and-chips joint and ordered a portion to go. At the British fort, a survivor of the 1692 quake and still an impressive historical monument, they sat among the cannon as Lake filled his face. Matt had brought along a copy of the *Gleaner* to tutor Frank on the plan of attack. He carried with him a small parcel.

Wolfing his food, Lake was unable to stifle a belch.

"Easy, Friar Tuck," Matt grunted. "Didn't you eat lunch?"

"Want some?"

"Lesson from the world of advertising," Matt said, drawing Lake's attention to the blood-spattered front page. "You have a football star or some gorgeous chick with tits out to here pose with your product. The glamour rubs off through simple juxtaposition. Pavlovian conditioning. Ring a bell, the dog eats. Next time it drools when it hears the damn bell."

"Yeah, I heard of that. Pavlov."

"Same thing works on the down side. So next to this picture of blood in the streets we get the editor to place a column on Manley... some puff piece that suggests he's up in an ivory tower while the masses are suffering and getting gunned down in the streets. Maybe that's a policeman lying there in a pool of blood."

"This how you brought down Allende?" Frank snickered.

"What are you laughing at, Tuck? Didn't you take Psych 1A? The work we did with *El Mercurio* in Santiago laid the ground for the overthrow of Allende. We'll do the same here. Propaganda is powerful business and this subtle stuff is just the tip of the iceberg. We'll hit it at all levels."

"Well, if you put the column on the PM in the middle and the bloody photo over here on the left, how about on the right you put—"

"A column on the economy going into the tank," Matt cut him off. He had a thing about being first and best in everything.

"I'm starting to see the beauty of it," Frank said, licking chips grease from his fingers. They strolled the old fort's quarterdecks, the fresh salt breeze from the open sea mingling with the redolent waters of the harbor, at the entrance to which the notorious pirate Calico Jack had been hung in 1720 as a warning against brigandry. They walked by the old barracks and parade grounds to Fisherman's Beach and ducked inside the Castle Keep bar, an atmospheric establishment on the waterfront pungent with tobacco and four hundred years of history, of which remnants abounded—a section of whale baleen, a ship's steering wheel, a barebreasted wooden mermaid from a ship's maidenhead, a rusted old anchor and sundry other *objets d'histoire*. The barkeep made change from a miniature "treasure chest" as a Skull-and-Crossbones rippled in the breeze of a small fan. Looking down from a shelf was a patch-eyed wooden buccaneer with a green parrot perched on his shoulder, a bit of kitsch among the genuine artifacts.

Frank and Matt eschewed the relatively well-lit wooden bar for a dim table in the back and waited for White to show. The setting called for grog and they ordered glasses of white Appleton rum. A bent and gnarled old man appeared from nowhere with a bag of "shark's teeth" which would, he swore, grant their possessor mighty powers, but Matt could see they were the teeth of a cow or goat. Rebuked, the man slunk away casting daggers and silent curses.

White arrived and joined them at their table. He was a reedy thin high-brown fellow, soft-spoken and mannerly. The mulatto middle class had arisen originally from liaisons between white master and black slave, the likkle tawny bastards brought into the house and afforded opportunities not granted their pure-blood black half-brothers and sisters left to their mothers' provenance. Matt produced the parcel, a box of Havana cigars, and the three smoked and drank rum. Matt wasn't a heavy smoker but he enjoyed a fine cigar on occasion. Knowing how coveted a good Habanero was, he gifted White with the remainder of the box. The *Gleaner,* the assistant editor said, would be a willing ally to Gallagher's propaganda campaign and welcomed opening a weekly column for a case officer to write scathing criticisms of Manley and the PNP.

Several days later the front page of the *Daily Gleaner* was laid out much as Matt Gallagher had prescribed, a puff piece on Manley getting a new car, "A Cadillac for the Prime Minister," flanked by bloody images of death in the streets on one side and news of a nose-diving economy on the other. With ten million dollars to spend, the boys at the Company would have bought the fucking Cadillac and given it to Manley if they had to.

Hell, maybe they did.

7

Mid-October 1980, Santa Barbara

It was past two as he tucked Marva's photo back in the drawer and crawled into bed. He'd been up late as usual practicing the music. His abode was undeniably shoddy and this Westside neighborhood was far from the best part of town, but it was home and he liked the unpretentious vibe and privacy, the small grassy yard enclosed by a seven-foot wooden fence. The two-bedroom unit was rented out of funds left him in his mother's will, which while not making him rich gave him a leg up while he got his act together. The place was filled to the brim with artifacts and memorabilia from Jamaica, as if he'd wished to bring a chunk of the Rock home to Santa Barbara and turn his pad into a mini JamDown-West. There were tourist posters of pretty girls in bathing suits at Dunn's River Falls and lush waterfalls and on the beach at Negril (where no building could stand taller than the palm trees). There were images of the Blue Mountains, the harbour at Kingston, coffee plantations. Rafting on the Rio Grande. Maps and album covers, Rasta tams, T-shirts, a carved ironwood bust of an African-looking woman with flaring nostrils. A large Jamaican flag, black, gold and green, adorned the wall to his left. Pictures of Bob abounded, dreadlocks flying, and some of other reggae stars too. These pieces of the Rock made his home into a sanctuary and shrine that linked him emotionally and spiritually back to his time in Jamaica and kept those days alive within him, soothing his restless soul if not conjuring actual memories to part the veil of the Lost

41

Time. All the memorabilia in the world couldn't do that. Neither did he keep abreast of current events on the Rock—only by best friend Zack informing him did he learn of monster Hurricane Allen ravaging the northeast coast this past August, its 39-foot storm surge destroying lives and most of the banana crop. Jamaica would remain for him an idealized tropical paradise uncorrupted by inconvenient truths and that was that. Yet his palace was also his prison. If he didn't absolutely have to be somewhere he stayed in, night after night.

Tonight, bitten by nostalgia for his days in South America, he'd set aside his good guitar, a Gibson Les Paul like Bob played, and taken up the old acoustic Victor had given him in Santiago, Chile back in '73. Victor was a grown man who would sit in the plaza and strum and sing *Guantanamera* and other cool songs. He'd recognized thirteen-year-old Scott's keenness for music and gifted him with the inexpensive beginner's instrument.

Scott's mind was filled with nonsensical chatter and sleep eluded him. He thought of Doc M, the strangeness of the man, the glint in his eye that seemed eerily familiar, an aloofness or *something* he'd seen somewhere, now lost to the ages.

From the stillness there came again that banshee whine. The previous night he'd spread rice about the place again, only to vacuum it up in the morning.

A tapping sound came from the front of the house. He grabbed the baseball bat from the closet and tiptoed in his underwear to the front room.

"Who's there?" he cried. "Someone there?"

The tapping again… sounded like the kitchen window. Taking a slugger's grip on the bat, he edged to the window and pulled back the curtain.

He got the fright of his life. Glaring at him through the glass—the face of the devil.

"FUCK!" he jumped back, knocking over chairs. It came to him that it was a human face that he'd seen, not demonic. A black man he'd never laid eyes on before.

"I've got a gun!" Scott shouted. "I'll blow your turkey head off!"

"Yuh name Scott?" a voice said. "Scott Gallaghuh?"

"Galla*gher*. Who the fuck wants to know?"

"Nah mean yuh nuh harm, sonny. Doan need nuh gun."

"Don't call me sonny, asshole. What do you want?"

"Me come with message from Jamaica."

"In the habit of barging in on people in the middle of the night, are ya?"

"I-man carry a thing from Jamaica fe yuh. From yuh friend Jesse James."

"Who?"

42

"Can let I in, sonny? Nah gwine hurt yuh."

"Hurt *me*? With your head bashed in by a 34-inch Ernie Banks? Stay where you are." Scott threw on jeans and came back to the kitchen.

"Stand back, hear? Louisville Slugger don't make no soft bats. And don't call me sonny, yuh old goose."

"Open the door, man. Where yuh manners?"

As Scott opened the door, he had a sense of déjà vu. Sonny? Someone used to call him that and it sure as hell hadn't been his father.

Standing outside the door was a black man, looked Jamaican… he had that island look about him, somehow. Scraggly beard and 'stache and world-weary wisdom in his eyes.

"What's this all about?"

"Told you," said the man, "yuh friend in Jamaica send me."

"My friend Jesse James," Scott scoffed, but the name had a familiar ring to it.

"Yes suh, Jesse James. Say yuh remember him fe sure."

"If it was so important why didn't he come himself?"

"Me come America fe work, him stay a yard. Can give I-man a beer?"

"Ain't got no beer."

"Visitor come and nuh refreshment yuh offer? Man gotta comport himself more hospital than that."

"Hospit*able*. Now it's me being rude."

"Howard never tell me it a gwan like this," the man shook his head ruefully. "Me say me never wan' chase down no white bwoy in America."

"All right, for crying out loud. Those shoes dirty?"

The man looked down at laced-up boots that seemed a permanent fixture on his foot.

"Just leave them on," Scott sighed. He led the man into the kitchen and put on hot water for tea.

"Sit down if you like," Scott said and the man sat at the kitchen table. "I do vaguely remember a Jesse James. Tall guy, right?"

"Nah too tall."

"Stubby Afro?"

"Dreads."

"Hmmm."

"Scar over him left eye. Him work at that time fe yuh father."

"My father."

"Say yuh father pay him to keep watch over yuh."

"Cha! Raasclot nah watch me bumboclot ass."

"Howard say fe sure yuh remember."

"Howard?"

"Jesse birth name, Christian name."

43

"How come he needs a phony name?"

"Them Kingston youth like fe take them tough-guy name."

"I remember that somehow. What's your name?"

"John Wayne."

"The toughest of them all.

"Name cyan't make man tough. John Wayne me birth name. John Wayne Elliston. Howie brother."

"So you're the real deal. Guess I'm lucky to be alive."

The man grinned. The teapot whistled and Scott got up to check the cupboard.

"Peppermint okay, Duke?"

"Peppermint. Yes I."

"So how'd you find me?"

"Howie say yuh live up this way and ride bike." The Jamaican slurped his tea and set it down to steep.

Just then came again that banshee whine. That same eerie alley-cat-from-hell moan. The Jamaican startled, and Scott saw in his eyes his own fear mirrored back.

"Howie wan' me give yuh this," Elliston said, as if hurrying to conclude his business. He reached to his shirt pocket and produced a small photograph which for Scott instantly blotted out everything else. It was a black and white snap of himself with Bob Marley.

"Bob!" he exclaimed. "I remember this. It was at his home in Kingston. Your brother give this to you? Jesse James?"

"Yes man."

"Where did he get it?"

"Say yuh must a drop at Smile Jamaica."

"Smile Jamaica. There was a concert."

"Yes I. Biggest concert ever in Jamaica. Remember?"

"Not really. God this is maddening!"

He couldn't take his eyes off the photo. Bob's infectious warm smile seemed to jump out and light up the room.

"Damn he looks great," Scott marvelled. "Wonder where he is right now. With some beautiful woman, no doubt."

"Sonny, uh, Scotty, me haffi gwan." [*I have to go.*] Elliston took a last sip of tea.

"You can sleep on the couch if you want, Duke."

"Gwine be all right?" the man asked. Again Scott had the impression the visitor was possessed of a sudden fear.

"Why wouldn't I be all right?"

Elliston reached out and brushed his fingers under Scott's whispy chin beard. He smiled in kindly amusement.

"Beard like Bob Marley himself."

Scott beamed at the ultimate compliment. "Thanks for the photo," he said and led the visitor out the door and through the gate.

"Your brother say anything about the CIA?" Scott asked as they stood quietly beneath the stars.

Elliston wrinkled his face enigmatically and stared off.

"He did, didn't he."

"Tek care a yuhself, sonny."

"You take care, Mr. John Wayne."

The alleycat picked that moment to let out a bloodcurdling shriek.

"Yard nice wit' some lily plant around the fence," Elliston said furtively. "*White* lily."

With that, Elliston disappeared into the night. Scott went in, dug a Wailers album out of the crate and slapped it on the turntable. He rolled a joint and *Duppy Conqueror* rolled around on the box. The lyrics nagged at him and through the floodgates of memory a story washed into mind. Bob Marley, the tale went, had been haunted by a cat crying outside his window back in the struggling days at Studio One, when he was sleeping on the floor in Coxsone Dodd's back room. The cat was really a ghost, a *duppy*, sent by an Obeah man and capable of doing grave harm. Rita saved him by smuggling him into her room at night.

Obeah. African black magic brought to the New World by slaves. Whatever it was called, Voodoo in Haiti, Santeria in Cuba, Obeah in Jamaica, it was as terrifying as the night that swallows the day. Slave masters and colonialists had lived in fear, for an Obeah master held the power of life and death. Hysteria rose to Salem witch-hunt levels, with Obeah men and women pulled out of churches and burned at the stake. Any black found in possession of fetish objects was subject to immediate hanging. The greatest Obeah masters were as powerful on the side of blacks as Jamaica's governor-general was for whites.

Even today Obeah was a force to be reckoned with. An Obeah man or woman could sic a ghost on you. Elliston had sensed it, you could see the fear in his eyes. That devil-cat had shrieked and he'd taken off fast. Obeah could fuck you over, mess with your mind, make you do crazy shit. Make you jump off the planet. Don't mess with Jamaican black magic.

Scott got up and spread more rice. A Jamaican remedy to ward off ghosts. White lilies served the same purpose. Casting the grains didn't make him feel safe, but at least he understood now why he was throwing it on his floor and a little something about Elliston's sudden interest in horticulture.

8

Phil Mitchell rinsed the vomit taste from his mouth. Another couple bottles last night. Karen had started the two of them drinking fine wines and it was all he had left of her (other than the outdated bellbottoms and flowery shirts she'd favored him in). With his practice going down the tubes, and ill able to afford the $200 varietals they'd once indulged in, he pretended his $5.99 Trader Joe's specials were her favorite vintages. Last night, a Napa Cab posing as a fine Valpolicella from Verona. A codeine nightcap to help him sleep but he still felt exhausted. He popped a Valium but it didn't take the edge off.

Waiting in Mitchell's office, Scott Gallagher inspected the photos on the far wall—dated black-and-white portraits of stuffy-looking souls in quaint finery, ghosts from a bygone time—as Mitchell blew in like a dark cloud.

"Hey, Doc," Scott greeted. He pointed to one of the photos. "Who's this guy?"

"Mesmer or somebody," Mitchell grunted in disinterest as he flopped into the big leather chair behind his desk.

"Mesmer?"

"Anton Mesmer, as in mesmerize, hypnotize. Sit down."

"Psychologists, aren't they?" Scott said as he sat. "Who's your man?"

"Used to like Jung."

"Used to."

"Good, Jasmine made coffee." Mitchell got up and poured himself a cup.

"Do you believe in the world beyond the veil, Doc? Karma, ESP, things like that?"

"Believe in that crap? Hell no."

"Because I think I've solved the riddle of the Lost Time. Why I can't remember."

"Let's hear it."

"Someone fixed my business."

"Come again?"

"Black magic. Someone threw a spell on me."

"You're not serious."

"Jamaicans believe it."

"You're not Jamaican."

Scott laid John Wayne's photo on the desk.

"I'll be darned," Mitchell said, eyeing the photo. "You really did know Bob Marley."

"Knew you didn't believe me," Scott rolled his eyes.

"How did you meet?"

"I was walking down by Cross Roads after school one day when I sees this likkle girl carrying a bag of something. Guinep or mangoes, I don't remember, some kind of fruit. Out selling on the street, a higgler. Ten years old oughta be in school. Selling on the street to help her mother buy rice 'n

46

peas for the evening meal. Life rough in Jamaica, yunno? So I'm standing there in my punky school uniform buying a mango, I guess it was, and all of a sudden this big silver-blue BMW pulls up and who gets out but Bob himself. Robert Nesta Marley, in the flesh. Got this stare that just pierces right through you, dreadlocks tumbling down. Takes your breath away, dig? Like looking into the face of a black-maned African lion. Magnificent, just magnificent. A force of nature."

"What did you do?"

"Pissed my pants and shit my britches. Froze up like *huevos* on a cold toilet. Next thing Bob's back in the Beamer and I'm going, 'You blithering numbskull. One time in your life Bob Marley is standing in front of you and you can't open your lily-liver mouth.'"

"So what happened?"

"Remember Henry? The guy I got in a fight with?"

"He accused your father of being with the CIA."

"I go back and dicker for a bike. 'Fuck off' he says, but I flashed some money and he saw the light. So I'm cruising Kingston and come across this cool old place with Rastas playing football in the front yard. Soccer football. I take a good look and there's Bob racing up and down like greased lightning in sneakers. Holy shit. I get off my bike and waltz in the gate like I'm somebody, know what I mean? Big old place with lots of trees and grounds for soccer. House trimmed in red, gold and green, the Ethiopian colors. They're running around like it's the goddamn World Cup…."

"Watch 'im! Watch de man dere!" the frantic chap in goal cried as bodies rushed upfield toward him in a mad scramble amidst a cacophony of hooting and shouting. Colorful characters in dreadlocks jockeying for position, *yes I*, them a ziggy-zaggy this way 'n that, natty in them cris' jerseys and tams, some barefoot on the hard paved surface.

"Me on 'im, Fams!"

"Watch Skipper dere! Jump! Gilly! See 'im dere!"

The man called Skipper worked the ball across the yard, weaving his way deftly past defenders and toward the increasingly frantic Fams bouncing around in goal.

"Me say watch Skipper! Him a come fast!"

"Me 'ave him mon, yuh nah hear?" the one called Jumpy cried testily.

The Skipper, a wiry short fellow with hair tucked under a purple tam, feinted to freeze Jumpy and passed the ball off to a teammate, who booted a shot high and over the fence to a chorus of hoots and hollers. Someone had to go fetch and in the meantime the man called Gilly retired from the game and went into the house.

"Oy Joe," someone shouted. "Play football?"

Scott blanched. The brown-skinned locksman calling him was the Skipper—Bob Marley himself.

"You're… wow," Scott gagged. "I…."

"Yuh play or nah? Need a man."

"I'm in, I'm in." Scott shoved his bike aside and joined in.

"Nah, Skip, him just a kid," someone protested.

"Why ya worry so? Ain't CIA. Yuh CIA, Joe?"

"Scott. No CIA here."

"Him play Skill side. Gwan now."

Allan "Skill" Cole, a professional footballer and world-class athlete, shoved Scott into the backfield as Marley's team worked the ball up field. Here came Bob on the dribble gunning straight for Scott, who ran up to challenge. Bob, who loved playmaking more than taking the shot himself, froze the kid with his eyes, deked quick as a cat and scooted by to set up a goal. Scott was left scratching his head. The man had game.

"Stay in front of him, Joe," Cole barked. "Skip go by like yuh flip yuh bamboo an' make a wish."

"It's Scott," Scott said.

Onlookers had a laugh at his expense, even the guy out on Hope Road hovering over his motorcycle as if it were having some mechanical problem. He'd been tailing Scott ever since he'd left school. His name— what he called himself—was Jesse James and that was his job, keeping an eye on the kid for his old man.

Scott broke loose down the right side and Skill Cole, pumping those massive thighs like supercharged pistons, drove upfield and worked the ball to him. With one man to beat—Bob—Scott dribbled forward but was tentative and Marley easily stripped the ball away and set up another goal.

"Cha! Stay wit' him mon!" Cole chided.

Here came the play again. Bob got the pass and drove toward Scott, who by now felt a burning need to prove his *cojones*. He went aggressively for the ball and hooked Marley's right foot, sending him sprawling on the pavement.

You'd have thought it was the crashing of the Hindenburg. Someone had tripped the Skipper. *The humanity.* Horrified gasps rang out and everyone swarmed over.

Wha'ppen dere? Wha'ppen fe Skippah?

Bloodclot white bwoy mash him up!

Raasclot knock him onna ground!

Cha! Y'all right, Skip?

"Nothing," Marley said through teeth clenched in pain as he was helped to his feet.

Skill Cole turned to Scott with a raging eye.

"Ain't American football Joe. Cyan't tackle the man like a fucking Miami Dolphin."

"Sorry... didn't mean to...." Dejected, Scott got his bike and started to walk off. As Skill and the others helped Bob limp to the house, Marley called out.

"Hey, Joe. Come eat a likkle thing with we."

"Thanks anyway." Scott walked on, head hung low.

"Nah trouble yuhself, seen? Take some I-tal stew fe yuh belly."

"Really?"

"Yes, man. Make yuh bamboo strong as iron."

Scott hustled back as Bob hobbled to the porch and took off his sneaker. The right big toe shone an angry shade of purple, but the skin wasn't broken.

"There blood I-man skin yuh like goddamn goat," Cole glared at Scott as he wrapped Bob's foot. Scott went pale and there were chuckles again at his expense.

"Hurt this here foot last year," Marley said. "Mashed up same toe playing football over Boy's Town field. Take long time fe heal."

"Better take care of that," Scott said.

"Doctor Joe say take care o' dat," Skill said with supreme sarcasm. "Where I and I send the fuckin' bill?"

"Name nah Joe," Marley said. "Him say Scott, nah so?"

"Scott, that's right. Pleased to meet you, Mister Marley."

"Mister Marley," Cole scowled.

"And that's how I met Bob Marley," Scott said to Dr. Mitchell. "Tripping the man on his bad foot. What a horse's ass."

"What happened after that?"

"We sat on the porch and I got initiated."

"Into what?"

"The club...."

The guys settled on the veranda near the Tuff Gong record shop and talked over the game as the sun sank low in the west, an afternoon breeze picking up. Bob Marley's scuffling ghetto days were over. He had come far for a brown-skin half-caste rudeboy, son of a black country girl and a white Jamaican who'd served in the British West Indies Regiment. Two years ago—despite a string of major hits in Jamaica—Marley was practically indigent, without a cotch of his own to rest his head. Now he lived further uptown than the prime minister in a colonial-era great house that harkened back to the days of slave owners. The Rasta elders had worried about that for a while, fearing their troubadour truth teller would lose his spiritual bearings in his fancy new digs. But Skip was roots all the way. Sure 'nuff

49

the place had acquired its own Rasta-fied, ghetto-licked personality, from the lively record shop and Queen of Sheba vegetarian restaurant tucked off by the front gate, to Rastafarian colors and iconography splashed across the fences and walls--*Yes, I-yah, Jah guide yuh going out and coming in*—to the guys themselves with their proud beards and wildly sprouting locks-vines, marvelously free and uninhibited. Their Queens wrapped in African prints and headdresses, black and proud and lovely.

Marley doffed his tam and shook out his locks; he'd been dread two years now since letting his Afro grow out in the *Natty Dread* period. Gilly Gilbert, a barrel-chested dreadlocks giant with handsome smiling face—a fine cook and football player nicknamed "General Gwan" and "Stonewall Jackson" for his defensive skills, a hard man to get past—ran in and out with smoothies whipped up in his blender from Jamaica's endless treasurehouse of fruit—mango, papaya, soursop, sweetsop, passionfruit, ugli and lots more. From nowhere appeared a huge spliff rolled in what looked like dried cabbage leaf. In speechless wonder Scott stared as Marley took rapid, massive hits, bellows-lungs pumping and flaming that blunt like a blowtorch. It seemed he would surely exhaust the whole humongous cigar in one fell swoop. Scott felt privy to a sacred rite... Bob Marley standing in front of him smoking a J.

Ganja, collie, ilie, herb, grass, Alaska, wisdom weed, kaya--marijuana had arrived in Jamaica in the mid-19th Century with indentured servants from India. The word *ganja* was said to stem from the same root as *Ganges*, the sacred river of Hindus, where *Cannabis* grew wild. Ganja is mentioned in the Vedas and a common Jamaican term for it, collie or "kali," reputedly comes from Kali, the Hindu goddess and consort of Lord Shiva. Rastas said the plant had grown on the grave of King Solomon and was the "holy herb" mentioned in the Bible—the vehicle to cosmic consciousness, key to expanding awareness of oneself, the universe and God.

Psalms 104:14. *He causeth the grass to grow for the cattle and herb for the service of man, that he may bring forth food out of the earth.*

The High Priest of Herb took a monster hit, held forever and blew out like he was the god of the west wind disappearing behind the clouds.

"Smoke herb, Scott?" Marley asked, his eyes glinting under narrowing lids though somehow he seemed ever more aware of his surroundings. "Jamaican herb strong. Sinsemilla. Cyan't hurt yuh none... first time maybe mess with yuh mind a likkle."

"I'll be fine."

Sinsemilla was weed that was not pollinated and grew without seeds—*sin semilla*—and oh baby but it packed a wallop.

Bob passed the rapidly shrinking spliff to Scott. Stoked to try the fabled weed, in the presence of Bob Marley yet, Scott took a big draw—and

50

promptly blew it out with a deep railing cough, drawing yet more tittering from the guys.

"Healing of the nation," Marley said. "Alcohol kill yuh, herb build ya."

"Truth."

Someone came out with a camera and snapped a shot of Scott and Bob sitting together on the veranda and flashing big smiles. Scott hit again on the joint. The burn wasn't as bad this time. The weight lifted from his shoulders and he floated off on a cloud, flowing into the great stream of energy that connects all living things. The Wailers' mammoth sound system was cranking *Slave Driver* so loud the ground beneath his feet trembled.

"Come, we go a house," Marley said and everyone went inside. Rasta elders had gathered in a room to the left of the gorgeous wooden stairway, reasoning and smoking the chalice, so Bob and the guys settled into the room on the right. Someone fetched ice for Bob's foot. More spliff was torched and Scott smoked his share. Bob and crew didn't usually pass spliffs around like American hippies; they smoked so much everyone just held his own. Hitting off the sweet Sinsemilla, Scott felt at one with the cosmos, moving and swaying with the rhythm of the music. It even seemed he could understand the Jamaicans' thick patois better now. *T'row 'way dem shoe mi breddah anna trod de earth like natural mon. Seen? Sight.*

Seeco Patterson came over holding a water pipe as intricate and impressive as Scottish bagpipes. With his roughly-hewn face, the Wailers percussionist looked like a proud Indian chief straight off the back of a Yankee nickel. Seeco had tutored original Wailers Bob, Bunny and Peter on the subtleties of cadence and tempo and gotten them the audition with Clement "Sir Coxsone" Dodd that launched their careers. In summer of '64, in the shade of the mango tree behind Studio One on Brentford Road in Trench Town, Peter Tosh, Bunny Livingston, Junior Braithwaite and Beverley Kelso backed Bob on lead vocals on a little number the group had cooked up called *Simmer Down*. Dodd knew he had a hit on his hands. Within days the group was back in studio recording on a one-track Ampex 350 tape deck, backed by a second female singer, Cherry Green, and the best ska band in the world, the Skatalites. The record was pressed immediately and that same night the tune was blasting on sound systems all across Kingston. *Simmer Down* was two months Number One on the Jamaican charts but Dodd paid the band a pittance. On the Rock, producers had musicians by the balls (hence Marley's persistent efforts to launch his own *Tuff Gong* label.

Seeco fired up the water pipe, took a long bubbly draft and offered it to Scott.

"Lick up the chalice," Patterson said, emitting a cloud of smoke like Geronimo emerging from a sweat lodge.

51

"Lick it?" Scott asked.

"Lick it, man, lick it."

"Is it licorice?" he said as he eyeballed the black rubber tubing.

"Smoke the damn pipe," said Tyrone Downie, laughing until tears ran down his face. They called him Jumpy for his hirky-quirky kinetic personality.

Scott took a blast and the warmth of human love and compassion spread over him. Ganja was illegal, Bob Marley said, because when you smoked you didn't want to war.

Feeling no pain, Scott sat on the couch next to the handsome short-haired chap who'd played goalie, the one called "Fams." A Rasta without dreads.

"Family Man, right?" Scott said. "Aston Barrett, Wailers bass player?"

"Yes, man," the genial fellow replied in a voice as deep and sonorous as the famous twang of his bass guitar. The nickname came from the multitude of pickneys that called him daddy, a "conscious African" like Fams eschewing birth control as the white man's evil scheme to keep the black man down. Local legend had Fams with more pickneys running around even than the Skipper, who tended to get first choice and who'd gotten angry at former squeeze Esther Anderson for wanting to use contraceptives. As a youth, like Bunny and untold other aspiring ghetto musicians, Family Man had made his first guitar from a stick, a sardine can and a strand of stripped electrical wire. You made do in Jamaica, made do with a lot of things.

"You must be Carly," Scott said to the thin, almost gaunt fellow sitting at Family Man's side.

Carlton Barrett nodded. The Barrett brothers were the heart of the Wailers rhythm section, Family Man on bass and younger sibling Carly on drums working the one-drop riddim to make even Sly and Robbie sit up and take notice. Yes man, the one-drop! Nice up the dancehall with the sweet reggae beat. Omit the first beat in a 4/4 measure and you got it. Carly had virtually invented the riddim. Bob loved it so much he stole the Barretts from Lee Perry's studio band the Upsetters right under Scratch's nose (settling a score for Perry selling off the rights to a batch of Wailers records to distributors in England without paying the guys a penny). Marley + Upsetters would prove to be a match made in heaven.

"Yuh love reggae music?" Carly asked, a burning joint in his hand.

"Me love it, man," Scott said.

Gilly Gilbert called the crew to eat. He had cooked up some I-tal stew Jamaican style in a big bucket out back. I-tal, Rasta-speak for "natural" or "vital." Rastas, following scripture, were health food fanatics, shunning foods like pork, shellfish, and salt, the latter believed to interfere with

52

spiritual experience. Big Gilly ladled the steaming ambrosia into calabash bowls made of gourds. Scott took his portion into the living room and sat next to Bob.

Scott wolfed great mouthfuls of stew from his gourd-bowl until Marley patted the back of his hand.

"Nah eat so fast," Marley admonished. "Too craven gravalicious."

"Mean don't eat like a pig," Family Man said.

"Right," Scott shifting down a gear. "You guys play good soccer."

"Skill play Santos Jamaica," Bob said. "Last September him lead them bwoy over New York Cosmos right here a Kingston Stadium."

"Kick Pele ass too," said Fams. "Jamaica win 1-0."

"Really? Pele?" Scott gazed over at Skill Cole with new wonder in his eyes, taking in the solid torso and tree-trunk thighs, the cool confidence in his demeanor.

"Skill totally rule Pele," Bob said. "Was day after I-man hurt this here foot playing football over Boys Town field. Rusty nail prick same big toe."

"Skip didn't play music he could play ball," Cole said. "Damn near good as me."

"Yuh come from America, nah so, Scotty?" Bob asked.

"Yeah. Been living in South America though."

"Down dere where?"

"All over. Bolivia. Venezuela. Chile. Argentina."

"What yuh daddy do?"

"Works at the embassy."

As if a switch had been thrown everybody immediately stopped eating and went stone cold silent. Suspicious glances and whispers filled the room, brows arched, postures stiffening defensively.

"What's wrong with that?" Scott said. "What, you think he's CIA or something? They do passports and visas, stuff like that."

"Passports," Skill Cole snorted derisively.

"Folk think CIA hide in there," Bob said.

"No way. My father doesn't work for the CIA, I promise you."

Tensed brows slowly eased, conversations and dining resumed, but the mood had shifted several notches toward the sedate end of the scale. Scott sat quietly, finishing his stew, as if alone in the room. He couldn't stand it.

"Why would the CIA be in Jamaica?" he burst out.

"Them nah like Manley."

"Come on."

"Election year a come. Them wan' it fe go the way them wan' it fe go."

"You really think the CIA is worried about an election *here?* Their hands are full with Russia and China, places like that. Nobody's getting bent out of shape over a little island in the Caribbean."

"Nuh place onna de earth them cyan't reach," Skill said. "Jungle of Vietnam to gold mine of South Africa. Cyan't hide from CIA."

"Man in Chile," Family Man said, "what him name, Allmendes?"

"Allende. *Ay-yen-day.*"

"Look what happen fe him."

"What about Chile?" Scott demanded.

"Man there wan' help him people," Marley said. "Mean yuh must take money from rich folk and Babylon nah like that. Them call him socialist, communist, everything like that an'--"

--"Tsssst." Skill slashed at his throat. Salvador Allende, president of Chile, had died in a coup d'etat on September 11, 1973, less than three years before. Scott and Matt were residing in Santiago at the time. Only thirteen, Scott had not really grasped what was going on but he'd heard the planes attacking La Moneda, the presidential palace, the country obviously in upheaval. A couple months later he and his father moved to Buenos Aires.

"You really believe the CIA had something to do with that?"

"Everybody know," said Family Man and all nodded.

"Them a try same thing in Jamaica," Marley added. "Manley too much like Allende... building school, hospital, road. Babylon a downpressor man. Always it a gwan so; only the place change. Cuba, Chile, Jamaica."

"The United States doesn't overthrow governments," Scott stammered. "We help everyone. We're the good guys."

The Jamaicans looked at each other aghast. Some cried in astonishment or rolled in belly laughs, others cursed aloud and slung anti-colonial diatribes (some of the choicest coming from Skill Cole).

Bloodclot! Raasclot! Bumboclot!

Devil massa backra. Babylon a gwine fall.

Yessuh, must gwan so, prophecy a fulfill.

Scott was bewildered beyond words. Bob and his pals had it all wrong. Everything he'd learned growing up had instilled in him the certain knowledge that his country stood unflinchingly for the Good and Noble. The occasional lapse only served to cast Uncle Sam ever more firmly in the bronze of mythic virtuousness. Scott had to believe that he had the truth, not the Jamaicans, but he couldn't bring himself to argue the point. Why alienate Bob and his new friends?

"Nyam, nyam," Marley said—*eat, eat*—and the matter was dropped. Eyes avoided Scott's for a while but he was not shunned and there were no overt hard looks. *White bwoy haffi learn the truth.* The message of Rastafari was not only the wickedness of Babylon System and the black man's redemption through Haile Selassie I, but love and I-nity (unity) as well. Scott was not an enemy to fear but a child to educate.

Each one haffi teach one. One Love, yunno?

Aha, Phil Mitchell said to himself, *he's getting this from the Rastas. Credibility issue here.* He figured to give the kid free rein and let him hang himself.

"Went back two days later," Scott said. "Rita was throwing a party for Bob's birthday. All kinds of people showed up, many top stars and singers, a full-on Who's Who of reggae...."

The sultry tenor of Bob Marley backed by Family Man's booming bassline blasted like Olympian thunderbolts as Scott rode into the Hope Road yard. The music came from the Wailers' humongous sound system in the rehearsal room in the old slave quarters behind the house and seemed to shake the very earth, it was that loud. To Scott it was like heralding trumpets announcing entrance into a fantastic new world, magical and forbidden. He ditched his bike and gimped in, limping slightly from an injury suffered playing soccer in PT at school the day before. Bob and the guys called a friendly *"Yes I"* when they saw him but there was too much going on to pay him much attention. People were flooding into the yard and moving to the beat like a gracefully flowing tide. It seemed half of Kingston was here, spilling out onto the veranda, roaming the grounds, leaning up against an almond or mango tree smoking spliff. Among them was musical genius to make the Grammies look like a high school talent show: "Jumpy" Tyrone Downie talking keyboards with fifteen-year-old prodigy Bernard "Touter" Harvey, who'd promised his mother he'd do his homework when he got home. Rita, Bob's dreadlocked Reggae Queen, and fellow I-Threes Judy Mowatt and Marcia Griffiths, the Wailers backing singers and marvelous soloists in their own right, were conspicuously present in long dresses and Ethiopian scarves.

Here was Big Youth, one of the giants of early reggae and a forerunner of American rap music, chatting heavy patois with future legend and tragic figure, big-bellied Jacob "Killer" Miller... Tabby, Bunny and Judge of the Mighty Diamonds, a dulcet roots trio if ever there was one... Johnny Clarke, his voice rich as mountain coffee... Ja-Man Junior Byles and I Jah Man... Bob's good friend Steven "Cat" Coore from Third World Band. Linval Thompson and a young Dennis Brown. Here was the awesome dread from St. Ann, Rodney Winston the Burning Spear. Bad boy Gregory Isaacs with his long narrow face and handsome Freddie McGregor with his dreads and beautiful high forehead. There were Abyssinians, Ethiopians, Congos, Gladiators and a Wailing Soul or two. Even a few ska era old timers like Alton Ellis and Derrick Morgan, greats who had gone before and paved the way.

Strutting in now like a banty rooster was Bunny. A feisty runt in dreads was he, devout Rasta, herbalist, farmer, sweet-voiced roots crooner. Bob's face lit up at the sight of one of his oldest friends in the world. Neville O'Riley Livingston, known as Bunny and since the breakup of the original trio with Bob and Peter Tosh as Bunny Wailer. They'd grown up together as barefoot boys in rural St. Ann and later as ghetto rudies in the same Trench Town tenement, where one thing led to another and soon they shared a sister, Pearl, from the congress of Bob's mother Cedella and Bunny's father Taddy, the indiscretion occurring right under the nose of Taddy's common-law wife.

"Wha'ppen, Bunny?" Bob called. *(What's happening, friend?)*

"Yes I," Bunny greeted as he came grinning over for a hug and shake. "How keeping, Nesta? Praises to His Majesty for the all of we a come together fe this upful occasion."

Sauntering in after Bunny was Joe Higgs, former vocal coach to original trio Bob, Peter and Bunny and major influence on their musical development. On Joe's heels were Wailers' manager Don Taylor and Chris Blackwell of Island Records, whom Bunny disparagingly called "Whiteworst." Mingling with the musicians and industry people were ghetto rankings like Mathews Lane bad boy Bucky Marshall, packing hardware.

Reigning Miss Jamaica Bikini Cindy Breakespeare, a dazzling fair-skinned beauty, was in the house. She and Bob had taken up with each other lately but Cindy was radiating icy vibes. Something about Bob diddling her girlfriends that upset her. The evening's hot topic of gossip: *Will Peter show?* Peter Tosh having ditched the Wailers in a snit over Bob singing most all the songs and getting most all the accolades when he was bursting with his own material to get out there.

A long table had been laid out with homecooked Jamaican food, ackee and saltfish, Red Stripe chicken with coconut cream, calaloo, bammy, fried plantain, cassava pudding and jonny cakes among the myriad culinary delights. Rita's friend Minnie, who with her ran the Queen of Sheba veggie shack, had baked a large carrot cake—I-tal with all natural ingredients— which she was busily slicing up for the pickneys, including the Marley brood of Sharon, Cedella, David (Ziggy) and little Stephen. None wore dreadlocks, which were strictly not allowed in the public schools. Rastas were regarded as little more than trash on the streets in the social hierarchy: whites on top, high brown and coloreds in the middle, blacks on the bottom and Rastas the lowest of the low. (The island's original inhabitants, the Arawak Indians, were long gone, wiped out by treasure-seeking Spaniards and warlike Caribs.) Despite their peaceful ways Rastafarians, like a small sect sprouting in the Palestine desert two millennia before, were much despised social pariahs, the target of considerable violence—mostly from the police.

The candles in Minnie's cake were lit to great applause and choruses of *'appy birthday, Skippah, 'appy t'irty-one.*

"Make a wish, daddy," oldest son Ziggy, 8, said in crisp schoolboy English.

"I-man wish my father's will can done on earth as it is in heaven," Marley said, blowing out the candles with a mighty huff.

"Wish haffi secret, Skip," Wailers art director Neville Garrick said with a grin.

"My father work cyan't secret," Bob declared and all nodded in agreement.

Ziggy bounded over to give Bob his present—a new Rasta tam Rita had knit.

"Handsome man," Rita said, coming up to smother him in a bear hug, Bob looking sheepishly over her shoulder for Cindy. She was across the room talking to Big Youth, the red, gold and green jewels inlaid in his front teeth his Rasta credentials. *Ites gold and green*, the same colors as Bob's new tam. Marley winked at Cindy but she pretended not to see.

Other presents came forth. Most people, having little cash to spend and knowing Bob wasn't into material possessions, gave simple things: a half bushel of yam, a crate of mangoes, a bag of ackee... Judy and Marcia just gave a hug and kiss and their best wishes. The guys in the band came up with an eight-inch spliff, drawing oohs and ahs. Chris Blackwell presented him a framed certificate for sales of one Island album or another though Bob was too distracted with Cindy to pay it much attention.

Scott didn't stay late and Rita packed up early as well to get the kids home on a school night. Bob asked Neville Garrick to see them home safe. Garrick got in behind the wheel of the BMW to let Bob and Rita have a moment alone. In a few days it would be their tenth anniversary. Married February 10, 1966, at eleven in the morning by the Justice of the Peace. They'd been performing together even then, Rita and her Soulettes singing backup on the guys' 1965 Studio One album *Wailing Wailers*, their first. Rita would later recall (perhaps incorrectly) that the Wailing Wailers opened for the Jackson Five at National Stadium on their wedding night, the emcee coming out on stage and announcing the blessed event to the whole world.

Not that Rita was overcome with happy remembrances just now, what with Bob and Cindy carrying on so.

"Yuh a come home tonight?" Rita asked in a plaintive tone. Bob usually spent nights at Bull Bay with the family. It was peaceful out there away from the grit and grime of Kingston and the hangers-on at Hope Road and he liked being near the children, on whom he doted. It had been Bob's tenderness toward Sharon, whom Rita had borne before Bob came on the scene, that had convinced her this ghetto rudeboy was a gem in the rough. She'd bring the baby to recording sessions, back in the days at Studio One, and despite Bob's intense focus on the music he would always make sure Rita kept to her feedings and got her rest. Tonight his mind was on other things.

"Wan' work a thing with Fams and Carly," Bob answered. "Get the riddim right on couple song fe the new album."

"Yuh mean work a thing with Cindy," Rita scowled. "Think me a fool, man?"

"Everything must cool fe lay down track inna de morning at Harry J."

"I-Three can stay and sing. Me ask Marcia and Judy."

"Take me pickney home," Bob shook no. "Doan need I-Three tonight."

Rita had another card to play. Noticing Cindy standing on the verandah talking to Joe Higgs, Rita came around the BMW with Stephen in her arms and kissed Bob smack on the mouth, then glared regally at Cindy as she walked back and got in the car. Cindy stormed off in a huff and Bob went for her.

"Cin, where yuh a go? Slow down man."

"Me haffi work tonight. Told you already."

"Them find 'nother girl."

"At the last minute? Be reasonable. Happy birthday, Bob. Hope you got nuff kisses to last you."

"Is yuh kiss I-man want."

"Call your wife. She's a wonderful kisser."

"Why yuh gwan so? Why yuh treat I so?"

"Ah, it's *me* treat *you* bad."

"Wha' me do?"

"Yuh know what you did."

"Eh?"

"Jennifer. Kayesha."

"What about them girl?"

"You *slept* with them." Cindy stopping to face off with Bob by the front gate.

"That why yuh screwface? Think me serious about them girl?"

"Serious enough to grind your bamboo in them pom-pom."

"Why yuh gwan so? Jah Jah nah want him son and daughter a fuss 'n fight over every likkle thing."

"Every likkle thing," Cindy repeated in a thickly ironic tone, rolling her eyes. "It hurts, yunno?"

"I-man talk with them girl now?"

Cindy shook her head.

"Think me love them more than yuh?"

"No," she said softly, bowing her head.

"Nothing can come between we, yunno."

"You're sweet talking me, Robert Nesta Marley."

"Is sweetness from me 'eart. C'mon, smile fe Bobby."

Cindy fought it but a smile cracked at the corner of her mouth. Bob took her hand and swung it along in a carefree manner like lovers do as they strolled out the gate, going for Cindy's car.

Just then a voice called: "Bob." Coming up the street were Prime Minister Michael Manley and his wife Beverley.

"Michael me brother, wha'ppen?" The two men embraced warmly. Marley shunned politics, but the $150 a night Wailers earned on the stump with the PNP in '72 was more money than they'd ever seen in their lives.

Beverley was stunning in a simple white dress, Manley casual in khakis and a Kariba shirt. Upon assuming office one of his first actions was to declare clothing suitable to the tropics acceptable for official government work in place of the traditional three-piece suit of the West. A symbolic statement that Big Brother to the North was no longer making all the rules around here, right down to the appropriate attire.

"Are we late?" Manley said. "We wanted to come by and wish you a happy birthday."

"Nah late. Know Cindy?"

The moment was mildly awkward. Manley had advanced the cause of women with maternity centers and by ending gender-based job discrimination and the stigmatization of illegitimacy—the Bastard Law. He'd also terminated government funding of beauty contests because of their universal bias for fair-skinned girls with European features and "good hair"—like Cindy. For too long in Jamaica blackness had been a mark of shame when black pride was ordained in the Jamaican flag itself—green for the land, gold for the sun, *black for the people*. Had Marcus Garvey, that great apostle of Black Pride and African consciousness, lived and died for nothing?

Manley thought back to his morning run. He had happened along the most beautiful white woman he'd ever laid eyes on in shorts and halter top with green eyes and breasts that merited enshrinement in a museum. They'd jogged along a ways and chatted. Claudia Candiotti was her name, an American girl of 25. She'd batted her eyes in such coquettish manner that Manley knew she was ripe for the plucking. She'd pointed out her apartment as they passed, adding that she lived there alone.

"Evening, Cindy," Manley greeted.

"Mr. Prime Minister. Mrs. Manley."

"Cindy," Beverley Manley greeted coolly. Rita was a friend of hers and she didn't approve of Bob's running around.

Breakespeare went off to work and Marley led the Manleys through the gate onto his property.

"Chris Blackwell's old place, isn't it?" Manley said. "Island House or something?"

"Nah Island House nuh more," Marley said. "House of Dread now."

"House of Dread, I love it!" clapped Beverley. Island Records' Blackwell had transferred the Hope Road property into Marley's name as payment toward albums already produced and as a place where Bob could meet the press, who weren't about to go into the Wild West streets of Trench Town to get their interviews.

Reaching the front door, Manley held back.

"You go in, Bev. Okay if we walk the grounds, Skip?"

"I and I can do that."

Beverley went inside to mingle and smoke a little ilie as Michael and Bob strolled about the property.

"Strange things a gwan, Skipper," Manley said. "Guns never before seen in Jamaica showing up out of nowhere. Automatic rifles, machine guns, M-16s, an endless supply of ammunition. The average Jamaican doesn't have money to buy bulla and cheese let alone fancy weapons and bullets to load them. But there they are out on the street shooting and killing... it come like a plague out of the Old Testament."

"Too much blood a run, me see it my brother."

"My security officers are convinced hired gunmen are involved. Outside agitators. Shipments of rice and flour poisoned... 17 dead from tainted flour in St. Thomas alone. Parathion, long banned in Jamaica. Labor strikes crippling the economy, the bauxite industry reeling and as bauxite goes, so goes Jamaica. All signs of an orchestrated program to disrupt the economy. Someone is stirring things up."

"A wickedness, man."

"I know a thing or two about strikes," Manley went on as they walked under a spreading almond tree. "Cut my teeth on labor actions. These strikes seem less about improving the lot of workers than bringing Michael Manley and democratic socialism crashing down. I admire Fidel Castro but have no intention of following in his footsteps—nor has he encouraged me to do so." Manley seeming to need to unburden himself. "Does it make me a communist to think Jamaica's natural resources should benefit the Jamaican people? That an able-bodied man should not have to work like a dog all his life in the bauxite mines just to enrich the board members of AJ Reynolds and Alcoa? We've never threatened to cut off foreign investment. I've steered Jamaica on an independent course, a third way in the tradition of Juan Peron. These hissy-fits all het up over Castro seducing me into going communist never stop to think old Manley might just bring El Jefe over to democratic socialism. The guttersnipes."

Manley was no Marxist. He'd studied Fabian socialism at the London School under Laski, the gradualist brand of socialism favored by George Bernard Shaw, H. G. Wells and other social reformers and despised by hard-core communists as detrimental to the cause. He'd even supported the expelling of Marxists from the PNP under his father's rule.

"Skip," Manley said softly, "this is in strictest confidence. Jamaica is in real trouble. The United States has cut off all aid because I didn't turn my back on Castro at the UN. Production of sugar and bananas is down, violence is scaring tourists away in droves even though it's almost exclusively confined to the Kingston yards far from the beach resorts. The world oil crisis has sent the price of imported goods sky high and our foreign exchange has been spirited out of the country as middle-class cowards flee to Miami. Where will we find money for the basic necessities of life? Food, medicine, schoolbooks? If I go hat in hand to the World Bank and the IMF in five years we'll likely find ourselves buried under a mountain of debt such that our miseries of today will seem mild in comparison. But if I don't take their money people will starve to death *now*. We'll have to close the schools and hospitals and lay off every factory worker in the country. I'm trapped Skipper and there's no way out."

"A tyranny, man." By now they had circumambulated the house and stood by the circular turnaround by the front door.

"If the leftists in my own party thought I was even *considering* dealing with the IMF they'd have my scalp. Can't *imagine* what Bev would do. My nether regions would be dangling from the city gates."

"Is nah from I-man she learn these thing."

"Thanks, Skip. Think it'd be all right to speak with the elders?"

"I and I can do that. Come, we go reason now."

They went inside and heads turned at the presence of the prime minister.

"Power to the people!" someone shouted and voices chanted: "PNP! PNP! PNP!"

Manley raised a fist in salute. He and Marley entered a room on the left of the handsome wooden staircase where a circle of Rastafarian elders and disciples were having a reasoning, *talking truth*. Rastafarians believed in the divinity of Haile Selassie, the recently deceased emperor of Ethiopia, born Tafari Makonnen. Ras Tafari was anointed Emperor in 1930 as Haile Selassie I ("Might of the Holy Trinity") and bestowed the titles King of Kings, Lord of Lords, Conquering Lion of the Tribe of Judah, Elect of God and Light of the World. A prophecy attributed to Marcus Garvey said "look to the East for the crowning of a black king"—and here he was. Selassie was said to be the 225th monarch in the line of King David and King Solomon. To disciples Haile Selassie I was not the prophet but God incarnate. The "I" in his title was vocalized alternately as "the First" or I as in "I and I," i.e., "you and I are indivisible, of the same spirit." That Selassie I was astrologically a Leo explained the proud "lion strut" of ardent followers like Marley, "coming not to bow but to conquer." So too was the bold and booming reggae bassline like an awesome leonine roar echoing over the African savannah.

Marley had recently gravitated to a branch (or "mansion") of Rastafari founded only eight years prior by a Kingston visionary, the Prophet Gad, who sat now at the head of the circle. Twelve Tribes of Israel dogma held that the twelve sons of Jacob, whom Jah (God, Jehovah) sent down into Egypt, were the ancestors of all persons alive today. Members were assigned to one of the tribes according to date of birth. February-born Bob belonged to the tribe of Joseph. Sacred doctrine held that only 144,000 believers would be saved on Judgment Day, 12,000 from each of the dozen tribes.

Also in the room was Bucky Marshall, ranking gunman from Mathews Lane wearing sunglasses and a gold chain around his neck. Marshall was no devout Rastafarian, but who was going to tell him he wasn't welcome to join the circle and smoke ganja with the brethren? Not with that god-awful scar running down the side of his face all the way to his jaw.

"Evening, Mister Prime Minister," Marshall greeted. "The people love yuh, suh. Joshua beat down them Jericho wall."

"I appreciate all you've done to help," Manley shaking Marshall's hand. That a prime minister should be beholden to a ghetto tough would most places be beyond comprehension, but not in Jamaica. Not long before, Manley had attended the funeral of a ranking who when snipers opened fire one day in JLP territory had sheltered Mike and Bev from harm with his own body, ready to give his life to save theirs. Standing together now, Manley, Marley and Marshall were as different as three men could be: the near-white, London-educated head of state; brown-skinned Bob, who had ridden music up from the ghetto; and coal-black Bucky, still trying to shoot his way out.

The three joined the circle of elders. The pipe was passed, the prime minister taking a small toke out of respect.

"Brother Michael wan' speak now," said Marley. Prophet Gad nodded approval and Manley stood.

"I'd like to form community self-defense groups to deal with the violence," Manley said. "Will the people accept this? We can be quite sure the opposition will crow that the communist sonuvabitch Manley wants to turn Jamaica into a police state."

The elders leaned together and mulled it over. Finally Prophet Gad spoke.

"I and I think more gun nah good idea."

"No, sir," Manley said. "These would be *unarmed* civilian patrols. No guns."

The Rastas conferred again.

"Say no gun?"

"Not even a peashooter. They'll work in coordination with armed officers. Peacemakers, not soldiers."

"Then de plan maybe can work."

"What do you think, Bucky?" Manley asked.

"Cyan't work without gun," Marshall said. "Genie outta the bottle already."

"Respect," Manley said, bowing his head to the Elders to take his leave.

"Yes I. Respect."

There came a commotion... enter Claudie "Jack" Massop, don of Tivoli Gardens and four of his lieutenants. JLP enforcers. Marley tried to steer Massop toward the food and away from Marshall, but the two saw each other and faced off, hands edging close to guns tucked beneath shirts.

The two rankings stared each other down. Massop and Marshall were big-hearted men who showered kindnesses upon the sufferahs in their districts but wouldn't hesitate to kill their enemies. Yuh born in tough environment yuh grow up tough. When Massop noticed Michael Manley coming out of the side room any hope of peaceful co-existence blew up in smoke.

"Wha' gwan now?" Massop cried in outrage. "The Gong get political with PNP?"

In the blink of an eye guns were drawn. People ducked for cover. Marley quickly interposed himself between the gunmen.

"Me nah step on nuh politician side, Jack," Bob said coolly, the guns pointing directly at him.

Striding quickly forward and calling on every ounce of his diplomatic savoir faire to help defuse the situation was Michael Manley.

"Claudie, I'm here for the same reason you and Bucky are here, to wish Bob a happy birthday. Nothing political going on here at all."

"A true, Jack," Bob said, and though Massop received anything the prime minister said with mistrust, he was inclined to believe the Tuff Gong.

"Take something fe yuh belly, man," Bob said. "Plenty food there, nuff spliff. Cool, cool."

Massop put up his gun and an uneasy truce was in effect.

"One love, brethren," Bob said. Massop and crew went about feeding their faces as the guests climbed out from behind couches and chairs. The Manleys, Bob and Bucky Marshall exited the house. Marshall got on his motorcycle and rode off into the night. Bob walked along with Michael and Bev back toward Jamaica House.

"A likkle thing if yuh get time from yuh trouble," Bob said to Manley. "Why the police haffi come down so hard on the Rastaman? Peter and Bunny both beat and put in jail for smoking herb. Beat bad."

Rastafarians were vexed that marijuana had not been legalized. A commission had revealed that a high percentage of Jamaicans smoked, far more than half, typically for energy to do their daily chores. The hysterical stereotype of users as social misfits and lazy idlers didn't hold at all. Dr. Manley West had developed treatments for glaucoma and asthma from cannabis extracts and many Jamaicans claimed beneficial effects of smoking on all manner of ailments. De-criminalization was recommended, but the United States with its un-nuanced drug war mentality wasn't going to stand for that. Manley took the blame in the eyes of the Rastas.

"I'll try to cool them out a likkle," Manley said, but many of his officers were JLP and he knew that if he were to catch a bullet one of these days there was a good chance it would be from the gun of a soldier or policeman. Those charged with preserving law and order had always been the greatest danger to ghetto dwellers, far above the threat posed by the criminal element. Marley, Marshall and Massop had lived with that all their lives. The irony was that now the same held true for the prime minister as well.

It was late now and quiet. Bob stripped to wash off the grit of the day under the water pipe out back. He left on his birthday tam to keep his dreads dry—he'd go up Cane River tomorrow and give them a good washing. Toweling off he ditched the tam, shook out his dreads and ambled along under the fruit trees in the warm Caribbean night. Standing naked, his bare feet planted firmly on Jah's fertile earth, he plucked a low-hanging grapefruit and peeled it. Such plenty in Jamaica and yet such want. The lingering shadow of colonialism. Violence born of deprivation and injustice. It had been a sweet day and Marley's star was rising but how could he rest when his people suffered so?

Unseen, one pair of eyes looked admiringly upon Bob's fine naked form, the taut sculptured buttocks, lean muscular legs, the back that shone golden brown in the heavenly illumination. The tapered waist and washboard abs of a weightlifter. Not a tall man, he stood straight and proud, his masculine feet solid in their stance upon the earth, his dreadlock ropes falling Medusa-like to his shoulders. The muted sound of gunfire in the distance.

Out of some sixth sense Marley turned to see coming toward him the naked form of Cindy Breakespeare, Miss Jamaica Bikini *sans* bikini. She moved in graceful stride, her eyes fixed upon his, Marley drinking in the vision of her loveliness, the ripe breasts, full rounded hips well suited for baby-making, the tiny waist that in its tapered recesses cast her feminine curves in breathtaking relief. Bob opened his arms to encircle and receive her skin to skin, her breasts brushing lightly against his chest in their soft fullness, loins pressed firmly together as the two bodies swayed as one, eyes wide with wonder as they peered into each other's essence. Bob held the last piece of grapefruit under Cindy's nose. She took fruit and fingers into her mouth and then Bob was kissing her, tongue and lips and fruit in a bouquet of sensual delights, the world of guns and madness fading into the ether. Life was good. Jah was great.

9

Matt, Frank Lake and a core group of case officers sat around the big new table in the Company section of the embassy, on which were several record albums, a small hi-fi system and a recent copy of *Time* magazine. The propaganda campaign against Manley was feasting on the arrival in country of 280 Cuban workers to build the Jose Marti High School. In the *Daily Gleaner* and North American press it was played as if Cuban guerrillas had descended from the Sierra Maestra and encamped on the lawns at Jamaica House, Castro and Manley inside smoking Havana cigars and plotting a communist take-over of the Western Hemisphere.

Labor actions in concert with the AIFLD, the American Institute for Free Labor Development, said to be a CIA front, were going well. In the first six months of 1976, strikes running 35, 43 and 81 days against Alcan, Alpart, and Alcoa, respectively, decreased Jamaica's bauxite production by 400,000 tons, severely impacting the already struggling economy. On February 11, a gang of terrorists rode into the Alcoa plant in Clarendon on motorcycles and shot it up, causing the plant to close. Three days later the Jamaican Tourist Board announced massive tourist cancellations. The multinational corporations urged the American press to castigate Manley for increases in the price of new cars, though most of the surcharge went into the pockets of boardroom bigwigs. As with the earlier gunning down of the two policemen at the US Embassy, many thought the Americans were behind the Clarendon shooting.

"We have here," big-bellied Lake stood to say, "albums from the Jamaican reggae group Bob Marley and the Wailers. We got *Burnin'*, *Natty Dread...*"

"That mean something, *natty dread*?" asked Matt.

"Dreadlocks is the Rasta hairstyle."

"Those matted ropes? What, like 'spiffy... *spiffy dread?*' What the hell does that mean?"

"Have a listen." Frank proceeded to play several tracks from the albums, drawing Matt's attention to lyrics he found "incendiary and inciting." Marley singing in grave, ominous tones about revolution, blood, brimstone and fire.

"Brimstone and fire, my ass," Matt scowled. "Who does this guy think he is, Elmer Gantry?"

"Preaching revolution," Frank said.

"Preaching is easy. Doing is another matter."

"*Time* is calling Marley a political force."

"Let *Time* come run the station. What else you got?"

"Check this." Lake put on *Burnin' and Lootin'* from the Wailers' second album as Marley sang in a coolly controlled rage of curfews and men in uniforms and burning the town down.

"But this is what we want, don't you see?" Matt getting a little impatient. "Burning and looting only makes Manley look worse. As long as we can channel whatever shit goes down back to the PNP it's all gravy. Guy's not out giving speeches for Manley, is he?"

"He played music on the stump for him in the '72 campaign," said Lake. "Tries to stay neutral now but—"

"Small potatoes, amigo, small potatoes."

"—they remain friendly… practically next door neighbors."

"Let it go."

"But—"

"Let it the fuck go, Tuck. Do we have a bug in the Cuban Embassy yet? How about a postal intercept of mail in and out? Have we turned any of their agents? There's enough work to do without worrying about some pantywaist singer, for crying out loud."

Lake stared at his hands and said nothing.

And that night in the ghettos of the city, in the streets and tenement yards, there was burnin' and lootin' a-plenty, chaos and conflagration, vehicles overturned, tires erupting in thick plumes of blue-black smoke, police shooting, women screaming, babies crying, fires raging, blood seeping, people dying. Weapons would later be recovered, automatic rifles and powerful handguns the likes of which until recently had never been seen in Jamaica. Michael Manley, on the scene with the Security Forces, raised his eyes to heaven and his voice to the Lord as he cried in anguish:

"Where are these fucking guns coming from?"

10

Halloween Week 1980, Santa Barbara

On his lunch break on the job at the UCSB bike shop Scott walked over to the student center, outside which in the quad a large assembly had gathered, students, professors, activists, youth chanting, shouting, some running around barefoot with painted faces and T-shirts or placards saying "US OUT OF EL SALVADOR." Less than one mile distant along the path to Isla Vista was the Bank of America that had been burned down by antiwar activists in 1970. The social consciousness of the '60s and early

'70s lived on in pockets across the land, Santa Barbara, Berkeley, Madison, in isolated hearts everywhere, a sacred flame flickering in the cold winds of a decade destined to make the Me Generation look like the height of compassionate altruism.

Scott looked around for Zack, who was into this kind of thing. Zack had the knack of showing up with his woolly dreads and baby blues and quickly rounding the prettiest girl, or *girls,* out of the herd. Today he didn't disappoint, two extremely attractive coeds hanging by his side.

"Shari, Zelie," Zack introduced. "You guys know Scotty dread?"

"Dread Scott, is it?" the girls giggled. His locks too were a chick magnet.

"Scott's the lead singer in our reggae band," Zack said. "Come out and dig the vibes sometime."

A student leader grabbed the microphone and got the show rolling.

"Hello Santa Barbara," the bearded activist said. "We start with a few words from Tom Hayden before we hear from a journalist who has recently visited Salvadoran refugee camps along the Honduras border. Tom."

Hayden was greeted warmly as he took the mic. Sitting behind him, his wife Jane Fonda.

"It's five years now since United States military forces left Vietnam after fourteen years of war," Hayden said. "People are surprised to learn that when Dien Bien Phu fell in 1954 the United States was footing 80% of the costs of France's war effort. This didn't all start in El Salvador in the 1970s. It's long-standing US policy of supporting brutal right-wing military dictatorships that terrorize their own peoples. El Salvador, Guatemala, Honduras, massacres are occurring constantly, gruesome, inhuman atrocities. The violence is worse even than Argentina, which is just off the scale. We're shipping tons of arms down there, from M16s to helicopters to everything else."

Argentina? Scott thought. *M16s?* Memories keyed in—he remembered an M14, but hadn't he also held and fired an M16? They looked quite different the two weapons, even felt different in your hands, it seemed to him. But Zelie was making eyes and sexual fantasies filled his mind.

The next speaker was David Blount, a journalist with the London *Sunday Times*, a proper Englishman in suit and tie. He stepped to the mic holding a newspaper.

"This is the *New York Times* from March," Blount said. "The front page spread is about the 'fruit of change' in El Salvador. The newspaper of record would have you believe that life for Salvadoran peasants is on the upswing, things are getting better and we—and by *we* I mean *you,* the United States—*we* may applaud ourselves for the good *we* are doing."

Blount lowered his arm and waited for the right dramatic moment.

"Rubbish," he said. "Absolute rubbish." A cheer went up and chanting broke out:

"The people, united, will never be defeated. The people, united, will never be defeated."

Blount held up his hand and the crowd quieted.

"The very day this article appeared," he said, "600 peasants attempting to flee to safety across the border in Honduras were massacred at the Lempa River. Hacked to death with machetes, bayoneted, beaten senseless by the butts of soldiers' rifles. The week before, 700 killed. A month later another massacre at the Sumpul River. There is overwhelming evidence of atrocities committed by the Honduran and Salvadoran armies and government militias, trained and supplied by the United States in what can only be called a campaign of genocide. The mass extermination of aboriginal peoples."

"Question," Zelie shouted, raising her hand and finally being recognized. "If things are so bad under the so-called 'human rights administration' of Carter, what can we expect if Reagan wins?"

With the election just days away, Carter was in deep trouble. Reagan had run rings around him in their recent televised debate, zinging him with "There you go again" and asking the American people "Are you better off today than you were four years ago?" With the misery index (unemployment + inflation rate) at an all-time high, Carter was dead in the water. The disastrous attempt to rescue the Iran hostages, ending with two aircraft down and eight US servicemen dead, hadn't helped, nor had extending asylum to the Shah—the act which had infuriated Muslim extremists and provoked the seizing of the embassy in Teheran in the first place. The Shah's Savak hands down among the world's most brutal police forces.

Zelie's question elicited loud hooting and Blount held up his hand for quiet.

"Imagine if Reagan were to order a US invasion or aerial bombing," he said. "Could be another Vietnam." Reagan had railed against Jimmy Carter for daring even to speak out against the atrocities in Argentina.

A contingent of right-wingers and ROTC types raised a ruckus with much pushing and shoving. The campus police arrived and the rally broke up. Zack and Scott and the two girls walked through the student center onto the grassy slope overlooking the lagoon as waddling coots pecked about for insects and crumbs of cookies. Beyond the lagoon, lined with giant eucalyptus trees, was the beach at Campus Point.

"So everybody's voting for Carter, right?" Zelie said.

"Scott doesn't vote," said Zack. "Like the Rastas. Bob Marley."

"You don't vote because Bob Marley doesn't vote?" Zelie gasped in indignation.

"I try to stay above the fray," Scott growing defensive. "Not get dragged into the dirt."

"Didn't you hear the guy say how bad it would be if Reagan gets in?"

"It's the system," Scott said. "System has to change."

"So you give up and let the crazies take over?"

"Let's forget politics for now," Zack said.

"I'm out of here," Zelie steamed. "Come on, Shari."

"Guess I shouldn't have said anything," Zack said as the girls disappeared from their lives.

"Yeah," Scott said, but in truth he breathed a sigh of relief. He was used to going home alone at night to his Jamaica-West sanctuary and practicing Bob, there was always oceans more to learn and perfect. Safer that way too. A woman was more terrifying than a ghost any day. Unless she was a Jamaican girl. Nothing like an *irie daughtah* with her golden black skin, glistening white teeth and strong body, a girl who could walk the street barefoot or blow you away in heels and a low-cut gown. A girl like Marva.

And coming to mind, images of an M14 and M16....

February 1976, Kingston

Scott stared out the window as the LTD clipped through Kingston traffic—in Jamaica they drove on the left as in England—and out of town past Caymanas racetrack to a patch of bush on deserted coastline at Green Bay.

"What are we doing, dad?" Scott asked as his father pulled off the road. "Middle of nowhere out here."

"Just come on. This'll be fun."

From the trunk Matt took two rifles and a holstered .45 revolver, which he belted around his waist.

"This here," Matt said, indicating the rifle with a wooden stock, "this is an M14. And this one here"—the other rifle of plastic and metal construction—"this is an M16. Give me either of these babies over an AK-47 any day."

"Those from Vietnam, dad?"

"Hold this."

Matt held out the M14 toward Scott, who thought it much the more attractive of the two weapons, with its fine burnished stock and more natural appearance compared to the modernistic M16.

"Be careful, it's loaded."

69

Scott swallowed hard and took the rifle and gingerly cradled it in his arms. He was sure he would trip over his own two feet and kill the both of them. Worse would be having to endure his father's disappointment.

Matt led Scott over a rise to a clearing between brush and sea. This was the police outdoor shooting range, targets scattered around like a miniature golf course. As Scott clutched the M14 like a angrily clawing cat, Matt set down the M16 and opened up with the .45 on a bull's-eye fifty meters downfield.

Blam! Blam! Blam!

Scott could hardly believe his eyes. His father was like some fast-draw desperado in a Western movie. Now Matt was scrambling, blasting four shots at a new target. Scott imagined he could see the bullets ripping into the target, dead center. Kill shots. Matt rolling on the ground to a prone position and firing afresh.

Adrenalin pumped into his bloodstream and Scott's mind swirled in a haze of unreality. Bullets seemed to fly in slow motion. He was awe-struck at his father's skill.

"Put down the rifle," Matt said, unholstering his weapon and strapping it around Scott's waist. He cinched the holster cord tight around his son's right thigh.

"How's that feel?" he asked.

"Little heavy."

"That's real artillery there. Forty-five Smith and Wesson. Feel its heft in your hand."

"I don't know, dad, I...."

"It won't bite you. Keep the business end pointed where you mean to shoot. Come on, son. Take the gun out of the holster."

Scott gingerly lifted the .45 out of the leather holster. The barrel pointed at Matt momentarily and he pushed it aside.

"This isn't rocket science," he said in some annoyance. "Pick a target and shoot."

"Should I put it back in the holster?"

"You're a fast draw artist now? Just point and shoot the damn thing. Let's not make a federal case out of this."

Scott aimed at a bull's-eye, scrunched up his face as if he were yanking a festering tooth and pulled the trigger. The .45 kicked hard and the bullet flew off over the blue-green Caribbean. He felt overwhelmed.

Matt showed him how to squeeze the trigger. Balance the piece in your hand, feel its weight, take control of the weapon. Smooth slow squeeze. You can do it.

"I don't know, dad, I—"

"Point and shoot, what's so hard about that?"

"Yeah, uh...."

"It's part of growing up and becoming a man. Learning to defend yourself. A rite of passage."

"It's not my thing. I don't want to shoot anybody."

"What are you going to do when they come for you boy, wave flowers? Shoot the damn gun."

Scott aimed and pulled the trigger. Again the bullet raced well wide of the target.

"That's a little better," Matt grudgingly commended, struggling to strike a positive note. "Let's try the M16."

Matt took up the modernistic-looking rifle, the M16.

"First thing is set your feet and get your balance," he demonstrated. "Nestle the butt into the crook of your shoulder, lock on your target and shoot."

Matt fired off a volley and Scott gasped at the sheer power of the weapon and the mastery of his father as he shredded a bull's-eye stapled to a tree trunk one hundred meters down range. Matt dropped to his knee and squeezed off another volley and again riddled the target.

Matt handed Scott the gun. By now Scott had figured the best way to get through this was to shut up and give the appearance of trying, at least. He planted his feet as his father had shown him, picked out a target and pulled the trigger. The weapon kicked hard and the bullet flew astray.

"You shoot it, dad," Scott said, yielding the weapon back to his father. "I can't do it like you do."

"You have to believe in yourself, son. There's nothing a man can't do if he puts his mind to it. Now the M14," Matt took up the other rifle. "Excellent sniper rifle. This baby'll pick a flea off a dog's back at four hundred meters."

But things went no better with the M14, shots going wide of the mark in more ways than one.

11

Halloween Night 1980, Santa Barbara

Moonlight slanted through the windshield and danced upon her hair in a strangely familiar way. In his mind's eye he saw another ravishing creature twirling a lock around her finger, laughing and smacking him a kiss. *Marva.*

"Here, Dread?" she asked. "Scotty?"

"What?" he snapped to, the old memories bursting in the air like cartoon dialog boxes.

"Should I turn here?"

"There by the mailbox."

The young woman driving the VW Variant fastback leaned forward to follow Scott's pointing finger. It was dark, the streetlight way down at the end of the block, and it was late, the Trick-or-Treaters long gone home to rot their teeth with their night's bounty.

"There it is, Suz," said Nadesha, riding shotgun in the front.

"Got it."

Suzette turned into the driveway by the mailbox and drove past the front property to the back unit. She and Nadesha constituted the We-Two vocalists, Reggae Rockers' background singers. Tonight's gig at the Coyote Grill had been the band's first go in a month since Scott had fallen and mashed up his lip. In his mind it had been a screaming success.

"Ladies want to come in?" Scott offered as he grabbed his guitar and they hopped out. "Long ride back to LA." He imagined himself tangled up in four breasts and two pairs of thighs. It had been a long time and that Suzette was a fox.

"I gotta pee," said Nadesha.

"Come in and smoke a joint."

"I like the flowers," Suzi said. "Lilies, aren't they?"

"What?" Scott spun on his heels.

Suzi gestured toward the narrow strip of earth running between the wooden fence and driveway. Scott stared in shock to see three small Calla lily plants *that hadn't been there before.* Had he simply failed to notice them? Did they just spring up? Had someone planted them? *Did John Wayne cause them to sprout just by speaking their name?*

"Let's get inside," he said, ushering the girls in and closing the door tight.

"Will you look at this," Suzi gasped at the abundance of Jamaican memorabilia. "Did we take a wrong turn and end up in Jamaica?"

"That would be a right turn," Scott said with a wink.

"Can we put on some music, Scotty?" Nadesha asked.

"Is Babylon wicked?" He put on water for tea.

The girls dug into the album crate and came up with Dennis Brown, "the Crown Prince of Reggae" destined to take over when King Bob stepped down to fulfill his dream of moving to Africa to be near his holy father, His Imperial Majesty Haile Selassie I. Scott rolled a spliff and the girls freshened up in the bathroom as the Crown Prince wailed on about having money in his pocket and still not finding love anywhere. The girls had been a great addition to Reggae Rockers since coming aboard three months ago, their angelic voices complementing Scott's tenor lead vocals much as the I-Three did for Bob. Suzette was slim and shapely where Nadesha was buxom and sturdily built, a former basketball player at Cal State Dominguez Hills with a low center of gravity. Both were African-American and exotic, Nadesha in braids and Suzette with her long flowing tresses. They lived in LA and drove up for local gigs.

His hands trembled as he rolled the joint, imagining pleasures sacred and profane. It had been *much* too long.

The girls came out of the bathroom and sat with Scott on the tattered sofa.

"Good show tonight, eh guys?" Scott finished rolling the joint, hit on it and passed it to Suzette.

"Great to have you back," Suzette said, toking up and blowing out smoke like an old pro. "Lip okay?"

"No problem."

"Nuff ladies checkin' you out tonight, Dread," Nadesha said. "Better put them pretty lips to work."

"That sleaze with her tits spilling out her dress?" said Suzette. "Scott can do better than that."

"I don't mind tits spilling out."

"Scotty, we need to talk," Suzette said. "The guys want us to have a little talk."

"So that's why Canada was giving me dirty looks all night."

"Nobody was giving you dirty looks."

"So spill."

"The guys, all of us, we don't want to be no Beatle-mania band."

"Beatle-mania?"

"Bob Marley-mania."

"My stash must be laced with psilocybin. Sounded like you said Bob Marley-mania, which makes no sense whatsoever."

"That's the whole point. You go up there like it's all your show. Like you're on a mission to prove you're Bob Marley or something. Look, Scott, you are a good singer, and you've got Bob down, but we don't want to be about being somebody else. We want to do our own thing, push the envelope and see what we can be and not settle for what's already been done. We can't grow doing it the way the Wailers would do it."

"Wee, wee, wee. Sound like the three little pigs."

"Like those Elvis impersonators," Nadesha jumped in. "Copycats in capes and sideburns."

"I don't believe this," Scott fumed. "*Copycats?* We are a reggae band. We're not going to sing Bob's songs now?"

"That's not the point. See, we knew you wouldn't get it."

"So fucking enlighten me."

"It's getting late."

"Like tonight," Nadesha said. "Your 'woy-yoys' in *Get Up Stand Up* are too much like Bob... it's so obvious."

"We don't want to be about copying anybody, not even Bob," said Suzette. "You dance like Bob, throw your locks the same way... it's too much. Even rub your forehead the way he does. It's phony."

73

"Phony? How can you say that?"

"Be yourself, man. Stop trying to be someone else. Come on, Nadeesh."

"What you see is what you get," Scott snapped, but the girls had collected their things and were out the door, leaving him frozen on the sofa like a carved stone figurine.

He went to his bedroom, studied Marva's photo a moment before picking up from the nightstand the recent edition of *Reggae Magazine* with its cover photo of Bob Marley and accompanying headline—

"Wailers US Tour Cancelled:
Exhaustion? Or does Marley have cancer?"

It's exhaustion, Scott thought with certitude. *The Tuff Gong is indestructible. His Majesty protects him.*

Suddenly his toe began to ache, big toe/right foot. He'd injured it in Jamaica the day after he tripped Bob Marley in the soccer scrim at Hope Road. Even now it bothered him from time to time and he limped as he went to shower off the grit and grime of the day. Standing beneath the steaming spray, his toe throbbing, he was inundated with images of a woman dying of cancer, her body eaten away by the dread disease. Foul, leprous, rotting skin. He went weak at the knees. He couldn't make out the woman's face but he knew in his bones it was his mother. Her DNA was in his body, passed down from mother to son. Her susceptibility to cancer was inside him. He longed for Marva, for Zelie, for anybody, consoling himself with the thought that biology was not destiny. He wasn't a female with breasts and uterus, wasn't his mother's daughter. This was not a death sentence. If you took care of yourself you could prevail over biological predispositions. Eat healthy I-tal food, exercise, mellow out with good Sensi and maintain a spiritual connection to the cosmos. Mind over matter. Natural mystic. Like Bob.

Stepping from the shower stall, Scott stared at his misted reflection in the mirror above the basin. It seemed a metaphor for his clouded memory and lost past. Without contemplation or intention, standing naked and wet, he lifted his arm and with the tip of his finger made a large letter *C* on the fogged surface of the mirror.

In the crescent-moon swath traced by his finger he saw something. His own white skin reflected back to him… but something else too, behind and hovering over him. Black. Blackness. Black skin?

He spun around expecting to see Bob or Marva or an Obeah man casting spells but there was nothing but a wet towel on the floor. Images flashed into mind… a recording studio… a name coming to his lips: *Jesse James*….

74

March 1976, Kingston

Rising spring temperatures soaked the armpits of Scott's brown school shirt as he raced up in a cloud of dust to Harry J's Studio in Uptown Kingston. Forget school. Bob had given his okay to sit in on a recording session. The algebra test in fifth period he really shouldn't miss but that wasn't until after lunch and he could do math in his sleep. A squared plus B squared, ho hum.

Harry J's was one of the independent studios that were popping up to challenge the longstanding dominance of the Big Three: Studio One (Coxsone Dodd), Dynamic (Bunny Lee) and Federal Records (Ken Khouri). Nearly all were located within one square mile in downtown Kingston, an impoverished zone in a Third World nation producing far more than its fair share of the planet's best music. Like legions of others, Harry Johnson had apprenticed with the legendary Dodd at Studio One before moving on to open his own joint here at 10 Roosevelt Avenue. The Wailers had started recording at Harry J's with 1973's *Burnin'* album and since last summer, Johnson having upgraded to a state-of-the-art 16-track mixing board, had been working on their new platter, *Rastaman Vibration*.

Harry J's may have been uptown but an armed guard was posted at the gate nevertheless. The hulking brute scowled at the bicycle cowboy with his scrubbed white face.

"Wailers recording session," Scott said. "Scott Gallagher."

The guard glared with equal parts menace and indifference.

"Gallagher, Scott," Scott said again, glancing about the kiosk for some list showing his name. "Skipper would have called me in. Bob Marley. Gotta be there."

"Gwan wit' yuh," the guard dismissively waved the kid in. Scott chained his bike and went through the gate. He could hear Wailers rocking out inside. He knocked and then thought the act frivolous and let himself in, a wall of sound and a cloud of ganja fumes slapping him in the face as he opened the door. For a foreigner such as Scott, entering a Kingston studio was like venturing to a different world, a wonderfully eccentric realm of creative genius, wild, wooly and unabashed, where deals were settled with fisticuffs and a producer like Duke Reid drew his revolver and fired a celebratory live round into the ceiling at Treasure Isle when the artists hit the right note. Harry J's did not disappoint—the scene was raw and raucous, music blasting, the riddim fresh and captivating to Scott's ears as Bob sang about *war*. The air thick with smoke, human-like forms appearing eerily from the dense haze as if in a dream. Dreadlocked faces floated like disembodied souls, Medusa-haired Rastas curious at the presence of the young white intruder. Engineer Sylvan Morris, one of the best in the biz, was in the booth working magic at the instrument panel as the Wailers jammed in the recording room, the full band—including the I-Three and three additional horn players—crammed into the tiny space. Scott sucked up the second-hand smoke and grooved with it.

From out of nowhere big man Gilly Gilbert came over with a rapscallion grin and a monster joint.

"Oy, Scotty," the bearded giant boomed. "Wha'ppen, mon?"

"Cool runnings, Gilly," Scott shouted above the music. "So this is Harry J's."

"Hardest studio in town. Sensi?"

"Thanks." Scott hit on the joint like he'd been sleeping in a hammock in the back hills of St. Ann all his life growing yam and letting his dreads grow. He promptly coughed his head off.

"Good herb," he rasped.

"The I haffi get him lung in shape," Gilly laughed. His attention was drawn to a dread he didn't recognize over by the door who seemed out of place, like he'd wandered in off the street.

"Scotty, likkle later, hear?"

Gilbert wandered off to check on the incongruous dread. Scott followed with his eyes as Gilly cornered the man by the door.

"Until now me never see the I in this place," Gilly said. "Who is you, man?"

"Them a call me Jesse James," the dread replied. Across the floor Scott caught a glimpse of the stranger, a knapsack slung over his shoulder and a wicked scar over his left eye glistening in a stray mote of light.

"Yuh gunman?" Gilly grilled the newcomer.

"Me peaceful man, my brother."

Jesse James, a carver by trade, was Frank Lake's man. Matt Gallagher was paying him good money to keep a sharp eye on his son (though he quietly continued to report to Lake, who hoped for ammunition to use against Gallagher if ever the shit hit the fan). Matt had installed him at the corner shop down from the house, the proprietor, Chinaman, being sympathetic to US interests. James, 38, would sit out in the yard whittling at blocks of wood and monitor Scott's comings and goings. He was a ruggedly handsome, wiry fellow with strong hands and an instinct for survival earned by paying his dues on the street. He'd been a rudeboy on his way to prison or the morgue when his gun jammed in the mouth of a rival and seeing the terror in the man's eyes he glimpsed as if for the first time the humanity that links one person to another. Withdrawing into a period of contemplation, he emerged with a new path in Rastafari—*Mama forsake you, Papa forsake you, Rasta take you,* the wisdom went. He wasn't the most devout Rasta that ever lived—wasn't about to give up his rum, for one thing—but Jah's grace befell him nevertheless.

76

Like many Kingston youth infatuated with the romance of the American Wild West (and gangster era of the Roaring Twenties) Howard Elliston had adopted an alias, a *nom de guerre* befitting his tough guy self-image. The trophy scar above his left eye was a keepsake from a street scuffle, but compared to the young men terrorizing the yards these days he had a heart of gold and detested violence. He devoted himself to providing for his two girls, whom he adored, that they might have a better life. His corruption would come not from ghetto gangsters but the inscrutable white men who gave him the extra income that kept his girls in shoes and lunch money.

"Me come fe hear brother Bob play music," Jesse James said, "and offer I and I brethren Lamb's Bread."

"The I carry Lamb's Bread?" Gilly perked.

Lamb's Bread was the best ganja in Jamaica and perhaps anywhere, certainly better than Columbian Gold, Maui Wowie or Oaxacan. Jesse James reached into his knapsack and produced a rolled spliff. He didn't see any reason he shouldn't hustle a likkle herb business on the side. (A free sample had gotten him past the guard outside).

"Control this," Jesse James said, offering the spliff to Gilly. "I-man have plenty more if it meet yuh stan-*dard*."

Gilly took the spliff and examined it, smelled it, rolled it lovingly in his fingers. Jesse James flicked his lighter and Gilly took a hit.

"Yes, my brother," Jesse James said, "the finest Lamb's Bread."

"Not bad," Gilly said as he blew out a wall of smoke.

Jesse James reached into his pouch and came up with a baggy of marijuana—what in America would be called a four-finger lid. He jiggled it in his hand to show its heft.

"Only twenty dollar for so much."

"Make it go like this," Gilly said. "I-man give yuh price and the I pay twenty dollar fe the music."

Jesse James' wide grin disappeared like jonny cakes at Sunday breakfast. Grudgingly, he handed over the baggy of Lamb's Bread to Gilly.

Coming in just then from an afternoon at Caymanas race track betting on the ponies were Skill Cole and JLP bad boy Claudie Massop. Some thought the Tuff Gong was playing both sides of the political aisle, hanging with JLP and PNP alike, in case Seaga whipped Manley in the election. In truth, rudeboys like Massop and Bucky Marshall idolized Bob, who treated them like brothers and never objected to their coming round. He would sit and reason with them, rapping about Rastafari and the travails of being black in a white man's world, hoping to guide them out of the dead-end street of their violent lifestyles. It didn't matter what side they were on in the tribal war.

Bob and the crew played songs for the new album. *War* had its origins in a speech condemning racial prejudice and discrimination that Haile Selassie I gave at the United Nations in 1963 and which Skill had brought to Skip's attention. It warned that as long as the belief prevailed that one group was superior to another, war would rage on this earth. To Scott's ears it was as good as anything the Skipper had ever done, up there with *Trench Town Rock* and *Belly Full*. Shit, this was as good as *Concrete Jungle*. Snooty purists said the band's best days were behind them, that the miraculous harmonies of the original trio of Bob, Peter and Bunny could never be matched, but the argument fell mute on sweetly sated ears intoxicated by the dulcet backing tones of the I-Three.

Another song shook Scott's world to its foundations. In *Rat Race* Bob was slinging impenetrable Jamaican slang... but what was this about the CIA... about Rasta not working for the CIA? The lyrics revealed in no uncertain terms the Rastafarians' fear and distrust of the US spy agency. Bob was calling it clear—Rasta didn't abide politicians with their *poli-tricks* working for the *shit-stem*, a wicked system that turned human beings into rats in a maze.

Scott's head began to spin. He felt dizzy, nauseous, had to sit down. Was there something to this CIA paranoia after all? Everyone was looking at him, he could feel their eyes dissecting him, dicing him up like guilty peas in a pod. Flushing hot and red, he took off without saying goodbye, Jesse James trailing out soon afterward.

After dinner that night, as Maddy went to her room where she stayed during the week, Scott confronted his father.

"What do you do at the embassy, dad?" he asked.

"What are you talking about?" Matt said, looking up from his *Daily Gleaner*.

"Simple question. What do you do?"

"Who you been talking to?"

"Where do you go at night?"

"A lot of government business gets done in the evenings. Meetings, dinners, entertaining foreign dignitaries and local politicians or businessmen. Not that it's any of *your* concern."

"Every night of the week?"

"Man can't go out for a drink with his buddies?"

"People say the United States is trying to control what goes on in Jamaica."

"Somebody's filling your head with crazy ideas."

"Are they crazy? Jamaicans believe them."

"Get this straight, mister. I do not work for the CIA. Got it?"

"I didn't say anything about the CIA, dad."

78

Matt's mind whirled. For an instant he thought he might have given the game away. He'd been meaning to tell Scott the truth about what he did, his chosen career, but clearly this was not the time.

"You think I don't know what people are saying?" Matt said, the veins in his neck blowing up. "That there's a CIA agent under every rock? Think I'm deaf?"

"What about Chile, dad?"

"What are you talking about, Chile?"

"Allende."

"Allende was overthrown by the Chilean military. We didn't have anything to do with that. What the hell are you thinking?"

"Who's *we*? Who's *we*, dad. The CIA?"

"Don't be an idiot. Allende was purely an internal affair. The people rose up to overthrow a Marxist dictator. Jesus Christ, my sixteen-year-old kid still wet behind the ears gets a load of some cockamamie gossip and comes home to lynch his own father."

"Dad," Scott whined apologetically, but his father knew how to make a timely exit.

"I'm going out," Matt said. "Do your goddamn homework." With that he was out the door and disappeared into the Kingston night.

12

Friday "happy hour" found Gallagher and crew hanging at the pool bar buffet at the Hilton Hotel. Good food and bikini babes to ogle in celebration of the successful bribing of a high-level employee at the central post office. The deal was for all mail to and from Cuba and the Cuban Embassy in Kingston to be diverted to the station for processing. The mail would be steamed open, read, analyzed and returned to the post office for delivery within 24 hours. It was a tremendous return on the paltry $200 a month payola to the postal employee. No luck on planting a bug inside the Cuban Embassy as yet, but big news at the top—George H. W. Bush had replaced Bill Colby as Director of Central Intelligence.

Matt sat back in the chaise lounge in his Hawaiian shirt and pleated slacks, enjoying his rum punch and cigar and the warm Caribbean evening. His .45 was holstered around his waist and if anybody made a fuss he claimed diplomatic privilege. If that didn't work he stared them down. He was the lord of all he oversaw, the alpha male, big chief bad ass, a human flying wedge of ego and conviction, fully focused and invested.

On the surface at least. Deep down, Matt Gallagher was not quite the well-oiled machine he presented himself as. Occasionally a gal in the way she smiled or moved or with a toss of her hair reminded him of Linda and recalled sweet days together, leaving a gnawing hollowness inside. Haunted by the memory of his Lost Lenore he hadn't been able to develop a

79

meaningful relationship with a new woman. Beyond that, Vietnam had left painful scars, buried so deep that for the most part he wasn't aware of them. Nam had been distilled in his psyche down to a central mythological core of Righteous Glory with the dirty details swept under the rug. Too many bodies blown apart, too many napalmed children, villages razed, livestock obliterated, far, *far* too much suffering for anyone other than a dyed-in-the-wool sociopath to tolerate without massive defense mechanisms kicking in. Matt Gallagher was no sociopath. His psychology fell more within the parameters of Hannah Arendt's "banality of evil" and Erich Fromm's "sane society." (Question: Is a "well-adjusted" person in a sick society sick or healthy?) Gallagher's psyche was akin to Dante's seven hells, the wickedest demons relegated to the deepest depths, locked away in labyinthine chambers, their dungeon cries surfacing in morbid nightmares that tormented his sleep and left him a powder keg with a lit fuse.

Lounging around the pool also were Frank Lake and operations officers Frederick Douglas (Freddy) McGinnis and John Morgan, all single men. New man McGinnis, only 27 and that rarest of creatures a black CIA case officer, was the man of the hour, the Cuba mail score having been his achievement. The only downer was the failed bait-broad operation with Claudia Candiotti.

"Sonuvabitch turned his nose up at a gorgeous broad like that?" Matt said. "Thought you said he was a ladies' man."

"Turns out he likes dark meat," Lake said.

"Oh for the love of—you mean he passed up pussy because he loves chocolate?"

"Seems he has a thing about being fair-skinned and leading a nation of blacks."

"The prick feels inferior about being *white*?"

"More or less, yeah."

"Pardon my naïve assumption but as the world's premier intelligence-gathering organization shouldn't we know that?"

"We fucked up."

"*We* did, didn't *we*."

"Okay, me. I fucked up."

"All right," Matt sighed, "have HQ send us a *black* girl. Barefoot country wench who picks her nose and wrestles pigs. Christ Almighty."

As the alcohol flowed the men grew boisterous, except McGinnis, who indulged in moderation. Even Matt, who could drink most men under the table, was feeling it. The sky darkened and they moved inside to the Junkanoo Room. Over more rum punch the conversation degenerated into gutter talk.

"Gal the other day caused a twelve-car pile-up," Frank Lake said with boisterous machismo. "Looked like a black Sophia Loren, I kid you not.

80

Hey McGinnis, you're bleeding." Lake tilted his head at the new man's open shirt collar. "There on your chest."

McGinnis peeled back his collar to reveal a bright purplish-red tattoo of four hearts on the upper part of his smooth and hairless left pectoral, one central large heart and three smaller ones dangling below rather like a pendant necklace. Inside each heart was a single droplet of water falling on a brightly-colored flower.

"Isn't that romantic?" Lake jested. "Freddy's got a girlfriend and three squeezes on the side. Or a mother and three sisters."

"It's personal, thank you," McGinnis retorted.

"Ah. Four boyfriends. I get it."

"You don't get squat."

"Oh, will ya look at the knockers on that one," Lake said as a voluptuous dark-skinned woman took to the dance floor with her partner.

"Chocolate milk on tap," Lake jived. "Jamaica has it all."

Everybody laughed except McGinnis, who forced a smirk but found this type of humor offensive. His patience was tested as Lake continued in a crude vein.

"I'd shoot my wad all over those puppies," Frank quipped.

"All right," said McGinnis.

"What's the matter, Freddy? Bet these black girls give good blow jobs, eh?"

"You'll never find out, Frank."

"And why's that?"

"They discriminate."

"Prejudiced against whites?"

"Against whale bellies."

"Bet they just love big cheesy black dicks though don't they."

"Cheesy you know; big you'll have to dream about."

"Let's see it then."

"Easy, Frank," cautioned Matt.

"No, let's just see the damn thing if it's so fucking spectacular," Lake spewed, bursting to his feet. "Come on brother man, whip it out."

"You'll need to stand back," McGinnis dished back. "Don't forget to brush your teeth when you're done."

"Black sonuvabitch," Lake whispered aside to Morgan, though he might have pegged his volume a little high.

"Sit down and shut up, Frank," Matt said.

"Go on, express yourself," said McGinnis, who had graduated Princeton. "But choose your words well, my ambergris-laden grampus, because the wrong one will get you killed."

"You shut up too, McGinnis."

"What language is this guy talking?" Lake blustered aside to Morgan, not realizing McGinnis had (again) called him a fat whale. "Did he just call me his grampa?"

"Stow it, I said. On the same team here, guys."

"Yeah, well he can just—"

"And apologize to each other."

"Fiddle di fucking dee," Lake grumbled and Matt cast him a sharp look.

"You do not want to test me," Matt warned.

"All right," Frank threw up his hands, "I apologize."

"Well, don't be talking about black women like that," said McGinnis.

"Let it go, McGinnis. Now shake hands."

Lake slowly got up and went around the table.

"Sorry Freddy," he said, "got a little out of line there. Didn't mean what I said." Lake didn't think of himself as racist and he'd had too much to drink… but it is not only what men do in their finest hours that belongs on their character resumes.

"Same here." McGinnis didn't think of himself as racist either but damn, white people sometime.

They shook hands, the firmness of their grasps more a matter of saving face somehow than an outpouring of brotherly love. Shortly Lake and Morgan left, the latter having to get up before dawn for an attempt to bug the Cuban Embassy.

"Frank's a little uptight about work," Gallagher said. "Don't pay him any mind."

"That's *so* white people," McGinnis shook his head. "Guy makes an ass of himself and it's 'he didn't mean anything.' Black man tried that he'd get tarred and feathered out of town."

"Slow down, Geronimo, just keeping the peace here. Come down off your warhorse."

"You're right. It was over and done. I should have let it go."

"Thirsty? Where can a man go for a little fun in this one-cow town?"

"Know just the place. Walking distance too. Unless you think it'd be safer to drive over."

"Safer is for sissies. Lead on, Hiawatha."

"Hiawatha, is it?"

It was midnight as Marley and Skill Cole arrived at Dandy Disco. Bob parked the BMW in the Hotel Parisienne lot and he and Skill took the lift up to the top floor of the hotel where Dandy was located. The place was jumping on a Friday night with a long line at the door. It wasn't Bob's style to take cuts but the bouncer waved them right in. Reggae blared on the sound system, people dancing and having a raucous good time. Women styling, drinks flowing, dudes scheming, bullshit flying.

The bouncer, a mammoth fellow named Buster, conducted Bob and Skill inside to their favorite booth by the window in Cindy Breakespeare's area. The booth already taken, Buster asked the occupants if Bob and Skill might join them. Buster asked exceptionally politely, for the two men sitting with their ladies were Al Capone and Wild Bill Hickok, ghetto gunmen of the most dangerous kind—mid-level toughs itching to shoot their way to Top Ranking. Capone and Wild Bill hailed from the yards of West Kingston and never went anywhere without their cannons (no doorman, not even a behemoth like Buster, so foolish as to attempt to take them away). When the gang lords saw who Buster was leading over they made a show of inviting the two stars to join them.

"Yes I!" greeted the boisterous Al Capone, whose real name was Petey. "Siddung, brethren, siddung right dere. Make I and I enjoy we-self up in this here establishment. Wha' yuh wan' fe drink, Gong? Rum, Skill? I-man order it fe yuh."

Marley scanned for Cindy and spotted her loading up with drinks at the bar. Stewing about his continuing dalliances with her girlfriends, she avoided making eye contact. Finally she came over, stiff-shouldered and formal.

"Something to drink?" she queried, all business. "The usual for you, Mr. Marley?"

"Yuh look nice tonight, Cin," Bob said, flashing a warm smile.

"That's one fruit punch," Cindy burying her nose in her order pad. "Allan?"

"White rum. The good stuff."

Cindy pivoted and disappeared back into the crowd and Bob let off a big sigh; he had his work cut out for him tonight if he wanted to get back in Cindy's good graces. Out the window, the shiny streets of New Kingston—a world apart from the tenement yards of his youth. Still, it was yardies he related most easily to, not Michael Manley and the politicians.

In due order Cindy returned with the drinks. Al Capone threw down cash and neither Bob nor Skill made a fuss. The four albums Wailers had put out since signing on with Island Records—*Catch A Fire*, *Burnin'*, *Natty Dread* and the *Live* Lyceum concert—had been critically acclaimed but sales were disappointing and touring didn't bring in much either. Bob was better off than he'd ever been but a lot was riding on the new album to be a moneymaker.

"Sit and talk a spell," Marley said, pitching woo. "Come siddung beside Bobby."

"Yuh mad, man?" Cindy snapped. "Cyan't see me busy?"

Cindy snatched up the money and ran off. Marley noticed a table across the floor, at which sat two men, one black, the other white and wearing a patch over his left eye. Foreigners.

"So what is the story behind your tattoo?" Gallagher asked McGinnis as they sipped their drinks, Matt going with rum and Freddy a Red Stripe beer.

"Before I answer that, or not," McGinnis replied, "what do you know about Alabama?"

"From there, ain'tcha."

"Yes sir. Birmingham, sir."

"Knock off this sir business, McGinnis. No back of the bus here."

"Uh huh."

"I don't know," Gallagher pursed his lips. "Grow cotton down there, don't they?"

"That's what I thought."

Cindy stopped by the table with the two foreigners and seemed to linger with the white man with the eye patch. He rested his hand on hers, drawing sensual little circles with his fingertips on her soft smooth skin. She sat and talked and threw back her head in laughter.

Bob got fed up and signaled Skill he was ready to go. He sauntered over in his fiercely proud leonine fashion to say goodnight and get Al Capone's change, sending a tsunami of excitement rippling across the floor, women making eyes and throwing out their chests, men wishing they had a fraction of his charisma. Cindy was rising to get back to work as Bob arrived at the table. The black foreigner flashed a smile of recognition though Bob didn't know him from Adam. The white man he didn't look at.

"'Scuse me," Bob said, "ah, Cin, yuh nah bring Petey him change."

"Lady's busy," Gallagher said forcefully. Matt was not tipsy but had reached a gray area where the lower demons sometimes escaped their chains and animal instinct took over for better judgment. His unlimited sense of his own power meant that he knew no bounds in drinking or anything else, despite the close calls he brought down on himself from time to time.

Marley didn't take his eyes off Cindy. He had no quarrel with the men—guys hit on her all the time and it was her job to be nice to customers. To a point.

"Didn't tell me what time you get off," Gallagher said, clasping Cindy's arm. "Let me take you to breakfast."

"Thank you, but I have to go home and get a good night's sleep," Cindy said as she searched Bob's eyes, fearing she may have taken her little game too far.

"Give me your phone number," Matt said. "I'll take you to a nice dinner."

"Really busy. Sorry."

"I insist, pretty lady."

"May I have my arm back, sir? Be right over with your change, Bobby."

Cindy twisted free and hurried off to the bar. Gallagher turned to see Marley giving him the evil eye.

"What are you looking at?" Matt said with a contemptuous glower.

Marley glared at the white man long enough for Gallagher's psyche to interpret it as a threat and kick in his jungle mentality. Bob didn't want to make trouble on Cindy's shift and decided to let it ride, spinning on his heels to go, but Gallagher wasn't through with him.

"It's *Bobby*, is it?" Matt said with cutting cynicism. Bob stopped and stared hard at this alien intruder on his home stomping grounds. Back at the booth, Skill and the gangsters were watching on closely.

"Bob Marley," he said. "Cindy my girlfriend."

"Bob Marley, the reggae star," Freddy McGinnis said with a sanguine smile. "How you doing, Bob? Saw your show at Max's Kansas City in the Big Apple back in '73. Opened for Bruce Springsteen and totally stole the show. A night I'll never forget, believe you me."

"I don't care who the fuck he is," Gallagher said. "What do you mean, boy, interrupting me when I'm talking with a broad?"

Now Marley loosed upon the one-eyed man the full force of his screwface, the gnarly-beast/don't-tread-on-me scowl that had been his first line of defense growing up in the ghetto (just before pulling out the ratchet knife). Gallagher met his eyes with the channeled power of his testosterone-driven animus and the two males locked in a stare-down. On the other side of the club Skill and the gangsters read Bob's body language and were up and hustling over.

"Yuh disrespect I-man in me own country, yuh bloodclot white man," Marley spit through clenched teeth, "me say fuck you yuh fuckin' hypocrite."

Matt flushed with rage and almost lost it. With his last remaining shred of self-control he realized that a scene here would reflect poorly on US presence on the island. Anticipating trouble, McGinnis produced a hundred dollar bill he'd stashed in his billfold for just such an occasion, just as Skill Cole and the ghetto bangers showed up, guns drawn.

"Fellas, fellas," McGinnis said, waving the Yankee C-note at the rudeboys, "my buddy has had a little too much to drink. We all know how that is, right? Let me buy you a round of drinks. Respect."

Al Capone pointed his revolver and watched for an excuse to shoot, an arrogant arching of the brow, a disrespectful twitch of lip, the slightest insult. Revelers nearby ducked for cover. McGinnis extended the Greenback toward Al Capone.

"Some nice champagne for your lady friends."

Al Capone crumpled the bill and threw it aside, then spit in McGinnis' face. Gallagher raged again, ready to fight and die for the man he'd treated so condescendingly earlier. Guns were leveled in his face. Matt instantly calculated that if he drew he would lose unless he took evasive action like diving behind a table, in which case the blood of bystanders would likely splatter the walls. McGinnis froze and hoped Gallagher made the safe play or they would both die.

Marley quickly stepped in, for the second time in days interposing himself in the midst of an imminent gunfight.

"Come, brethren," he said, "make I and I light spliff and dance with the daughtahs. Nah wan' Cin get nuh trouble."

Al Capone's concentration flickered and Matt calculated the odds were good he could outdraw and kill the two scumbags. But his better judgment was returning and he started thinking strategically. A scene would make an ugly mess for the Company. And *hombres* this bad could be of use some day.

"Round of whatever they're having," Matt said, snapping his fingers. "With my compliments."

Al Capone's thirst for blood wasn't quenched but going against the Tuff Gong would be a bad move. The gunman lowered his weapon and his sidekick followed suit.

"Let's went, amigo," Matt said as McGinnis wiped the saliva off his face, his C-note long gone in someone's pocket. "We'll catch up with Marley later."

First thing Monday morning, Gallagher instructed Frank Lake to open a file on Bob Marley. Which of course he had already done, on the sly.

13

November, 1980, Santa Barbara

The people had spoken. As the sun rose over the Santa Barbara foothills, morning in America had officially arrived. California Governor Ronald Reagan had been elected president of the United States. Reagan, whom no less than Henry Kissinger derided as a gunslinger and whose "voodoo economics" even George H.W. Bush had ridiculed. The outgoing Carter Administration had issued a "Global 2000" report warning that the world in the year 2000 would be crowded, polluted, ecologically endangered and subject to strife and conflict, but the Reagan crowd would pay no heed. If you've seen one redwood you've seen them all, let the bloodbath begin now. Ideology was more comforting than science anyday, all one's cherished beliefs confirmed in the face of all controversy. Scott's friends were going on like it was the end of civilization. Lost in thought as he rode over for session with Dr. M he was almost flattened by a Buick pushing the yellow at State Street. There was a chill bite in the air but he was warm enough in the ubiquitous Marley Tee and denim overshirt.

Arriving at Canon Perdido Suites, he took a seat in the waiting room as Dr. Mitchell was running late. Scott grabbed the morning paper, flush with election analysis, and tossed it aside with merely a glance. Images and memory fragments continued to pound nightly at the battlements of his psyche: A machete slashing down hard in the dark. A coconut shell with a face like Caravaggio's *Medusa* lopping round and round on the ground like the freshly sundered *cabeza* of a Jacobin beheading. That Quasimodo hunchback manipulating fetish objects as if performing mystical rites in the dead of night. He saw Simon Bolivar, the great statesman, and his Jamaican friend Henry, his face contorted in deep emotion. Anxious under the weight of the invading images, he maintained strict adherence to his nightly regimen, smoking weed and practicing the music with religious fervor, studying Bob, getting him down ever more perfectly.

At 10:25 he glanced over to Jasmine.

"I'm sure the doctor will be here any minute," she said.

At 10:34 a Porsche 911S roared into the parking lot and thirty seconds later Doc M rushed in in a disheveled state.

"Sorry I'm late," he said and asked Jasmine for aspirin. "Touch of flu."

"Cancel today if you like, Doc," Scott said.

"I'll make coffee," Jasmine said.

Mitchell hurried off to his office and plopped heavily at his desk. His weekend had started Friday morning with Bloody Marys at breakfast and a 10:00 tee time at Canyon Links. The day before he had administered a lengthy test battery to an insurance patient—a lucrative part of his practice—and promptly written up his report. He rewarded himself with a round of golf, got off to a good start—bogey/par/bogey—and went easy on the flask between shots. He carded a 99, the first time he'd broken 100 in a long while. Pleased with himself he went out and bought a pair of New Balance running shoes and a lime green sweat suit and got up early Saturday to run the track at City College.

For five minutes he was a lean mean machine. For an 880 he was Kip Keino burning up the track. Then a knife was stabbing at his flank and his lungs gasping for oxygen. A splitting headache finished him off. The rest of the weekend was a laundry chute to the basement. He retreated to the safety of old routines. Wine and *The Man Who Shot Liberty Valance* until three in the morning. Nipping at the cough syrup straight from the bottle. A Valium to help him sleep and this morning a wrenching bout of constipation. Payin' the piper.

"You look beat, man," Scott said. "Go home."

"And miss our session?"

"Think you just did."

Jasmine knocked, let herself in and made coffee. She dropped two tablets of aspirin into Phil's palm and exited. Mitchell washed them down with a glass of water.

"Oughta smoke some ganj," Scott said. "Alcohol kill ya, herb build ya. Bob said that."

"No birth of consciousness without pain. Jung said that."

"The guy you used to like."

Scott noticed again that odd, vaguely familiar glint in Doc M's eye. It was more than just the inability to hold his gaze and look him directly in the eye... there was some secret sadness or longing or hard-won wisdom he couldn't put his finger on.

He got up and poured a cup and brought it to Mitchell, who held it in two hands and sipped.

"You look a little beat yourself," Mitchell said, studying his patient. "Something on your mind?"

"Ah, this girl in the band gave me a load of shit. Said I copy Bob."

"Do you copy Bob?"

"No way. It just comes through me. Natural mystic kind of thing."

"How's that go?"

"Natural mystic. That's Bob. Like one time he and I drove over in the Beamer to Rita's place in Bull Bay. Bob wanted her to check on a pickney he'd had with another woman—Rohan, I think. The mother left Rohan with his grandmother while she went off to work and Bob was worried he wasn't getting the care he needed. Skip wandered down the lane a moment to check on his Rasta brethren and Rita and I chatted. She told me Bob knew things other people could never know. As a barefoot country boy in Nine Mile he blew people's minds reading palms, so right on it took their breath away. Maybe children have a power and we lose it as we grow up, I don't know. Bob never lost it. He gave up reading palms when he was little—came in one day and told his mother he was a singer, he was singing now. But he never lost that ability, that sixth sense, that *connectedness*. His visionary powers lay in his African bloodline. His grandfather Omeriah Malcolm was a healer and magic man much respected in those parts. That's why Bob's music is full of a deeper wisdom, also why he's so driven. Rita said he senses he won't live past 36 and he's hurrying to get his message out there. One love, yunno?"

"Is this a roundabout route back to this Voodoo business?"

"Voodoo's Haiti, Doc."

"Didn't Marley play at the Bowl last year?"

"Great show. Year before too."

"Did you go backstage and visit him?"

"Uh, no." Scott squirmed, growing sullen.

"Marley was in Santa Barbara and you didn't look him up? Didn't you want to renew old acquaintances?"

"One question at a time, Doc."

"Did it end badly between you two?"

"Don't push, all right?"

"I don't believe anyone can see the future. All that crap."

"I don't copy Bob. I'm an *artiste*. Why can't people believe me?"

"I believe you."

"No you don't. Suppose that makes me paranoid."

Mitchell let that one hang in the air a moment.

"Rita ended up taking that pickney in herself," Scott said, shaking his head in wonder. "Jamaican women, man. The best. Biggest hearts in the world."

"Did you have a girlfriend in Jamaica?" Phil asked.

"A girl the gods would fight over," Scott lit up. "I'm seeing her in this gorgeous purple dress that really showed off her, you know…."

"Assets?"

"*Great* assets. Front and rear. Inside too."

"Did this Helen of Troy have a name?"

"Troy," Scott rolled his head back and scratched his neck. "That rings a bell too."

"Tell me about her."

"Marva. Her name was Marva, marvelous Marva. Man oh man oh Marva."

"Sounds like you were quite taken."

"If you'd a seen her, Doc, if you'd a seen her."

"How did you meet?"

"Sound system."

"Come again?"

"Radio in Jamaica doesn't play much local music. Gotta go to the sound systems to catch a sweet reggae beat. A Jump, a street bash."

"The stations don't play Jamaican music?"

"They're run by The Man, the Anglo establishment. This was a British colony not twenty years ago, don't forget. The white elite own the airwaves, BBC, RJR. Radio Jamaica Rediffusion. Play bubblegum pop shit, Herman's Hermits, Freddy and the Dreamers. The Supremes. Bob and them used to joke about their gangster buddies threatening the DJ with life and limb to get them to play their songs. Going right in to the station while they're on the air and pulling the guy out of his headphones. Enterprising souls like Coxsone Dodd rigged up traveling sound systems and drove into the neighborhoods to do street parties. Dodd supposedly had five different systems going out every night of the week. It's a hoot, everybody dancing and making out in the shadows. Jamaicans know how to party."

"You really come to life talking about this. Go on."

"One Friday night Henry—same Henry who sold me my bicycle; we got pretty tight after that—he and I hooked up to dig some tunes. But I gotta get out of the house first. Dad's home and he's been on my case lately. We talked about Bolivia, no, Argentina, it was Argentina...."

April 1976, Kingston

The crack of gunshot in the ghettoes was muffled this far uphill and all was peaceful, on the surface at least, as Maddy served the evening meal of meat loaf and Irish potatoes with carrots. American food for the white Americans. She kept her eye on Scott. He'd been a picky eater lately and she was concerned. The sliding glass door to the patio open to receive the ambient breeze, ceiling fan cranking. Wasn't the heat, it was the humidity. At least in summer there was plentiful rain to cool things out a likkle, but those tender mercies were a couple months off still.

Maddy was a big woman of dark complexion, unassuming in her ways—when the man of the house was around. With Matt it was always "yassuh, mistah Matt" and "thank yuh kindly, mistah Matt," but with Scott a more rounded portrait emerged. First and foremost she was the matriarchal Big Mama taking him by the ear and sitting him down at kitchen table to do his homework. At other times she became the nurturing Madonna who laid out his school clothes, brushed his hair and cooked his favorite meal; this after all was a 16-year-old baby who'd lost his mother and needed to be doted on. Then again she was the sensitive big sister who guided him through the rough patches of adolescence, not to mention the hazards of life in Kingston, tough neighborhoods, hotty-totty Jamaican girls, wily street boys. Maddy took these motherly chores not as an unwritten part of her job description but as a commandment of the Lord to carry out with love and selflessness.

Not quite all was peaceful. The relationship between father and son could hardly be so described in the best moments. Matt buried his nose in a weekly *Gleaner* column one of his case officers was writing that issued a steady stream of diatribes against Manley without the slightest basis in fact. Scott fiddled with his food, eating around the meatloaf.

"Yuh nah like Maddy meatloaf, Scott honey?" she said, wiping her hands on her apron. "Stomach upset?"

"I'm sure it's delicious, Maddy," he said. "Just... you know... meat. Going I-tal now."

"I-tal?" Maddy shrieked. "What nonsense fill yuh mind with this I-tal business? Meat keep yuh body strong an' healthy. Only crazy Rastafarian nah eat meat. Them a blackheart man live inna gully an' steal likkle pickney, nevah see dem again."

"Rastas aren't crazy, Maddy and they don't steal children. They're good people."

"There, see that," said Matt, raising his nose out of his newspaper. "Good news out there if you know where to look. And you should know," he glared at Scott, "since you lived there."

"Lived where?"

"BA. You have no idea there was a coup in Argentina last month do you."

"There was a coup down there?"

"Isabel Peron was running the country into the ground. Thank God we've seen the last of the Perons."

"Who's the new guy?"

"The military has taken over. They'll end the silliness, you can be sure of that."

"Aren't the government and military supposed to be separate things?"

"If a fool like Peron is running things you have to step up."

Juan Peron, in collaboration with his remarkable second wife Eva (Evita) had implemented many policies to achieve social and economic justice in Argentina, inciting the ire of the United States, which over the last three decades had trained more than 4,000 Argentine military personnel and wasn't about to let this jewel of the south slip away so easily. The CIA played their usual role but third wife Isabel—taking over after Peron's death—was so inept she did their work for them. The military junta, in collaboration with real Nazis who with the Americans' help had escaped postwar Europe via the rat line, would become notorious as one of the most brutal regimes of the latter Twentieth Century.

"Isn't it up to the people to vote the fools out?" Scott asked. "Thought that's what democracy is all about."

"Can't let the country go down the tubes just because the people are stupid."

"What if the generals are stupid?"

"Stop making a fuss and eat your dinner."

"I don't eat the flesh of dead mammals."

"Then go to your room."

Scott went to his room, Maddy calling after him, "Scotty honey, Maddy make yuh a nice sandwich, hear?"

"Let him be," Matt said.

"But suh, boy him age haffi eat decent meal."

"He's old enough to be responsible for his actions."

91

About nine o'clock Matt picked up the phone and called Dandy Disco. He was working his charm on Cindy when Scott emerged from his room and headed for the door in his stepping-out clothes.

"Hold on a minute, Cindy," Matt said, covering the mouthpiece with his hand. "Thought I sent you to your room."

"Didn't say stay there forever," Scott said. "Soon come."

"Don't give me soon come. Where you going?"

"Out for a little music. No big deal."

"At night with all this shooting going on? I don't think so." Matt knew that with a number of operations planned around town this was a bad night to be out. "You're staying in, buddy. Still there, Cindy?"

"Come to Jamaica and live like prisoners, eat American food?" Scott flared up. "Are we supposed to be better than black people or something?"

"Don't be taking that tone with me, mister. I know who I am. Do you?"

"What's that supposed to mean?"

"It's my job to bring you up decent and that's what I'm going to do."

"*You* go out all the time. Seem to have made it through all right."

"*I'm* not the subject of this conversation."

"Come to Jamaica and sit in your room. Don't go out on a Friday night like normal kids. Don't experience the culture."

"*Culture?* You want to experience the *culture*?"

"I knew you'd say that."

"You're not going out. Discussion over."

Scott stomped off to his bedroom and slammed the door behind him. By now Cindy had hung up and Matt returned to his reading. Some moments later he grew irked at Scott's radio and knocked on his door.

"How about turning that down? Up early tomorrow."

He knocked again and tried the door knob—it was locked.

"Scott, open this door, hear me?"

Matt pounded on the door but there was no response.

"Shit!" Matt raced out the front door and around to Scott's bedroom window. The room was empty.

"Little prick," he cursed. "I'll kill him."

Fifteen minutes earlier Scott had eased out the same window and ridden off on his bike. Soon he arrived at Half Way Tree Square, where once farmers bringing produce to Kingston market had rested under the shade of a spreading cotton tree. Standing in the place of that tree since the early 19th Century was a clock tower dedicated to King Edward VII—tonight's meeting point.

He looked up and down but Henry was nowhere to be seen. It was eerily still, like the calm before an earthquake. Shadows lurked in doorways, angry shouts came out of the night. An unseen dog barked fiercely. Gunshots rang not so far away.

A job, he scowled in silence. His father had claimed in angry spite it was his "job" to raise him. Punch the clock and put in your time. Could've been training dogs or packing meat. Shoveling shit.

At 16, Scott had passed the age when bonding with his father was the overriding issue in his life, but there remained an unfulfilled yearning, not to say emptiness. His father had been absent during the key formative years of his life between the ages 5 and 10, when Matt was in Vietnam. After Scott's mother died in 1967 he lived with Aunt Sylvia until 1970, when Matt came back from training at Camp Peary and took his son to Bolivia with him for his first assignment with the CIA. They'd been together ever since, though their togetherness was far from the normal intimacy of father and son. Much might have been remedied had Matt been of an emotionally giving nature, but the distance between them was growing rather than shrinking, however much both, and particularly Scott, might have wished otherwise.

From out of the night came a sputtering roar as a souped-up VW bug raced up with its lights off—to save the battery, the thinking went. Poking his head out the passenger's side door was the handsome face of his friend Henry.

"Get in, Scott Man," he said.

Scott hopped in. At the wheel was a huge Jamaican male who seemingly shouldn't have been able to fit inside a VW.

"My older brother, Hog," Henry said.

"Howdy, Hog. Where we headed?"

"Trench Town," Hog said.

"Musical center of the universe," Henry said, lighting a joint.

There was unvarnished truth in Henry's claim. In the decrepit yards of West Kingston was an efflorescence of musical genius to make Memphis and Motown pale in comparison. It was the Golden Age of reggae and Dylans of the ghetto were not only producing thrilling tunes to dance to but brilliant sociological portraits of the culture, with poignant commentary on life on the far side of the tracks as well as biting dissections of the *shit-stem.* Raw, incisive, profound, the songs of the poet laureates of the tenements established a body of literature that transcended time and place to become mythopoeic chronicles of life in the Third World in general. Overwhelmingly the music was created by Rastafarians, who injected a pervasive spirituality meant to guide the black man's struggle against Babylon while promising redemption in the next world. It was a conscious *roots music* that connected to the earth, the Great Mother, to the ancestors and ancient wisdom, the teachings, gods, griots and nature spirits of Africa. Greatest of the Bards from Yard was Bob Marley. The voice of the Third World was a skinny ghetto youth with ratchet in pocket who hadn't finished high school but wrote from the heart, informed by scripture and the wisdom of folk culture. His lyrics pricked at the conscience of the West, and though Babylon wasn't listening he kept beating the drum. Meanwhile the music scene in the United States was descending into the wasteland of disco.

Trench Town was a short drive down Half Way Tree toward the harbour. The streets were largely deserted when they should have been teeming with people.

"Don't look right, man," Henry said. "Turn there."

Hog turned down a small lane running into the Trench Town ghetto. Henry hollered to a youth loitering on the corner, who hollered back.

"Say them move over Tivoli Gardens," Henry said. "Gwan, Hog."

"Why would they move?" Scott asked.

"Police come roustin' through or them afraid PNP district like Trench Town get shot up."

"Why would it get shot up?"

"Little shootin' never hurt nobody," said Hog, who wasn't called Hog for being the smartest pig in the poke.

"Tivoli should be safe, right?" Scott said and Henry and Hog laughed.

As they drove down to Tivoli close to where the old United Fruit Company wharves had once stood they were relieved to see people milling about. The music was definitely on. With the election-year violence any nocturnal gathering carried some element of risk but the people of Kingston weren't about to lock themselves up for twelve months and pretend the year 1976 never happened. Music was in their blood and soul and sometimes it was all that made life worth living.

Hog turned into a small lane. Roofs and walls of corrugated "zinc"—rumpled aluminum sheets—were everywhere and every corner was spray-painted with the neighborhood's political allegiance: "JLP." Anti-Manley slogans abounded.

"What would happen if I came here alone?" Scott wondered aloud.

"The brothers would take you to school," Henry warned. "Don't go wandering off."

Tivoli Gardens had come into existence in 1966. Four years earlier a young Lebanese-Jamaican returning from overseas won his first seat in parliament in the district. Edward Seaga, who didn't have a drop of black blood in him, had been raised in the United States and educated at Harvard. He earned street cred by having been a reggae producer and for bringing home to Jamaica the bones of Marcus Garvey. His constituency was Back O' Wall, a shanty town of Rastafarians and desperate squatters living in tin-can lean-tos made of scraps scavenged from the streets. A young Bob Marley took his first lessons in Rastafari here. But the people were PNP supporters and non-voting Rastas who eschewed politics and were of no use to Seaga. Bulldozers and soldiers with fixed bayonets were sent in and the community flattened to dust. Seaga launched a major housing project with apartments awarded to JLP supporters and the new district of Tivoli Gardens became the enduring party base. Government tyranny or community development? In Jamaica it depended upon whom you asked.

Hog parked and the guys walked down toward the action. Music was in the air and rounding a corner they entered a different world—hundreds of people were collected around a flatbed truck loaded with a hi-fi system and massive speakers stacked high. Vendors sold beer and jerk chicken from pushcarts and makeshift stands. To Scott, it was magical and exotic, an urban Shangri-La casting its spell of enchantment, beckoning him forth.

"Anybody want a Red Stripe?" he said.

Henry jerked Scott's forearm violently.

"Don't NEVER mention that brand of beer in a JLP district, man. Wanna get us all killed?"

"I don't get it."

"Red is PNP color. Want beer you buy Heinie."

Duly admonished, Scott slunk over to the beer vendor and bought three Heineken—which in a PNP neighborhood would have been equally taboo, for green was JLP color. Any PNP faithful present opted discretely for a green bottle of Heinie.

Matt Gallagher dashed from the house in his stocking feet and put his shoes on in the car, forgetting to grab his gun. Matt had snuck out a window or two in his time but he wanted to whip the living tar out of his kid.

Music playing somewhere? he hollered up at the corner shop where Jesse James hung out—and where the hell was the damn guy when you needed him?

Try Trench Town, someone shouted.

Matt sped down Old Hope Road toward the harbour district. The closer he got to downtown the more raucous the streets became, the cars either old clattertraps or tricked-out hells-on-wheels with blasting stereos and some guy trying to get lucky in the back seat. Jeeps with rudeboys cruising alongside and giving him the evil eye. He beamed it right back at them. Working his way to Trench Town he found no music and asking directions got only shouted curses and disbelieving stares. *Gwan Tivoli,* a kindly woman finally said and he turned the car around to a pelting of rocks that spider-webbed the windshield. Reaching Tivoli he parked and wandered into the ghetto on the same narrow lane the three boys had entered earlier. Angry voices called out from the shadows.

"*Galang, bloodclot white mon.*"

"*Gwine lost y'othah eye tonight, white bwoy.*"

"*Yuh fool, mon. Gwan wit' ya.*"

Other voices had a different bag of goods to sell.

"*Got the sweet pussy fe yuh, sugar.*"

"*Suck yuh bamboo all night, hun.*"

Instinctively, Matt reached toward the gun he usually wore on his hip. Gun or no gun, he knew no fear and plowed ahead. A couple guys came at him from the sidelines and Matt spun on his heels and made for them like a one-eyed apostle from Hell. The two backed off, but these were not the baddest of the bad, rudest of the rude, just youth throwing out their chests in a show of territorial imperative. Not the ones who would shoot you just to watch the life ooze out of you. Scott's fair skin and blonde hair would make him easy to spot, but the crowd was thick and it was dark. Matt sensed he was here somewhere. What he saw next prickled the hairs on the back of his neck.

Scott and Henry sipped their politically correct Heineken and watched as a well-built masked man in a silver superheroes outfit vaulted onto the sound system truck. The crowd went wild as he strutted about the makeshift stage spouting lyrics in rapid-fire patois. Two ammo belts crisscrossed his shiny slick breast and strapped around his waist was a fancy holster with ivory-handled revolvers tucked in butt forward.

"Prince Galactic," Henry said.

Prince Galactic, cutting an impressive figure with his broad chest tapering to a schoolgirl's waist, spun records and "toasted" over the hardest tunes by the hottest artists. One of Coxsone Dodd's DJs, Henry said.

People were moving and grooving to the sounds and as Scott was with a Jamaican nobody paid him any mind. Suddenly there she was, dancing with her girlfriends, a tall dark-skinned beauty in a tight sweater to put Gina Lollobrigida to shame. Her smile lit up the night and melted that white bwoy's heart.

He boogied closer to the bronzed goddess, eyes tactfully averted. As Prince Galactic dropped Burning Spear's *Marcus Garvey* he flashed a casual smile. She smiled back. Her hair was woven into thick braids that made her look like an Indian princess, and in fact she was part Indian. Gandhi, not Geronimo.

Closer still he dared, the radiantly divine creature moving with him, shadowing his steps, following his lead. Then Prince G dropped Big Youth's *S 90 Skank* and she put it in high gear, leaving Scott in the dust. She wined her hips in raw sensuality, with uninhibited eroticism that was pure

Jamaican from her black island blood and culture. Off in a corner some guy was pushing up against his girl like he was Jah's gift to womankind but that was nothing compared to the heat this dancehall queen was throwing off. His heart pounding in his ears, Scott pressed nearer but prolonging the pursuit the coy doe elegantly sashayed and scissored out of reach.

"I'm Scott," he hollered.

"Marva."

"You dance great."

"Do all right yourself."

"Hey, would you like a Red... I mean Heineken?"

"All right."

Boisterous shouting broke out and Scott looked around to gauge the situation. Henry signaled to keep an eye out. This kind of shenanigans went on all the time, hired provocateurs paid dollars and beers by a rival sound system to talk trash and disrupt the performance. But with election fever burning, no telling what might happen. Marva danced on, not about to let some idiot ruin her evening. She slowed and again moved in sync with Scott as under her spell he forgot about the beer.

Matt Gallagher glued his eyes on the man not forty feet in front of him. Black man, ratty snaky hair... it was that guy from the helicopter, the runty one, what was his name? Thunda or some damn thing. *Pocket Thunder.* What the hell was he doing here? Matt wasn't aware of any operation this evening in Tivoli. Shooting up JLP territory to cast blame on the PNP wasn't implausible—but dammit, he had to be kept briefed.

Was that mean-looking guy here too with the equally strange name? *William the Conqueror,* that was it. Matt scanned the crowd... yep, there he was on the other side. Something was going on all right.

A bottle shattered, a woman screamed. As mob emotions boiled, Scott pressed his pelvis between Marva's swaying hips. He reached around to the small of her back and held her flush against him as they moved together as one. It seemed like a dream, he'd never been that bold with a girl before. The sultry Caribbean night drawing it out of him.

And then gun shots rang out. *Bam. Bam. Bam. Bam.* The panicked crowd ran like stampeding stallions. Scott grabbed Marva's hand before she was borne off in the torrent. He pulled her into a dark recess, kissed her and groped at her crotch. Marva moaned and gave herself to his touch for an instant before pulling back.

"Come on," she cried and led him from the bedlam.

Automatic weapons bursting from all directions, Matt crouched into a dark corner. If it was those two jokers shooting off their guns with his boy

97

walking around out there they'd be sorry. Three bodies lay on the ground. Matt had failed to save his wife and win the war in Nam, would he now fail to protect his son? Seeing that Scott was not among the fallen, he pushed deeper into the ghetto.

Suddenly a Jamaican big as a tree and brandishing an upraised machete charged at him. Matt hit him low like a football linebacker and using his foe's own momentum threw him over a three-foot high planter overgrown with weeds. By the time the guy hit cement Matt was gimping with his bad leg down the bumpy narrow path, hugging the sides of tenement walls and zinc fences, looking everywhere for Scott. Moving deeper into the concrete jungle and further from his vehicle, his way out.

Marva and Scott stumbled hand-in-hand through the chaos, laughing and crying out and pulling each other along. They wound their way through a maze of dismal dank back alleys that opened into a neighborhood of sturdier dwellings with proper yards and further still to a quiet middle-class district, where they belayed to gasp for breath.

"You all right?"

"Yes, man. You?"

"Alive, I think."

"C'mon."

Marva led Scott around the corner and into the walled courtyard of a modest free-standing home. A light on inside.

"This your place?" Scott asked. "Someone there?"

"Mama waiting for her baby to get home."

Scott frowned. "Thought we were going somewhere we could... you know... hang out."

"Ask me for a date."

"*A date?* We're here now, the time is right."

"My mama didn't raise no port-in-a-storm."

Scott swallowed hard and remembered his manners.

"You're right. Moving too fast. A date... when's the next riot?"

Marva laughed. "Please, no more nights like this!"

"Tomorrow."

"Tomorrow is church. Weekend best. But how will you get home?"

"Catch a taxi or something."

"Better stay here."

"Thank you God," Scott clasped his hands.

"Don't start licking your chops. You're sleeping on the floor. Me nah give it up on the first night... especially to jail bait."

"What are you, all of seventeen?"

"I'll be nineteen in—"

Before she could finish Scott pulled Marva close and kissed her and didn't quit until she snapped her head back.

98

"There a fire in you, bwoy," she gasped, "but yuh still gwine sleep on the floor."

Marva led Scott around to her bedroom window.

"Wait fe me signal," Marva said. "Bathroom's close to mama's room so pee out here. Gotta do more than that I don't know what to tell you. Find a pile of leaves or something."

"I'm fine."

Marva held her finger to her mouth to shush him and went around to let herself in the front door. A light went on in the bedroom and she appeared at the window silhouetted behind the drapery. Scott held his breath as she disrobed and put on her nightgown. She disappeared and returned moments later and raised the window. Scott climbed in.

Marva led him on tiptoe into the darkened living room to use the phone to call home. Nobody answered. Scott whispered a message saying he was staying the night at Henry's. He wondered where dad was so late.

Dad was up to his neck with staying alive as Tivoli Gardens exploded in gunfire. Clawing his way through zinc alleys in search of his son, he took an unlucky turn toward the outskirts of a PNP district and ended up in a crossfire as rival cadres brought out heavy hardware and blasted away at each other behind street-corner barricades.

The *pop-pops* of Friday night specials and staccato *rat-a-tat-tat* bursts of M-16s gave Matt a sweet adrenaline fix. The more blood spilled, the quicker Manley would be out on his ass. He just had to avoid getting his name or picture in the paper... in the wake of the Senate Church Committee's dirt-digging into CIA shenanigans, the Company didn't need any more embarrassment. Dying out here wouldn't help either.

The big guns had the street pinned down and avenues of escape were closing off. Matt ducked into a tenement yard thinking to climb a wall and jump down on a gunman, take his weapon and shoot his way out. Suddenly a huge dread brandishing a stalk of sugarcane like a club came at Matt with wide yellow eyes. Matt flushed with animal excitement— someone that enormous would be a challenge, at least. He was about to counterattack when the man spoke.

"I-man get you out safe."

The bearded goliath motioned Matt to follow him. Matt held back.

"Move quick, hear?" the dread cried. Matt cautiously followed him to the darkened archway of a tenement. The man held up his hand for quiet as footsteps ran past.

"This way," he said, entering the dwelling, where a dim light flickered. Matt hung back calculating the odds someone was in the next room waiting to blow his brains out.

"Come now if yuh wan' live."

Against his better judgment, Matt followed the black behemoth to the back room. There in the low light of a small lamp a woman sat bare-bosomed, an infant nursing at her breast and another small child clinging to her leg. The woman looked up at Matt without the slightest trace of self-consciousness or shame and smiled; Matt's eyes lingered upon her full milk-laden breasts. In the midst of these decrepit paved gardens she radiated an almost spiritual calm and acceptance, a Raphael Madonna in ebony.

The dread showed Matt to a rear door opening to an enclosed yard.

"Gwan an' nah look back," he said. Matt glanced into the gentle giant's eyes an instant and without a word fled the dwelling, scaled the wall and got the hell out of Tivoli.

Scott tiptoed to the bedroom trembling with visions of Marva's naked body, but she had laid a sheet and pillow on the floor for him. She averted her eyes as he stripped to his undies and took to his bedroll.

"Good night," Marva said and leaned over to kiss him. She turned off the light and he lay back and listened to her breathing.

"You'd give it up if I was older, is that it?" he said but there came no response. Scott stared at the ceiling as he grew drowsy and finally closed his eyes, only to wake with a snort at the tickling of a mosquito on his nose.

Only it wasn't a mosquito. The filamentary loose ends of Marva's braids were brushing lightly upon his face as she bent low over him.

"Shhh," she shushed and lay down next to him. She kissed his cheek and danced her tongue to his lips. Scott's hand found her crotch but Marva pulled back.

"Just hold me, okay?"

"Okay." He removed his hand.

"We can go on the bed," she said, and there they spent the night snuggling close, his white Penney's briefs pressed in agonized ecstasy against her exquisite backside. It was a night he wished would never end and of course such nights never did.

14

The salty sea breeze licked at his nostrils as Scott walked Henry's rickety bike along the oceanfront. Marva had said eight o'clock, hadn't she? Victoria Pier where the cruise ships come in, or used to anyway? He walked up and down in a fret after his frantic bike ride across town, busting his butt to arrive at the appointed hour until he remembered about *soon come,* which usually translated as "don't hold your breath" but he took to mean "hold your horses, I'm on my way." Looming in front of him was a large bronze statue of a black man rising from a massive stone plinth, as if breaking free of shackles. Situated at water's edge—the very spot where slaves had arrived from Africa.

An old Ford pickup truck rumbled around King Street onto Ocean Boulevard, a good-looking young buck at the wheel. The rickety jalopy grinded to a halt and out stepped an irie daughtah poppin' style in tight blue jeans and pink t-shirt with rainbow butterflies and *Dunn's River Falls* embroidered on the front.

"Like it?" said Marva, grabbing a small daypack off the seat before the pickup sped off, the bronze Adonis casting a broad grin back through the rear window.

"Hey, Marva. Who was that in the truck?"

"That was Troy. Handsome, don't?"

"You think?"

"Relax. He's my brother."

"Like what, the statue?"

"*Negro Aroused,* by Edna Manley, Michael's mother. Jamaica's Michelangelo. Commemorates the 1938 worker strikes that like to burn the country to the ground. Black man rising and ain't it about time. Wood original's in the National Museum. Welcome to Kingston Harbour."

Marva swept her arm out toward the blue if less than pristine waters. "Seventh largest natural harbour in the world. Used to be six forts and one hundred forty-five cannon standing guard. Horatio Nelson was the captain at Ft. Charles before he put his thing down and became *Admiral* Nelson. Out there is Port Royal, what's left of it. The Sodom and Gomorrah of the Caribbean—pirates and buccaneers drinking grog, whoring, gambling."

"Sounds like spring break." Scott scanned across to the Palisadoes and remaining structures of "the wickedest city on earth."

"Earthquake of 1692 sank her below the sea," Marva said sadly. "The wages of sin, Scotty, the wages of sin. The Lord giveth and the Lord taketh away. Fire, hurricanes, cholera, more earthquakes, it come like an Old Testament apocalypse. Port Royal has seen it all. Then they built Kingston, named for one of them British kings... William of Orange. C'mon, we've got a long day ahead of us."

Marva led Scott up King Street, the main thoroughfare from colonial times lined with imposing greathouses with their verandas and stately columns. Slavemaster homes. *Massa backra.* They arrived at a large square at the center of which was the green oasis of William Grant Park.

"Here we are at the Parade," Marva said. She was perfectly fluent in both patois and English, but spoke mainly the latter with Scott. "Redcoats would muster here, used to be hangings, whippings, all manner of goings-on. See that blue dome over yonder? That's Ward Theatre, where Norman Manley started the PNP in '38 in the wake of the big worker strikes."

"Manleys, Manleys everywhere."

"Norman Manley is one of Jamaica's seven national heroes. A great, great, *great* prime minister, rest his soul. Michael's going to be even greater.

101

Long way to go but we'll get there. 'One-one coco fill basket,' we say… one step at a time. Want a coconut water?"

Nearby was a vendor with a cart full of coconuts. Marva ordered two and the fellow licked the tops off with his machete. Marva took hers with a straw while Scott drank straight from the shell, "Jamaican-style."

"Yummy," Scott lit up as he tasted the milky-sweet liquid for the first time.

"Coconut water wash de 'eart," the vendor said, counting his money.

"C'mon," Marva said, taking Scott's hand, "we won't see much of Kingston at this rate. Remember, could be a pop quiz at any time."

"In that case was it seventh harbour and six forts or sixth harbour and seven forts?"

Marva laughed and led him around a corner and straight into a raucous scene—a street-full of marching women shouting down Manley.

"No Cuba! No communism!" they chanted, waving homemade placards and banging pots and pans as if to symbolize Manley's failure to feed the children. Many had been persuaded to join in by $10 bribes extended by Matt Gallagher's men. PNP supporters heckled as they passed along, acrimonious shouting flying back and forth.

"I don't like this," Marva said. "These things have a way of getting out of control. Let's keep moving."

They ran back to the Parade, where they caught a bus up into the hills. There was a nice hike with a waterfall, Marva said, and they could stop along the way at Nelson's Lookout.

The House of Dread was on cool runnings. West Indies time. *Soon come.* Early morning jog around the Mona Reservoir and back to bliss out over Gilly's strawberry-and-passion fruit smoothies. Bob and Family Man had returned from mixing the new album in Miami, *Rastaman Vibration* was a wrap and the pressure was off. *Nah fret yuhself, mon.* A paint-splattered Neville Garrick in overalls was working on a colossal drapery of Emperor Haile Selassie I to use as a stage backdrop for the upcoming concert tour. The rest of the crew were scattered, some helping out on Peter's and Bunny's debut albums.

Moments like this were ideal for songwriting and Bob sat on the veranda strumming his guitar, singing and scatting lyrics as they came into mind. He sang of the human condition and the black man's struggle, informed by folk wisdom and the teachings of Rastafari. Since the departure of Peter and Bunny he wrote virtually all the band's songs, though often with helpful contributions from bandmates, friends and even people passing on the street. "Try it this way," someone might call out and toss off a riff. Esther Anderson claimed to have pitched in on *I Shot the Sheriff*, as did Lee Jaffe, "the white Wailer" from the States who played harmonica on *Rebel*

Music. Reggae truly was the people's music, "heartbeat of the nation." Family Man, in orchestrating the instrumental accompaniment, deserved a good deal of credit for the Wailers sound too.

Cindy showed up and sat on the porch, Bob lighting up in a big smile. It was a rare few moments of privacy, but they had more company than they realized. Across the street in a second-floor apartment—recently rented under a phony name—a CIA surveillance team was watching their every move, alert to all comings and goings. Binoculars and telephoto camera were trained upon the property and manned around the clock, twenty-four-seven, two-person teams taking four-hour shifts. All intelligence recorded in a notebook. Matt Gallagher now having *two* white whales to obsess over.

Bob and Cindy had patched up their differences but beauty queen Breakespeare was out of it this morning. She sat mute and preoccupied, running her bare foot along his as he sweetly sang and skatted as the spirit moved him. Noting her apparent malaise, he shifted into the song off the *Natty Dread* album that was fast becoming a reggae anthem, *No Woman No Cry*.

She remained still and passive as a stone.

"Why yuh nah sing, Cin?" he stopped and said.

"Oh, Bobby," she sprang to her feet. "You *live* these words. Sitting in the government yard, Georgie building the fire, eating cornmeal porridge. Life in the yards, hard times on the street. We from opposite sides of the track you and I. So much me cyan't ever share with you."

"Why yuh gwan so, Cin?"

"We apples and oranges, man. Me wan' wear jewelry and make-up and I know it nah set well with your Rastafarian beliefs."

"Wearin' make-up so important?"

"It's not the make-up," Cindy said softly. "I want to know what the future holds for us."

"Only Jah know."

"Marriage?"

"Just a paper, man."

"It's more than paper, Bobby. It's all about commitment."

"Love the only important thing."

"Girl wants a nest. Family."

"Me love fe have baby with yuh. Wan' see black pickney like sand onna beach."

"But Rita--"

"Rita like sister, yunno? Sing, man. Sing and everything be all right."

A colorful clattertrap of a VW van drove in the gate like a float in some surreal Rose Parade, Rastafarian iconography and graffiti plastered all over it. A crew in dreadlocks and splotchy overalls hopped out hefting brushes and buckets. Across the street in the surveillance post binoculars were raised.

"Oy, Foot," Bob hailed the crew leader, a graybeard nicknamed for his deformed, enlarged foot, on account of which he everywhere went barefoot. Bob had hired the crew to paint the House of Dread red gold and green, the Rasta colors... *ites gold and green.*

"Oy, Skippah." Foot hippity-hopped over.

"Carry new man?" Marley asked, noticing an unfamiliar face.

"Reg'lar man catch sick," Foot said and hollered over. "Oy, Doc. Come meet the Skippah."

The new guy hustled over, a paint bucket in each hand. Young kid in dreadlocks, about twenty. He set the buckets down to shake hands.

"Pleasure fe meet yuh, Mistah Marley," the young locksman said.

"Name Doc Holiday," Foot said, "like inna shoot-out corral."

Marley studied the kid as he slapped him some skin. He wasn't a true Rastafarian. Bob could smell that a mile away.

Across the street in the surveillance post, Fred McGinnis trained in his binoculars.

"There's our man," McGinnis said.

Jangling in the oversized pockets of Doc Holiday's work trousers were three spoon-shaped, radio-activated cavity transmitters—the same kind of bug the Soviets had secreted inside a plaque of the Great Seal of the United States presented to Ambassador Averell Harriman in August 1945 and which had hung undetected in Harriman's Moscow office until 1952, picking up every word that was said.

Doc Holiday nervously fingered the bugs. Normally a case officer or technician would make the installation, drilling holes to secret the devices inside a wall then resealing and repainting with matching paint. No one however had come up with a feasible plan for inserting a trained man or team into Marley's residence, where the action never stopped and heavy characters patrolled day and night. The best shot seemed to be for someone like Holiday to slip the bugs inside a potted plant or under a piece of furniture.

"Come, Cin," Bob said, jumping to his feet, "make we gwan a beach while dem work."

Bob pulled Cindy to her feet and she dashed inside to freshen up. Since Michael Manley had desegregated the beaches, a black man like Marley was free to go to any stretch of shoreline he pleased—even with a white woman. An ordinary scuffling Rasta, though, would still be taking his chances.

Bob went around back where Neville Garrick was painting a lion on his huge drapery of Haile Selassie I—the "Lion of Judah."

"It a come nice, bruthah," Bob said. "Seen Skill?"

"Upstairs, me think," Garrick said. A long lanky galoot almost as handsome as the Skipper and with that same scraggly under-beard, Garrick had come under the tutelage of Angela Davis while studying at UCLA College of Fine Arts. As Wailers art director he was also designing the album cover for the new LP —which he conceptualized rather like Bob posed as a guerrilla fighter ala Michelangelo's David staring down Goliath.

Marley found Allan Cole lazing in the hammock in the long enclosed balcony off the upstairs bedroom.

"Skill, keep yuh eyes open while me gone," Marley said.

"Trouble, Skip?" Cole sat up.

"Stranger a come me house, seen?"

"Sight."

The First Annual US-Jamaica Friendship Charity Golf Tournament was this day hosted by the US Embassy at Caymanas Country Club near Spanish Town. Spanish Town had served as the nation's capital for almost two hundred years following the demise of Port Royal in the 1692 cataclysm; now, well it had seen better days. Net receipts from the tourney were to be donated to the Kingston Boys Club. Melody Raines, the new broad sent down by HQ, a beautiful black girl no less ravishing than Claudia Candiotti, walked around looking stunning in a tight dress that clung to her million-dollar backside like a miser to his money. It was hoped that Michael Manley would show up and take the bait.

By no coincidence, in Matt Gallagher's foursome was Major Garrett Anderson of the Jamaica Defense Forces, successor to the British West Indies Regiment. Intelligence had Anderson as a vitriolic JLP sympathizer. Matt introduced himself on the putting green before tee-off.

"Matt Gallagher with the American mission," he greeted warmly, hand extended.

"Garrett Anderson." Anderson was a ruggedly handsome man with muscles bulging out his lavender golf shirt. Sliver of mustache riding atop his upper lip.

"*Major* Anderson, isn't it? With JDF?"

"That's right."

"I believe we are in a foursome together."

"Excellent."

"It's all about the kids."

"Indeed it is. Well done, sir."

Their foursome was called and they met the other two members of their group. David Doty was an executive for a US bauxite mining concern, while Freddy Wang, a rotund and friendly fellow, was owner of Wang's Supermarket. Chinese had come to Jamaica, like the indentured workers from India, in mid-19th Century, many eventually becoming shop-owners and incurring the resentment of their black fellows, though some like Wang were beloved for the selfless kindnesses they extended in their community.

"Gentlemen," said Matt, "shall we say a $10 Nassau?"

"Too rich for me," said Wang.

"I only bet on sure things," said Doty. "IBM, for instance."

"Anderson? Straight up, no handicaps."

"But, uh…" Anderson glancing at Matt's eye-patch.

"I play by sense of smell," Matt deadpanned, and winked.

"You're on."

Anderson teed up and ripped the ball two-eighty straight down the fairway. Matt, a naturally gifted athlete who had picked up golf in his one year in junior college and whose depth perception and hand-to-eye coordination had adapted well to the loss of one eye, managed a decent drive thirty yards back in the playable rough. He would have to outplay Anderson at the short game if he hoped to win the wager.

Which of course he didn't. The plan was to lose and butter the major up. Nurture that resource. Gallagher didn't bring up politics at all over the first nine holes, which somehow he managed to win by a stroke (not wanting to be *too* obvious). Anyway, a come-back victory would really put the major in a good mood.

"How do Jamaicans feel about Manley sending his police force to train in Cuba?" Matt finally tested the waters as they walked down the tenth fairway to their tee shots. The *New York Times* was fulminating over this incendiary new development, though Manley had sent only a small crew to learn the fine art of body-guarding from experts who protected Castro.

Anderson answered by hocking and spitting noisily.

"Maybe Manley will get voted out in the upcoming elections," Matt said and Anderson banged his three-iron thirty yards over the green.

Marva and Scott rode the bus four thousand feet above Kingston into country painted shades of green so luminous and intricate in their infinite variegations only the Great Artist Himself could have managed it. These southern slopes of the Blue Mountains were pockmarked with farms and coffee plantations but there were still patches of virgin forest, cedar, mahogany, teak, giant Cyathea ferns, dogwood and evergreens, especially higher upslope. The 7000-foot range and neighboring John Crow Mountains blocked the northeasterly "doctor breeze" from reaching Kingston and took the brunt of the torrential rains that hit the north shore during the summer hurricane season, though there was nothing to stop monster storms blowing in from Africa from sneaking in the backdoor on the south side of the island.

They got off at Guava Ridge and ate a bite at a Rasta's stall under a sprawling silk cotton tree near the trail head. Scott had never tasted such wonderful food--ackee and saltfish, calaloo, fried plantain and jonny cakes, washed down with Irish Moss, an invigorating seaweed concoction. He wondered why Maddy never cooked like this.

Marva told him that the Arawak (Taino) Indians had carved their canoes out of silk cotton trees like the giant specimen they were sitting under. In such had they rowed out to greet Columbus. When on his 1504 Fourth Voyage the "Admiral of the Ocean Sea" was shipwrecked and stranded on the Rock for a year, Indians rowed two canoes across the open Caribbean to Hispaniola to summon a rescue party. With an almost indistinguishable shudder Marva added that duppies lurked amongst the tree's massive roots.

Whoo. Whoo. There came the hooting of an owl from atop the 120-foot tree.

"Pattoo," said Marva, using the old West African term, her voice laden with a cautious gravity as she tilted her head to steal a glance. "They say owls are messengers between spirit worlds. Symbols of death."

"Don't worry. I'll protect you."

"Aren't you sweet," Marva lit up.

Scott paid the bill and left a generous tip to the friendly proprietor, receiving one in return.

"Take the daughtah fe the third falls, friend," the Rastaman whispered aside, a twinkle in his eye. "Fe real."

The Rasta held up a small jug, a broad grin breaking across his face. "Take a swig of strong-back, likkle brother. Make yuh bamboo like iron."

Scott took a big swill just in case.

"Yes I-yah!" the Rasta cried in mischievous delight. "Yuh pistol gwine shoot bullets of fire an' melt dat girl heart."

Marva took his hand and they set off along the trail. At this elevation it was pleasantly cool and clouds were building in the distance but Marva assured him that heavy downpours were rare in April, though May was a different story altogether. Jamaica has no poisonous snakes or large land mammals to speak of but they delighted in sightings of rare Swallowtail butterflies big as a man's hand and—*See 'im there!*—"Doctor Bird" hummingbirds with a lancet-like red beak and streamer tailfeathers that called to mind the ridiculously wonderful long cloak of a 19th Century doctor. Marva was a bright, talkative sort who relished sharing her country and culture with her new friend and seemed to never run out of interesting things to say.

"Arawak Indians used to say Doctor Birds are reincarnated souls of dead people," she said, sending a shiver down Scott's spine. He remarked reflexively about the "heavy death vibe in the air today."

They tramped on and Marva spun tales of Anancy, the half-man/half-spider folk hero who used his wits and cunning to solve problems—the trickster, a universal Jungian archetype, like the Native American's coyote. Son of Nyame the sky god and Asase the earth goddess, Anancy brought the rain to quell forest fires and taught the ways of agriculture to humankind. The spider-man was a heritage of Old Africa that like his cousin Brer Rabbit in the American South had survived the Middle Passage to keep alive the *roots* of the ancient mother culture, passed down to generations of Jamaicans by mothers and grandmothers telling bedtime tales, sometimes attributed to "Aunt Nancy."

Marva told him how the clever Anancy had collected all the stories in the world as his own, as Anansesem or "Anancy stories."

"His father Nyame told Anancy to have the stories he must bring back the python, the leopard, the hornets and the dwarf. Anancy tricked Onini the python into lying down on a branch so he could measure how long he was and tied him up. He dug a hole and the leopard fell in and Anancy offered to get him out with his web."

"Tricky," Scott said.

"You get the idea. Catching the hornets was really clever. He poured water out of his calabash like it was raining and said they could stay dry inside the empty jug."

"And the dwarf?"

"Anancy made a doll, covered it with sticky tar and put a yam in front of it. The dwarf came and ate the yam and thanked the doll. When the doll didn't reply the dwarf got mad and hit it with his hands and got stuck."

"Reminds me of Uncle Remus and the Tar Baby," Scott said.

Soon they were at Flamstead, the ruins of Horatio Nelson's estate, and Scott gasped in awe as his eyes beheld the view. The entire city of Kingston lay sprawling downslope, from Barbican and Beverly Hills to the harbour and open sea all the way to South America.

"Wow," Scott gushed in awe. They rested and Marva told how the great admiral had come down with yellow fever on a sea voyage to Nicaragua that claimed 90% of his men. Marva said that a woman from these parts had saved his life, a free colored versed in natural remedies named Cubah Cornwallis.

"There's folks out here that's got *the power*," Marva's voice swelling with pride. She added with a hint of indignation, "World doesn't know what Jamaica and Jamaicans can do."

They set out again and soon arrived at a lovely waterfall where a dozen or so Jamaicans frolicked and reposed.

"Rasta said there's a bitchin' falls up ahead," Scott said. "Wanna go for it?"

"You Tarzan, me Jane."

Fifteen minutes later they came to an even more splendid falls with fewer people. Marva slipped off her shoe and dipped her foot into water tinted a deep green from the verdant surroundings.

"Ooh, nice," she cooed. "What was that word?"

"Bitchin'. Don't think he meant this one. Can always come back."

"After you, bwana."

The trail grew steep and thick with growth but soon enough they arrived at a setting like the biblical Eden lush with twining vines and giant ferns and a waterfall that plunged some fifty feet into a basin of cool clear eddying pools. Best yet there wasn't a soul around. If this wasn't paradise it hadn't yet been created. And they had it all to themselves.

Scott felt a giddy surge of energy originating in the small of his back that radiated to fingers and toes and set a fire burning at his loins. Was it the Rastaman's herbal potion?

Or was it that Marva had peeled off her clothes and stood naked in front of him?

"Aren't you going in?" she asked.

"Uh..." Scott had never gone skinny dipping with a girl and fumbled at his buttons in a rush. When he was finally disencumbered Marva took him by the hand and they jumped feet first into the inviting blue waters. They paddled and splashed and laughed in unfettered joy.

"Did you call me bwana?" Scott teased.

"Uhh-uhh," she purred, eyes a-twinkle, "me nah dun dat, *nah suhhhhh*."

They stood under the falls and let the cascading water pummel their shoulders and backs.

"It's Or-*ange*," Scott said. "That British king... William of Or-*ange*. City in France."

"I knew that."

"What else do you know?"

"I know you have a nice cock."

Marva took Scott by the hand. She felt his trembling and wondered if it was his first time. She led him across the pool to where they had left their clothes, which she gathered up to make a blanket. With a pocketknife from her pack she sliced a ripe mango into two juicy pink halves and they fed each other, kissing open-mouthed and gorging on the slippery wet fruit.

Then Marva was on her back on the mattress of clothes and Scott welled with an ancient energy both sacred and profane, the daytime sky filling with crescent moons and shooting stars like the painted ceiling of a Renaissance Cathedral of Love.

At the House of Dread the three cavity transmitters were burning a hole in Doc Holiday's pocket. He wanted to plant the damn bugs and get the hell out of there. But every time he looked around muscular Allan Cole was looming, slapping a machete against his thigh. First chance he got he slipped off the property and disappeared.

Heineken bottles collected on the table as Gallagher and Major Anderson sat at the 19th hole at Caymanas Country Club and replayed their round. The beers were on Matt's tab. Clashing priorities had come in to play as Matt was on course to break 90 for the first time ever. He swallowed hard and pulled his putt on the 18th hole, settling for a 90 and giving Anderson his chance to win. Anderson blew two short putts to card a 91. Gallagher made a mental note—*chokes under pressure*.

Talk turned to Michael Manley.

"We were better off under the bloody British," Anderson grunted.

"Can anything be done?" Gallagher asked.

"Things *are* being done, I assure you."

"We might be able to help. Money. Materials. Can almost promise."

A foursome came in off the course and they hushed up.

"I'll be in touch," Anderson said, standing to go.

That evening Scott joined the Morrison family for dinner. Marva's mother Winny was black Jamaican and an ardent supporter of Michael Manley, her father a jewelry shop owner of Indian heritage (East Indians impolitely called "coolies") who was a party faithful but believed Manley overplayed his hand. Marva, a high school grad, worked in the family shop. Winny, a buxom woman who seemed more than her puny husband could handle, served curried goat, festival dumplings, steamed bananas, and bammy with rice 'n peas. Scott started to eat but stopped abruptly as everybody joined hands for grace.

"Humble we are in yuh sight, Lord," Winny began, head bowed. "Thank yuh fe yuh many blessing. Thank yuh Lord fe yuh bounteous earth that sustain we, yuh mighty rivers that refresh we, yuh sweet sun that brighten we day and yuh bright shining moon that guide we through the darkest night. Lord, we thank yuh for Scott and pray yuh keep him safe. Amen."

All chanted "amen" in reply.

"Nice," Scott said and everybody dug in to the wonderful food. Scott didn't touch the curried goat.

"Nah like me goat, bwoy?" Marva's mother asked.

"He's going I-tal," said Marva. "Growing out his dreads."

"Bwoy grow him locks? Lawd, lawd."

Everybody laughed, including Scott.

"Rasta don't drink beer either," Marva said. "No Red Stripe and *certainly* no Heineken."

"Heineken?" squawked Winny. "Yuh support JLP, bwoy?"

"Uh, no," said Scott, eyeing Marva. "PNP sounds good to me."

"Jamaica nothing without PNP," Winny said. "Michael Manley keep wolf from door fe plenty folk."

Later, as Scott and Marva sat smooching on the veranda, she told him another Anancy story. In the psychology of a culture faced with the horrors of slavery, the folk literature of the trickster gave a measure of redemption in outsmarting Massa and his wicked system. Yet Anancy was sometimes "too devious for his own good" and Marva wanted to relate a tale with a nicer message.

"Anancy wanted to hoard all the wisdom in the world," she said, "so he got a calabash and went around and gathered it all up. He wanted to hide it at the top of a tree—a silk cotton tree like where we had lunch—so he tied it around his stomach and started climbing. He couldn't shimmy up with the darn thing around his belly so his son Ntikuma suggested he tie it around his back. Anancy was so shocked the likkle boy's solution was wiser than his own that he dropped the calabash and it smashed and all the wisdom got out. A rain came up and washed the wisdom to sea where it spread around the world, and now there is a little bit of wisdom in everybody."

"A happy ending after all," Scott said. Suddenly the front door flew open and a handsome young man blew in barefoot, shirt unbuttoned to the waist. It was the guy who dropped Marva at the pier that morning. Her brother.

"Oy, Troy," Marva said. "Come meet Scott."

"Soon come," Troy said, hardly breaking stride as he disappeared down the hall. Moments later he emerged cleaned up and wearing shoes and a laundered shirt.

"Likkle later, hear?" he tossed off an easy grin and the dark-skinned Adonis was out the door.

"Nice guy," said Scott. "Terse, but nice."

"Lotta jerks out there take advantage of nice guys," Marva frowned.

"Wish I had a family like yours."

"My family is your family," she said, and the warm feeling in Scott's heart was like the embers of a winter fire.

One week after the charity golf tournament the US Embassy presented a check for $3900 to the director of the Boys Club at the monthly foreign diplomats dinner. Michael Manley showed briefly for the photo op and Melody Raines, flaunting cleavage, flashed coy smiles whenever the prime minister glanced her way. Matt Gallagher swore that if Manley passed on this one he would personally put a bullet right between the man's eyes.

*

111

Blindfolds were snug as the VW Beetle rumbled through the twists and turns of the winding country road. Garrett Anderson downshifted into second to accommodate an unpaved stretch as it narrowed into a thick arboreal patch that sent leafy tentacles slapping against the side windows. Beside Anderson in the front passenger seat was Joseph Stewart, chief of police for St. Andrew Parish; in the back were Matt Gallagher and Freddy McGinnis. A fat moon shown bright overhead but Matt could discern no clues where they were. "For your own protection," Anderson had said of the blindfolds. At least, thought Gallagher, the Jamaicans were taking measures to ensure secrecy.

Gallagher and McGinnis were quite the odd couple in the backseat. Gallagher liked McGinnis for his spunk and intelligence but feared he was too morally nuanced to make it as a case officer. McGinnis was equally ambivalent about his chief—he respected his strength and drive, perhaps unconsciously wished to prove himself in his eyes, but growing up black in Birmingham, Alabama he'd had plenty experience with sonsabitches and there was no doubt in his mind Gallagher and Lake were exactly that.

On the other hand, he'd been taught as a boy to give people a chance and that meant allowing them an opportunity to be better than shown thus far. Even white people. Did making an ass of yourself once or twice make you a racist? Experience teaches wisdom but sometimes you had to take your lumps to get the point. McGinnis had had his share of fistfights growing up but as a former seminary student he took seriously the golden rules of turning the other cheek and doing unto others. And these two guys were nowhere near the sonsabitches he'd come across back home. That was some major league evil right there. It had been the assassinations of Martin Luther King and Medgar Evers that had turned him from a life in the church and set him on the path that would lead to the CIA.

"You can take off your blindfolds," Major Anderson said.

Gallagher and McGinnis removed their blindfolds but the foliage was so dense it was like being in a submarine in an underwater forest of kelp. The Bug emerged into a clearing where a dozen or more vehicles were parked by an old country manor. Men with automatic rifles came forward, flashlights and muzzles glistening.

Anderson lowered his window and spoke the password: "Rice 'n peas." They were waved through. The men got out and were approaching the old two-story dwelling when another armed guard came forward and Anderson uttered the second password:

"Cornmeal pudding."

They were allowed to enter. Inside was a motley assortment of ghetto rudeboys and Uptown types in slacks and shirts. The curtains were drawn and reggae music played in the background. Matt noticed Pocket Thunder and William the Conqueror smoking weed in a corner. He stared and the two glared back. The rudies had denied having anything to do with the shooting at the Tivoli street bash, claiming they'd merely gone out to enjoy a night of music. Matt suspected they were mercenaries without allegiance or honor, if not outright PNP spies, and not to be trusted.

The two Americans, Anderson and Stewart met in a side room with an olive-skinned man drinking Appleton rum. Charles Darnell was deputy leader of the Jamaica Labor Party, a ponderous and paunchy man who stood six-foot-five.

Darnell opened a briefcase, took out a stapled ten-page document and set it down on the table like it was the Holy Grail.

"The major has written something up," Darnell said, nodding toward Anderson, who stiffened his chin proudly. Gallagher picked the document up and leafed through.

"'Operation Werewolf... equipment and supplies... arms, explosives... cache points... personnel.'" Matt looked up in astonishment. "You're plotting a coup against the Manley government."

"I was led to believe the United States would be sympathetic," said Darnell.

"We are with you every step of the way. What is your plan?"

"Cut off the head and the beast will die," said Darnell.

"Yes, but *how,* exactly? Your operation must be carefully thought out to the last detail and executed with precision. Nothing can be left to chance."

"We are open to suggestion."

"How many men do you have?"

"As many as we need."

"I'm talking *field-trained* men. Marksmen, explosives experts, guerrilla fighters. The shock troops that will spring like lightning and seize control of the government."

"Well, uh…"

"Police, military? In what strength? Entire units or individuals plucked here and there?"

"Yes, of course."

"How many are prepared to revolt against their government? How many will remain loyal? It's all gotta be worked out. Take stock. Get your numbers. Organize your squads. Know who you can trust."

Darnell leaned back into his chair, leg over knee, and scratched his chin. Stewart madly jotted down notes. Anderson sat taking it all in. Freddy McGinnis was impressed how Matt took over like Patton in a steel pot.

"Group your men into squads," Matt said. "I will personally conduct their field training. We'll keep the guns and ammo flowing. How much explosives materiel do you have?"

"Fifty sticks of dynamite."

"I'll try to bring in a top explosives expert I worked with in Chile. Cuban with spit in his eye. Ghetto rats can help with the psy-ops but watch out for mercenaries who might stab you in the back."

"Psy-ops?"

"Psychological operations. Propaganda, labor actions, strikes and protests, economic sabotage."

"Economic sabotage?" Anderson cringed. "I don't like the ring of that."

"SOP for any serious attempt to remove a despot from power. Like softening up the beach with your big guns before you commence landing. A weakened economy gets the people screaming for change, brings the military and business leaders into your camp. You want public opinion on your side. Look, if it was up to me, I'd put a bullet through the cocksucker's head and be done with it. But if your coup fails—and a million things could go wrong—there's still the chance the people will rise up and vote the Commie-loving sonuvabitch out of office. Economy's sailing along, the masses won't give a damn about Communism, they'll go with the status quo. Squeeze the economy so the people feel the pinch and bingo, it's champagne time."

"Give me an example of this economic sabotage," Anderson demanded.

"Stuffing dirt in the gas tanks of city buses. Shooting up the offices of the bauxite companies. Tear up the roads so people can't drive. Bomb every power plant in the country. Blow up key bridges. Poison the food and water supply."

"But this is terrorism against the domestic population," Anderson protested, folding his arms across his chest.

"Can't pull your punches if you want to win," said Darnell.

"Win *at what cost*? By destroying the country's infrastructure and crippling the economy? Making people's lives even more miserable than they already are?"

"Has to be done," said Joe Stewart.

"Might seem heartless, Major," Matt said, "but it's the kindest way. Much greater suffering will ensue if Manley is allowed to stay in office another four years and build his coalition with Castro. Whole damn Caribbean could go communist. Mexico falls and all of Central America is lost. From there it's an easy step into South America where the ghost of Bolivar is waiting to rise up and rally the people. We have no choice, gentlemen. This is a war we have to win. A little cinching of the belt now will prevent wholesale tragedy later."

"We are ready to move forward," Darnell said, as Stewart nodded in agreement. Anderson thought he saw a spark of understanding in the black

American's eyes, a hint that he harbored the same deep-seated qualms, but the foreigner said nothing and the major bit his lip in silence.

"One other thing," Matt said.

"Yes?"

"This hooligan reggae singer."

"He means Marley," said McGinnis.

"What about him?" Darnell asked.

"He's trouble."

"Bob Marley is enormously popular in Jamaica," Darnell said. "He has the protection of powerful people on both sides of the fence. It's a suicide mission. The man is untouchable."

We'll see about that, Matt thought.

15

Thanksgiving, 1980, Santa Barbara

Aunt Sylvia cooked turkey for Thanksgiving and had Scott over to her Goleta home. He allowed himself a little poultry for the occasion with the usual fixings. Rastas weren't always strict vegetarians. The crucial foods to avoid were pork and shellfish, bottom feeders and scavenger and predator fish. Salt, as it was believed to repel the spirits. Alcohol, especially rum and hard liquor.

"How's it going with Phil?" Sylvia asked.

"Dr. M?" Scott said, washing down his aunt's steamed carrots with a sip of water.

"Are you comfortable with him?"

"He's okay, I reckon. Little square. Something about him though. Expression in his eyes nagging at me."

"There's a problem?"

"No, nothing like that. Just something mysterious about him."

"Are you getting into interesting things?"

"Guess so."

"You don't sound too enthused."

"Poking around stirring things up seems like asking for trouble."

"You've got to get it out, Scottie. Sometimes people who go through hard times, real hard times, like a Holocaust survivor that was in the camps, they won't talk about it, not ever. They lock it inside, just too painful. Then one day for some reason they start to talk and it all pours out of them, all the bottled-up pain, and they bawl like a baby. Just sobbing uncontrollably. Could be fifty years and like it was yesterday. It's not weird, it's just the way humans are, the way the mind functions. We have to suffer our losses fully before we can move on. Jung says our hidden dark side is the key to new growth, but only if we give it expression. If you hold things in you only make it worse, even make yourself sick."

115

"Mitch likes Jung too. Used to, anyway."

"You should read him sometime. Want me to give you some books?"

"I'm okay."

"Tough nut to crack, aren't you?" Sylvia smiled. "Ready for some pumpkin pie?"

"Sure. Should I tell you about my dream?"

"Absolutely. Whipped cream?"

"No thanks. There was this black woman, like a gypsy, you know, beads and mystical potions."

"Uh-huh."

"She was an Obeah woman. Hands me a bundle of herbs and says put these under your pillow and you will dream of your sweetheart. Worked too. Made me dream."

"Who did you dream about?"

"Marva. So you know what I'm going to do?"

"What?"

"Dream about Marva putting herbs under her pillow so she'll dream of me."

"Maybe she already is dreaming of you and made you think of her."

Scott's face lit up. He would have never thought of that in a million years.

"You never told me what happened with her," Aunt Sylvia said.

"Let's not go there, okay?"

"Don't you think it's time you let go, hun? So many nice girls out there." Scott frowned and she sweetened her tune. "Why don't you go to Jamaica and settle things in your mind? How about you and I take a trip down there sometime? Would you be up for that?"

"Maybe someday."

"Let me know when you're ready." Aunt Sylvia dished out two slices of pie and spooned whipped cream on hers.

"Sure you don't want some? Gotta live a little."

"None for me, thanks."

The day after Thanksgiving Scott stopped by Sound Spectrum on lower State Street. He went not to the reggae section but two rows over in classic rock, where he riffed through the stacks under "B" and lifted out an album, paid for it and rode his bike home to the Westside. He'd finally put his finger on that puzzling expression that fluttered into Doc M's eyes every now and then. He'd had a vague certainty that he'd seen that look before and now he'd figured it out, or thought he had.

It was a look of despair—the same despair Scott had seen in the impoverished masses in Jamaica. They'd used to gather at Hope Road when

116

Bob was in town. People on the edge, pushed to the brink by the ravages of cruel circumstance and a wicked system. He'd seen them there often, these *sufferahs*, perhaps even that first time at the House of Dread. Yes, he was sure of it....

He sat on the couch next to Family Man, mellowing into the vibe. Smoking herb with Bob Marley—it blew his mind just to think of it. Sound system blasting Wailers tunes. Carly hitting on a spliff, big Gilly up shaking his butt to the music, everything cool-cool. But where was Bob?

"Seen Skipper?" he asked to anyone in earshot.

"Him outside attend the *sufferah*," said Family Man in that deep and sonorous voice that was like an aural massage of the spirit. "Gwan, check it out."

Scott went out front where he saw that a large crowd had gathered in the yard. There was Bob in the midst of them, barefoot and limping from Scott's tripping him in the soccer scrim. He listened on as Bob talked to a distraught woman carrying an infant with a small child clinging to her skirt.

"Wha'ppen, sis?" Bob asked.

"Greetings, Bob," the woman said, her upper lip trembling. "Me nah wan' trouble yuh none but my man him get shot dead and there no food in the house. The youth-them belly ache and them a cry."

Her eyes, Scott thought, were sinkholes of agony.

"Nah trouble your mind, seen?" said Marley, cupping her head in his hands and kissing her forehead. "Baby take the breast?"

She nodded tearfully as he palmed her a fistful of "J," Jamaican dollars to buy food for her brood.

"Listen now," Bob called to the waiting masses. "Need food fe eat move over this way and make line. Need something else gwan other side."

These were poor downtrodden folk with nobody to take their problems to except Bob Marley. These were the *sufferahs* of Kingston and beyond.

As always there were far too many achy bellies for Gilly to feed alone so Bob slipped a thick wad of money to a trusted youth to buy box meals from vendors on the streets. It would take an hour or more to round up enough to feed the throng. Bob always dropped whatever he was doing to minister to the less fortunate. For many it would be the only decent meal they would eat all day. And it wasn't just food but school shoes and packs and everything else. They came from miles around, from all across the island, as if making pilgrimage to a holy site, to beg help from the only person who would listen to their plaints and do what he could to relieve their woes. Every day was the same.

Scott put the newly purchased album on the box and lit a joint. Eric Burdon and the Animals. The '60s British Invasion. What was that Burdon song Doc M said he liked that first day? *When I Was Young*, wasn't it? Was there something to that? How could a Porsche-driving psychologist with a house on the hill and the world by the tail have anything in common with some of the most under-privileged people on the face of the earth? He set the needle on *When I Was Young*. Did the music you listen to say something about you, something profound? Any other song and he might not have bothered, but this one suggested a going back to the roots, a thread tying present to past.

The song came on with short instrumental rifts that sounded like a World War II fighter plane and a '60s muscle car. Then Burdon hit it, his voice strong and clear and bluesy. He sang of cold rooms and hard times growing up the son of a soldier, losing himself in cigarettes and girls and learning the old-fashioned way, through harsh experience in the school of hard knocks. It was a boy's initiation into the sordid side of life, Burdon's tone elegiac, almost tragic in mood. The lyrics were definitely tracing back to the roots in a deeply personal way. Hard times, dad in uniform… off to war, perhaps? What was Burdon getting at and what was Doc M keying in to? Everything was more intense in those halcyon days of youth, pain more torturous and laughter more joyous, the senses baptized with the awe and beauty—and sometimes the horror—of the world. It was a wistful look back at a time when life was fresh and new before nerve endings deadened, protective shells were erected and innocence was lost, leaving the adult to cry, *Oh God, what has become of that wide-eyed child that once was I?*

Scott hit on the joint. The words packed a wallop. Maybe a song was just a song. A cool tune to sing along to. Not a Rorschach inkblot, a projective revelation of the mind's deepest secrets. But this was the *favorite*, the one that sprang to mind. Doc M had said something once about Freud's colleague Alfred Adler, who'd maintained that one's earliest memory in life hinted at the course of development his/her life had taken. The lyrics of *When I Was Young* suggested more than a nostalgic walk down memory lane. They spoke of lost faith and the death of hope. Disillusionment. A rotting on the vine.

Is that it, Doc? Has your sloe gin lost its fizz?

Metamorphosis: The former empty suit, Philip Mitchell, Ph. D., clinical psychologist, the high and mighty Doc M, was instantaneously transformed into a living breathing human being with hopes and dreams and memories, flawed and fallible, a grownup child with a past and his own unique story to tell. A person, like Scott himself.

Johnny Carson had long since signed off and the old John Wayne flick *The Searchers* come to its denouement, the Duke rescuing his long lost

118

niece, a young Natalie Wood, from faceless wild Indians. Phil Mitchell sprawled on the couch, idly clutching his practice putter. A bottle of wine and several nips of codeine had not conjured the solace of sleep. He'd lately added Vicodin to his arsenal of mood-altering substances. He'd taken the drug years before for a knee injury and gone to his orthopedist to plead, quite untruthfully, that the knee was acting up and could he please have something for the pain.

How many would constitute a fatal dose? he wondered.

Using his putter like a cane—as if his knee really did hurt—he tramped out to the deck of the hillside Riviera home he'd shared with Karen for nine years. The deck jutted out over the canyon on tall stilts, a magic carpet of wood floating in midair. The lights of the city down the chaparral-dotted slopes lit up the moonless night, the little harbor, the dark expanse of the Santa Barbara Channel with its giant oil platforms strung across like a silvery bracelet twinkling in the night. The Mission with her twin towers cloaked in shadows, the "Queen of the Missions" they called her. At the twenty-one such settlements the Franciscan fathers founded in Alta California, Indians were converted at gunpoint, often, whipped if their piety was found lacking and hunted down if they fled. The vast darkness stretching to the horizon made Mitchell anxious. There were sharks in those waters. Man-eaters. What if you were out there alone bobbing up and down with gray fins of death slicing toward you? Any expanse of water unsettled him. Even the redwood hot tub made him uneasy and he hadn't been in since Karen had flown off, not once. He'd only learned to swim because Karen had wanted to go scuba diving in the Bahamas. As long as she was there, he'd never felt afraid.

Life seemed past the point of no return. Once he'd bristled with enthusiasm for Jung and the humanistic psychologists, Maslow, Rogers, Fromm. Like them he too had believed that a child, properly nurtured, its basic needs met, would like acorn producing oak naturally develop his/her full potentials as a good and loving being. Now, with his life path seeming more in the past than future, he wasn't so sure that the Skinnerian behaviorists weren't right that humans were nothing more than the products of their environment, scurrying mindlessly about like lab rats in a maze. Living for the next reward fix. Unthinking automatons maximizing pleasure and minimizing pain. This goddamn Gallagher kid a lost cause. Another whiny loser. Once the kid had seemed the Grail, the key to new life, but redemption was not to be found. The thread had been lost. Where was there to go from here? Why not take a handful of Vicodin and suck down the whole damn bottle of Codeine and get it over with? Didn't Freud say the ultimate goal of life was death? The oceanic bliss of nothingness. A Jungian return to the Mother. Ashes to ashes, dust to dust.

119

He peered down to the shadowy ravine one hundred feet below. It would be easy enough to jump. Would death come instantaneously? Would there be awareness of pain? What if you survived as an air-sucking vegetable with tubes jabbing in you, voiceless and unable to express your pain?

A tinge of vertigo forced him back from the edge. The instinct to live had not died away. He played these maudlin little games knowing he didn't have the nerve to go through with them. Where was the strength of character which had sustained him all these years? Putting himself through school, working weekends and summers, TA-ing through the graduate program, hustling his licensing hours. This was not the record of a weakling. Should he have been out in the "real world" driving a truck?

16

Late April 1976, Kingston

Nine pm, Cinnamon Lounge, Hotel Caribbean. Five-star luxury in Uptown Kingston. A pretty high-brown vocalist with "good" hair wearing a flowery evening dress was belting out Cole Porter and Duke Ellington tunes to the accompaniment of a five-piece jazz band. The clientele, mostly white foreigners and light-skinned Jamaicans, were sloshing back drinks and enjoying themselves in fine style.

At a quiet table off to the side, Matt Gallagher ordered another round of drinks. Sitting with him were Frank Lake, Freddy McGinnis and a tall Cuban, handsome, strong-jawed, Caucasian. An old friend of Matt's and fellow warrior from days in South America, he had just flown in from Caracas on his private plane, spit in his green eyes and burning hatred in his belly.

Luis Posada Carriles, 48, was head of the phony ICI "detective agency" in Caracas, which wasn't a detective agency at all but a front for a terrorist group dedicated to anti-communist actions. Posada had been a classmate of Fidel Castro at the University of Havana, but where Castro had taken to the Sierra Maestra to wage revolution against the oppressive regime of Fulgencio Batista, Posada became an officer in the dictator's secret police. After Castro and his 300 overthrew Batista, Posada fled Cuba and trained with the US Army at Ft. Benning, Georgia, in 1963 graduating 2nd Lieutenant, a crack marksman and explosives expert. Later he was installed at the behest of the CIA as chief of operations for DISIP, the Venezuelan secret police.

The waitress delivered four Cuba Libres, properly served in highball glasses. The rum-and-Coke, twist-of-lime beverage was said to date to the Spanish-American War, when Teddy Roosevelt and his Rough Riders rampaged across Cuba freeing the island of European hegemony only to replace it with the latest American version.

"Cuba libre!" Posada toasted and everybody lifted his glass. Posada's consuming passion in life was to free Cuba and her people from the clutches of Fidel Castro. More than the women who flocked to him, more than the common pleasures of life, he lived for one thing—to see Castro dead and rotting in the ground. The other bearded dog Che had been disposed of and now it was Fidel's turn. Anyone who stood in the way was fair game. Anybody not against Castro was an enemy. Some claimed that Posada had been in Dealey Plaza on November 22nd, 1963 and was the man who killed John F. Kennedy. Or one of the men. Cuban exiles enraged over the Bay of Pigs fiasco. Posada had the skill to make the shot.

"Thanks for coming, Bambi," Matt addressing Posada by one of several nicknames, Solo being another (after Napoleon Solo from the *Man From UNCLE* TV show). Matt was buoyed by the presence of Posada after bugging attempts on Jamaica House, Marley's residence and the Cuban Embassy had all been botched. On top of that, the black girl sent down from HQ, Melody Raines, had failed to lure Michael Manley into her amorous web. Raines had halitosis or poor hygiene or hair on her chest or who-knew-what-the-fuck wrong with her and Manley wasn't biting. Raines was sent home and Matt and the guys determined to give it one more try and find the bastard a Jamaican honey. If the stuff about him being a ladies' man wasn't a bunch of baloney.

"Nice to see you again Matt." Fluent in Spanish and English, Posada spoke in the language of the *gringos* for the sake of the other two men.

Posada's methods were bloodthirsty, pure terrorism. He roamed the Western Hemisphere in his airplane targeting politicians and governments the least bit sympathetic to Castro. Cuban embassies were a favorite target—those in Kingston and Mexico City had been bombed seven times in 1974 alone by him or his comrades.

"Bambi and I go way back," said Matt. "Caracas, Santiago, fighting the good fight--"

"—covering each other's ass," Posada grinned.

"You couldn't get hold of Mother Teresa?" Matt asked.

"Haven't seen him lately. He spent a lot of time in Europe last year on the Leighton hit."

"Bernard Leighton… Allende's VP, popped outside his apartment in Rome."

"Nine-millimeter Beretta head shot. Got his wife too. Unfortunately the bastard and his whore survived. MT said they should've used a .22."

"MT wasn't the trigger?"

"Italian Fascists."

"What about MT?"

"He's whining about being out of country so much, away from his family. Married a Chilean girl, two brats."

121

"Mother Theresa" was Michael Townley, a white American expatriate working for DINA, the Chilean secret police. A hit man specializing in explosives and a rabid anti-communist, Townley had been tasked by General Juan Manuel Contreras, head of DINA and a paid CIA asset, with eliminating dissidents against the regime of Augusto Pinochet.

"To have the three of us together again, eh, compadre?" said Matt. "What miracles we could work here."

"We will work them still."

They clinked glasses and Matt moved in close.

"Did you bring any goodies with you?" he whispered.

"A couple boxes of dynamite and a few rolls of fuses were all I could manage on short notice."

"We'll pick up the slack."

"How can I help with your program?"

Matt leaned closer still and the two spoke in Spanish.

"I want you to help me train a squad of men to perform public service."

"*High* public service?"

"The *highest.*"

"When would this service be undertaken?"

"Soon. Before the elections."

"It will be done, so help me God."

"Knew I could count on you. How much time do you have?"

"Not long. Something is in the works. The call could come at any time."

"What's up?"

"A major meeting of minds under the auspices of Generalissimo Pinochet. We are going to take the cause to a higher level. A united front is to be formed, a spearhead which can accomplish truly great deeds... actions that will turn the enemy's heart to stone."

Just then a paunchy white man and a beautiful black woman whirled onto the dance floor like Fred Astaire and Ginger Rogers. Someone began to clap and the crowd joined in. As he watched and remembered gay times in old Habana, sadness came to Posada's face.

"There was a time, my friends," he said bitterly in English, "when people danced in Santiago de Cuba, in Havana and all across the *isla bonita* of my birth. In the streets and ballrooms, in their homes, they danced. There was a time when, how do you say, the *joy of life* filled the hearts of my countrymen. With my last breath I will fight to bring those days back again."

"To freedom," Matt toasted, and the men clinked glasses.

In the following days Gallagher and Posada began training Operation Werewolf foot soldiers in guerrilla warfare. Matt started with hand-to-hand combat and Posada with marksmanship. The Cuban didn't get far before his call came in. The secret high-level conclave of anti-Castro groups was on for the first week of June in the Dominican Republic. Anxious to make preparations, Posada got back on his plane and returned to Caracas, promising to return to Jamaica at first opportunity and pick up where he'd left off. In his absence, Matt Gallagher continued the training.

17

December 1980, Santa Barbara

Paranoia strikes deep. On December 3, 1980, four United States church women—three nuns and a lay missionary—were raped and murdered in El Salvador by the National Guard. This coming seven months after the cold-blooded murder of Archbishop Romero as he gave mass in a hospital chapel in San Salvador (the Salvadoran army days later shooting up the funeral, killing dozens of mourners). The church, in its concern for the poor and downtrodden, had become an enemy of the rich and powerful. Romero had pleaded with Jimmy Carter to stop funding the right-wing militias, begging him "Christian to Christian" to no avail. Persons involved in both outrages graduates of the US Army School of the Americas in the Canal Zone. Research would show that the more courses officers took at SOA, the more likely they were to engage in atrocities and human rights violations. No doubt some had been trained by Matt Gallagher.

In Santa Barbara, December brought weather that was cooler but still the envy of most of the nation. Cycling over for session, Scott saw in Doc M's parking space not a Porsche 911S but a BMW 2002tii, primed for repainting but still magnificent. He ran his hand lovingly along the full length of the car's body as he passed and thought of how Bob used to say BMW stood for "Bob Marley and the Wailers." Another year or two and he'd have enough saved to buy a Beamer of his own.

He was admitted to Dr. Mitchell's office to find him standing hunched over in putting position aiming at an overturned plastic cup on the floor.

"Get that par," Scott said. Dr. M stroked the ball a good foot wide of its mark and off the fringe of the Persian or Turkish or whatever kind of rug it was and onto the bare wooden floor.

"My bad," Scott apologized, astounded that a putt could be missed so badly.

"Ridiculous sport," mumbled Mitchell, weak from another breakfast missed, the DTs coming on. "Grown man knocking a little ball with a stick. Come, sit down."

They sat in their customary places, Mitchell hiding his trembling hands as he assumed once again the farcical mantle of wise man and healer. A whiteboard had been rolled into the room that wasn't there before.

"The walrus is dead," Scott said.

"John Lennon," Mitchell said grimly. The former Beatle had been gunned down in New York City by a crazed fan outside the Dakota apartments where he lived with Yoko Ono.

"Why kill Lennon?" Scott asked. "What did he ever do beside sing give peace a chance?"

"Peace can be subversive," said Mitchell. "But let's talk about you."

"What about that song of yours, Doc? *When I Was Young.*"

"Eric Burdon."

"Mean something to you?"

"Not really."

"Your father was a soldier, times were tough." Scott stared as if an explanation were due.

"It's just a song I like, man."

"Was your father a soldier?"

"Navy man, actually," Mitchell said softly.

"Now we're getting somewhere. Tell me about him."

"Let's get back to you, shall we?"

"Times were hard?"

"Hard enough, I guess. How about you losing your mother at an early age?"

"Didn't see your car out front."

"You changed the subject."

"Whadja do, trade the Porsche for a BMW?"

"You did it again. Talk to me."

"The girl called back. Suzi from the band."

"The girl who accused you of copying Bob?"

"Yeah. She tried to make nice. Not a bad kid. Suzette Scarlett. Is that the best name ever or what? Good-looking too. Nice teeth. Looks a lot like Marva."

"Now we *are* getting somewhere. What happened after that night at the street dance?"

"We started going out a lot, especially after the Wailers took off on tour. Did a lot of neat stuff, went up to Ocho Rios, Port Antonio, explored Maroon villages in the hills. It was awesome being together, like getting so high on spliff and righteous tunes that you explode through the space-time continuum into a whole new galaxy of experience."

"Yeah," Mitchell said.

"Been there, Doc?"

"Everybody—*ahem*," Mitchell cleared his suddenly parched throat, "everybody who's ever been in love has been there. What came between you guys?"

"I don't know. That's Lost Time."

"Let's try something, shall we?" Mitchell vigorously rubbed his palms together in a show of enthusiasm. He rose and wheeled the whiteboard over, took up a marker and began to write.

"I'm writing down people you've brought up," he said, speaking aloud each name as he made a list on the left side of the board:

"Your *father*

Henry

Maddy

Michael Manley

Bob Marley

Marva"

He turned toward Scott. "What was John Wayne's brother's name again?"

"Jesse James."

"Ah yes, who could forget Jesse James." Mitchell added the name to the list.

"Anybody else?"

"Quasimodo."

"The hunchback with the walking stick." And Mitchell wrote "*Hunchback*" on the board and held out the marker to Scott.

"Make any notes you want," he said. "Shuffle names around, arrange them as you like, whatever occurs to you."

Scott took the pen and stood before the board, crossed his arms and studied the names. By "*Father*" he wrote "*Dickhead*" and drew a small heart next to Marva's name.

"Anything else?" Mitchell asked and Scott shook his head.

"Nothing at all?"

"Is this what they call an impasse, Doc?"

"Things don't just happen, you know," Mitchell snapped in frustration. "You gotta reach for it, make it happen."

"No need to get bent out of shape."

"Let's try something else, shall we? I'll help you relax a bit and we'll talk some more."

"Maybe I'm not the only one that needs to relax. You mean like hypnosis?"

"Something like that. Letting go and relaxing a bit."

"Whatever you say, man."

"You can lie down on the couch if you want."

"I'm fine."

"Suit yourself."

Phil came around the desk and sat in the chair next to Scott. Mitchell, who had become adept at hypnosis during his clinical training at UCLA, began to speak in a soporific monotone intended to induce a light trance.

"Imagine a heaviness coming into your body. Seeping into your feet and working its way to your ankles, up your calves and thighs, through your pelvis, stomach, into your chest and back, your arms, up to the top of your head. You are very relaxed and heavy... your eyes are closing by themselves."

Mitchell continued in this manner until Scott's head bowed and his eyes fluttered shut. He seemed to be one of those highly susceptible individuals, the 15 or 20 percent who went under easily and deeply—the kind stage hypnotists picked out of the audience.

"You are very relaxed now," Mitchell continued. "You feel fine and are completely safe. You can talk easily and stay deeply relaxed. Do you understand?"

"Yes."

"Good. Now I want you to go back to Jamaica. You and your father are living in your house on the hill in Kingston, you're in school in Miss Williams' class, you have become friends with Henry. You've met Marva at the street dance and think you've seen Jesse James at the recording studio. You remember all these things, don't you?"

"Yes."

"What comes to mind about any of this now?"

Scott sat quiescent and unmoving, though his eyes fluttered under their closed lids and his chest rose and fell noticeably as he breathed in and out. Signs of incipient anxiety.

"You remember Marva in her purple dress, don't you?"

"Marva. Marva."

"What do you see?"

"People."

"What are these people doing?"

"Singing. Dancing."

"Go on."

"Burned-down houses," Scott increasingly manifesting symptoms of distress—a quivering of the lips, swallowing, tense hunching in the shoulders.

"Where Marva is are burned-down houses?" Mitchell probed.

"Barb wire."

"Barb wire? Where are you?"

"Have to tell her. Where is she?" Scott's head rolled side to side in building panic.

"What do you have to tell her?"

"Not coming. Not coming. Have to tell her."

"Tell *me*."

"Simon Bolivar. Henry. Tell Marva."

"I don't understand. Simon Bolivar, the statesman? Who's not coming?"

Scott fidgeted in his seat and clenched his teeth. His eyes seemed to bulge beneath their lids as if distended by a pressure inside his head. He droned in a disaffected monotone: *"Smile Jamaica... Smile Jamaica... Smile Jamaica."*

"This has to do with your father, doesn't it," Mitchell queried and Scott tightened up like a steel drum. "And why you fell that day."

"Death... dying."

"Is there some danger?"

"Danger!" Scott rasped in a dry wheeze and as it had that first day in office his hand came down the front of his shirt in discrete hops suggesting the nurturing ministrations of his mother. Phil didn't want to push too hard or take the kid too deep too fast but thought a little catharsis might be salutary.

"Scott, I'm your father sitting here next to you. What would you like to say to me?"

"Father?"

"Big Matt. Dickhead. Your father, sitting here in front of you. You can tell him anything you like. It's perfectly safe for you to talk. You want to tell your father something."

Scott mumbled something under his breath.

"Speak up, son," said Phil. "This is your father speaking."

Suddenly Scott's eyes popped open and without coming out of trance he burst to his feet and thrust his right arm over his head. He clenched his fist and slammed it down into the palm of his left hand. He did this repeatedly while ambling robotically up and down on the rug, creating the impression in the psychologist's mind of someone striking down with a heavy object or club. A machete, even.

"Are you angry?" Mitchell queried. "Give voice to your feelings. What do you wish to say?"

"Filthy lying cunt-whore!" Scott shouted.

"Say it to me," Mitchell said. "Tell it to your father."

Like lightning, Scott's left hand shot out and grabbed the doctor's forearm, adrenaline pumping through his veins and giving him superhuman strength.

"Filthy lying cunt-whore!"

"Easy, friend," Mitchell laughed in nervous embarrassment. He could not loosen the kid's powerful grip, his raised right arm poised to strike. The situation was getting out of control. Somebody could get hurt.

"Wake up, man. Scott, wake up." Phil tried to walk patient out of trance. "I'm going to count backward from five. When I reach one you will be perfectly awake and--"

Before Dr. Mitchell could finish his hypnotic suggestion Scott's right hand grasped Mitchell's other wrist—now he had vise grips on both arms. Befogged eyes rolled down and stared through Mitchell like he wasn't there.

"Wide awake!" Mitchell cried. "Wide awake now. Wake up, dude. Five-four-three-two-one. Scott! Scott!"

On the verge of panicking, Phil realized he had gotten exactly what he asked for and that there might be more to gain from this yet. It was a dangerous game, but the adrenaline was flowing in him too and he felt excitingly *alive*.

"I told you to stop hanging around those filthy Rastas," he barked in his most authoritative, patriarchal voice. "Go to your room and don't come out until I say so."

Scott exploded like a beast unchained, releasing Mitchell's arms and in a split second digging his hands into his throat. Driving with his legs, he pushed the therapist backward, the older man desperately trying to set his feet, like a person slipping down a precipitous slope, the muscles of his legs straining, weak and unexercised as they were. He brought his arms in close and tried to force the lad's hands apart but it was useless. Futilely he pushed against patient's chest. Struggling with a deep-seated prohibition against doing a patient harm, he overcame his scruples and punched at Scott's flank, but it was as if slapping the hide of an elephant, having no effect. Meanwhile Scott had backed Mitchell up against the wall behind the desk, pinning him with a loud thud—sending Dr. M's mind spinning about what Stan and Jasmine would say if they came running and found him like this. Patient's hands dug ever deeper into the doctor's throat as he mindlessly screamed "filthy lying cunt-whore!" The fear took hold in Mitchell that he might die right here in his own office in a few short minutes, and would certainly do so if no one came in or he didn't manage somehow to break free. Tensing over his entire body at the spectre of imminent death he brought his knee up into Scott's crotch. The kid flinched without letting go his grip, but Phil was able to twist away from the wall—only for Scott to dig his toes in afresh and screaming at the top of his lungs drive Doc M across the floor and slam him into the wall with the portraits, one falling and shattering on the floor. Scott banged his head hard and came out of trance.

"What the fuck?" he cried, scrambling to his feet, his eyes regaining their lucidity.

128

"Are you all right?" he reached down to help Mitchell up. "Jesus, doc, what weird shit is going on here?"

Mitchell was on his knees, huffing and coughing and rubbing his neck.

"We... struggled," Mitchell gasping for air as he found his feet. "Let me... catch my breath."

The door opened and Jasmine ran into the room. "Doctor, are you all right?" she cried. "Mitch?"

"We're fine, Jaz. A little... [*panting*] autogenics training is all. Breath... control."

Mitchell laughed a demented little laugh at the irony—so utterly winded while practicing breath control!

"Oh, Freud broke," Jasmine lamented, picking the shattered 9 x 12 portrait up from the floor.

"Old Siggie's seen better days," Mitchell deadpanned.

"I *thought* that was Freud," Scott said.

"A shame," said Jasmine. "Sure everybody's okay?"

"Yes, yes, autogenics never hurt anyone."

"Autogenics," Jasmine echoed vacantly, as if her mind couldn't wrap around the concept. She ran for a broom and swept up the broken glass before leaving again.

"So what the hell just happened?" Scott said.

"You grabbed my arms... pushed me into the wall."

"How do I know you didn't grab *my* arms and push *me* into the wall?"

"Look at these marks, man."

"That's not proof."

"It's my fault. Tried to take you along too fast."

"Told you this was bigger than both of us," Scott said, pacing up and down on Dr. M's putting rug of unknown origin. He stopped of a sudden and stared at the white board a long moment before picking up the marker. Mitchell watched as the pen flew across the board. Finally Scott stepped back and they had a look.

Scott had drawn a square inscribed within a circle and with two intersecting lines divided the square into four equal quadrants. Written inside the four cells:

BOB   DICKHEAD

MARVA   JESSE JAMES

At the intersection of the horizontal and vertical lines that formed the quadrants, in the very middle of the configuration, he had drawn a small

129

circle. The circle had the psychological effect of linking the four quadrants and four persons named therein. At the same time, it seemed like crosshairs in a rifle scope. Inside this small circle at the center of the square Scott had written: CIA. The larger circle within which the square was inscribed was labeled OBEAH.

"Where did that come from?" Mitchell said in astonishment, though he had repeatedly seen the unconscious manifest in mysterious ways during his career. Just when you think you've seen everything, something more amazing yet occurs.

"I don't know," Scott shrugged.

Mitchell studied the board. "Bob, your father, Marva, Jesse James. The four central figures at the heart of it all. And tying everything together is--"

"The CIA."

"You were singing a song. Something about Jamaica."

"That's Bob Marley. *Smile Jamaica.*"

"Didn't you say there was a concert?"

"That's right. There was."

Scott scanned the board and again took up the marker. Underneath the circle and inscribed square he drew a rectangle, as if to serve as the foundation for the edifice above, and labeled it SMILE JA.

"Good work," Phil said. "I hope this helps you organize your thoughts."

"Maybe shoot a little higher. How about world peace?"

"Let's take ten. I need a smoke. You can lick your chalice or whatever it is you do."

Mitchell grabbed his jacket and the two marched past a bemused Jasmine to the back parking lot. Phil lit up a cigarette and gazed toward the hills of Santa Barbara. Scott followed his eyes to the semi-arid slopes dotted with fancy homes and eucalyptus.

"Harder for men to let go, you know," Phil declared, blowing out a cloud of smoke. "Mother-son relationship just so primal. Jung built his whole psychology around it."

"That guy Jung again."

"Gotta let go," Phil said softly, as if chanting a mantra for his own ears. "Gotta let go."

"Married, Doc?"

"Not anymore."

"What happened?"

Mitchell stared at the impatiens in the flower bed.

"Didn't mean to be a buttinsky," Scott said. "What about this struggling business?"

"We'll work it through. Think Suzette might be worth a shot?"

130

"Maybe."

"Nice teeth."

"Yeah."

"Let me know how it turns out. One thing."

"Yeah?"

"First thing that comes to mind. Ready? *Smile Jamaica.*"

"Machete," Scott replied instantly and Mitchell's body trembled from fingers to toes.

"Feel that breeze?" Scott said, the wind in his face. "Sudden warm breeze. Jamaican will tell you that's a ghost."

Scott mounted his bike, casting Mitchell a disquieting look before riding off, as if he were still in his unconscious and possessed by dark forces. Back in his office Phil tucked the letter opener away in the drawer, smirking at the thought that he too was becoming paranoid.

18

May 1976, Kingston

It was dark by the time William the Conqueror finished his business with his woman. Putting his clothes back on, he slipped her a few J$ and felt pleased with himself. Money in his pocket and after tonight there'd be a whole lot more. Simone and the kids could eat for weeks off it. There was nothing Simone could say about the revolver she watched him tuck into his waist; whatever he was doing he was putting food on the table for the youth—end of story. All she could do was pray he would live to return another day to her Tivoli Gardens tenement. She would have prayed harder if she'd known where he was going or if she'd seen the big guns that would be broken out that made the revolver in his waist look like a child's popgun.

"Wan' I fix yuh supper?" Simone asked as she sat naked on the edge of the bed.

"Me catch a meal later, man," he said. Simone reached out to squeeze his hand and William left. He rode off on his Yamaha motorbike heading east past Coronation Market and around the Parade, skirting the central downtown PNP stronghold dominated by the powerful Tel Aviv gang (named after the impregnable Israeli city in the movie *Exodus*). Following a side street until it dead-ended at Barnes Gully he turned right on Fleet Street and pulled up at a small yard with a mangy dog tied in the corner. He entered through the rickety gate and went around back, drawn by the aroma of chicken and breadfruit smoking in hot coals.

In the rear, beneath a spreading mango tree, Pocket Thunder tended a smoldering fire in a metal bucket.

"Oy, Pockie."

131

"Gwine live long, Conqueror," Thunda uttered the proper greeting for when a person you were just thinking of suddenly showed up. "Hungry?"

"Me can eat. Woman fire me appetite."

"Have a cool Heineken and rest after yuh labor. Fowl 'most done."

Thunda too was feeling spry with a big payday imminent. Even the dog would get meat tonight. Pocket Thunder (whose real name was Cordell Cooper) had gotten his nickname from an uncle who went to Toronto to work and developed an appreciation for ice hockey, but due to his contrary nature rooted for the Montreal Canadiens rather than the hometown Leafs. When he returned to Jamaica he raved about the exploits of Henri Richard, whose older—and bigger—brother was Maurice "The Rocket" Richard. Uncle Tibor went on and on about the "Pocket Rocket" scoring the championship-winning goal in overtime of Game Six of the 1966 Stanley Cup finals versus Gordie Howe's Detroit Red Wings. Cordell adapted the moniker to fit and wore it well. Quite the explosive little bundle was he.

Thunda and Conqueror feasted and talked over old times as they drank their green-label Heineken. Their friendship predated their gang affiliations—Thunda from the Southies, aka Renkers, William the C from the notorious Shower Posse, both JLP-affiliated and not in any major squabbles with each other at present. Hardened street fighters though they were, they waxed nostalgic about the old days before the violence got so out of hand, a time when neighbors shared and laughed and cried together.

At midnight Thunda got on the back of William's motorbike and they rode down to the West Kingston docks, deep in JLP territory. Running a maze of dark deserted streets, they pulled into a lot, closely observed by snipers positioned in the shadows. Continuing around to the back they were stopped by armed guards with M16s who escorted them inside a dark warehouse.

With the arrival of Thunda and Conqueror everyone was present and accounted for—a total of fifty men… many hardly more than boys, down to 13-year-old Colin Vaughn, who having dropped out of school looked for guidance to the tough guys who ruled the streets. Running the show was Police Chief Joe Stewart, who huddled the squad together in a windowless room where the light of a kerosene lantern would not be seen from outside.

"Everybody stay in position and nah shoot nuhbody, hear?" Stewart went over final instructions. "Horn beep three time, hustle yuh ass back in the van lickity-split. Anybody miss bus on 'is own."

A floor panel was wedged up with a crowbar to reveal a cache of weapons. Top Rankings got M1s and M16s… little Colin Vaughn reached in his thumb and came up with a sawed-off Winchester double-barrel shotgun, his chest swelling like Dirty Harry. You could blow a hole clean through someone with that sucker. Quite a plum.

At one o'clock the fifty men piled into vehicles loaded with gasoline-filled glass jugs with rags stuck down their necks. Headlights off, the caravan pulled out of the yard and away from the docks. Their route followed backroads up to Allman Town, close to National Heroes Circle in PNP territory. Nobody spoke. The moment for jokes and laughs had passed. If there was a season for every purpose, the time had come for burnin' and killin'.

Earlier that evening...

Maddy had cleared the table and was doing the dishes as Matt sat in his easy chair and silently read a speech Che Guevara had given at the UN in 1964. It was important to study the mind of the enemy. The Argentine's *foco* revolutionary theory was based on the idea that a small band of guerrillas could spur a revolution, as had occurred so spectacularly in Cuba. The prevailing wisdom, ala Mao Tse-Tung, held that it was necessary first to marshal a counter force of equal strength. How had Castro and his ragged band of 300 defeated the whole Cuban army? Che claimed that if a small band of guerrillas could with stinging hit-and-run attacks goad a cruel and repressive government into taking draconian countermeasures, the people would rise up and sweep the bastards out of power—a strategy finding success in Cuba in no small part because Batista was so reviled that even the army turned against him. For a moment Matt imagined himself as a "good Che" freeing the people of Jamaica from the tyranny of Manley.

Scott was in his room strumming along to the new Wailers album, *Rastaman Vibration*. The foreign tour in support of the album was now in full swing. Bob's mom, Cedella, remarried now to a man named Edward Booker, had driven down from her home in Delaware for the Philadelphia concert. She'd never seen her son perform before a live audience and that night at the Tower Theater her Nesta reached deep into his soul and gave it all he had. You could see God in Bob that night said Mother B, totally blown away.

There came a knock on Scott's door and his father poked his head in.

"Hey," Matt greeted.

"Too loud?" Scott turned down the volume.

"It's fine. Mind if I come in?"

"Come on."

"Practicing?"

"Pickin'. What's up?"

"Just being sociable. New album? This it here?"

Matt picked up the album cover and studied Neville Garrick's cover artwork showing Bob posed like David staring down Goliath.

"Bob Marley and the Wailers... Jamaican, aren't they?"

"They live right here in Kingston. Guess what? I met him. I met Bob Marley, dad. Wait, I'll show you a picture."

"Lay it on me, buddy."

Scott took from his shirt pocket the photo of Bob and him that had been snapped on the veranda at Hope Road, Bob with a monster spliff in his hand. He kept the photo with him wherever he went. He showed it to his father.

"I'm riding around on my bike and stumble on his place," he swelled with pride. "Cool old house over on Hope Road. They were out playing soccer in the front yard. I played soccer with Bob Marley, dad."

"Cool. Hope Road, you say?"

"Yeah. Bitchin' old place. Always a million people over. Rastas, musicians, politicians, journalists from all over the world, even... uh..."

"Even what?"

Even ghetto gunslingers, Scott had started to say.

"Even toasters," he said instead. No sense *asking* for trouble.

"Toasters?"

"DJs who talk over the music rather than singing... it's really cool. Some of the top artists are toasters... Big Youth, U-Roy, I-Roy, Jah Stitch."

"What do they talk about?"

"Everything. Current events, politics. Big Youth is called 'The Human *Gleaner*' because ghetto people who can't read get their news from him."

"Well. That's quite something."

"A Rasta Eden in the heart of Kingston. Big ol' place with trees and everything."

"Marley's a Rasta? One of these pothead marijuana smokers? Is that a marijuana cigarette he's holding?"

"It's not like that, dad. Ganja is part of their religion."

"Every skid row junkie claims smack is his religion."

"They're not *junkies*. Oh my God. They have lives like anybody else. Normal productive lives."

"*You* don't smoke, do you?" Of course Matt by now knew quite well from Jesse James' reports that Scott smoked.

Not wanting to lie, Scott said nothing. Matt flipped over the *Rastaman Vibration* jacket and studied the track listing.

"Let's see what we got here. *Who the Cap Fit...* what's this? *War?* He's singing about *war?*"

"Bob sings to *end* war. But sometimes you gotta kick ass. Stand up and put an end to the bullshit."

"I'm sure we're all trembling in our boots."

"Bob can change the world," Scott said. "Gonna happen too. Might take a while, but we'll get there. One-one coco fill basket, Jamaicans say."

Matt struggled to control his rage... here he'd given an eye and a chunk of his leg to the fight for freedom in Nam and his damn bratty kid was worshipping a fucking ghetto rat.

"So Marley likes soccer?" he said.

"Good too. Went right by me even with his bad foot. They say he could play pro."

"What's this now... bad foot?" Matt's ears perked.

"Nasty sore toe... soccer injury. Like an idiot I go and trip him. Stupid klutz."

"Sore toe on his shooting foot?"

"Yeah, big toe on his right foot."

"Big toe, right foot—just like your injury."

"Weird, huh? I hurt it in PT at school the very next day. Did you want something?"

"Just being sociable. I'm going out for a while. You all right?"

"Yeah."

As Matt left and closed the door behind him, Scott wasn't sure what had just happened. He and his father had managed to talk about Bob and Rasta—even ganja—without tweaking each other out. There'd been a shaky moment but the levees had held. Maybe they'd make it as a family yet.

Matt went to his bedroom and put on a shirt. He wanted to beat sense into his son—consorting with black radicals, smoking marijuana and not being honest about it—but there were issues of national security at play here. Scott had penetrated further into Marley's inner circle than any agent in the employ of the Kingston station. He had already provided intelligence about the reggae singer's associates as well as his injured foot. Every weak link was vital information.

Matt strapped on his holster. A major Operation Werewolf action was on for tonight. He would go to the embassy in case anything came up. Maybe a quick stop at Dandy Disco to check on Cindy now that the Rastaman was out of town.

Ten minutes after Matt left the house Scott walked merrily out the front door and hopped on his bike to ride over to check fe Marva. He hadn't gone far when the thought slapped him in the face:

Why was his father snooping around asking questions about Bob Marley?

The convoy drove up from Tivoli past the Parade and onto Love Lane. *The Love Lane Caravan of Death.* At New North Lane they jogged right and then left onto Stable Lane, which opened after a long block onto Heroes Circle, a broad avenue ringing the large green oval of National Heroes Park. The lead vehicle stopped and waited for the column to form up. Off to the right was the Shrine of Monuments, memorials to all seven of

Jamaica's national heroes from Nanny of the Maroons to Norman Manley; just beyond that in an island on the boulevard was a statue of Simon Bolivar, a gift from the government of Venezuela. In case anybody cared to glance over and ponder their cowardly intended actions in the light of true heroism.

At the head of the line, Joe Stewart waved the column forward onto Orange Lane, one long block of tenement yards teeming with PNP supporters, hundreds of persons crammed into dozens of units. Inside the vehicles, matches and cigarette lighters were struck.

Suddenly, doors were thrown open and bodies scrambled out on the fly. Shooters with automatic rifles posted up as others heaved the Molotov cocktails into tenement buildings up and down the block. The homemade bombs burst and sent angry flames licking at walls and doorways. Soon the entire street was on fire as the sky itself seemed to erupt in the inferno. The gunmen opened up with their big guns, shredding the sides of buildings and shattering windows. Terrible screams rose up. Children wailed and mothers cried in horror. Men came out and were blown away in their underwear. Anyone trying to escape got shot at. Little Colin Vaughn fired his Winchester shotgun at anything that moved, man, woman, child, dog, tree branch. His heart racing so fast there seemed no space between beats.

A fire station was a couple blocks away and responded quickly. Turning onto Orange Lane, the engine truck came under heavy fire. The brigade was forced to pull back and await police assistance. When the police arrived, they too were pinned down by the gunmen. Eventually they fought their way forward and the marauders jumped into vehicles and raced away. By this time the entire block had burned to the ground. When the sun rose and the smoke cleared, five hundred persons had been rendered homeless. Eleven bodies were recovered from the scene. One had been felled by a police bullet—thirteen-year-old Colin Vaughn, his fingers clutching his prized sawed-off double-barrel Winchester shotgun.

And the angels in heaven wept that grown men, black men and white, Jamaican and American, that grown men and an evil system had put such a weapon in the hands of a child of Jah.

19

Following the regimen he had learned during his apprenticeship at previous stations, Matt had his case officers begin their working day with a set routine: reading the local newspapers and familiarizing themselves with incoming and outgoing cables—including State Department cables—as well as any documents that came in through the diplomatic pouch. After that everyone was to go over the passenger flight lists with special attention paid to Cubana Aviacion and other airlines servicing Cuba or Eastern Bloc countries. Morning too was a time for writing intelligence reports and propaganda articles. Lake had come up with an attractive Jamaican girl to plant on Michael Manley's staff, but Matt's patience with that operation was sorely tried.

Just before lunch Gallagher, Frank Lake and Freddy McGinnis huddled around the hi-fi to listen to Bob Marley's new album—and not because they'd suddenly become fans of his music. They listened as Marley sang of crazy baldheads and bum-beds and drumming the bastards out of your camp.

"Baldheads?" Matt grunted, sitting back with arms folded across his chest. "That's not us is it, crazy baldheads? Better not be us."

"Are looking a little thin on top, Big Dog," said Lake with a smirk.

"So it's natty dreadlocks kicking ass on the short-haired infidels, is it? Goddamn welcome to try. Isn't going to be any revolutions on my watch, so help me God. Crazy baldheads, my ass."

The secretary buzzed for Matt. There was someone to see him.

Arriving moments earlier at Oxford Road, Scott secured his bike and entered the Mutual Life Building. He rode the lift to the third floor with several African diplomats wearing fine suits, he clad in his brown school uniform. As the door opened and the Africans were met by the Marine Corps guards, Scott slipped past. The receptionist called him over and buzzed the chief. A minute later his father appeared, not looking pleased to see him.

"What are you doing here?" Matt demanded. "Why aren't you in school?"

"Thought I'd drop in and say hello."

"We're busy here Scott. You can't just drop in like this."

"Why not? What's the big secret?"

"This is a government office, not the public library. Business is conducted here that involves the affairs of two countries. Now you said hello, go home."

"What are you afraid of, dad?" Scott raising his voice a notch so the secretary would overhear. "Don't have anything to hide, do you?"

"Of course there's nothing to hide. All right then, damn it. Five minutes and you're on your way. Got it?"

"Fine."

Matt led Scott down the hall to the unmarked door of the Kingston station of the Central Intelligence Agency.

"Wait a moment," Matt said, opening the door and stepping inside, closing the door behind him while keeping a firm grip on the doorknob. When the secretary had buzzed a moment earlier, he'd instructed everybody to stash any sensitive materials—the lie detector, steamed-open letters to the Cuban Embassy, files on PNP leaders. He noticed now the Marley album out in plain sight and signaled Lake to remove it. Within thirty seconds, everything was shipshape and Gallagher opened the door for Scott to come in.

"Hey everybody," Matt announced. "This is my son, Scott."

"Hi, Scott." Shit-eating grins all around.

"Hi." Scott glanced around the place. There were maps, globe, files, cabinets—an office much like any other. Small hi-fi system on the table. A portrait of President Ford on the wall.

"See?" Matt said. "No bogeyman here. Just hard working civil servants."

"What do you do up here, dad?"

"The work of the United States government."

"Visas?"

"Visas are handled over at our Cross Roads office. This is the political section. The ambassador's office is here. That kind of thing."

"*What* kind of thing, exactly?"

"Meetings, diplomacy, international relations. All kind of state business goes on here you wouldn't begin to understand and I wouldn't care to go into. So don't be a pain in the ass, all right Sherlock?" Matt grinned to show his colleagues he was kidding but Scott knew he was dead serious.

"How come this part is separate from the other side?" Scott asked.

"Going through a door makes it separate? Maybe you'd like to meet the ambassador on your way out."

"Sounds like a real kick in the pants."

Matt led Scott back outside the door to the embassy proper and to the office of Sumner Gerard, outside which sat another secretary, a white American woman.

"Sumner in?" Matt asked, knocking on the door.

The door opened and there stood the ambassador.

"Hey, Sum. This is my son, Scott."

"Hello, Scott. Ambassador Gerard. Pleasure to meet you."

"Likewise I'm sure." Scott was struck by an indefinable similarity between the ambassador and his father. Was it that both were bold, headstrong men of action? *Boat burners.*

"No school today?" Gerard asked.

"Field trip," Scott said.

"Smart ass," Matt said.

"I learn more seeing things with my own two eyes than sitting in a classroom all day."

"Got a live one on your hands here, Matt," Ambassador Gerard grinned. "We're all a bit rebellious at that age. You must channel that energy, young man, put it to good use."

"How would you suggest?"

"Serving your country," Matt interjected.

"That's the best one can do," Gerard concurred.

"What about countries like Jamaica? What happens to them?"

"What's good for America is good for the world," Gerard said. "Serve your country and you automatically serve Jamaica and all the other poor countries."

"How does that work?"

"You see, son," Gerard explained, "there are two paths in this world, the path of freedom and the path of enslavement. Socialism is nothing more than slavery at the will of the State. Jamaica has to choose which road to go down and right now it's being led astray by its own foolish leaders."

This from a Nixon appointee. Before Watergate, the Nixon administration had distinguished itself for awarding ambassadorships to the highest bidder. Where Gerard had earned his appointment with years of public service, his predecessor Vincent de Roulet bought his with a $75,000 contribution to Nixon's election campaign. He arrived in Jamaica aboard his 90-foot yacht and had seventeen racehorses shipped down for his amusement. He was overheard to use derogatory language to describe Jamaicans, demanded visa applicants wait in endless lines in the hot sun and forbade access to the bathroom on the grounds that "Jamaicans take pleasure in flooding the toilets." Manley finally got fed up and expelled the sonuvabitch.

"I think we've taken up enough of the ambassador's time," Matt Gallagher said.

At home that night, Matt laid into his son.

"What kind of a prank was that you pulled today?" he said the moment Scott walked in the door, as if waiting in ambush.

"I stopped in to say hi to my father," Scott said. "Why is that a prank?"

"You were snooping around."

"What would I be snooping for?"

"Don't be a twerp."

"What was with the stereo sitting on the table?"

"Some people like to listen to music. You ought to be able to appreciate that."

"Wouldn't it be easier to listen to the radio?"

"They don't like reggae. Talk about paranoid. Getting just about fed up." Matt spun on his heels and walked away.

"Dad," Scott whined, suddenly unsure of himself.

It wasn't until hours later, as Scott lay on his bed staring at the ceiling, that he realized his father had been lying.

20

June 1976, Bonao, Dominican Republic

Powwow time in Hispaniola. Luis Posada Carriles flew into Santo Domingo in his private plane for the all-important CORU planning meeting. Among his comrades in arms was Orlando Bosch. Like Posada, Bosch had attended University of Havana with Fidel Castro in the '40s, fled Cuba after the revolution, taken military training with the US Army at Ft. Benning and gone on to become a paid CIA agent. Bosch too was a marksman said to have been in Dealey Plaza in November 1963 boiling with hatred toward the traitorous JFK and with the skill to make the shot. As obsessed as Posada with Castro and communists, in 1968 he fired a bazooka at a Polish ship docked in Miami harbor. Also present were agents of the Chilean secret police (DINA) and virtually every right-wing military and paramilitary organization in Latin America. Mother Theresa was here too. Many if not most if not all were connected in some fashion to the CIA. This was Operation Condor.

Fifteen months earlier, Chilean dictator Augusto Pinochet had promised five major factions of Cuban exiles funding if they would unite and join with the South American dictatorships in the fight against the red menace of socialism. The five factions were now linking hands in one unified front, the Coordinating Committee of United Revolutionary Organizations, or CORU (*"El Coru"* Spanish for "Condor"). Operation Condor would wage bloody terror against union activists, farmers, leftist politicians, students, professors, the clergy, anyone advocating for the poor and downtrodden. It was a campaign of rape and pillage worthy of the Middle Ages, with deaths in the tens of thousands, many more tormented, tortured, traumatized. Computer systems and communications for tracking down and eliminating dissidents provided by the CIA through the Canal Zone command center. Brazil, Paraguay, Uruguay, Chile, Bolivia and now Argentina safely in Condor's talons.

Some of the many enemies to be dealt with:

--Orlando Letelier, former Chilean government official under Salvador Allende and tireless critic of Pinochet, exiled and currently residing in Washington;

--Carmelo Soria, a Spanish diplomat who arranged asylum for Chilean exiles;

--Pascal Allende, nephew of the deposed Salvador, who had already survived an assassination attempt in Costa Rica (for which Orlando Bosch had been arrested);

--US Congressman Ed Koch, who had proposed cutting military assistance to Uruguay on human rights grounds.

Many others had already been disposed of. General Carlos Prats, head of Chilean armed forces and VP under Allende, blown away in a

September 1974 car-bombing in Buenos Aires that also killed his wife— Mother Theresa taking honors on that one. Assassinated just in the last month were a Chilean diplomat, two Uruguayan statesmen and mere days ago General Juan Jose Torres, former president of Bolivia and that rarest of creatures, a military man beloved by the people for wanting to improve their lot. CORU leaders were eager to up the ante with a spectacular action that would strike fear into the heart of communist sympathizers everywhere. Something really big, like blowing up an arena or skyscraper or knocking down an airliner.

Meanwhile, the Organization of American States, the OAS, convened its Sixth General Assembly in Santiago, Chile. Addressing the body on the subject of, impossibly, *human rights*, was Henry Kissinger. Mr. K took the opportunity to meet privately with Generalissimo Pinochet and wink away any concern about bloody methods of repression. When Pinochet complained about Orlando Letelier and the stink he was raising in Washington, Kissinger reassured the dictator not to be unduly concerned about lofty concepts like human rights.

"We are sympathetic to what you are trying to do here," Kissinger said. "We support your methods."

Jamaica House eased into the stillness of evening. Beverley was off at a PNP Women's Movement conference, Natasha asleep in the care of her nanny. The nightly distant gunshots passed unnoticed in the prime minister's downstairs study as Michael Manley sat at his desk and pondered the dangerous path he was contemplating.

On Manley's desk was a wooden case, a near-sacred object contained inside: The *Rod of Correction,* a three-foot-long ivory-handled wooden staff, a gift from Emperor Haile Selassie. Manley gently lifted the Rod from its case and ran his fingers along its smoothly carved length. During the campaign of '72, Manley had invoked the numinous authority of the Rod to splendid advantage, wielding it like the staff of Joshua and sending the faithful into frenzied ecstasy, the Promised Land dawning nigh. He was waiting for the right moment to unsheathe it once more and call on its magical powers to carry the PNP to victory anew.

Manley set the Rod down and flicked off the lights to rest his eyes. Why would anyone want this job? The blackboards at Trench Town Primary School and the screens at the downtown theaters riddled with bullet holes, the economy collapsing, civil society verging on ruin. Recent events had put Jamaica at risk of becoming an embarrassment on the world's stage. The last fortnight had started off well enough. In Port-of Spain Manley had secured a loan for $80 million from CARICOM partners Trinidad and Tobago, Guyana and Barbados that would keep Jamaica solvent a few months at least. Fifteen Cuban doctors had arrived and were busy saving lives (despite the usual firestorm of criticism from the press and opposition party).

But now this. Peruvian Ambassador Fernando Rodrigues murdered in his suburban Kingston residence. Knifed to death by common thieves as his fourteen-year-old daughter cowered in her room. Never before in Jamaica had a foreign diplomat been slain.

But what if it wasn't common thieves? On the bookshelf behind Manley's desk were Philip Agee's *Inside the Company: CIA Diary* and Marchetti and Mark's *The CIA and the Cult of Intelligence*. The authors were former CIA officers describing the spy agency's secret machinations, Agee in particular charging "the Company" with waging "destabilization programs" to topple foreign governments. Manley and his CARICOM colleagues at the Port-of-Spain meeting had agreed that such programs were in effect in Barbados and Guyana as well as Jamaica. Kissinger denied it. Ambassador Gerard denied it. Deputy Assistant Secretary of State William Luers denied it before a House investigative committee. At least they had their story straight.

How many democratically-elected leaders had been overthrown for implementing progressive social programs to improve living standards for their peoples? Mossadeq, Iran; Arbenz, Guatemala; Arosemana, Ecuador; Allende, Chile. All he wanted from Chilean copper, Allende said, was that every child in the country could have one glass of milk a day. For such heresies IT&T had put a million dollar cash bounty on his head. The old order of oligarchy and privilege had to be maintained at all costs and in this endeavor the CIA would find an able partner in Operation Condor. They were two fists, one of iron and the other of steel, united in cause, and if the left one didn't get you the right one sure as hell would. Lumumba. Bosch. Goulart. Sukarno. Manley knew his name might soon be added to the roster.

He went to the small bathroom and rinsed his face, leaving the light off. Staring at his shadow in the mirror he imagined lustrous black skin covering his body. More than anything he wanted to be a black man, for his fellow Jamaicans to see him fully as one of them, an ebony-skinned Jamaican of African heritage, son of slaves. A *brother* in blood and struggle.

But now it was time for decision. The forces of chaos and terror were winning, violence dragging the nation down. There seemed nothing left but to come in with "heavy manners" and kick ass. Things were too far gone for half measures. Dare one say "martial law?" The thought of it sent a shiver down Manley's neck. Imposing martial law might well end his political career. The struggling tourism industry would be dealt a crippling blow and deepen the country's economic woes. The press and opposition would eat him alive.

Manley sipped tonic water and wondered what his father would do. The legendary Norman Washington Manley, against whom he would forever be measured. "Pardi" had always been a fighter. His battle to found a Caribbean League, a Third World alliance of poor island nations that would stand united against powerful bullies, was to have been the crown jewel of his life's accomplishments. It had ended in bitter defeat, haunting him to his grave. Michael thought of his own even more grandiose project, the "New International Economic Order" in which the developed North would share technology and resources with the undeveloped South. A bold proposal that would give billions of poor the opportunity to have decent lives. Gaining support from Robert McNamara, Willy Brandt and the UN General Assembly, the program had a real chance of pushing through. It was what kept him going when things seemed the bleakest. But change as big as this did not come without commensurate risk and Manley knew a fate similar to his father's might be in the cards... if an assassin's bullet didn't take him first.

A sudden creaking of footsteps snapped Manley to attention. His security officers had warned of assassination plots and unauthorized persons detained on the property. He fumbled in the darkness for something to defend himself with. Too late to shout or phone for help.

Quiet. Footsteps on the red-carpeted staircase....

He assumed a defensive crouch and prepared himself. The footsteps kept coming.

Entering the study.

Manley raised his right arm to striking position.

"Mike?"

Manley switched on the light. Before him in bare feet and nightgown, holding a folded copy of the *Daily Gleaner*, was his wife Beverley.

"For Christ sake, Bev, what are you doing sneaking around like this?"

"What are *you* doing down here holed up in the dark like a renegade Maroon? And why in God's name are you waving the Rod of Correction like a bludgeon?"

Manley, brandishing in his upraised hand Selassie's wooden staff, flushed red and lowered his arm.

"Damn it, Bev, I thought you were a JLP assassin. I was about to beat you into submission."

"Mike, stop your work and come to bed. Seriously."

Beverley Manley wrapped her arms around her husband, the strain in his eyes evident.

"You're working too hard, honey. Let yourself breathe."

"This is bigger than just me, Bev," he said, holding tight to his wife. "I can't take my eye off the ball now... one false step and we go under and everything will have been in vain."

"You can't tie every loose end yourself. There's a limit to what one man can do and I'd say you passed yours long ago. Save a little for us."

"I'm not finished yet by a long shot."

"Let's go to Nyumbani this weekend. It's been ages."

Every Friday there wasn't official party business to hold them, Michael and Beverley collected Natasha and headed for their retreat home in the hills above Kingston ("Nyumbani" Swahili for "home"). There among the trees and fresh air Manley tended his award-winning roses, the pressures of office waning for the moment with the cool waxing of the moon over the Blue Mountains. Perhaps tending roses was a metaphor for what he wished to do for Jamaica—dig his fingers in and husband the struggling shoots to blossom. But even here he could not escape the ghost of his father, for this was family land, parceled off from the patriarch's estate.

"Things are hectic just now," Manley said. "Be up soon, I promise."

"Have you seen the *Gleaner*?" Bev tapped the newspaper to Michael's chest. "Might want to have a quick look."

Bev padded upstairs as Manley scanned the front page. More of the same old... *wait a minute, what's this?*

June 16, dateline Johannesburg: Schoolchildren in the South African township of Soweto, a ghetto as stark as any in Kingston, had risen up against the apartheid government's decree that school classes were henceforth to be taught in Afrikaans, the language of the minority white elite. It was as if Anglo children in the United States were suddenly to be instructed in Spanish. Enraged youth took to the streets to protest this latest attempt to exterminate their culture and squash their aspirations. The state struck back in force. In came the halftracks and soldiers with their rifles and the ground ran red with the blood of children; casualty lists were kept secret. Thousands of teens and adolescents would be jailed, beaten, tortured and killed in a siege that lasted thirteen years of pure terror. The courageous sacrifice of these young freedom fighters was instrumental to the eventual defeat of apartheid. As photos like those of twelve-year-old Hector Pieterson hit the papers—the boy shot in the back and dying in the arms of an older youth as his sister ran alongside—the world could no longer avert its eyes. International sanctions would be implemented and South Africa become a pariah on the world's stage (the apartheid regime defended to the last by Ronald Reagan and his ilk). Pictures of Colin Vaughn would not be appearing in the world's press.

Manley knew now what he had to do. If schoolchildren could stand up against the colonial system he could do no less. The lives of Jamaicans were more important than lost tourist dollars, most of which would be siphoned off by foreign interests anyway. He couldn't in good conscience turn his head and let business go on as usual. He ordered Governor-General Florizel Glasspole to declare a State of Emergency effective immediately

144

across the island—essentially, martial law. Tanks rolled into the streets as the security forces cracked down with heavy manners. Michael and Beverley stuck close to the office, Nyumbani having to wait another day.

Operation Werewolf was in a shambles. On June 18, Herb Rose, a JLP insider, quit the party claiming "its whole strategy was based on violence as a means of obtaining victory at the polls." Rose accused JLP deputy leader Charles Darnell of plotting terrorist actions against the government. Manley ordered police raids and a small arms cache was uncovered in Trench Town; Darnell, Major Garrett Anderson and several other JLP party members, as well as a PNP candidate who appeared to be in cahoots with the opposition, were detained in police custody. Darnell was found to be in possession of tape recordings of police and military transmissions dating back to May 19, the date of the Orange Lane fire. Most incriminating was a recovered document entitled "Operation Werewolf—St. Ann Parish" in the handwriting of Garrett Anderson. The obviously subversive material included the following inventory:
- --22 trained men
- --100 submachine guns
- --2 barrels of gunpowder
- --50,000 anti-government pamphlets.

In a separate action, 257 sticks of dynamite and 25 rolls of fuse wire—enough to take out every power plant and water reservoir in Jamaica—were captured near Montego Bay. Anti-Manley newspaper editors turned a blind eye and hushed it up.

21

Wrapping up the *Rastaman Vibration* Tour with a rousing show in Manchester, England, Bob Marley and the Wailers flew in to Norman Manley International about the time tall ships were sailing in to New York Harbor for the American Bicentennial. The United States was finding itself once more after the squalor of Watergate and Vietnam, winning gold at the Montreal Olympics, *Viking 1* zooming toward Mars, Microsoft and Apple founded this year. The American Dream was alive and well with *Rocky* winning Best Picture, though *Taxi Driver* and *Network* depicted the dark underbelly of the beast, Ron Kovic's *Born on the Fourth of July* and Alex Haley's *Roots* doing the same in literature. Australian Rupert Murdoch purchased the *New York Post* for $30 million and would become a conservative force in US political thought, or what passed for it.

In Kingston the summer sun beat down mercilessly on a city under martial law, people living for the afternoon showers that cooled pavement and tempers for a few blessed hours. A measure of national pride was found in Donald Quarrie taking a gold and silver in the sprints at Montreal. Tourist cancellations were up but violent crime down. Home guard training had begun and photos of new recruit Michael Manley at the shooting range appeared in the newspapers. Polls showed overwhelming support for the State of Emergency; fewer people were dying and by that measure the lockdown had to be deemed a good thing. Security forces had detained hundreds.

Absent from the returning entourage was Allan Cole, who had gone on to Africa. Marley and Cole had planned to travel together to Ethiopia, the Rastafarian fatherland, but Bob was forced to cancel as hostilities raged between Ethiopia and Somalia over the territory of Eritrea. Cole, fearing that gangsters on the Rock were lying in wait to kill him over a gambling debt, went on anyway. Rather African warlords than Kingston rudeboys any day.

At the airport waiting to welcome the Wailers home was a legion of adoring fans. Cindy Breakespeare was there to give Bob a hug and kiss and hell if Rita was watching. The satchel Bob picked up at the carousel carried virtually the same exact contents as at the start of the tour two months before. Bob Marley was not dazzled by America's cheap and abundant material goods. What did glitzy things matter to a man on a holy mission to spread his God's message of love, equal rights and justice?

A big tour was always a grind. Two months on the road in Europe and North America and Bob was always first on the bus and last to go down at night. He ran sound checks and pushed hard at rehearsals, often signalling "one more time" when everyone else was eager to call it a day. He expected one hundred percent and gave a thousand. Marley hit it like an athlete, warming up so vigorously before shows he was drenched in sweat before coming out to hail the audience with a joyous "Jah Rastafari" or other Rasta greeting. On stage he wore whatever he had on, but when it came to the music it had to be immaculate.

Nor was a Wailers tour a matter of "do as the Romans." The Rastas stayed true to their convictions, didn't frequent fancy restaurants or make do with junk food. Bob requested suites with a kitchen so Gilly could cook I-tal stew and blend up his fruit smoothies. A soccer ball was always on hand for the guys to go out to the nearest park and get up a game. Rasta stays fit. Ganja had to be available—Bob had it written into his contract with Don Taylor that Wailers were to be kept stocked while on the road. A special treat was Ziggy and Stephen coming out on stage to dance to their father's music.

Everybody bid each other "likkle later" and Bob and Cindy slipped away to her apartment to make joyful love. Afterwards over a light lunch of steam fish and bammy they caught up.

"The tour was good, Bobby?"

"Yah, good." The *Rastaman Vibration* album would be the highest charting Wailers record during the Island period (1973-1981), reaching

146

number eight on the Billboard charts. The Wailers were declared "band of the year" by Rolling Stone Magazine. What a year for reggae, with *Rastaman* as well as debut solo albums from Bunny (*Blackheart Man*) and Peter (*Legalize It*) and yet a second great offering from Tosh that fall (*Equal Rights*). Not to mention Burning Spear's milestone *Marcus Garvey* and outstanding albums by Abyssinians, Augustus Pablo, Gladiators, Max Romeo and the Upsetters, the Mighty Diamonds and others. From amongst this sea of riches, the Grammy for Record of the Year went to George Benson's smooth and utterly forgettable *This Masquerade*. Best New Artist: Starland Vocal Band. Bob Marley would not win a Grammy during his lifetime.

"How was the Roxy?" Cindy asked. "I recall last year George and Ringo showed up."

"Other one an' dat Japanee girl."

"John and Yoko?"

"Yeah man. Bob Dylan."

"Bob Dylan was at your Roxy show? Lawd, lawd."

"Him fucking good, man. Really say it clear." The Roxy, an intimate supper club on Sunset Strip in West Hollywood, was a great place to see a concert—it was like having the Wailers in your living room. The '76 show that had Warren Beatty and Jack Nicholson dancing on the tables in Bacchanalian revelry would be remembered as one of Bob and the band's best performances.

Cindy dropped Bob at Hope Road and a football scrum was shortly underway. Scott Gallagher showed up and worked himself into the action. Soon a yellow VW bug puttered into the yard. Rita got out as if bearing bad news and spoke privately with Bob. She left and Bob went in to the house and came out wearing fresh jeans and shirt. He got in the BMW and started it up. Halfway down the driveway, Bob poked his head out the window.

"Oy, Scotty. Haffi do yuh homework?"

"Fuck that shit." Scott dashed around and in the passenger seat before Marley could change his mind. Bob turned right on Hope Road and headed toward downtown.

"Hear 'bout this Gun Court business?" said Marley as the Beamer hummed along.

"Not really."

"Get catch with gun, automatic life sentence."

"If you shoot somebody?"

"Nah haffi shoot *nuhbody*. Them find yuh gun them lock yuh up and throw away the key."

Marley turned left on Half Way Tree Road, headed toward Cross Roads.

"Woman friend of Rita son get lock up. Only 18."

147

"Eighteen and life in prison. Damn."

"There always gun in Jamaica, but nuh like so. Dam a go bust. Rifle, handgun, machine gun... folk think CIA bring them in."

"Nah, I don't..." Scott began, stopping short as Bob glanced over with a bit of a screwface.

"Why do people lie?" Scott asked.

"Them afraid of the truth."

The BMW passed Cross Roads en route to Up Park Camp and there was Gun Court: a big red monstrosity in the heart of the city, a prison-camp with armed guards on watchtowers and big bales of barbed wire atop the walls. Michael Manley's heavy-handed attempt to deal with the spiraling violence.

As Marley approached the wire-fence gate with the words GUN COURT emblazoned in huge letters, Scott snapped to attention. Two women were standing outside the gate arguing with a guard.

"Look!" Scott cried. "It's Marva."

Scott stuck his head out the window and called to her. The young woman turned but got back to her business with barely a frown of recognition.

Bob pulled the BMW over and Scott hurried to his sweetheart.

"Marva, what are you doing here? Hi, Mrs. Morrison."

Mrs. Morrison scowled as darkly as her daughter had done an instant before. They were dressed in their Sunday finest and looking none too happy.

"What's up?" Scott asked.

"My brother got mixed up in some trouble," Marva said.

"Troy? That cool guy who dropped you at Victoria Pier that day?"

"Yeah."

"You all right?" Scott taking his girl by the arm.

"No, I'm not all right. Why did Joshua have to start this stupid Gun Court? Yes, there's violence but don't lock the youth up. Why should they have to pay?"

Marley came over and read the pain in Marva's face. He clasped her hands firmly in his.

"Keep a song in yuh heart, likkle daughter," he said. "Jah Jah see yuh through."

Marva's sad eyes took flight as if a soothing balm lathered her soul. A pedestrian door in the gate opened and Marley was waved in. A guard came over to chase the women away but Marley held up his hand like a magic wand and they all walked in together. Once inside the women had to wait as Bob and Scott were ushered into the lockdown area. Scott followed as Bob was passed through several locked doors and into the office of the prison warden. A young black in prison garb was promptly shown in. Scott

148

was shocked—the kid couldn't have been any older than he was. Marley gave his testimonial, saying the youth, Mikey D, had been known to him since he was a pickney, a decent bwoy who had never been in any trouble until he'd gotten involved with the wrong crowd. Marley asked about a pardon or early release. Finally the prisoner was led away and Bob and Scott were shown out. Marley asked the warden to grant audience to the women waiting outside for—

"What that boy name, Scotty?" Marley asked.

"Troy Morrison."

Exiting, they passed Marva and her mother on their way in. Scott gave Marva's hand a squeeze for luck.

Back in the BMW, Marley started up and drove.

"Why all this violence, Skip?" Scott asked. "I don't get it. Why don't people appreciate living on this beautiful island? Jamaica is paradise, yet there's so much hatred. You say the CIA is behind it. In America we have a saying, 'guns don't kill, people do.' Who's pulling the trigger? It's not Americans, it's Jamaicans. Don't see how you can hang this on Uncle Sam."

"I-man show yuh something. Check it out."

As they neared Heroes Circle, Marley turned onto Orange Lane and drove slowly past the smoldering charred hulk of what once had been peoples' homes.

"Orange Lane," the Tuff Gong said. "Hear 'bout the fire?"

"Little bit," Scott said as he stared at the desolate ruins that stretched on and on.

"Ten, eleven people die here. Baby asleep him bed, old woman... them a run out get shot."

"How could anybody do this? See, this is what I'm talking about."

"Baby nah born with hatred. Pickney must learn fe hate."

"Do they know who did it? Marva says it was the JLP fighting against Manley but I read where the deputy leader of the JLP claimed trucks came in earlier that day and evacuated all the PNP supporters. That true?"

"Who know? All them politician fuckin' liar. Show yuh something else."

Marley turned from Orange Lane onto the main Orange Street thoroughfare, heading for the yards of West Kingston. He purposely drove past the worst slums in the city, where human beings were jammed like cattle-car herds into festering zinc-roofed hovels and cardboard lean-tos. Marley slowed to let his young born-of-privilege friend get a good look at the hollowed cheeks of emaciated children, their swollen malnourished bellies, the vacant hopeless stares of crushed souls living lives of utter desperation, their numbers reduced but by no means eliminated by Michael Manley's social programs of the last three and a half years.

149

"Fuck," Scott cringed at the gut-wrenching squalor.

"Satan make easy work on empty belly," Marley said.

"Why doesn't somebody do something? Government, Red Cross, *some*body."

"Poli-tricks. Devil work through the system. *Shit-stem.* Nothing ever change beca' shit-stem never change. Gun only thing the youth-them know."

Some thought that it wasn't poverty alone that corrupted the ghetto youth. More than a few pointed at movies and TV bringing American programs glorifying gunslingers and ramming material gluttony down the throats of young people who saw for the first time what they didn't have and could never get. It was like whiskey to Indians as white men killed off the buffalo and drove them off their land.

"One more thing I-man show yuh," Bob said.

Marley turned the BMW toward familiar streets of his youth—the Ghost Town section of the Trench Town ghetto. They arrived within minutes. A slum, it was nevertheless a couple steps up from the abject misery of the worst garbage can alleys. The place had a life to it despite the deplorable conditions. People smiled and waved joyful greetings as Bob passed. He parked in the shade of a mango tree and got out, leaving the car unlocked with the keys in the ignition.

"Want me to watch the car?" Scott asked.

"Nobody bother I ride."

As they walked the streets, folks kept coming up to slap Bob some skin.

"Wha' gwan, mi bruddah?"

"Yes, Rasta."

"The I make de hardest music, fe true."

Scott was dumbfounded that in the midst of such suffering, in these godforsaken snake pits of human existence, this Calcutta of the Caribbean, there could be such a spontaneous outpouring of life, call it nothing else. Raw, orgasmic, sweat-and-guts-and-never-say-die life. The human longing to endure and prosper. Blood-in-tooth-and-claw animal instinct alongside all the lofty higher human values. It was bursting everywhere, this crackling, slapdash, ragamuffin life. A woman singing as she hand-scrubbed her clothes. Another tremendously fat woman waddling naked under a backyard water pipe. An industrious fellow re-soling raggedy sandals with a patch of tire tread. Men playing dominoes at the corner shop, slapping their pieces down on the board, *wham!* Barefoot pickneys threading string through an old plastic bottle and calling it a toy; older kids, equally shoeless, playing cricket in a bumpy zinc-fence lane with a twig of wood for a bat; folks moving and grooving to riddims blasting from a boombox somewhere.

150

Jamaicans living hand to mouth and eking out a life in poverty, but rip-snorting alive. This too was the ghetto and Scott looked and learned.

Bob led Scott to a decrepit tenement yard on 2nd Street. The tenements, running from First through Ninth Streets, were public housing projects built after the devastating 1951 hurricane (the word coming from the Arawak god of storms, *Huracan*). Typically three small units were arranged in a horseshoe around a central courtyard. Far from mansions, the tenements at least put a roof over your head.

"Momma and me live in this yard here when me likkle boy," Marley said. "Bunny live over there. Nuh electric, nuh running water… one likkle standpipe fe thousand, two thousand people. Momma 'n me move here from 'nother place cross town nuh so nice."

This is nicer? Scott shuddered.

"We come a Kingston from Nine Mile in St. Ann when me 10, maybe 11. Bunny and him faddah come 'bout then too. The garden parish them say, St. Ann. Marcus Garvey hail from there. Me white father run off an' leave we, cyan't remember what the bastard look like. Used to sing here, me and Bunny and Peter, or over Third Street at Joe Higgs' yard or First Street at Tata's. Peter come a country too, from Savannah-La-Mar out Negril way. Joe Higgs teach we harmony so we three young voice come together and make sweet sound. Stay all night singing, vocalizing. Georgie make the fire blaze fe we drink coffee 'n eat likkle bite and push on. Plenty time we catch music on radio from New Orleans, Miami if the signal blow on the wind. James Brown, Curtis Mayfield, Sam Cooke, Fats Domino, all dem great ones. Elvis, Ricky Nelson. *Go Jimmy Go,* know that one? We listen all dem silly love song. Brook Benton, Drifters. Get Cuban riddim from Havana too. Later I and I brethren go a studio and cover dem record in island riddim, ska, rock steady, roots, rockers, ragamuffin, everything."

"Cool."

"Me and Rita grind da wood first time over Tata place," Bob said with eyes aglow. "Me n' Bunny n' Peter used to walk over by Rita place on our way to Studio One. Down 2nd Street, along West Road past old Calvary Cemetery and over Trench Town Gully to Greenwich Park Road by the new Calvary Cemetery. Rita live over there, she be standing by the gate when we three pass. Alfarita Constantia Anderson. Face shining black as night, big smile. Peter like her first, then me 'n her gravitate natural like to each other. Her brothers wan' chase I off beca' me skin brown. Nuh wan' them sister mix them pure black blood with half-breed like me."

"A true?" Scott boggled.

"Prejudice flow up, down, every which way." Before he'd become comfortable in his skin, Marley as a youth—like Michael Manley—had wished to be darker, blacking his hair to be "more African-looking."

151

"Any regrets, Skip?" Scott asked as they walked back for the car.

"Only that His Imperial Majesty visit JamRock only time ten year ago an' me in Delaware doin' shit-work fe get the music going back a Yard. Me leave JA day after me 'n Rita get marry an' two months later His Majesty come. Them say when Selassie-I plane a come, big flock of white dove appear inna sky an' alla sudden His Majesty plane break through them cloud. Man! Greatest day fe Jamaica until now. Bredren run round outta dem blessed mind in frenzy. Plenty thousand a them. Elder Mortimo Planno haffi move them back so His Majesty can come outta the plane."

By now they had arrived back at the car, which had emerged from the mango tree's shade into the orange-rind glow of late afternoon. Everybody knew Marley's ride and no one would think of messing with it, but Bob was distressed to see several youth ogling the BMW with covetous eyes. It was just wheels—Skill had thought it'd be a sturdy vehicle to ply the rugged backroads of St. Ann on ganja runs. It wasn't about luxury and ostentation. No one cared less about status symbols and such nonsense than the Skipper. But the youth-them ogle.

Red-checked apron tied around her plump midsection, Maddy prepared two Saturday breakfasts—bacon and eggs with hash browns and coffee for Matt and Jamaican peanut porridge, roast breadfruit and fresh juice for Scott. Different meals, different appetites, different worlds. Matt hidden behind his morning paper.

"How's work?" Scott asked, drawing no response.

"Oughta try this breadfruit," he tried again and Matt mumbled something behind his newspaper.

"I SAY, the breadfruit's good."

The newspaper came down. "What are you squawking about?" Matt said

"The breadfruit. Know where it came from?"

"Maddy's backyard I suppose."

"Originally. How it came to Jamaica."

"I wouldn't have a clue."

"South Pacific. Tahiti. Captain Bligh brought it back. Cheap source of food for slaves in the colonies."

"Mutiny-on-the-Bounty Captain Bligh?"

"Yep. They were five months on Tahiti collecting plants and heading back to Jolly England when the men mutinied. Bligh and eighteen faithful got dumped off in a seven-meter dinghy with a sextant and pocket watch. They made it to Timor in forty-seven days. Thirty-six hundred nautical miles, an incredible feat of seamanship. Bligh returned years later and got his specimens and that's how breadfruit came to Jamaica. Apple too. Tahitian apple, otaheite."

"Balls," said Matt. "That's what it takes, big brass *cojones*. Want something bad enough you can't piss off first time you run into a brick wall. You climb over or go around or ram through the damn thing. Wanna go shooting today? Give it another shot, pardon the pun."

"Not really."

Matt scowled and the paper wall went back up.

"Ever think about mom?" Scott asked and down it came again.

"What kind of a question is that?" Matt said. "I think about her all the time. Don't you?"

"Can't remember her much."

"She used to brush your hair one hundred strokes every night before bed."

"She never got to eighty-five and gave up?"

"No way. Not your mother. She wasn't like that. You could count on her for anything. Your mother wasn't like everyone else, run of the mill and ordinary. She was *extra*-ordinary. Not even sure she was human. Like she was from some higher place sent down for a visit and the angels took her away again."

"I remember making a Valentine for a girl in kindergarten… someone helping me glue a red heart. Can't see her though."

"Probably was your mother."

"What did she look like?"

"Like Cleopatra of the Nile," Matt said, his face lighting up in a way Scott had never seen before that made the lines in his father's face vanish. "Like a princess from the movies. Skin white as Michelangelo's marble, long black hair flowing in curls down to her shoulders. I wish…."

"What?"

"Nothing."

"You wish she were still with us."

"That's not what I was going to say."

"What then? Really, I'd like to know."

"I should have been there for her. Maybe it would have made a difference."

"You were in Vietnam. No use worrying about it now."

"I did what I thought was right at the time. Don't know, maybe I'd do it the same way again." He was quiet for some time and cleared his throat before speaking again.

"Sorry you never really got to know her," he said finally. "Sorry…."

"Forget it, dad. It's not your fault."

"No, it's never anyone's fault," Matt said with a tinge of remorse that caught Scott off guard. "That would be too much to ask."

"Things get complicated."

"How's that girlfriend of yours, what's her name again?"

"Marva."

"Make sure you use a rubber. Don't want to get one of these native girls pregnant, even if she looks white."

"What the hell is that supposed to mean?"

"Don't go getting attached either. Never know how long we'll be here."

"Aren't going anywhere, are we?"

"Never know."

"Why can't you have a job where you stay in one place?"

"That's the way it is. Deal with it."

"I won't leave. I'll stay here with Marva."

"Sounds like it's your first pussy. This your first piece of ass? Everybody gets a little pussy whipped the first time. Well, I didn't. If you're that whipped better cut it clean."

"I'll marry her," Scott snapped. "Know what else? She's black. We'll get married and have little brown babies, how would that do you? Maybe I'll go gay too."

Before his father could respond Scott stormed off, wondering why things always ended up like this and if he was to blame.

Scott was riding down the hill on his way to Hope Rope when he had the feeling of being followed. For some time he'd been suspicious of a dread that was always hanging around the corner shop chiseling wood. Catching a glimpse of someone on a motorcycle that looked like him, he stopped and the guy stopped too. When he turned and made for him, the dread scurried away down a side street.

Next morning he took a different route down the hill, going far out of his way to descend the back side and circle around so as to come up on Chinaman's shop from below. He caught the dread in the yard chipping flakes off a block of wood and glancing up the hill as if watching for someone. He took him completely by surprise.

"Who are you?" Scott demanded, storming in the yard. "Why are you following me?"

"Whoa now, sonny boy, me nah--"

"Hey… you were at Harry J's that day."

"Nah suh."

"Cut the crap, okay? Who the hell are you?"

"Me nah follow yuh, sonny. Work here a shop."

"Bull shit. Is my father putting you up to it?"

"Doan know yuh faddah from Adam inna de Bible."

"Name's Matt Gallagher. Works at the embassy. If you lie I'm going to know and you'll get in trouble, so fess up. Following me, aren't you."

154

"How trouble find me?"

"Trouble nah find you if you tell the truth."

"The one-eye man?"

"Sonuvabitch! I knew it."

"Him worry 'bout yuh sonny, that's all."

"Don't call me sonny, all right? You follow me everywhere I go?"

"Is I job."

"To school?"

"Mmm."

"At night? To Marva's house?"

"That righteous Jamaican daughtah?"

"You *didn't* follow us to the waterfall that day?"

Jesse James grinned from ear to ear.

"YOU SAW US AT THE WATERFALL?" Scott flushed beet red.

"The I carry himself with the daughtah like a man. Nah reason fe shame."

"Sonuva-fucking-bitch. You tell my father everything? Whether she gives head or not, you tell him that, huh?"

"Nah fret yuhself, sonny."

"Don't fucking call me sonny."

"Sorry, suh. Nah tell yuh daddy, seen?"

"Can't pretend I never saw you now can I."

"Please, mister, two likkle girl me 'ave. Yuh daddy job can let them eat. Jamaica rough, man."

"Hope he's paying you fair and square."

"Make I and I work a deal. I-man keep me distance and nah bother yuh. Just gwan 'bout yuh business. Please, suh."

"Ain't getting off that easy. I want to know what my father does, where he goes, who he sees… the whole ball of wax. And don't call me sir either."

"Me nah know anything about that."

"So you find out."

"Mean say follow the man?"

"Ain't like you'd have to learn a new skill."

"But sonny boy, suh…."

"Heck, you must be curious what the guy's story is."

Jesse James scratched his head in consternation and broke into a wide grin.

"Deal," he said and the two shook on it. "Jesse James I-man name."

"I'm… well, you already know my name. Now listen up, Mr. Jesse James. Don't even think about carpetbagging me. Wanna keep a lid on things you find out what my old man is up to. Might be whoring or drinking with his buddies, I don't care. Just be honest with me."

155

"Honesty the word, likkle man."

On July 2nd Luis Posada Carriles flew in to Jamaica with a fresh supply of C4 plastic explosive, dynamite, fuse wire and detonators picked up from Cuban exiles in Miami. Matt Gallagher welcomed him over lunch and Cuba Libres in the Cinnamon Lounge at Hotel Caribbean. Shadowing them in the patty shop across the street was Jesse James, who chatted up the chubby daughtah behind the counter and waited for them to come out. When Posada and Gallagher finally emerged and Jesse James got a good look at the big stranger, he had the impression he was Cuban. A woman passing along the street angrily spit the word "ass" as she laid eyes upon him and she looked part Cuban as well. The guy wasn't one of the workers at the Jose Marti School the Cubans were building and sure as heck didn't look like any doctor either. Many Kingstonians believed Cuban exiles were behind the bombings at the Cuban Embassy over the last few years. What business did Mister Matt have with such people?

Forming hit squads of Operation Werewolf personnel, Posada blazed a trail of destruction across the city: July 3, two bombs set off in Olympic Gardens; July 6, a huge blast forced closure of the Alcoa bauxite plant, causing millions in damages and injuring eleven; July 9, a bomb exploded in the baggage handling area of Cubana Airlines at Norman Manley Airport, only a delayed flight preventing a major tragedy. Posada got back on his plane and flew to Barbados, where within twenty-four hours an explosion rocked the Cubana Air office. Matt knew Bambi had arrived safely.

Around this time a flood of high-level intelligence came in to the Kingston station. Spanish diplomat Carmelo Soria had been murdered in Santiago in a Condor hit after being brutally tortured at Villa Grimaldi. (Where Pinochet's iron hand was so ruthless he ordered hanged a guard who in a casual aside had expressed sympathy for victims and their bloodchilling cries of agony. Others tortured included a young woman who would later become the country's president, Michelle Bachelet.) An assassination of US Congressman Ed Koch was reported in the works and warning was posted of a possible bombing attempt on Cubana Airlines Flight 476 from Panama to Havana on June 21.

It was learned that Michael Manley was to give a speech in September to the large Jamaican community in Toronto. Realizing that security precautions were sometimes lax in unfamiliar settings and that any trouble could be spun as the work of disgruntled Jamaican expatriates, Matt Gallagher immediately contacted Luis Posada in Caracas. A plan was made for Manley to be assassinated in Toronto by Cuban exiles and headquarters in Langley gave a back channel OK. President Ford's executive order ending sanctions against foreign leaders would be ignored, just as the

156

congressional ban on supplying the pro-apartheid armies in Angola would be flaunted with the shipping, under Director of Central Intelligence George H. W. Bush, of at least twenty planeloads of arms into the African hotbed. The CIA held itself above the law, as fundamentally it was intended to be— its funding hidden in the budgets of other executive agencies and still largely exempt from Congressional oversight despite recent efforts to rein it in. Bush did not inform Koch of the plot against his life and no one made any attempt to warn the Cuban government of a possible attack on its national airline.

Posada had to pass on taking the Toronto hit on Manley personally as a major operation was in the works on the life of Fidel Castro. Infuriated by the massacre of schoolchildren in Soweto, the Cuban leader had dispatched military advisers to Mozambique to train South African freedom fighters. It was another slap in the face to the West—the Washington elite wanted the Bearded One dead so much they could taste his blood in their mouths. When it was learned he was to travel by boat to Africa in September for the first anniversary of the Angolan revolution, a commando under Posada and Orlando Bosch was formed. The Kingston station was advised to be on the alert for any information regarding Castro's travel arrangements. The bait-broad operation was ratcheted up to top priority on the possibility that pillow talk from Castro's buddy Manley would yield pearls of intelligence. Gallagher's team had come up with a girl, but they should have done their homework. Manley already had a squeeze on the side.

July ended with American Bruce Jenner winning the Olympic decathlon. The Montreal Games had gone quietly without the Black September horrors of Munich '72 or the "Black Fist" salute of Tommie Smith and John Carlos at Mexico City '68 (a gesture that outraged pundits in the United States while the police slaughter of hundreds of unarmed student protesters incensed over the cost of staging the spectacle when poor people were starving went largely unnoticed). In quite another way, however, the Games of Montreal made an historic statement. Twenty-two African nations had boycotted in protest of the New Zealand rugby squad's tour of South Africa. Black people were coming together, African consciousness was rising—and Bob Marley was the revolution's troubadour, chanting down the walls of Babylon.

22

Christmas Week 1980, Santa Barbara

The Good Ol' Boys 'n Sweet Young Things bar was rocking out. Tucked away in the corner of a small shopping center in Winchester Canyon up past Isla Vista on the road to San Francisco, the joint drew a fair mix of customers, from UCSB students to real cattle-wrangling cowboys, from stock brokers to the occasional movie star driving over from Montecito in the Lamborghini. Jimmy Messina dropped in from time to time and locals swore Jackson Browne sang *Running On Empty* for the first time there. Tonight was reggae night and nuff joints were passed in the back of vans in the parking lot while coke was the drug of choice in Beamers and Porsches. On stage the Reggae Rockers were kicking it to Dennis Brown, with Scott's lead vocals backed by Suzette alone while Nadesha sat home in LA nursing a sore throat. Scott had reluctantly agreed to add songs by various reggae artists to the playlist—as few as possible—and couldn't help breaking into Marley mannerisms during all Wailers tunes, and in fact most of the others. It just flowed out of him. Give him a mic and he did his thing.

After the gig Scott caught a ride home with Suzette, who was unusually sedate.

"So how'd it go tonight?" Scott asked as they cruised 101 through Goleta.

"Okay," Suzette said, unconvincingly.

"Not too Bob Marley-mania for your taste?"

"You're still doing it."

"We did Dennis Brown, didn't we? I gotta be who I am, man!"

"Right."

"Was it a good show or not?"

"That's not the point."

"How can that not be the point?"

Suzette quietly studied the road.

"So I'm a prick, right?" Scott said.

"No, you're not a prick."

"Halleluiah."

"Can I ask you something?"

"No."

"Shut up. How come you never ask me out?"

"Go on."

"Really. How come you never ask me out?"

"We're in the band."

"So?"

"So we're in the band."

"Oh brother. What is this lame act of yours, going on like you're better than everybody else?"

"That's not it at all."

"Kiss me."

"You shut up."

"No, really. Kiss me."

"You're driving."

"There's no one on the road."

"Yeah, well…."

"Doesn't have to be Burt Lancaster rolling on the beach with Susie White Tits. Give me a little kiss. Hurry up before a car comes along."

Scott leaned over and put his lips to Suzette's. She opened wide and swirled her tongue around his in a most delicious manner. He broke to catch his breath before she was done with him.

Suzette checked her mirrors. "Again," she said.

Scott leaned back over and kissed her a second time. Again her tongue went exploring. She took Scott's hand and brought it to her breast. He was slipping his fingers inside her blouse when a Camaro Z28 came upon them at 120 mph, blasting its horn. Suzette swung the wheel of the Variant sharply to the right.

"Asshole! You all right, Scotty?"

"Fuck," he gasped.

"Sorry to scare you."

"No. You kiss good."

"I do a lot of things good."

"*I* need a cold shower."

"That's not what you need."

"What do I need?"

"Come to LA with me and you might find out."

"Tonight?"

"We can stop and get your things."

"Just bomb down to LA."

"Do you have other plans? Course if you don't want to."

"Let's think about this a minute."

"If you have to fucking think about it."

"Just… you could stay here."

"At your place?"

"We could hang and you go back on Sunday."

"The man has a plan. What would we do? I mean, besides…."

"Besides what?"

"You know what."

"Out with it, emancipated woman."

Suzette flashed her perfect teeth and broke into song, lifting up her sweet and lilting voice in Bob Marley's *Stir It Up*. After a couple verses Scott came in with his nasally tenor and they harmonized beautifully together. The sizzling eroticism of the lyrics melted the frozen distance between them, or rather, it thawed Scott's icy resolve. They laughed and Suzette rested her hand on Scott's knee. He dared imagine the strange cold loneliness of these last four years coming to an end this very night. Maybe it would make the banshees howling outside his window go away.

159

Back at his pad, Scott slipped *Catch A Fire* onto the turntable and set about rolling a bomber joint as Suzette put on the kettle for tea.

"Mind if I take a shower?" Suzette asked.

"Sure. Gussy yourself up."

"Want to take one with me?"

"Soon as I roll this Colossus of Rhodes spliff."

"Don't know what you're missing, boy. Watch the kettle."

Suzette went off to take her shower as Scott plopped on the couch and took up rolling papers. As he contemplated events immediately to ensue, his hands began to shake and his throat went dry. Images of Suzette soaping her breasts sent his heart pounding. His head ached, his mind went numb and a sense of dread came over him. He felt as if to barf. Frantically he stuffed weed into the rounded-out rolling papers, spilling much with trembling hands that betrayed his inner terror. He lit and hit hard and fast.

In the bathroom Suzette disrobed and studied her nakedness in the mirror. She rotated left and right to view herself as Scott would soon be seeing her, admired the contours and curves to reassure herself he wouldn't fail to be driven to distraction. Posters of Bob Marley were tacked up even in this confined space. And what was this on the sink? Bark?

Oh, that's right, she thought, *Bob uses bark to clean his teeth.*

Scott's fascination with Bob Marley, she feared, went too far. Something was wrong there. A friend of hers had become so smitten with Luther Vandross after he winked at her at a concert that she followed the man around like Little Bo Peep, certain a great love affair was destined between them. She'd nearly ruined her life.

Flaming ash raced down the length of the joint like a dynamite fuse as Scott drew repeated deep drafts. The herb was having a strange effect. It seemed like he'd slipped out of his body and was hovering ten feet above, looking down and taking it all in, seeing everything, his jittery hands, the sloppily rolled joint bobbing in his mouth, even the roiling of his stomach and crashing of his heart. His sudden fear that he was a crazed murderer and didn't know it.

Suzette pranced wet and naked into the room. Scott almost audibly gasped—with her clothes off she looked all the more like Marva, same lithe legs, the well-turned ankles and cute feet, breasts equally as magnificent, same narrow waist. Similar shoulders even. She jiggle-wiggled over and backed her callipygian buttocks down onto Scott's lap.

"Nice joint," Suzette said, smacking a kiss over her shoulder and taking the spliff. As she sucked down a healthy drag, she didn't see that Scott's expression was clouded and confused. She turned back and kissed him with open mouth and for the next several minutes they traded hits and kisses as they finished off the joint. Suzette thought it odd that Scott sat there like a knot on a pine not touching her when he could be caressing her breasts and thighs. Odder still was the squishy flatness where the ship's mast should have been. But slow hands were a virtue and they did have all night.

She hummed and trilled Marley's sensual *Stir It Up*, her voice seductive and raw, eyes gypsy hot as she turned and pulled the Marley tee up and over his head. She kissed him and pressed Aphrodite's voluptuous peaks softly to his face, reaching her hand behind his head to hold him close, as if to say "your woman is here and everything's gonna be all right."

He tensed and pulled back.

"You all right, baby?" Suzette asked.

"I want, uh...."

"*I want* to give you head," Suzette kneeled before him, loosened his red-gold-and-green hemp belt and wrestled his jeans to his knees. She brushed her face softly into his white Penneys briefs; he was still limp but she had a way to deal with that. As she slid her fingers under the elastic band, Scott struggled to his feet and pulled up his jeans.

"Let's smoke more Sens," he blustered.

"Jesus!" Suzette cursed, throwing up her hands as Scott frantically rolled another joint. "I've seen some bad timing in my day, but this takes the prize."

She sat beside him on the couch.

"Why are you so nervous?" she said. "Don't you like sex? Not gay are you?"

"Fuck no I'm not gay. Little out of practice is all."

"Do you want me to put my clothes on?"

"I don't know."

"*You don't know*?"

"Just want you to be comfortable."

"I'd be more comfortable if you took your clothes off."

"Done." Scott finished rolling the spliff, his hands shaking as he held it up for inspection. Suzette resented that Scott made her feel something was wrong with *her*.

"Let me," she said, taking the lighter and flicking out a flame.

"Jah Rastafari," Scott chanted and touched the tip of the spliff to the fire. He took a long drag and passed it with trembling hand to Suzette.

"Bob would fuck me," she said.

"What?"

"Bob's never out of practice. He wouldn't jump out of the saddle to roll a flippin' joint."

"How do you know what Bob would do?"

"I know men. Bob is a lion. He'd fuck the shit out of me."

Scott stared at Suzette as if trying to decipher the words of a great enigma. Slowly he turned to gaze into the distance, losing himself in an ethereal fog, as if all systems had broken down. Feeling faint and swallowed

161

up, he lowered his head between his knees and sucked air, lungs pumping like bellows.

"Are you all right?" Suzette placed her hand gently to his shoulder. She regretted getting in his face like that.

Her words were blotted from awareness as pictures slashed through his mind—*a thunderstorm bursting from a clear blue sky… a bouquet of red and white flowers.* Jamaican symbols of death. His terror intensified.

Suzette leaned close, rested her head on his back, felt the quaking in his soul. His ascendant consciousness looking down with bemused indifference.

"I'm right here, baby. Breathe with me, come on now." Suzette pressed her chest tightly against Scott's back so he could feel her lungs expanding. Gradually his breathing began to deepen and flow in harmony with hers.

"That's it. In and out, in and out."

She thought now to invoke Bob in a more flattering way.

"You sing Bob good, hun," she said. "Really are a fine reggae singer, an artist like Bob. An *artiste.* I love when you sing *Stir It Up* and everybody's moving to the riddim, mellowing into the vibe like a groove thing, the ladies looking up at you with nasty sin in their eyes. Plenty times I wanted to drag you into the back room right then and there."

She began to hum and sing *Stir It Up*, which apart from the title's more general connotation of raking up trouble was explicitly, joyfully, erotic. She sang so tenderly it was like a mother's lullaby to her infant child, as soothing and comforting as mom's life-sustaining heartbeat. It worked like a shaman's magic. Finding new life and energy, Scott rolled over and nuzzled against her breasts, biological imperative reasserting itself. Detecting his arousal Suzette tugged down his briefs and he buried himself inside her.

"Fuck me, Skipper," Suzette commanded and Scott fucked her hard, but he wasn't really there, his movements robotic and strangely cold, devoid of the usual passion such intimacy entailed, his gaze removed, his greater consciousness looking down from above and seeing in this ultimate expression of life's longing only the promise of death.

Up in the hills of the Santa Barbara Riviera, Phil Mitchell studied the new LP he'd bought that afternoon: *Rastaman Vibration*, with its Neville Garrick-designed cover portraying Bob staring down Babylon. On the inside cover, the cheeky inscription: *This album jacket is good for cleaning herb.* On the back cover was the "Blessing of Joseph" from the Bible (Genesis 49:22-24 and Deuteronomy 33:16). It spoke of Joseph being aggrieved by archers who had shot at him, and hated him, but his arms were made strong by the mighty God of Jacob, and let blessings be upon his head.

162

A recipe for paranoia, Phil mused. Did this wax platter offer insight into the Gallagher kid and his Jamaican experience? Was he a full-fledged clinical paranoiac, a dissociative multiple personality, a hysteric with a tendency toward hypochondria, or simply a pathological liar? An imaginative bull-shitter? Or e) all of the above? A diagnosis of "mixed-up kid" only went so far.

Mitchell put the album on the stereo and sat back with his Trader Joe's wine. Marley sang of dreads and baldheads, war, the CIA, an "evil system." The music was catchy but Phil's impression was of an overriding sense of vulnerability, suspiciousness, distrust—in a word, paranoia. A primordial stew of paranoid postcolonial angst.

No wonder this Gallagher kid is so messed up, Phil mused as he finished his bottle of wine and took a Vicodin for his imaginary pain.

Scott woke before Suzette. He studied her as she lay next to him softly breathing in and out. A beautiful girl, intelligent, caring, loved reggae—what more could a guy want? Hot stuff in the sack too, a spirit of nature, wild child, sleek lioness in glorious naked splendor, untamed, free, eternal. A catch like this did not come along every day of the week. So why this aggravation in the pit of his stomach?

Suzette awoke and saw that Scott was watching her.

"Good morning," she said with a crinkly, sleepy-eyed smile.

"Morning," he replied, unable to hold her glance, his voice thin and brittle. He rolled onto his back and stared at the ceiling.

"How do you feel?" she whispered.

"Okay."

"Just okay?"

"Good, good."

She lay over him with her breasts lightly brushing against his chest. He looked everywhere but at her.

"Why can't you look at me?" she said.

Scott lowered his eyes to hers.

"I *am* looking at you," he said, in the next instant finding greater interest in the ceiling.

"I don't understand," Suzette rolled off in a snit.

"Suzette," he said, "why do you like me?"

"What kind of question is that? Why shouldn't I like you?"

"Is it because I'm white?"

"WHAT?" Suzette threw back the covers and sprang to a seated position. "What does being white have to do with anything? You think I'd suck Barry Goldwater's dick because he's white? So you like me because I'm black?"

"I don't know."

163

"YOU DON'T FUCKING KNOW?" Suzette spat in anger, her face contorting into a contemptuous scowl.

Scott sat up abashed.

"This is happening so fast," he said, groping for a handle on the situation. "Yesterday we were friends in the band and now...."

"It's not like we're married. Jesus, Scott."

"Just that... it's scary, you know."

"I know," the fire disappearing from Suzette's voice. They lay down and cuddled guardedly, Scott not quite sure what to do with his hands. After some time, he cleared his throat and spoke.

"The guys in Jamaica are so handsome, awesome bodies, magnificent dreadlocks. More gorgeous than the ladies even."

"So?"

"So why would a girl like a skinny white guy like me?"

"It's how two people click," Suzette said. "Being gorgeous isn't the important thing and color doesn't have anything to do with it. Gotta believe in yourself, my dear, or a girl with a hump and horn won't have you."

They dozed off in each other's arms, but after they got up they didn't touch each other and each pair of eyes repelled the accidental glance of the other. Suzette collected her things and without waiting for breakfast slipped out to the car. As the VW rolled down the driveway, Scott took out his guitar and sang Bob Marley songs, and Suzette drove home to LA alone.

Phil was in the garage bundling newspapers for recycling. It was a two-car garage but he usually parked the Porsche in the driveway and left his "fun" second car inside, a BMW 20002 tii. The Beamer ran well but was in need of a paint job and restoration. It leaked oil and Phil tiptoed around large stains in the cement. Having read his share of quasi-Buddhist literature—Alan Watts, Ram Dass, J. Krishnamurti—he tried to keep a Zen state of mind and not get caught up in the lure of the printed page as he shuffled the newspapers about. Meditation in action, focus on what you are doing, stay in the moment. He couldn't quite pull it off and frequently stopped to glance over items that caught his eye. He played a maudlin game of pondering whether he was worse off now or at the time the stories came out.

One of the brown paper bags ripped and papers flew everywhere.

"Fuck," Mitchell cursed, lighting a cigarette. Grocery bags never used to burst when Karen was around. He tramped across the street and gazed mindlessly out over the hillside canyon, a morning haze hanging low over the ridges. In the evenings you could hear the howl of coyotes, sometimes catch sight of them slinking through the underbrush hunting mice and overconfident house pets. Billions of years of evolution led to this moment... what the hell was the point?

164

Phil dragged his ass back and stared at the mess in the garage. He had half a mind to set it on fire and howl at the moon as it burned when words jumped out at him, a small column on the front page of a weeks-old edition of the *Santa Barbara News-Press* under the heading:

"REGGAE STAR COLLAPSES IN CENTRAL PARK"

The article was about Bob Marley. It said that Marley had been jogging with Allan Cole near the lake in New York's Central Park when his body suddenly "froze up" and he fell helplessly to the ground. It was a Sunday morning after a concert at Madison Square Garden with the Wailers sharing billing with the Commodores. Cole helped Bob back to his hotel room at Essex House.

Phil checked the date on the newspaper: Monday, September 22nd, 1980. Something about the date struck him... *September 22nd*. He remembered that the 21st was the Anderson-Reagan debate and the eve of Iraq's invasion Iran.

In the next instant Phil dashed into the house to his office in the den. He checked his personal calendar—when had been Scott Gallagher's first appointment? *October 5th*.

The kid had first shown up at the office a couple weeks after his fainting spell at City College... which would put the incident on September 21st—the same day as Marley's collapse. What were the odds of two such similar events randomly happening together in such close temporal proximity, especially given the kid's obsessive adulation of the reggae star? It seemed almost metaphysical, from the realm of witchcraft and sorcery.

He stopped by the city library and dug up a book on Afro-Caribbean religion. In the section on Jamaica, he read about the dread in which white colonialists had held practitioners of Obeah, who like Haitian masters of Voodoo were reputed to be able to kill as well as restore life. Slave rebellions that sprang up from time to time were often (correctly) blamed on Obeah men, who were so respected and feared by fellow blacks they held immense power, barefoot generals commanding unregimented "armies" as obedient as the legions of Rome. An Obeah man—or woman—who held the power of life and death at his or her fingertips could stir things up plenty.

Phil read of Plato the Wizard, an Eighteenth-Century Obeah man in the parish of Westmoreland who grew too much out of control and was burned at the stake. Before dying, Plato cursed his jailer and swore he would be avenged by a terrible storm. Within a short period of time the jailer died and Jamaica was hit by the fiercest tempest ever to strike the West Indies, the Great Hurricane of October 3, 1780, followed by earthquakes that leveled every building—*in Westmoreland*.

Mitchell finished his reading and put the book up. As he left the library in an otherworldly daze, a warm breeze picked up.

A Jamaican will tell you that's a ghost.

165

23

Mitchell awoke on the couch with the TV going and his mind lit up. There had to be a rational explanation for this business with Scott Gallagher. Witchcraft and sorcery—what silliness. Had the kid gotten that far under his skin? He was a psychologist, grounded in science, trained to plumb the depths of the mind, not dabble in potions and magic.

It was almost, he tittered, as if he'd come under a spell. Of course there had to be a logical interpretation. If the kid knew about Marley at the time he was jogging a psychological sequencing of events might easily be invoked. No need for metaphysics to solve this riddle, but what was left— the workings of the human mind—was just as intriguing.

When morning came he backed the Porsche out and drove to town, scanning window fronts on State Street. He had a vague impression of a particular store being somewhere along this stretch of road.

There. Black Star Liner.

Phil pulled to the curb and switched on the emergency flasher. On display in the store behind glass streaked red, gold and green were exotic items like smoking pipes, carved wooden masks and a Che Guevara poster. Entering the head shop—named after the steamship line started by Marcus Mosiah Garvey to carry Africans of the Diaspora back to the Motherland— Phil made his way through a maze of dashikis, Rasta tams, reggae cassettes, hemp belts, tie-dye and Bob Marley T-shirts and "Black Power" trinkets. The expatriate Jamaican clerk was ringing up a young black woman in braids and Phil queued behind her. The woman left and the clerk, a dark-skinned man with a stubbly beard and complacent expression, studied his receipts.

Phil cleared his throat and the man looked up.

"May I help you?" the chap said.

"Do you know Bob Marley?" Phil asked.

The guy stared as if Mitchell were a simple-minded fool. He detected the smell of alcohol about the well-dressed stranger.

"Not personally," he said.

"I heard he collapsed while jogging back in September."

"You a reporter?"

Mitchell dug up his business card and handed it to him.

"'Philip Mitchell, Ph. D.,'" the fellow read, examining the card as if a relic from outer space, "'the Suites at Canon Perdido.' Mmm-hmmm."

"And you are?" Mitchell offering his hand.

"George," the man said, shaking Mitchell's hand with less than the enthusiasm of Stanley greeting Livingstone.

"No, I'm not a reporter, George. I've recently discovered Marley's music and wish to know more about his life."

"Uh-huh. Well yes, it true, him take ill while jogging in Central Park likkle while back. Sunday morning after Madison Square Garden concert with the Commodores. Wailers did one more show two days later in Pittsburgh. After that the entire tour was cancelled. Everybody wonder whether Bob catch sick or just nuff nuff tire out."

"What seems to be the verdict?"

"Only Jah know."

"What do you think?"

"Only know they take him to the cancer ward in New York."

"Sloan-Kettering?"

"Couple days later Bob gwan hospital down Miami somewhere."

"Cedars of Lebanon?"

"Maybe."

"Rumor is him get baptize round 'bout November."

"I see. Any speculation what type of cancer it would be, if indeed it were cancer?"

"Heard melanoma. From toe he injure playing football."

"A toe?"

"Big toe, right foot."

"Thank you very much. Call me if you hear anything, would you George?" Phil's mind was spinning fast as he exited, not hearing George's parting shot:

"Buy something next time, Mr. Big Man."

Phil felt back on his game. If Obeah, like Voodoo, could kill, it was the victim's *belief* in the power of the curse that did it. It was a psychological phenomenon, not metaphysical. Voodoo reportedly could stop a strong man's heart—*if* that heart feared the witchdoctor's magic. Had the power of belief, or suggestion, for want of a better term, caused Scott Gallagher to collapse that day at City College?

The mind could play tricks on the body, no doubt about that. Mitchell thought of Freud's turn-of-the-century Viennese housewives with their "hysteria neuroses"… repressed sexual energy producing symptoms of physical illness in the absence of underlying organic disorder. The classic glove anesthesia of conversion neurosis, in which a loss of feeling in the hand was anatomically impossible given the actual wiring of nerves, proving the syndrome was "all in the mind." Hysterical blindness without any physical damage to the optic system. Most dramatic of all, perhaps, was hysterical pregnancy, in which a woman might show all outward signs of being with child, from swollen belly to labor pains, even though her womb was empty. If the mind could weave fantasies like that it was certainly capable of making a sensitive kid pass out and fall flat on his face. Especially a kid given to dissociative episodes.

How to approach treatment? The kid's overarching—obsessive?—adulation of Bob Marley presented a ready handle. He identified himself so closely with the reggae star that there was no room for his own identity to emerge. Scott had to be led to see that Marley's virtues were projections of his own buried potentials so that he could take Bob "back inside" and reclaim those virtues as his own. If it wasn't too late. Jung spoke of the healing power of the unconscious but warned that if its voice was ignored—if the wisdom of dreams, intuitions and other unconscious manifestations was not heeded—the healing function was lost and the psyche actually became dangerous, even deadly. This seemed to fit the Gallagher kid to a T—deep symbolism surfacing everywhere but with little evidence of self-awareness or reassimilation of the psychic elements back into the personality. If that assessment was accurate, the kid was a walking powder keg with a lit fuse.

Still, the handle was there and for Phil Mitchell the germ-kernel of hope bloomed anew, nurtured by the sunlight of fresh understanding, hope that this case might turn things around and he would prove to himself and the world he could take an ailing soul and work healing magic, thereby substantiating his own life and being. That night he stood a long time out on the balcony gazing at the stars, clutching by the neck a cheap bottle of California red, the oil rigs glistening out in the Channel. They said an acid-tripping Jim Morrison wrote *Crystal Ship* watching Platform Grace twinkle kaleidoscopically one night such as this.

Not long before he died.

24

Joint in hand, Scott sat back and listened to the Saturday night Roots Riddim show with DJ Spliff on FM radio. Spliff was playing old school jams and Studio One gems from the 60's and 70's and was about to bring on his special guest for the evening.

"We're here tonight with Lester Bangs from *Cream* Magazine," Spliff said, "talking about Bob Marley, the man and the music. Lester, what's the latest on Bob's health?"

"Good question, Spliff," Bangs replied. "There seems to be a shroud of secrecy enveloping the whole situation. Bob put on a helluva show at the Garden back in September, but he appeared exhausted giving interviews. Really wasn't himself, often letting Tyrone or Family Man do the talking. When Bob did answer he seemed confused, unable to carry a thought through."

"Might've had a good buzz on," Spliff laughed.

"He's tired from touring, you idiots!" Scott raged.

"I understand you have a tape to play, Spliff."

"Indeed I do, Les. This is Bob speaking from the hospital after the Wailers' North American tour was canceled following the September 23rd show in Pittsburgh. That would be two days after Bob collapsed while jogging in Central Park. Listen."

Scott turned the volume up on the radio. The voice of Bob Marley issued across the airwaves:

"Hail, Rasta. You think anything can raas kill me? I understand that writers and people in the press are very interested and concerned about my health. I want to say thank you for your interest and that I'll be back on the road again in 1981 really performing for the fans we love. Beautiful, yunno? It's Bob talking to yuh, have no doubt. Seen? Good."

"Bob Marley talking shortly after he was hospitalized at New York's Sloan-Kettering Memorial Cancer Center," Spliff said, "with what has variously been described as exhaustion or something much worse. Gotta tell ya Lester, Bob sounds pretty perky there."

"Yes," agreed the feisty Bangs, "but if all this was simple exhaustion, why would Marley bounce around from Sloan-Kettering to Cedars of Lebanon in Miami and back again to Sloan-Kettering in New York? And what are these rumors about Bob checking in to this alternative New Age health clinic in Mexico where Steve McQueen went before his death? I don't like those tea leaves."

"Point taken, Lester. Now back to the music with Augustus Pablo and his magic melodica dubbing it on *East of the River Nile,* coming at you on the Roots Riddim show with I-man DJ Spliff."

Sucking nervously on his own spliff, Scott looked down at his bare right toe, suddenly throbbing. To his eye it appeared red and swollen. Seemed like he was always stubbing it. Was it a coincidence that he'd injured it the day after he tripped Marley playing football that day at the House of Dread? Bob had mildly aggravated the toe he'd mashed up the year before, but what Scott couldn't know was that Bob banged the toe again but good playing soccer against a pickup team of French journalists in Paris in May 1977, at the start of the European leg of the *Exodus* tour. Bob had taken a rough tackle from a guy wearing cleats, the toenail was torn off and wouldn't heal. A French doctor cut away a jagged remnant of toenail, dressed the wound and ordered Bob to stay off his feet, but Marley was having none of that—cancel a major tour over a toenail? *The Tuff Gong?* The show went on and every night after electrifying performances before packed houses Bob would limp backstage and find his right sock drenched with blood. After the tour wrapped up an assistant to Chris Blackwell took Bob to see a doctor in London. The date was July 7, 1977....

169

They shall not make baldness on their head
Neither shall they shave off the corner of their beard
Nor make any cuttings in their flesh

--Leviticus 21: 5

The Rastafarian community in Jamaica was in a state of frenzy. The prophesized fall of Babylon was nigh. In Revelations, St. John had foretold of the inevitability of the final Apocalypse, when the seven angels would unleash the seven plagues. Joseph Hill, a devout Rastafarian and lead singer of Culture, had recently released a record entitled *Two Sevens Clash*, a clear allusion to scriptural unfolding. Since at least the time of Pythagoras, numbers had possessed mythical status, the number seven in particular symbolizing perfection and eternity. And now it was 7/7/77.

In Kingston, the Security Forces were on maximum alert. Streets were deserted of rich and poor. Rastas had held intense Grounation reasonings of late to consider the prophecies and examine the signs and now the day was come.

Four thousand miles away on this day of imminent catastrophe, Bob Marley limped into a London doctor's office to have his injured toe examined. The doctor took one look at the festering digit and immediately ordered a scraping for microscopic examination. He wasn't pleased at what he found.

"Mr. Marley, there are cancer cells on your slide."

"What say?"

"I examined the scraping from your toe under the microscope—"

"Uh huh."

"—and there are cancer cells in your toe."

"Does that mean I have cancer?" Bob so shocked he used proper Queen's English.

"I'm afraid so. The toe should be amputated as a matter of highest priority. We'll have to take some of the foot as well to make sure we get all the diseased cells."

"Nuh blade shall cut the flesh of Rasta," Bob scowled. Such radical surgery was against his religious beliefs. Cutting of flesh and hair was prohibited in the scriptures... besides, how could he sing and dance on stage with a big hunk of his foot whacked off?

"In the interest of your health," the doctor advised, "I urge you to reconsider."

Marley limped out cursing the doctor's blasphemy. Someone from Island Records called back seeking clarification of options; with the *Exodus* album poised for great success no one wanted to see the booked-out North American leg of the tour cancelled.

170

There was one alternative to amputation, but it was a long shot: cutting away a small part of the toe, cleaning the wound and treating the infection. Bob would have to stay off his feet for six months. But there would be a considerable risk that all the cancer wasn't removed.

And the amputation?

A much shorter convalescent period of only one month would be required. Bob would never be quite as nimble on stage again, but at least he could get up there and sing and the tour could go on. People who had money riding on the tour pressured Bob to go with the amputation.

In the end, Bob's Rastafarian beliefs held and he refused the amputation. He flew to Miami to consult with a black orthopedic surgeon, Dr. William Bacon, who performed a skin graft on the toe. The North American tour was postponed until the fall. Bob, down and out for one of the very few times in his life, called his mother. Mother B was disturbed at the anguish in her son's voice.

Why Jah Jah let me have cancer, momma? he beseeched her. It was not a question even the wisdom of motherhood could answer. Marley flew to Miami to recuperate in the home he had bought for his mother there.

25

January 1981, Santa Barbara

Arriving at Dr. Mitchell's office for session, Scott noticed on the wall a group portrait hanging among the individual shots of Freud and the rest. The portrait obviously had some history about it, capturing some bygone era, perhaps around the turn of the century. It showed an assemblage of several dozen quaintly dressed persons, mostly males full of themselves, preening peacocks in suits and ties posing for the camera.

"Ah yes," Mitchell said, looking on with his patient. "Twentieth anniversary celebration at Clark University, 1909. Freud and Jung bringing psychoanalysis to the New World. Here they are front and center, at the height of their powers, still close friends. Adler here. Otto Rank, Sandor Ferenczi. American pragmatist William James. Frau Jung. Jung's mistress Toni Wolff close by."

"Man had skills. Juggling squeeze and old lady like that."

"Come in, sit."

Scott mentioned his date with Suzette.

"How was it?" Phil asked, morning sunlight streaming in the window behind the desk.

"Good and bad. She stayed the night."

"That would be the good."

"A few anxious moments along the way but turned out okay."

"And the bad?"

"Kinda pushed her away. Started feeling uncomfortable. Cramped. Couldn't breathe."

"What turned you off?"

"I don't know, man. Got a bad feeling about all this anyway."

"About all what?"

"This talking stuff." Scott shook his head woefully. "What does it mean to believe in yourself, Doc? I mean, how do you do it if you're not doing it already? How do you believe something you don't believe?"

"You have to do the work. Clear the soil and the tree will grow. That's what this business is all about. Digging up weeds."

"Sounds so easy."

"On the other hand the Buddhists say there is no self to believe in. It's all an illusion that separates us from the momentary flow of life."

"Now I'm really confused."

"Your first appointment was October 5th, was it not?"

"Sounds about right."

"You were admitted to the hospital two weeks prior... Sunday the 21st, is that correct?"

"Could be."

"What else happened that day?"

"What day?"

"Sunday the twenty-first."

"Nothing. What do you mean what happened?"

"Something important."

"Hell if I know." Scott fidgeted in his seat.

"Bob Marley collapsed in Central Park."

"Oh, that."

"Same day you fell and banged yourself up at City College."

"Was it? I wouldn't know."

"Why did you go jogging that day?"

"Rasta stays fit."

"But why twice in one day, the first and only time you ever did that? Did you hear about Bob *before* you left the house?"

"Why do I feel like I'm being cross-examined? Suppose that makes me paranoid."

"It must have been on your mind. *Something* drove you out there again."

"What exactly are you getting at?" Scott snapped.

Mitchell sat quietly, letting his patient see it for himself.

"You're saying I fell on my face to be like Bob Marley?" Scott said and immediately winced in pain.

"What's wrong?" Mitchell asked.

"Boot's a little tight around the toes."

"The toe you hurt playing soccer in Jamaica. Big toe, right foot. Same as Bob."

"Here we go again," Scott rolled his eyes to the ceiling and folded his arms across his chest.

"You worry you might have cancer."

"What a morbid thing to say."

"Your mother had it and now maybe Bob."

Scott exploded out of his seat so abruptly it startled Mitchell, who'd seen a similar reaction in this patient before.

"Nuthing can kill Bob Marley, fool!" he bellowed in angry patois. "Man a lion, y'hear? Protected by His Imperial Majesty Haile Selassie the First. Me cyan't abide this rubbish talk. Cancer nah kill Bob Marley."

"Sit down, please."

"I-man finish with this raasclot foolishness." Utterly indignant, Scott limped heavily toward the door, favoring his right foot, whereas he earlier had walked into the office quite normally.

"We're coming along nicely here," Mitchell said. "This is important material."

"Fuck off, yuh bloodclot Babylon vampyah."

"Wait. Don't go. *Please.*"

Scott froze. *Please?* Dr. M never said *please.* The man was begging. An intoxicating sense of power and control washed over him.

"We are onto something important here," Mitchell said, nervously lighting a cigarette.

"I'll stay on one condition," Scott's patois replaced by the crisp enunciation of a courtroom lawyer.

"Condition?"

"You smoke ganja with me."

"Impossible."

Mitchell flushed hot. If patient walked out that door, odds were good he would never return, just as they'd stumbled upon a breakthrough. The alternative was unthinkable—violating all professional ethics and giving in to patient's rude request. Smoking pot like some aimless ragamuffin? Dr. Philip Mitchell was no anti-establishment rebel. There was no choice but to let the kid walk out the damn door and to hell with him. Just when he'd gotten a handle on things. Would he forever botch things up?

"I can't smoke marijuana with you," Mitchell said.

"*Won't,* you mean."

"All right, won't. I'm not a goddamn hippy."

"Pussy. I'm out of here."

"You can't expect me to... you mean *right now? Here?*"

"This exact minute." Scott easing back into the room.

"Where would we go?"

"We'd sit right here on our fat babushkas."

"You have it on you?"

Scott reached into a pocket and pulled out a baggie containing two rolled joints. He yanked off his Rasta tam and flung out his locks.

"No no no, we can't... not a good idea." Mitchell dragging heavily on his cigarette.

"And you call *me* paranoid? Lighter."

"I didn't call you paranoid."

"I need your lighter. Mine's out."

Phil handed over his cigarette lighter. At this point, what could it hurt?

"Good Sinsemilla herb," Scott proclaimed. "Alcohol kill ya, herb build ya."

"Will it make me talk like a Rasta?" Mitchell joked nervously. Scott torched the joint and hit it hard before passing to Dr. M.

"Lick it, man."

Mitchell took the joint and studied it a moment, scrunched up his face, sighed, took a safe small hit and coughed out a tiny plume of smoke.

"Hold it in, Mitch baby."

"That's *Doctor* Mitch baby to you." Phil took another wimpy hit and coughed it out.

"Healing of the nation," Scott said. "Feel anything?"

"Not really."

"Lick it again."

Phil took a deeper blast and held a few seconds before rasping it out. A load seemed to lift from his shoulders, his whole posture loosening.

"How do you feel?" Scott asked.

"Heavy. Tingly. A little paralyzed."

"Your body's relaxing, man. Let the magic fumes part the veil of ignorance and take you to the balmy shores of Truthsylvania. Say that five times fast."

"Next door to Bullshitville, isn't it?"

"Herb reveal truth, man."

"So how do *you* feel?"

"Mellow yellow."

"Maybe mellow isn't always good. If it keeps you from getting out there and taking a risk."

"See there? Ideas popping out of you left and right. Bottle that shit and sell it, Doc Man."

They sat silently a few moments, puddle-hopping from one mind space to another, exotic new worlds bursting into consciousness like wormholes to secret universes.

"Why didn't you go backstage to talk to Bob when he was in town?" Mitchell asked. "There has to be a reason."

"I told you before--" Scott paused as a quizzical expression flooded over his face.

"Simon Bolivar was in exile in Jamaica," he said, as if tapping a font of forgotten knowledge. "Wrote an important document on the Rock. Did you hear what I said, Doc?"

"Not really," Mitchell flashed a rascally grin.

"Don't go spacey on me, man."

"Simon Bolivar."

"Yeah."

"Anything occur to you about that?"

"There's a statue in Kingston. Near Heroes Circle."

"Did something happen there... besides birds shitting on it?"

"Good one, Doc. Diggin' deep."

"Shall we put him on the board?"

Scott studied the whiteboard a moment, grabbed the pen and to the list on the left side of the board wrote *Simon Bolivar* below the name of *Marva.*

"We're getting somewhere now," Mitchell said.

"Yeah, nowhere, fast."

"What about Jesse James? You turned tables and had him follow your father. What came of it?"

"Got a bad feeling about that too."

"We'll dig it out. Want some pizza? I'm in the mood for pizza. The works okay? Suppose you're vegetarian."

"The munchies strike again."

Mitchell picked up the phone and buzzed Jasmine.

"Jazz honey, call down to Gina's and order a large vegetarian pizza, would you please. Have them deliver—"

"Whole wheat," Scott said.

"What's that?" Mitchell cupped the phone with his hand.

"Whole wheat crust."

"See if they have whole wheat crust. People eat that kind of thing, I guess. Captain Midnight, over and out."

Mitchell hung up to see Scott psychologically undressing him with his eyes.

"When I was young," Scott said. "What's it mean, Doc? Talk to me. Your Eric Burdon song."

"Nothing. Doesn't mean nothing."

"Times were hard, cold. Your father was in the army--"

"—Navy."

"The navy, and times were tough. You learned a lot. You were a likkle bwoy and wild shit was going down. Crazy wild shit. Laughter, pain, the whole shot."

"Sometimes a cigar is just a cigar," Phil said, folding his arms across his chest defiantly, not relishing being in the hot seat.

"Or a joint," Scott producing the second marijuana cigarette. "Talk to me, man."

Phil turned to the window, gazing out to distant nothingness, all silliness and frivolity dissipating into the ether.

"Your faith was stronger then, was it?" Scott kept pushing. "That's what the song says. How's it go—your faith was stronger, you believed in your fellow man. You were older then somehow. You had it going on and blew it. Talk to me."

Phil sank deep into silent contemplation, as if his defenses had been compromised and he'd retreated to a last refuge of shell-shocked denial. Scott squirmed, the mood suddenly thick and oppressive.

"My father was at Pearl Harbor," Mitchell said finally.

"Yes yes." Scott not immediately catching on.

"He's still there."

"Still where?"

"Went down on the Arizona."

Fuck, Scott cringed under his breath as Phil stared into the distant past. After a long awkward interlude of silence Scott fell back on the wisdom of Bob Marley.

"Come on, Doc," he said, springing up and bouncing about like Marley in all his free-wheeling elan. "Bob says to get up and dance away your sorrows and if anybody knows what he's talking about it's the Skipper. The Soul Rebel. Be a revolutionary spirit, a rebel like Bob, yunno? Don't be no stuffed shirt, man. Sing and dance and everything gwine be all right. Forget the bullshit, ya dig? Come on, Mitch. It's soul rebel time."

Mitchell remained seated and somber. There came a rapping at the door.

"Pizza for Captain Midnight," Jasmine called. Scott intercepted her at the door and took pizza, paper plates and a tall bottle of 7-Up from her.

"Everything all right?" she asked, trying to peek past Scott as he interposed himself to block her view.

"Absolutely. Love your hair." A flattered smile came to her lips and she self-consciously patted her coif as Scott closed the door in her face.

"Pizza," he announced.

Mitchell was staring out the window in a funk.

"I've behaved disgracefully," he said, shaking his head sadly. "Smoking marijuana with a patient... I'm a professional."

"You *were.* Just kidding."

"I've lost my authority... your respect."

"I respect you more now than ever."

Phil turned forward in his chair. "Respect doesn't come from here," he said, tapping his forehead. "It comes from down here in your gut. Like your fascination with Bob Marley. It isn't something you do intentionally. Of course you didn't go jogging planning to throw a fit and fall on your face. This stuff comes out of your core, your center, your unconscious mind. That's why we've got to dig in."

"So dig."

Mitchell glanced at Scott's T-shirt, the silk-screened image of Bob with dreadlocks flying, and sudden inspiration came to him.

"What color was your mother's hair?" he asked.

"What?"

"Just out of curiosity."

"Don't remember. I was six years old."

"Thought you said seven."

"Six, seven, what difference does it make?"

"It was black, wasn't it. Long and black like Bob's."

"It was blonde."

"Just said you don't remember."

"Why yuh wanna play this shit, man?"

"I know you can see her in your mind."

"You don't know what's in your own fucking mind."

Phil held his tongue lest he speak harshly and regret it later. He tried the pizza.

"I hope an Obeah man did put a curse on me," Scott said in remorse, his pleasant buzz derailed. "Otherwise I'm really fucked up."

"You're not fucked up. We are as we are for perfectly good reasons. And it isn't about ghosts."

"I had the inside track with a great gal and I blew it. That's fucked. Probably do the same thing all over. Sabotage myself again and again and again."

"Go back to your Simon Bolivar. The Liberator, 'he who brings liberty and freedom.' What does that mean to you? First thing that comes to mind."

"Escape."

"From what?"

"The past."

"Escape is not an option. We gotta grow through it and come out the other side."

"What do I do, Doc?"

"Be a rebel. Soul rebel."

"How?"

177

"By being your authentic self."

"How the hell do you do that?"

"Dig and reflect sometimes. Live in the moment the rest. Like Bob says, dance away your sorrow. Pizza's really good. Oughta try some."

Scott bit into a juicy, indulgent, tomato-cheesy, hardly I-tal slice of pizza.

"That is good," he said.

26

September 1976, Kingston

Bob Marley sat barefoot on the porch at Hope Road strumming his Gibson Les Paul as binoculars were trained on him in the observation post across the street. Trained in also was a new eavesdropping device that bounced an infra-red beam off a front window and back to receiving equipment in the post. The beam picked up voice vibrations from inside the house and carried them back to be decoded. This new bugging method wasn't working very well either, as music was always blasting mega decibels and the house was invariably full of people chatting heavy patois.

As Marley strummed, a grand idea floated around his mind. The last two years the Wailers had played benefit concerts in Kingston with Stevie Wonder and Marvin Gaye. Peter and Bunny had even come out for Stevie, reuniting the original trio for one last glorious evening for the cause, a local school for the blind. Music put in service to the greater good.

Maybe something like this could be done again, Marley reasoned, a free concert to help chill out the violence and bring the people together.

Marley hollered to the house. "Where Don Taylor? I and I must talk."

Diane Jobson, Island Records' in-house lawyer, got on the phone and an hour later Taylor's Datsun pulled into the property (duly noted in the surveillance log across the street). Out stepped a neatly-dressed black Jamaican, short-haired, presentable, toothy as Alvin the Chipmunk. A man who carried himself with the bravado of one who had fought his way up from humble beginnings. Don Taylor had hustled his entire life, as a boy diving for coins tossed by tourists from cruise ships, later as a young man pandering to foreigners on port call seeking the wet and wild. Finally catching on as valet for Anthony Gourdine of Little Anthony and the Imperials. By 1974, when Marvin Gaye came to town for the benefit concert at the Caribe Theatre, Taylor had finagled his way into a job as personal assistant to the R 'n B icon. He'd made it to the bigtime.

"Don Taylor," Marley hailed, "me wan' do concert in town fe Christmas. Cool everything out."

"Sounds good. Could be quite profitable."

"Raasclot Don Taylor, yuh bloodsucker. Me nah wan' scrape money off poor Jamaican back. I-man play fe the people and bring the country together."

"A free concert… okay, I see where you're coming from. Do you have a venue in mind?"

"Somewhere everyone a come together in peace, rich, poor, black, white, Chinee."

"Maybe the government could sponsor it. A real people's concert."

"Cyan't be about politics. JLP, PNP must stay out."

"Shall we run it by Manley?"

Jobson rang up the prime minister's office and handed the phone out the window to Bob.

"Bob Marley a call fe Michael Manley."

"Just a moment, sir," the female voice on the other end of the line said.

"This is Michael Manley," the PM came on. "That you, Bob?"

"Yes suh, is Bob speaking. Me nah wan' disturb yuh work there."

"Always time for you, Skip, what can I do for you?"

"I and I wan' make Christmas concert fe the people. Cool things out a likkle."

"Wonderful idea. Why don't you come over and we'll talk."

Bob laced on shoes and he and Taylor drove over to Jamaica House. The guard at the Hope Road gate waved them in and they proceeded up the grand entryway. Beefy security personnel at the front door patted them down and they ascended the leftmost of the two semi-circular red-carpeted staircases, past the Queen and Prince Philip, to the second floor.

"Why hello, Mr. Marley," exclaimed Miss Cathy Gilchrist, a charming young woman with caramel skin and "good" hair, her eyes dancing at the sight of the sexy reggae star. Gilchrist was Manley's personal assistant and traveled with him on overseas junkets.

Marley, ever the ladies' man, winked and smiled.

"The prime minister is on the phone with the president of Mexico," Gilchrist bubbled. "He'll be with you in one moment. Sit down, please."

Seconds later Manley appeared, greeted the two men warmly and ushered them into his upstairs office.

"Sit down, make yourself comfortable," he said. "Tell me all about your wonderful plan. A free concert to bring the people together, splendid."

"Christmas morning to make the spirit right," Marley said.

"Mr. Prime Minister," Taylor broke in, "we—"

"Please, call me Michael."

"Mr. Michael, sir," Taylor went on, "since it's a free concert, could the government help a likkle? Maybe oversee security, cut the overhead."

"That might be arranged," Manley said.

179

"Cyan't be 'bout politics," Marley stated forcefully. "Haffi keep PNP, JLP and this 'n that outta the thing… haffi neutral."

"Let's bring Arnold in on this." Manley had Miss Gilchrist summon Arnold Bertram, the minister of state, whose office was in a bungalow behind the main building. Bertram arrived shortly in Levi cords and sport shirt and Manley introduced him around. Gilchrist came in bearing a tea tray and set it on the small wooden table. She beamed a radiant smile at Bob on her way out.

"Bob wants to do a free concert, Arnie," Manley said. "How's Christmas morning?"

Bertram checked his date book, made a couple calls to his secretary, hummed and hawed and scratched his head and lo and behold, came up with a date.

"December 5 looks like the best bet," he said.

"Sunday, December 5th," said Manley. "Shall we go with that?"

Marley nodded and enthusiastic handshakes followed. The Smile Jamaica concert was on.

When Chris Blackwell learned of Marley's plan to do a free concert, he flew in from Nassau in his private plane to discuss the matter with Bob. Blackwell had strong reservations about doing the gig with elections coming up and he wasn't the only one. Heavy JLP people were trying to muscle Marley into canceling the event. Claudie Massop, the don of Tivoli Gardens, sent word from his jail cell that a lot of people would be upset if the concert went on as planned. *Very* upset.

Born a son to a rum fortune and properly educated at Harrow's in London—until kicked out for peddling booze and cigarettes to classmates—Blackwell had formed Island Records in the early '60s and though in those days they hadn't met had released some of Bob's first singles under license from Leslie Kong's Beverley Records. After early struggles, Island found financial footing in 1964 with the international ska smash *My Boy Lollipop* by teen wonder Millie Small, a Jamaican girl from Clarendon variously said to be anywhere from 14 to 18 years old.

In winter 1971 a trio of down-on-their-luck rudeboys from Kingston showed up in Blackwell's London office. Despite releasing huge Jamaican hits like *Simmer Down* and *Trench Town Rock*, Bob, Peter and Bunny had been unable to break into the lucrative US and UK markets and had nothing in their pockets to show for their efforts. They were under contract to Johnny Nash's company JAD and that too was going nowhere. Johnny Nash might have been seeing clearly now but the three rudies couldn't see past their next meal.

Warned that these hooligans would take the money and run, Blackwell—who'd dabbled as a professional gambler—knew a good bet when he saw one. Going with his instincts, he gave them 4000 English pounds to make an album. The three Johnny-Too-Bads returned to Kingston and in six months had crafted one of the great albums of all time, *Catch A Fire*. One boggles at the thought that had it not been for Millie Small and her infectious little multi-platinum *Lollipop* that kept Island Records from going under, the world may never have come to know the music of Bob Marley as it did.

Blackwell checked into the Sheraton and took a taxi over to Hope Road. Bob had been spending most nights lately with Rita and the kids out at Bull Bay, as Cindy Breakespeare was in London preparing for the Miss World competition—Bob was footing the bill—but he came back to the yard everyday for rehearsals and to hang with the crew. Blackwell and Marley sat in the shade of a mango tree out back, the Island top dog casual as usual in shorts and Hawaiian shirt. Tom Jones-handsome with wavy black hair, Blackwell looked like a Welsh sea captain.

"This Taylor's idea?" asked Blackwell, who wasn't the shifty Taylor's biggest fan. The story went that DT had shown up at the House of Dread on the Marvin Gaye tour and awakened Bob from a sound sleep to make his pitch to be Wailers' manager. His chutzpah impressed Bob but Blackwell didn't trust him a plug nickel.

"Is I come with it," Marley said.

"I don't like it, Skip. People are going to think you are shilling for the PNP. That's dangerous, man."

Blackwell leaned forward and lowered his voice. "Something I have to tell you. I was summoned to the US Embassy to meet with Ambassador Gerard. He said they were watching me. You too."

"Bloodclot!" Marley roared. "Them a damn fool."

"Be careful, Bob. This is Cold War politics. Jamaica has been elevated to the world's stage and is under the spotlight. Like it or not this is the United States' backyard and they don't abide anyone making waves. These are dangerous times. Wouldn't do the show if it was up to me. I'd cancel as fast as possible."

"Show must go forward," Marley said. "Cyan't worry 'bout them hypocrite."

"Then be sure the PNP stays out of it. At least do that much. Keep it as neutral as possible."

"So me think too. Haffi neutral."

"It's a magnificent gesture, Skip. I'm proud as hell of you."

"The killing must stop. If I-man can play music and chill things out, me love fe do that. One love, yunno?"

Word came that the show was scheduled for the lawn at Jamaica House, infuriating JLP cadres even further. Rita had a disturbing dream and begged Bob to go to Manley and change the venue. Manley agreed and

Smile Jamaica was rescheduled for National Heroes Circle Park. Same date, December 5, 1976.

In the breakfast room at Jamaica House, an agitated Michael Manley paced the floor in bathrobe and slippers, a sheath of handwritten notes in his hand. That night he was to address the PNP annual convention and wanted to include something for all factions of the party, not least of all the leftwing, which ever since the IMF-World Bank conference in January had been on high alert. Taking IMF or Bank loans, they feared, would mean the devil to pay: devaluation of the Jamaican dollar, crushing cutbacks in social expenditures, higher unemployment, more suffering. It would be a turning back on everything the party stood for—a selling out to the highest bidder.

"'We were trapped in a world system we call imperialism and a local system we call capitalism,'" Manley read from his notes. "'We realized there could be no change in this country unless we were prepared to change the system.'"

He stopped and looked to his wife. "Shoot, I say system three times. What do you think, Bev?"

"Sit down and eat your breakfast while it's hot," Beverley Manley said, shaking Pick-a-peppa sauce onto her calaloo and cabbage.

"I've got to get this right. There'll be twenty thousand people hanging on my every word tonight."

"Mike, you are the most stirring speaker this part of the world has ever seen. You'll be fine. Just cool, man."

"The people are suffering and depending on me to ease their pain. I'm the one who has to deliver the bad news that more hard times are on the way, maybe the worst yet. It all comes down on me."

"Tell it straight. Suffering is hardest when we're alone. Shared misery in the name of a cause is easier to stomach. Now eat."

"You're right as usual," Manley sat in the breakfast nook with his wife.

"What about the Rod?" Bev asked.

"Tonight? The Rod of Correction?"

"The people are dying for it to come out. Been four years now since they've seen it."

"Maybe I'll let it simmer a little longer."

That night, Manley and Bev drove to the National Arena, the nanny along to help with Natasha. The place was already standing room only and party faithful kept coming like it was games day at the Roman Colosseum. The decision was made to move across the street to the larger National Stadium, where three years earlier George Foreman had won the heavyweight championship by knocking Smokin' Joe Frazier into the middle of next week with a thundering right hand.

Like a shepherd tending his flock of thousands, Manley led the masses out the Arena and over to the Stadium. Bev walked along beside as the nanny carried Natasha.

"Any trick to addressing a crowd that surrounds you, Bev?" Manley sought last-minute counsel.

"Keep turning to include everybody. Think theater-in-the-round. Don't forget this." From a bolt of fine cloth she unraveled the Rod of Correction.

"You brought the Rod!" Manley cried, stopping in his tracks.

"If the spirit moves you." She slapped the near-sacred artifact into Michael's palm.

Watching from the shadows as the huge procession paraded past were Matt Gallagher, Frank Lake and Freddy McGinnis.

"What in God's name is wrong with these people?" Gallagher scowled. "Do they *want* to live in communist hell?"

"Maybe they just agree with Manley's policies," McGinnis said.

"Maybe you're in the wrong line of work," Matt snapped, glaring hard. McGinnis took no offense as he had been thinking the very thing himself, the massacre on Orange Street having raised grave doubts in his mind about the moral rectitude of Agency operations in Jamaica.

"He's got a point, Matt," said Lake, who'd been bending over backwards to be civil to McGinnis ever since their run-in at the nightclub. "We've got to work harder. PNP crowds are five to ten times the size of JLP rallies."

"Balls," Gallagher grunted.

Before a jubilant Stadium crowd of 40,000 strong, Manley exhorted his fellow Jamaicans to take strength in their shared struggle. Alluding to pressures to accept IMF and World Bank funds, Manley cast a poignant glance to Bev and D. K. Duncan and cried out words he knew would appease the party's leftwing:

"We are not for sale!"

The crowd roared and stomped its approval. When Manley brought out the Rod of Correction and waved it about like a wizard's magic wand, the huge throng broke into an ecstatic frenzy that shook the stadium to its pilings. Manley swelled with hope—the dream was very much alive. Much could be accomplished given four more years and if the New International Economic Order he championed were pushed through it would mark the start of a bright new day for the Third World. He didn't know that two fists were set in motion, one of iron and the other of steel, and that one of those fists was swinging for him.

September 9. Arch assassin Michael Townley flew in to JFK from Santiago on a Chilean passport in the name of Hans Petersen Silva. The thirty-four-year-old native of Waterloo, Iowa met with Condor-affiliated Cuban exiles and in the company of Virgilio Paz moved on to Washington and checked into a Holiday Inn. A DINA (Chilean secret police) surveillance team had jetted in two weeks earlier to gather reconnaissance but MT would spend a week conducting his own.

Target: Orlando Letelier, former Chilean ambassador to the United States and outspoken critic of the Pinochet regime. A tireless lobbyist against military aid to Chile, he'd spent a year in concentration camps after Pinochet's lackeys stormed La Moneda, the presidential palace in Santiago, on 9/11/73 and machine-gunned Salvador Allende to death. Now involuntarily exiled from Chile, Letelier worked at the Institute for Policy Studies in Washington and resided in nearby Bethesda, Maryland.

Townley, Paz and Dionisio "Pool of Blood" Suarez prepared a bomb in an eight-inch-square aluminum baking tin with TNT, C-4 and components purchased at Sears and Radio Shack. Townley was good with bombs, planting them under cars his forte, like the one that had blown General Prats and his wife to kingdom come in Buenos Aires.

September 19. Three two-man hit teams of Cuban exiles departed Caracas on a commercial jetliner bound for Miami. The six assassins had been handpicked by Luis Posada from his best men. From Miami the three teams would fly the following day to Toronto, where a DISIP (Venezuelan secret police) team had arrived weeks before to conduct reconnaissance and secure weapons—high-powered rifles with scopes for the snipers, handguns for the backup teams who would mingle in the crowd and shoot and run if the snipers missed their mark. Target: Michael Manley, Prime Minister of Jamaica.

The planned assassination of Fidel Castro while traveling to Angola had been busted up inside Cuba. It had seemed a good chance but plots against Castro came a dime a dozen. Freed of that chore, Posada thought at the last minute to insert himself as triggerman on Toronto Team 1, but was dissuaded by the need to plan for an even bigger action scheduled for October.

Shortly after midnight on the morning of the 19th, Townley, Paz and Suarez drove to Bethesda in Paz' Volvo. Townley, whom General Contreras had promoted to the nominal rank of major after the Prats hit, got out and walked up a cul-de-sac to the Letelier family home. In the driveway was Orlando's Chevrolet Malibu Classic, which others in the family often used, seventeen-year-old Francisco having driven his date to the prom in it. Townley crawled under the Chevy and attached the bomb to the cross

184

member with black electrical tape. The arch assassin threw the safety switch to "hot" and walked back down the cul-de-sac to Paz and Suarez, waiting in the Volvo.

September 21. Beverley Manley laced on jogging shoes and joined her husband on his early morning run around the reservoir. A girl had to watch her shape, especially with a ladies' man like Mike. Besides, she wanted to spend time with her husband before he left for Toronto. And when they did go out—even for a jog around the reservoir—they made sure that Natasha would be cared for if something happened to either or, God forbid, both of them.

After their run, Manley packed his bags for tomorrow's flight to Toronto. He invited Bev along, knowing she would be flattered but would almost certainly opt to stay home with Natasha. He much preferred it that way—and had his reasons.

On the TV was news out of Washington... something about an explosion on Embassy Row....

Orlando Letelier was running late that morning and wasn't ready when Michael and Ronni Moffitt, fellow employees at the Institute for Policy Studies, arrived in his car to pick him up for work. Letelier had loaned the Chevy to the Moffitts the previous evening when their car experienced mechanical problems. Michael and Ronni, newlyweds of four months, were passionate about working alongside people like Orlando for democracy in Chile, three years now under Pinochet's brutal military dictatorship. Letelier kissed his wife Isabel goodbye and they set out at 9:15. Michael sat in the back while Ronni rode shotgun. The day was drizzly gray.

As they passed the nearby Roy Rogers Restaurant, a late-model gray car pulled in behind the Malibu; in the car were Virgilio Paz and Dionsio "Pool of Blood" Suarez. On the front seat was Townley's homemade detonating device plugged in to the cigarette lighter.

By 9:30 a.m. they were in Washington. As they reached Sheridan Circle off Massachusetts Avenue, commonly known as Embassy Row, Paz and Suarez threw the switch on Mother Theresa's bomb.

Inside the Chevy, Michael Moffitt noticed a hissing sound, followed immediately by a flash of light over his wife's head. Then came the awful explosion.

The force of the blast launched the car off the ground. Letelier's legs were severed and he died almost instantly. A fragment of metal ripped open Ronni Moffitt's throat and she staggered to the curb. Michael Moffitt, shaken but not seriously hurt in the back seat, rushed to his wife and discovered to his horror that she was bleeding profusely and going into

185

convulsions. She choked to death on her own blood. She was 25 years old. Orlando Letelier was survived by his wife and four sons.

Joan Baez sang at the memorial service for Orlando and Ronni the following Sunday. George McGovern, Eugene McCarthy and Salvador Allende's widow and daughter were among those in attendance. Baez' choice of Violeta Parra's hauntingly beautiful *Gracias a la Vida (Thanks Be to Life)* was particularly poignant, for Letelier was remembered as a warmhearted man who loved to sing and dance and brought smiles to the faces of those who knew him.

Michael Townley promptly buried the identity of Hans Petersen Silva and returned to Chile on a US passport under the name Kenneth Enyart. The CIA under George Bush the Elder acted quickly to deny the Pinochet regime's culpability and the North American mainstream media uncritically reported the pap they'd been fed. Some have said an extensive network of right-wing journalists, codenamed Operation Mockingbird, was established after World War II through which history could be whitewashed even as it was being reported. Then again it may not have been necessary, given the ease with which sycophantic commentators swallowed the official line, the Woodwards, Bernsteins and Seymour Hershes few and far between.

The Condor directorate was ecstatic. They had assassinated a top diplomat and an American citizen in a spectacular car bombing one mile from the White House and were being given a free pass. There was nothing to stop them from planning even more daunting strikes.

"Now that our organization is in good standing after the Letelier job, we are going to try to do a few other things."—Orlando Bosch, from intelligence document submitted to Henry Kissinger, September 1976.

September 23. Michael Manley stared out over the ebony faces of the many Jamaican expatriates gathered in the large city square. *Torontonians*, people living in Toronto were called. Emigrating to the States, Canada or UK was almost a rite of passage for Jamaicans; thousands jumped the pond every year seeking work to feed their families back on the Rock. Pickneys left behind "a yard" grew up with one parent or aunty or grandma. If work came there'd be money for school uniforms and shoes; if times were good for lunch too. But times were seldom good. Bob Marley, Rita and Bob's mother had all gone this route. Some stayed and never went back.

The energy pulsing from the throng was electric. These were the moments Michael really came alive—he was at his most inspirational in front of a large audience, rallying the troops, sounding the battle cry: *Forward!* Smiling at him from the wings was Cathy Gilchrist, his traveling secretary, in whose embrace he'd spent the night. Quite a few nights, in fact, over the last several months. A beauty she was, with her caramel skin and ripe breasts.

Reggae tunes blared out over the PA, rendering a homey Caribbean feel. As the music died away and Manley stepped to the mic feeling safe and secure, there came a sudden breeze and with it the thought how easy it would be for someone out there with a rifle and scope to blow him away. He glanced again at Cathy and his fear subsided as it always did when she was near. Nobody, not even Bev, understood the tremendous pressure he was under, people's lives and the very survival of the nation hanging on his every move. He was feeling it from all quarters and the weight all came down on him. He was the loneliest man in the world and nothing lightened his burden for a few precious moments like Cathy's firm young flesh. No wife would understand that.

Manley's speech went off without a hitch. The assassins who had come for him had never gotten out of the airport: Six known anti-Castro Cuban exiles arriving en masse sent up all kinds of red flags with Canadian Customs. When word got back to the CIA, the bosses got cold feet and called the whole thing off. Manley, like a cat, had escaped with another of his charmed lives. Before the end of the year, his luck would be tested again.

On the upstairs balcony at Jamaica House, Bev Manley sat in the last rays of daylight and finished her reading assignment for her class in West Indian Lit at UWI. She gazed languorously over the wooded grounds that had once been part of King's House, the colonial governor-general's estate. Her imprint on these grounds was significant--a community vegetable garden there just beyond the roses; a basic school intended as a model for the educational system, which Lord knows needed improvement; a day-care center and "pocket park" for children (inspired by the First Lady of Venezuela, Senora Perez). Beverley hadn't come to Jamaica House to sit around putting on airs. Jamaicans pulling together could accomplish great things. Like her husband, Bev never gave up hope. God was merciful and surely saw it was time that African peoples got a square deal in life.

She got up to raid the fridge for a bowl of Cuban ice cream—Fidel had been sending over buckets of the delicious treat since last year's state visit to Cuba (Michael and Bev reciprocating with cases of Pick-a-peppa sauce).

A phone call came in on the private home line.

"Hello, Mike?" she answered.

"Where Manley?" a man's voice said.

"Who's calling, please?"

"Manley up there a Toronto… with a woman."

"*What?* What did you say?"

"Manley love young pussy, yunno."

187

"Bloodclot!" Bev screamed in patois. "Take yuh fucking bumboclot and never call here again!"

Beverley slammed the phone down, gasped for air. Knowing it was the absolute worst thing to do, she got on the phone to Toronto.

"Hotel Alouette," the man answered.

"Michael Manley, please. It's urgent."

"Is Mr. Manley a guest at the hotel?"

"He's the goddamn Prime Minister of Jamaica."

"One moment ma'am.... I'm sorry, Mr. Manley has left instructions not to be disturbed."

"Now you listen to me. This is the Prime Minister's wife and I want to speak to my husband right now."

"One moment please.... I'm sorry, Mrs. Manley, there is no response from the Prime Minister's room. Shall I leave a message with his key?"

Despairing, Bev dropped the phone and ran to Natasha's room where her daughter was in the care of the nanny. Bev picked up her little girl and held her close, needing to receive nurturance as much as to give.

At noon the next day, Bev and D. K. Duncan, PNP General Secretary and fellow member of the left wing, met at Amanda's, a cozy Indian restaurant in New Kingston. They sat on the bougainvillea-shaded patio and Bev ordered chicken tikka while D. K. had fish masala and coconut shrimp.

"What time does Mike get in?" D. K. asked.

"He's extending another day. Last minute meeting or something."

"Probably having supper with his old friend Pierre Trudeau. How's the chicken?"

"D. K., I think Mike is having an affair."

Duncan bowed his head and wrenched his hands.

"What is it?" Bev asked.

"I didn't want to say anything," Duncan said softly.

"*You knew?* Jesus, am I the only one in Jamaica that *doesn't* know?"

"Calm down, it's not that bad."

"Bad enough some fool calls me on our private line to rub my face in it."

"Bev, I'm so sorry you should have to put up with that. Listen, how about we go out on the town tonight, have a drink and some laughs? Night out would do you good."

"I couldn't, D. K. How would it look for the wife of the prime minister to be out with another man? Me cyan't do that to Michael."

"Cyan't do what him a do to you? Anyway, it'd be innocent."

"I know, but... how sure are you?"

188

"About the affair? One hundred per cent. First-hand knowledge. Anyway we are both public figures, no reason we shouldn't be seen together. For all anyone knows, we're on PNP business."

"Boozing it up at some nightclub."

"We'll sit in a corner and drink coffee. Spread charts and graphs on our table."

"You know what, D. K.? Why the hell not? Just for an hour or so. I'm not drinking coffee though, tell you that right now."

Duncan reached across the table for Bev's hand.

"Just know this, Bev," he said. "Me always there fe yuh."

The first lady looked down at D. K.'s hand resting gently atop hers and softly wept.

27

January 1981, Santa Barbara

The New Year brought the inauguration of Ronald Reagan and that bastion of liberalism Barry Goldwater warning against right-wing zealots blurring the line separating church and state. Japan was now selling more cars than the United States, where gas had doubled in price over the last two years to $1.20/gallon. Later in the year would come the first *New York Times* report of a "rare cancer in homosexuals" that would be named Gay Related Immune Deficiency (GRID), redubbed the following year Acquired Immune Deficiency Syndrome, or AIDS.

After his early morning jog, barefoot on cold and windy West Beach, Scott pedaled home and kicked the soccer ball around in the backyard, pretending he was working a give-and-go with the Skipper, until his toe began to throb. It seemed to hurt when he was upset or angry and right now he was both. Lester Bangs insinuating Bob had cancer. How could the Tuff Gong be sick? Skipper was tougher than any virus or mutating cancer cell. Lester Bangs could go fuck himself.

His throat was sore and he felt sick himself. The chilly beach run perhaps.

The phone rang.

"Hello."

"Hi Scott. Nadesha."

"Nadesha, hey."

"You sound out of breath."

"Just back from a run. What's up?"

"Big news."

"Marijuana is legal in all fifty states?"

"Not quite that historic. Guess who's opening for Peter Tosh at the County Bowl?"

"Batman."

"The unheralded but fast-rising Reggae Rockers."

"A true? Fe real?" Scott half jumped out of his skin, the pain in his throat and toe disappearing like magic.

"Isn't it great? Peter, Beres Hammond and us on the same bill."

"Too bad it isn't the Wailers."

"What are you copping an attitude for? Why do you have to get negative?"

"Just saying it's too bad—"

"--We're getting together this weekend to rehearse and plan it out."

"Suzette okay?"

"Why wouldn't she be okay? Girl's awesome."

"Just saying, say hi, you know."

"I can say hi."

"Great."

Blues stopped by to pick Scott up Sunday afternoon and they drove up San Marcos Pass to Zack's place: an old adobe *casa* belonging to Zack's uncle with a wooden barn out back. Blues was Reggae Rockers' bass player. The property was at the mouth of an oak-shaded canyon, the closest neighbors a mile away. There was no electricity so a generator was used to power up the amps. Scott's armpits soaked in anticipation of seeing Suzette.

Blues and Scott arrived and the band was all accounted for: Scott on lead vocals and guitar; Reggie, a dreadlocks black, background singer and percussionist; Canada, who'd pulled 29 in the draft lottery—a guaranteed ticket to Nam—and hidden north of the border for several years, keyboards; Zack on drums; and the We-Two of Suzette and Nadesha.

Everyone went inside the adobe *casa*. Built in 1905 by a Tarahumara Indian, it was cool on hot days and warm on cold—Native Americans the first environmentalists. *Uprising,* the Wailer's latest album, played on the boombox. Suzette studiously avoided making eye contact and Scott got the impression there was something going on between her and Reggie. He burned with jealousy.

Then from out of nowhere Canada dropped a bomb. He and the others wanted to add original material to the playlist for the Tosh concert, he said, with Reggie singing lead on some songs. All the great bands do their own songs, he added.

"You want to do songs nobody's ever heard of instead of reggae tunes by the top artists in the world?" Scott flushed in bewilderment. "Why change things when we're on a roll?"

"This is our chance to shine."

"Fuck, guys. Go with what got us here."

"It's like Peter coming in for Bob," Blues pointed out.

190

"Remember when they got their audition with Coxsone Dodd?" Scott fired back. "Junior sang a number and Dodd was going to give them the boot until Bob stepped in and sang *Simmer Down*. When the chips are down, go with your big guns."

"Two lead singers would add variety and depth."

"A band becomes identified with a sound. You can't throw Frank Sinatra into Black Uhuru, it won't fly."

"We don't want to change the sound, we want to make it richer, more textured. Like The Band, Levon and Danko both sing. All four of the Beatles sing lead sometime."

"Jesus H. Christ. You got Koufax on the mound with a zillion strikeouts, you don't bring in the right fielder because he's got a good arm to third base."

"And you would be Koufax with a zillion strikeouts?" said Reggie.

"I was making a point. Anyway, it's too late now. We haven't rehearsed."

"We've rehearsed," Canada said.

"Not when I was there we haven't."

"No. You weren't there."

"What? You've been rehearsing behind my back?"

Scott studied faces as Suzette averted her eyes and Zack examined his hands for calluses.

"You don't listen to what people tell you," Canada said. "This is a band, not a solo act."

"Fuck this shit." Scott stormed out and wandered up the canyon. Zack came out and hollered at him to cool out and come back.

"Rattlesnakes out there, man."

"Fuck off, Zack." Scott's right big toe hurting bad.

Intrigued by Dr. M's sudden "humanness," Scott enrolled in a Psychology 1A course at City College for spring semester. He was at home reading in his textbook about endorphins, the body's natural pain-killers, when the phone rang.

"Yeah?" he snapped, still fuming over the trouble with the band.

"Scott?"

"Who wants to know?"

"Phil Mitchell."

"Who?"

"Dr. Mitchell. This a bad time?"

"Dr. M? Hey, Doc, what's shaking?"

"Am I calling too late?"

"No problemo. What can I do for you?"

"I was thinking I might... um... that is, uh..."

"Spit it out, man."

"Thought I might buy some grass."

"*You* want to buy herb?"

"Couple joints, yeah."

"Hot shit on a stick. Doc M wants to buy herb."

"Maybe I made a mistake. I…"

"C'mon over, stoner. I'll hook you up."

"Sure I wouldn't be disturbing you?"

"You'll disturb the shit out of me, you worthless hippy. Just joking. C'mon by."

"How do I find your pad?"

Scott gave directions and twenty-five minutes later came the deep purr of a Porsche rolling into the driveway. The stench of alcohol effused from Mitchell's breath as Scott showed him in. Phil remarked on the abundant Jamaican memorabilia as Scott plopped down in the rocker with his stash, Wailers as usual on the stereo.

"So you want to buy herb," he said, rolling a joint. "Wake up and live y'all."

"Lot of things came up the other day," Mitchell said as he sat on the couch. A baggie of marijuana had been set out on the armrest. He picked it up and weighed it in his hands.

"This for me?"

"It's all yours, baby. You're in it now."

"Thought I'd explore using marijuana as an adjunct to psychotherapy. Facilitate the process. The way R.D. Laing used LSD. It seems to open things up."

"Don't have to make excuses to smoke ganj, Doc. Way better for you than booze, which by your breath you're no stranger to."

"I admit to having a little wine with dinner. Is this rice on the floor?"

"Don't ask." Lately Scott had been burning rosemary as well— another trick to ward off ghosts.

"You're going to have rodents the size of Cleveland."

Scott held his finished spliff up like it was a Dead Sea scroll.

"Let there be light," he said. Mitchell torched the spliff and they smoked.

"Maybe grass can help me cut down on my drinking," Mitchell said, coughing out fumes. "Booze is a dead end street, you're absolutely right about that."

"What else you doing? Uppers? Downers?"

"Come on."

"Don't have to wear a sign around your neck, stoner."

"Stop calling me stoner. Would you do me that favor, please?"

192

"Sorry."

"Do you know what Vicodin is?"

"Isn't that what they gave me for my lip? Opiate, isn't it? Geezo, Doc M is doing smack. Here I thought I was the counterculture rebel. Explain yourself, sir."

"Guess I haven't let go yet. My wife...."

"You got dumped."

"Like a load of crap."

"Don't do that to yourself, man."

"Sometimes I wonder if we ever really know a person," Mitchell sighed, shaking his head. "We build up these illusions of happiness."

"What do you mean?"

"Karen. She would get all revved up. 'Let's go wine tasting, let's try this new restaurant, let's go snorkeling in the Bahamas.' Then she would fire on me for not taking charge, not having ideas. Women."

"So it's not *physical* pain we're dealing with with this opiate shit."

"They want a homebody to build a nest... then expect you to be James Fucking Bond. Exciting and dangerous."

"Fuck it, Doc. Bitch doesn't know what she's missing. Can we call her a bitch?"

"She's off in Paris with some Frog prick with snails on his breath and I'm popping Vicodin like cough drops."

"Just fuck it, man. Say it loud say it proud. Fuck it."

Mitchell shook his head and they smoked down the joint.

"How old were you when your father died?" Scott asked.

"Three or four."

"Which is it? Perhaps you'd like to lie down on my couch and talk about it."

"I'll pass on the psychoanalysis."

"Bob lost his father early too. Never really knew him. Mother away in America working. He placed his trust in his holy father, Haile Selassie the First."

"Isn't Bob your Selassie?"

"Wh-what?"

"He's like a God to you."

"Man, don't you have *anything* positive to say?"

"Are you a Rasta?"

"I think black people should have a black god."

"You're not black."

"We all come from Africa originally, right?"

"There was a coup d'etat. Haile Selassie was assassinated."

"And Jesus was crucified. Cyan't kill God, Bob say."

"Do you go to church, Rasta church?"

193

"Herb is church. I read the Bible. Used to anyway."

"Rastas read the Bible?"

"Yes, man. Chapter a day they say. Give thanks in the morning and praises at night. Bob reads his Bible religiously, pardon the pun."

"I hear Bob was baptized not long ago."

"Rumors, Doc. Babbling in the wind."

"You say Bob is invincible. If I'm like Bob I'm invincible too."

"This how you intend to pay for the herb, Doc? Little midnight head-shrinking?"

"Nobody's invincible, man. We are mortal and vulnerable and that's the way it is."

"I don't want to talk about it."

"I think you've invented this fear you have cancer, like that sci-fi flick where the monsters are creations projected from the mind. Then having manufactured the enemy you conjure a hero to slay the dragon. Balm for your fears in the person of Bob Marley."

"Who cares what you think, dickwad."

"You hear on the radio that Bob collapses while jogging and you are so deeply identified with him that—"

"—Fuck off, man."

"—that you are driven to get up off the couch and go jogging yourself though you've already run that day. The fear is so overwhelming and your love for Bob so strong that you collapse like he did. Whether you passed out or not it works out the same. You *had* to fall. So stop kicking yourself in the ass and get on with it."

Rage welled up in Scott. Doc M had challenged the very foundations of his existence. But the rage was shortcircuited by the marijuana. As Bob said, when you smoke herb you don't want to war. Phil laid down two twenties for the baggy of weed and took off. Scott got up and put on *Rastaman Vibration* and sang and danced along with the Skipper.

He awoke from fitful slumber with images of a half man-half spider spinning a giant web that entrapped everything that came along, humans and armies and low-flying fighter jets. Budding forth from these eerie scenes was a plan. A scheme worthy of Anancy, boldly devious, that would save Reggae Rockers and show Suzette what she was missing all rolled into one. He got on the phone to Zack.

"Zack," he said, "I need your help."

"*I* need a blowjob," Zack mumbled, half-asleep, "but I don't call you at three in the morning to tell you."

"Listen up. You awake? This is crucial...."

194

28

September 24, 1976, Kingston

The DJ dropped Chuck Berry's *School Days* and Dandy Disco spurted to life, lights flashing, bodies out on the floor cutting a rug. Fifties music was the best, in Matt Gallagher's mind... everything was better before all this feminism and civil rights nonsense. He kept an eye out for those two ghetto bangers who thought they were so tough and drank Heineken in case they showed up. None of the women in the house tickled his fancy. Bloody Vietnam nightmares had him teetering on edge.

Things change and stay the same. The Jamaican economy was getting royally screwed, the people suffering worse every day, but despite everything Manley's popularity only grew. The Toronto fiasco, Operation Werewolf in disarray. Werewolf was overly large and unwieldy anyway; a small squad of good men was the way to go. A dirty dozen or magnificent seven. Operation Phoenix, Colby's Vietnam assassination program, had proved that.

Just then a dark-skinned woman entered, drawing his attention. Not blessed with ravishing looks or voluptuous figure, she possessed something much more attractive: incredible poise and elegance. This was *somebody*... and not just *any* somebody.

It was Beverley Manley, the first lady of Jamaica. At her side, a man. *Well, now.*

The man was someone from the government... Duncan or somebody. D. K. Duncan. The two sat in a booth away from the dance floor. The woman's graceful movement, her unpretentious dignity and ease at being in her own skin made him think of Linda and he flushed nostalgic. Matt waved Cindy over and had her dispose of the empty Heinekens and bring him a fresh Red Stripe. He ordered a bottle of French wine delivered to Mrs. Manley's table.

At the Castle Keep bar, Fred McGinnis and Frank Lake sat in a quiet corner beneath a wall-mounted shark's jaw and sipped Heineken. Theirs was an uneasy alliance. McGinnis felt even less comfortable with Lake, despite the latter's toadying attitude of late, than he did with Gallagher. At least with the chief he knew where he stood.

"Where you from, McGinnis? Alabama, isn't it?"

"Birmingham, Alabama. Yes, sir."

"Princeton's a pretty big leap for an Alabama boy."

"Oh, yes sir, it's a leap all right. Where you from, Frank?"

"Kankakee, Indiana."

"Indian territory."

"Not anymore."

"I think something's going on with the chief."

"Something what?"

"Like he's thinking outside the box. *Way* outside the box."

"What's wrong with that?"

"Depends on whether you think rules are to be followed or broken."

"What rules do you think he is breaking?"

"All of them."

"He is a sonuvabitch."

"I get the feeling he's planning a rogue operation outside Werewolf. Going outside proper channels."

"For Matt Gallagher, there are no proper channels."

Cindy delivered the bottle of French wine to Bev and D.K's table. Mrs. Manley turned his way beaming a warm smile and waved him over.

Arriving promptly, Matt bowed his head respectfully. Despite the difference in skin color Beverley's manner and style were somehow reminiscent of the lost Linda. He forgot about the troubles at the office. This was no longer about business.

"Mrs. Manley."

"Thank you so much for the wine," she said, extending her hand. "Forgive me, you are with the embassy, are you not?"

"Yes, ma'am," Matt cradled Bev's fingertips between his thumb and forefinger and kissed her hand. "Matt Gallagher, at your service."

"Matt, this is D. K. Duncan."

"D. K."

"Matt."

"Matt, the Prime Minister and I were so appreciative of the golf tournament the embassy hosted a while back. Mike sent a note expressing our thanks to Ambassador Gerard, don't know if you would have seen it."

"Seems I came across it."

"The folks at the Boys Club were grateful for the generous donation."

"Much appreciated," Duncan added.

"We are glad to do our small part," Matt said. Though the embassy's gesture was more about public relations than generosity, Machiavellian to the core, even Matt and the crew couldn't pretend not to see the wrenching conditions in which a great number of Kingston's youth grew up, and their wish to do a little something was not entirely self-serving. They saw no incongruity with their secret mission of making the economy scream until Jamaicans cried uncle.

Matt's ears perked as the DJ spun the old Beatles tune *Twist and Shout*. "There's a song I could dance to," he said. "If D. K. doesn't protest too much."

"No, no," Duncan said.

"Then may I have this dance, Mrs. Manley?"

"Well, I..." Bev demurred; this all seemed so strange. But she felt obligated to offer some small kindness in return for the embassy's gesture of goodwill. And this chap was handsome and strong and confident. His muscular arm and outstretched hand urging her forth.

"I would love to dance with you, Mr. Gallagher," she said, taking his hand.

"Please, it's Matt."

"Matt."

Matt led her onto the dance floor and he and the First Lady kicked it. Natural athletic ability made him a good dancer despite his bum leg and she moved gracefully as well. With each hop and bop she relaxed more and more, as if a series of invisible shackles lifted one after the other from her shoulders and she allowed herself to have a good time. For his part Matt was increasingly enraptured in the fantasy that it was Linda dancing by his side, casting her bewitching smile and lighting up the room once more with the glow of her personality and charm. As Bev let loose her inhibitions and moved more sensuously still, it suddenly was 1958 and he and his saronged Dorothy Lamour were dancing in some barefoot San Diego dive or Hussong's across the border in Ensenada.

They boogied through a couple more tunes and a slow number came up. He placed his hand on Bev's waist and then around to the small of her back. As they moved together, he rode the fantasy toward its ultimate denouement, as if *she* were still there. He pressed close to Bev and before she had time to think or react boldly he pushed forward with his pelvis. Her breath escaped her. She felt him *down there*—she hadn't bargained for that. Was she that desirable? Was he that hot-blooded? This was all so dangerous and exciting and she a married woman. The reflexive tendency to pull back was somehow stilled. Matt pressed into her and she felt almost penetrated and it was thrilling and primal. Hips locked and pulsed, her head against his chest, their hot breath intermingling. Bev trembled at the thought he would kiss her neck or nibble on her ear. The pain of Michael's unfaithfulness gave way to the sweet ecstacy of forbidden lust—and revenge.

Matt whispered raw words in her ear, an invitation to sin in words that left nothing to the imagination. She gasped and went faint, would have fallen to the floor had not Matt caught her and held her up. Women shrieked. Matt carried her to the booth as Duncan rushed forward to take charge.

"Mr. Gallagher please, give the woman some air."

Matt cast Duncan a look but he had lost the upper hand. Beverley was groggy but not unconscious and as D. K. fanned her with a drinks menu she gathered herself.

"Are you all right, Mrs. Manley?" Cindy Breakespeare asked.

Matt tried to move back close to repair with gallantry the damage he had done.

"Mrs. Manley, Bev," he said, "I—"

Beverley looked up and locked eyes on Matt. What had been thrilling a moment before turned loathsome. She felt violated. This man had nothing of her husband's sophistication and gentility. He was coarse and indelicate, his actions boorish and presumptuous. Overcome with shame and revulsion, she convulsed in nausea and vomited all over Matt's shirt and pants. Linda had done that once during a bad flu and despite his embarrassment he felt a warm glow as he turned and walked out of Dandy Disco.

At the Castle Keep, Lake called for the bill, but McGinnis hadn't gotten everything off his mind yet.

"Ever think about what we're doing here, Frank?" he said, studying the Skull-and-Crossbones fluttering on the wall above the bar. "In Jamaica, I mean."

"We're doing our job. Serving commander-in-chief and nation. Whadja have, three beers?"

"Our commander-in-chief outlawed assassinations."

"Scruples bothering you, Freddy? Goin' Commie, ain'tcha."

McGinnis had recently been meeting with a Cuban agent he'd met at a foreign diplomats dinner. It was all above board and legit—undercover officers often knew and interacted with their opposites from foreign countries in the interest of gathering intelligence and turning assets. The Cuban, Jorge Aguirre, hadn't been persuaded by McGinnis' praise of American democracy and recent advances in civil rights.

"In Cuba," Aguirre had said calmly, "everyone already possesses these rights for which your people in America strive so mightily."

Aguirre described the housing that was being built, the free education through university and universal healthcare Cuba offered while the rest of Latin America was sinking further into the abyss of inequality, the rich getting richer and the poor poorer. McGinnis pointed to the freedoms enshrined in the Bill of Rights. Aguirre countered that with its tremendous disparities in wealth between black and white and rich and poor, America was really two countries, one First World and another Third World, and that its glorious freedoms didn't mean much to the tens of millions in the latter group. Caught off guard, McGinnis wondered aloud if perhaps there wasn't some middle ground to be found between the two systems.

"Isn't that what Manley is doing?" Aguirre said. "Seeking a third way?"

Aguirre caught a glimpse of the tattoo under Freddy's collar, the four blood-red hearts strung like pendant and chain with flower and raindrop inside.

"Does that have anything to do with the bombing in Birmingham a few years back? The church?"

McGinnis was stunned into momentary catatonia. His "enemy" had correctly connected his tattoo to an incident every black adult he'd ever met knew well and not one white person had even heard of—the 1963 bombing of the 16th Street Baptist Church in Birmingham, Alabama by four members of the Ku Klux Klan. The bomb had been timed to go off on Sunday when church was in session to accomplish the most carnage and it had succeeded only too well—four dead, twenty-two injured. The four deceased were girls aged 11 to 14: McGinnis was himself 14 at the time and one of the fatalities, Addie Mae Collins, had been his best friend at school. (Addie Mae's sister Sarah had been hurt but survived.) The hearts tattooed on McGinnis' chest represented the four girls—Addie Mae, Cynthia Wesley, Carole Robertson, Denise McNair—Addie Mae the big heart in the center. The droplets falling on the flowers were meant not only as teardrops but also raindrops, as if to represent the possibility, somehow, of renewal, whether in this life or the next. It was one year before three civil rights workers were murdered in the celebrated *Mississippi Burning* case. Joan Baez recorded Richard Farina's *Birmingham Sunday* in memory of the four ascended angels, who would live forever in the annals of the civil rights movement.

"I had two beers," McGinnis said. "What about the chief's obsession with Marley?"

"Marley is trouble. Stirs things up, incites passions. Appeals to the herd mentality."

"The guy is a saint. If you pulled some shifts out at the surveillance post you'd see it. He's out there everyday, feeding the masses, taking care of his people. Does that make him a communist?"

"You're twisting things around."

"We hang this pernicious label on anybody who wants to make life better for the least among us. Priest, farmer, union man, anyone wishing to help the masses rather than the business elite. Once that label 'socialist' is appended you're a monster to be hunted down and destroyed. We'd take down Jesus Christ himself."

"You *have* gone commie."

"Come on, Frank, be honest with yourself. We all see the horrible disparities in wealth and land ownership in these poor countries. The Company line has always been that development that lifts the masses out of poverty is crucial to maintaining order in the system. Trouble is, any development only helps those that already have it made. For everybody else things don't get better they get worse. Marley's out there with his thumb in the dike helping people make it through the day and we get all bent out of shape. It's just music. Why take down a folk hero who's doing his damnedest to keep out of the fray?"

"You're a prick McGinnis but you make a lot of sense. Might be right about Chiefie too. Wouldn't put a rogue operation past the sonuvabitch for a minute. Just between you and me, Gallagher has one of my guys keeping an eye on his kid, but he still reports to me. Why don't you have a talk with him and see what you can find out?"

The car rolled up and doors opened and slammed shut. Someone spoke, baggage was shuffled. *Michael was home.* And standing in the doorway of Jamaica House like an Old West sheriff was Beverley Manley, still clad in the black dress she had worn to Dandy with D.K.

Michael Manley hustled forth, surprised to see Bev standing there.

"Still up, honey? It's half past one."

He puckered for a kiss and Bev turned her head.

"What's this all about, Bev? Why are you all dressed up?"

"D. K. and I went out for a drink."

"You went for a drink."

"After the Women's meeting."

"With D. K."

"That's right. With D. K."

"I'm away on government business and my wife is out in a black dress having a drink with another man."

"Is there something you want to tell me?"

"Bev, I'm exhausted. If you have something to say I wish you would--"

"Out with it, man."

"What in the world are you going on about?"

"I want the truth. Who is she?"

"She?"

"The woman you were with in Toronto."

"Oh... that."

"Oh that? What the hell does that mean? There are other sins I don't know about?"

"No, no... don't be silly."

"Is she someone on your staff?"

Manley bowed his head and was silent a moment before he nodded.

"You will fire her immediately," Bev ordered. "And you will ponder what this marriage means to you."

Beverley blew off up the stairs and secluded herself with Natasha in the guest bedroom, where she would spend the next week of nights. Michael's betrayal was a cruel blow... but she didn't know the half of it.

Matt kept going in to Dandy Disco in search of Al Capone and Wild Bill Hickok. Soon enough the ghetto bad boys showed, taking their usual booth. Matt had instructed Cindy that if these two came in she should immediately serve them bottles of Heineken and a platter of jerk chicken. As Cindy delivered the order and pointed back to Matt, he gave a crisp salute and held up his own green bottle in a toast. They made no reply.

Matt waved Cindy over and paid for two more beers and a tray of fruit for the Jamaicans.

"Tell them I want to talk," he said.

"Are you sure that's a good idea?"

"Intercultural relations."

"That went over so well with Bev Manley."

Cindy did as requested. Matt went to their booth and slid in next to Al Capone, whom Matt had discerned to be the dominant one. Capone reflexively leaned the other way without looking up. The two rudeboys remained aloof, engrossed in feasting on their chicken.

Matt slipped an envelope onto the table. Capone and Hickok glanced at the envelope and then at each other. And kept eating.

"Open it," Matt said.

Knowing the white man likely was CIA, the gangsters didn't dare push their snobbishness too far. Al Capone wiped his hands and took up the envelope. He opened to find five crisp one hundred dollar bills.

"Plenty more where that came from," Matt said in low voice. "Guns too."

He discretely palmed off a small plastic pouch to Capone. Big Al dipped the tip of his finger into the fine white powder. When he rubbed it into his gums, his eyes lit up like Time Square on New Year's Eve.

Ganja ruled Jamaica, but cocaine was establishing a foothold, thanks to the CIA. Already there were some who craved it more than weed and would do anything to get a snoutful. With Matt supplying guns, money and the White Lady, Al Capone and Wild Bill were his. He took them and their posse out to the Green Bay range before dawn for training with M16s with live ammunition. His rogue operation was in business.

29

By October, Bob Marley had finished composing a song for the upcoming concert entitled, not surprisingly, *Smile Jamaica*. The song was appropriately catchy and upbeat; like many of Marley's songs it incorporated Jamaican folklore into the lyrics so he could speak to the masses in simple terms they knew well and understood almost intuitively. Like the old aphorism to "throw water into the well and cast away the evil spell," or exhortations urging Jah to help his people. Lyrics that music critics might have dismissed as simplistic and child-like were in fact brilliantly attuned to the cultural Zeitgeist and worded to be unifying rather than polemic. The Wailers went first to Lee Perry's Black Ark studio behind his home in middle-class Washington Gardens and recorded a fast ska version of the tune. Perry had started sweeping floors at Studio One and gone on to dj for Coxsone Dodd's sound systems. Later he sang his own hit records and produced Wailers classics like *Duppy Conqueror* and *Trench Town Rock*. Scratch coached Bob, Peter and Bunny on their vocals, encouraged their socially conscious lyrics, cooled down the backing falsettos and pumped up the bass and drums. Chicken Scratch, Super-Ape, Pipecock Jackson, the Upsetter, Perry was as eccentric as they came—said once to have planted vinyl records in his garden—but was a major influence on the Wailers and reportedly the only person Bob ever called a genius.

Perry's ska rendition of *Smile Jamaica* was fine for Side A of the single, but Bob wanted to slow down the tempo with a bigger, rootsier version for the flip side. He got the troops down to Harry J's and dragged in Neville Garrick and Gilly to sing harmony with the I-Three, all backed by the Zap Pow horns (a trumpet, trombone and saxophone). During a break, as Bob listened to playbacks with his Twelve Tribes bredren, a troubled Judy Mowatt huddled with Marcia Griffiths to relieve herself of a bad dream she'd had the night before.

"Headline in newspaper say 'Bob got shot,'" Judy said, trembling under the weight of it. The lovely Mowatt pregnant with what everybody assumed was Skill Cole's baby.

"Shot?" Marcia gasped.

"Y'unnerstand what frighten me so? Paper say Bob shot for a song."

"Lord."

"And check it. Lyric we sing 'under heavy manners'? Lyric PNP slogan."

"Better tell Bob." From the very start Marcia hadn't liked the idea of the concert one bit.

Judy went to Bob, who hadn't been aware of the political association to the lyric. He took the matter to the Rasta elders.

"Bredren," Bob said, "how yuh think 'bout this lyric here?"

The Rastas conferred a moment before issuing a ruling.

"Lyric PNP political slogan," the venerable Rasta leader spoke, his dreadlocks down to the small of his back. "Maybe make trouble."

Bob studied how to rework the song and called everyone back to studio to record another version. The offending lines were struck, but Judy Mowatt would have more disturbing dreams. As would Bob Marley.

A cable came in to the Kingston station from the Western Hemisphere desk warning that a "former DISIP operative" in Venezuela had been overheard to say, "We are going to hit a Cuban airplane." Matt knew it was Bambi. He suspended all operations that involved sending agents to Cuba or flying Cubana Airlines. Like the earlier threat against Cubana 476 it was probably a false alarm, but with Bambi anything was possible.

October 6, 1976, Simon Bolivar International Airport, Caracas, Venezuela

Nancy Uranga Romagosa dozed as she sat in the boarding gate waiting area. It was too early to be up and she wasn't feeling well.

Someone tugged at her arm.

"Nancy, it's time."

"Oh, Milagro," Nancy yawned.

"Are you all right?" asked Milagro Pelaez Gonzalez, 21, Nancy's best friend on the fencing team.

"My stomach is doing cartwheels."

"We have to go. They called our flight."

Nancy looked up to see other members of the fencing team standing over her with their athletic bags slung over their shoulders. Everybody was excited, the squad having done exceptionally well at the championships in Venezuela, winning all three trophies in individual competition with Milagro taking the silver medal. Many of the twenty-four were teenagers, medals dangling proudly around their necks for the flight home. For Nancy, 22, it had been a busy summer and fall—first the Montreal Olympics and now these Central American and Caribbean Games here in Caracas. Now it was time to get back to her studies in biology at the University of Havana.

The Pan Am flight this morning would take them to Port of Spain, Trinidad, where they would catch a Cubana Aviacion plane originating in Guyana and island-hop home to Cuba. Nancy wondered why she was so tired; coming down with stomach flu, maybe. She had been a last-minute replacement on the fencing squad for 12-year-old Maria Gonzalez, who'd cried her eyes out over having picked the wrong time to get sick. She ducked into the souvenir shop and bought a gift to take home for Maria, a doll draped in the traditional plaited dress of a Venezuelan *chica*.

"Nancy, hurry up," Milagro said. "Do you want to walk to Trinidad?"

Nancy paid and stuffed the doll in her handbag. As she ran for the plane she knew the keepsake wouldn't ease young Maria's disappointment at missing out on the trip.

Cheddi Jagan International Airport, Georgetown, Guayana

Raymond Persaud's father pulled the car to the curb and hopped out to get Ray's bags. Raymond's mother embraced her son and showered him with tearful kisses, which Ray tolerated with some embarrassment knowing his parents loved him more than words could say, as he loved them. He wore his new suit for this most wonderful occasion, a suit he'd picked out himself (with doting hectoring by his mother). It was quite simply the greatest day of his life—off to begin his studies to become a doctor. He was one of six students from Guyana to win scholarships to attend medical school in Cuba, courtesy of the Cuban government. They came from all across the nation to travel today as a group, young, bright, filled with dreams. What would Havana would be like, the food, the people? Cuba, he knew, had an excellent medical system. How, only seventeen years since the revolution and throttled by a crippling US embargo, could little Cuba offer free medical training to students from all over the developing world while sending out her own trained professionals to improve the healthcare of poor countries, at no cost to the host nation? For Ray and his fellow scholars it was the opportunity of a lifetime. And if the girls were cute, that would be all right too. Such were the dreams of a 19-year-old boy off to become a man.

Raymond's father hunted up a redcap as Mrs. Persaud reminded Ray of everything he wasn't to forget while away in Cuba—to brush his teeth after every meal, be polite to his teachers, watch out for "that kind" of girl, go to bed and rise early. *For heaven's sake wash your hands after touching the cadavers.* Most important of all was to write often and call whenever possible. Ray's sister Roseanne kicked alongside hoping for an ice cream stand somewhere in this huge and scary building.

Through check-in and now it was time to board. More hugs and tears, dad's proud handshake, wave and onto the plane. Raymond dabbed at his wet eyes and glanced around at the other passengers. Several Guyanese not in the med school program were flying to Cuba for medical treatment. He checked his watch. The flight to Trinidad he calculated at roughly an hour. Another hour to Barbados, a longer leg over to Jamaica and the last quick hop to Havana. It would be a long day but at least there were no scheduled changes of airplane, it was Cubana 455 all the way—a DC-8 with plenty of room and those four beautiful engines. Tonight, when the bird alit at the end of its journey, he would enter a new world. And when all was said and done, after all the hard work was completed, exams passed, labs turned in and late-night cram sessions mercifully over, he would return home and place his training and skills in service of the people of his native country. Such need in Guyana. Now buckle up, a last look out the window as the Cubana de Aviacion DC-8 roared down the runway and left Georgetown and South America behind. Forever.

Piarco International Airport, Port of Spain, Trinidad

Cubana 455 arrived in Port of Spain around noon for a brief stop. A number of new passengers boarded, including twenty-four members of the Cuban national fencing team. Two of the girls sat in Raymond Persaud's row and seemed even more excited than he was. They introduced themselves as Milagro and Nancy, Milagro wearing her silver medal around her neck. Milagro. *"Miracle."* Raymond's adventure growing more magical with every passing minute.

Two other boarding passengers were Venezuelans Freddy Lugo and Hernan Ricardo, young men in their 20s. Both worked for Luis Posada Carriles's "detective agency" in Caracas, both were paid CIA operatives trained in explosives. They have checked their baggage through to Havana though had no intention of traveling to Cuba, where they would immediately be arrested. Ricardo carried two camera bags onboard.

At twenty-five minutes past noon, pilot Wilfredo (Felo) Perez Perez, 36, who had served alongside the freedom fighters in Angola, gunned it down the runway and the plane lifted off for Barbados. With him were two co-pilots, Angel Tomas Rodriguez, 36, and Miguel Espinosa Cabrera, 47, the latter having fought alongside Fidel Castro in the Sierra Maestra. Lugo placed one of his camera bags under his seat; it was filled with C-4 plastic explosive. Halfway through the short flight, Ricardo went to the rear bathroom and hid a tube of toothpaste under the sink—the Colgate in the tube had been squeezed out and C-4 inserted. Ricardo somehow locked himself in the bathroom and pounded on the door in panic. A flight attendant summoned one of the co-pilots, who kicked the door open. Ricardo, white with fear, returned to his seat. Pencil-type detonators on timers have been rigged on both devices.

Seawell International Airport, Bridgetown, Barbados
Cubana 455 landed at Seawell in the capital Bridgetown shortly before 1:00 to offload and take on passengers. Lugo and Ricardo were among those getting off, Lugo carrying only one camera case. By 1:10 the aircraft was ready to resume transit, next stop Norman Manley International in Kingston. The flight manifest listed 48 passengers, including the 24 members, coaches and trainers on the fencing team, the 11 Guyanese, 5 persons from North Korea, and 8 others; the crew numbered 25, for a total of 73 persons on board.

At 1:15 pilot Perez pushed it down runway number nine and the plane lifted off. Raymond Persaud and Milagro Pelaez delighted at the sight out the windows of Paradise Beach, crowded with people enjoying themselves on this perfect sunny day under clear blue skies. Nancy Uranga rubbed her tummy and belched. She had a good idea now why she felt so woozy.

At 1:24, as the plane reached 18,000 feet, the toothpaste-tube bomb went off and tore apart the rear bathroom. The interior of the plane was suddenly a blazing inferno.

"Fire! We have an explosion!" captain Perez shouted, struggling desperately to maintain control of the plane. One of the co-pilots frantically radioed for permission to return to Seawell as Felo fought desperately to limp back to land.

"You can make it! Felo you can make it!"

The screams of passengers—so many young people—stabbed at Perez like daggers but he could do nothing but fight his war at the controls and try to bring 'er in. Seawell was close, there was a chance they could make it... *Mother of God there is a chance!*

"Close that door!" Perez shouted as the firestorm raged close to the cabin. Would he see his wife and children again in this life?

At 1:30 the camera bomb under Lugo's seat went off and the terrors of Hell were magnified many times over. Captain Perez, seeing all was lost, turned away from the shore and Cubana 455 nosedived into the Caribbean Sea eight kilometers from land as sunbathers on Paradise Beach watched in horror. Heroically, Perez saved many lives on the crowded sands below, but all onboard were lost, their bodies mutilated beyond recognition. Bloody stumps were all that remained of the future doctors, the Olympic athlete, the freedom fighter who'd helped overthrow the Batista dictatorship and the others, Raymond Persaud's dream of a lifetime of helping his people blown to smithereens with his corporeal self. Seventy-three lives lost... seventy-four if the baby growing in Nancy Uranga Romagosa's young belly were counted. As of that date, it was the most grievous act of aviation terrorism in history.

Back in Bridgetown, Freddy Lugo and Hernan Ricardo checked in to the Holiday Inn where Ricardo placed frantic calls to Posada and Orlando Bosch (alias Senor Panyagua, "Mr. Bread and Water") in Caracas. Unable to reach either, he left a coded message:

"A BUS WITH 73 DOGS WENT OFF A CLIFF AND ALL GOT KILLED."

Alternating between elation at killing more people in one fell swoop than Carlos the Jackal ever had and utter despair—"Freddy, I have never killed anyone. I am lost."—Ricardo panicked. He and Lugo bolted for the airport and caught the next plane to Port of Spain, where they checked into the Holiday Inn under phony names and again tried to reach Posada and Bosch. Their behavior was so suspicious that someone tipped off police and they were taken into custody for questioning regarding the Cubana 455 bombing. Initially denying responsibility, one week later they confessed and claimed they were working for Luis Posada. Ricardo drew a sketch of the detonators used on the bombs.

On this same day, October 6, 1976, Director of Central Intelligence George H. W. Bush ordered the investigation into the Orlando Letelier

206

bombing-murder sealed (George W. Bush would extend the ruling in 2001). To an FBI inquiry about the explosives used by the Cuban exiles, Bush replied "forget about it." In 1991, under President Bush, the CIA destroyed its files on former asset Juan Manuel Contreras, the DINA chief who'd hired Michael Townley and who had met at least four different times in Washington with CIA Deputy Director Vernon Walters as Condor was forming. Better that the American public did not know what her friends around the world were doing.

Was Walters at the June 1976 CORU planning conference in the Dominican Republic? Why had it been necessary for Contreras, the head of a foreign nation's secret police, to come all the way from Santiago to Washington—5000 miles—to meet with the Deputy Director so often? Did Walters okay Letelier's murder, as Contreras maintained? Who really ordered the CORU conference, Pinochet—or the CIA? The documents were sealed and destroyed.

30

February 1981, Santa Barbara

The date of the Tosh concert rolled around and Scott rode with Zack in his VW microbus to the County Bowl. They smoked a joint en route but their conversation was far from relaxed.

"Let's think about this," Zack said.

"Don't weasel out on me, Zack-Attack," Scott admonished. "Stick with the plan."

"*Your* plan, not mine."

"We have to work together on this."

"You just want another shot at Suzette. You're thinking with your cock."

"You with me or not, friend?"

"Fuck."

High up on the Santa Barbara Riviera, Phil Mitchell was lazing on the deck, half asleep in the warm sun, when the phone rang.

"Hello."

"Dr. Mitchell there?"

"This is Dr. Mitchell. Who is this, please?"

"George from Black Star Liner."

"How you doing, George?"

"Information about Bob Marley a come from me brethren in Jamaica."

"What did you find out?"

"Him sick. The cancer real."

"Oh no."

207

"Say when him stumble and fall in Central Park it really a stroke."

"Oh dear."

"The cancer reach advance stage. Him gwan clinic in Germany for treatment. Them say him baptize fe real. Ethiopian Orthodox Church."

"I see. Thank you, George."

Santa Barbara County Bowl, originally the site of caballero shows of Old Spanish Days, was built in the manner of a Greek theatre against the natural slope of a small wooded canyon, just outside city limits. Intimate and cozy under eucalyptus, sycamore and oak, it was said to be Bob Marley's favorite US venue. Scott and Zack arrived early to set up and run sound checks.

Peter Tosh in concert in California—who would have thought it? Winston Hubert MacIntosh was an incredible talent second only to Marley in the annals of reggae, but his lack of enthusiasm for touring—coupled with Bunny's absolute refusal to leave the Rock—was the fly in the ointment that broke up the original Wailers trio. Now he was getting out there big time, major tours for the *Bush Doctor* and *Mystic Man* albums in the last few years and *Wanted: Dread or Alive* coming this June. But then it was different being the star of the show.

The climate gods were cooperating with crisp sweater weather, sunny, deep blue skies, a pleasant cool bite in the air. People were streaming in, the grassy infield filling up with hippy types and earth women in granny dresses, Caucasian mostly. Blacks in the States had been slow to warm to reggae; even black-owned media and radio stations looked down their noses at it as unsophisticated island music. Bob had made a point of playing the Apollo in Harlem to try and reach his bredren and sistren in America. 'Course in Santa Barbara there just weren't that many blacks around. Twenty-five rows up sat Aunt Sylvia and Phil Mitchell, courtesy of two comp tickets from Scott. Two people thoroughly in need of an evening out.

Scott watched Suzette out one eye and Reggie out the other. Feeling inferior to handsome, dark-skinned Reggie, he burned with jealousy and overcompensated in anger and spite. He regretted not having said more than "hi" to Suzette in greeting and wondered if he'd been too brusque even in that. A smile would have gone a long way. The One Love vibe wasn't flowing—and on this most special of days, in more ways than one.

At 5:45, Reggae Rockers took the stage to a polite round of applause. The band's allotted time onstage worked out to six songs—two with Reggie singing lead, a huge blow to Scott's ego, as he'd always sung all the songs. Even worse was the playlist, which the others, he felt, had stupidly bullied through, and wasn't militant enough to suit him. It included no Marley tunes or anything he could really shine on. As if they wanted to put him in a musical straightjacket. He took it as a personal affront. And that's where Zack came in.

Shifting into his stage persona, Scott swaggered to the mic, glancing over to Zack to see if he was with him. Zack shook "no" and avoided his eyes. Having no choice but to proceed, Scott raised his gaze to the masses.

"Greetings in the name of His Imperial Majesty Haile Selassie the First, Jah Rastafari!" he cried, raising his fist in salute the way Skipper would do it.

"We are Reggae Rockers. First we wanna give a shout out to our dearly beloved Bob on this day, February 6, 1981, his 36th birthday. Bob Mar-lay! Love and I-nity, yunno?"

He did not know that Bob was at this very moment at a last-gasp cancer clinic in the Bavarian Alps and that Rita, Mother B and Neville Garrick had this day thrown him a birthday bash, all the Wailers other than the Barrett brothers flying in for the occasion.

The crowd gave a rousing cheer. Scott counted out the cadence and the band kicked the evening off with Scott singing lead on Jimmy Cliff's *You Can Get It If You Really Want,* a lively sing-along that got the house rolling right off the bat. So far so good.

Next was Reggie singing his two original compositions, *Reggae Par-tay* and *Beach Jammin.'* Suzette smiled over at Reggie and Scott's jealousy burned hotter. The crowd seemed to be enjoying it, which didn't help.

The final three songs were supposed to be *Ninety-six Degrees in the Shade* by Third World, Freddie McGregor's *Sitting in the Park* and Jacob Miller's effervescent *Suzy Wong. Ninety-Six Degrees* told of Paul Bogle, Baptist deacon and son of a freed slave, who led the 1865 Morant Bay peasant uprising and was hung for his efforts. It was a great song and Third World's Bunny Rugs sang the hell out of it, but it was now or never. Time to spin Anancy's web.

Scott shook a fist at Zack. Once the drummer laid down the beat the bass typically had to follow and the riddim was set. Everything hinged on Zack. On *Ninety-six* there was no instrumental lead-in to the vocals, so when Zack gave a lick with the sticks everybody looked up in confusion.

"*Zimbabwe,*" Zack called out, as Scott had begged him to. Zack was in!

"Gwan now!" Scott cried. "One, two, three."

Zack hit the drum roll again. Bass man Blues shrugged and fell in line and from that point there was no turning back, the others had to follow. It was Scott's moment to win or lose. Moving forward to the very edge of the stage, he bowed his head and held his arms wide in crucifix position the way Bob had done at last year's concert and blown everybody away, looming over the masses like a dreadlock Christ, wings spread to embrace

209

the righteous, eyes lost in a deeper mystery as Family Man's rapturous bass line roared like the Lion of Judah, boasting of momentous things to come. Scott played it exactly the same, letting Blue's sonic booms sizzle the stew to the last possible moment before he looked up from his reverie and launched into Marley's great anti-colonial anthem. *Zimbabwe* chronicled and simultaneously inspired the struggle against minority white rule in the former Rhodesia and throughout southern Africa, pleading for the right of every man to make his own destiny and warning that arms would be taken up if necessary. It was one of Bob's best songs both lyrically and musically and to hear the Skipper sing it live was a never-to-be-forgotten experience. Scott had cut a tough row to hoe for himself but he held nothing back. This was about letting Bob Marley's heroic revolutionary persona rip through him like a prophet channeling his god. In fevered ecstasy he dipped and danced around the stage, flinging his locks like the Skipper, parading militantly, punching the air, rubbing his forehead and making all the facial gestures he practiced at home. He had made up his mind to do it his way—ala Bob—and if the others didn't like it, tough shit (all the while hoping Suzi would be dazzled by his rebel spirit and creative artistry). The crowd loved it, feeding off his vibe and boogying up a storm as beaucoup herb burned on the grassy infield and in the aisles.

As the song finished, Scott cued Zack and Reggae Rockers went in to *"War"* and segued from that into *"No More Trouble."* At one point he bounced over behind Suzette and Nadesha and scatted with them like Bob did with the I-Three, a hand on each girl's shoulder, pumping his knees up and down as if running in place, whipping his locks to the crowd's delight. Suzette cast a look back over her shoulder. Astonishment? Admiration? The crowd was on its feet as the tempo built in a cresting wave of excitement. By the final stanza Scott had them eating from the palm of his hand. The house erupted into a standing-O and he bathed in the adoration of the masses. Beres Hammond, one of Jamaica's top "lover's rock" crooners was ready to take the stage but the moment had a magic of its own and he waved Reggae Rockers on.

"Gwan man," Hammond shouted to Scott, "dem a call fe encore."

Scott lit up in a huge grin and called *"Get Up Stand Up."* He pumped his arms to the crowd and those who weren't already standing took to their feet as the instrument players laid down the riddim. The energy built in shimmering harmonic waves, flowing from stage to top row of the stands and reverberating back to the grassy infield like a musical tsunami, everybody bouncing and boogying and waiting for the beat to roll around to join in singing.

Just then a tremendous cheer rose up. Scott peered over his shoulder and there on the stage was Peter Tosh himself. The long lean puckishly charismatic Tosh on his unicycle smoking a monster spliff, *in your face,*

Santa Barbara. He pedaled the one-wheeler back and forth and up and down like a Flying Wallenda on the highwire. The incendiary Tosh, the legalize-it man, Stepping Razor, Red X, the original busted-and-beaten-and-coming-back-for-more Angry Young Man, lightning in a bottle, militant mystic man, *cha!*

Beres Hammond hopped on stage and he and Tosh, puffing nuff ganja, sang backup with the We-Two as Scott started in on *Get Up Stand Up.* The house was absolutely on fire and with Hammond and the great Tosh jamming behind him Scott's confidence soared. Bob's mannerisms and style, even his vocal intonations, came through with such a lack of affectation and self-consciousness that Scott was almost convinced he was the King of Reggae in the flesh, lashing the world with those righteous and mighty locks.

The part rolled around where Peter—who'd co-written the song—usually stepped in for Bob. Suddenly everything changed. Tosh wheeled to the mic to join in on lead vocals. As Peter sang in his deep and richly emotive voice, Scott grew intimidated and lost his way as well as the words, leaving Peter soloing. After soaring so high, he crashed like Icarus into the drowning sea of wounded ego. Scott felt himself pale to nothing under the shadow of the magnificent Tosh. Petty emotion flushed through him, paranoid insecurity, envy and rage, thoughts of death, jealousy of the Toshes and Reggies and Suzettes of this world with their dalliances and knowing looks. From nowhere, images of the warrior's M14 and executioner's machete flashed into mind, as if the consuming emotion could only be released in some act of violence. He raised his gaze to the bleachers and remembered being up there last year when the Wailers were in town and he'd been torn between utter delight at seeing Bob perform and inexplicable terror at going backstage and saying hi, as much as he wanted to, fear winning out in the end. Exactly the same had happened the previous year, 1978, at the July 23rd concert on Haile Selassie I's birthday. On both occasions he'd hid from his idol as if restrained by invisible shackles.

Tosh carried the song toward the finale where Bob liked to go into his "woy-yoy" riffs, the acme of orgiastic One-ness that a Wailers concert could be at its best. Just before the couplet that led into the riff, Peter stepped back to give Scott the spotlight, but Scott froze up and gagged. He stood alone, impotent and lost, the eyes of the world slicing him to shreds in his mute anguish. Peter had to jump in and save the moment:

"Dread!" Zack shouted. "What are you doing?"

Scott pulled dumbly within, into his protective shell, as Peter finished out the song, covering Bob's woy-yoys with aplomb. The place went crazy. As applause rippled down from the rows of happy revelers, Scott slunk off stiff-lipped and when Zack and then Suzette ran after to check on him, he ignored them and kept walking, guitar slung over shoulder, until he reached home. Beaucoup Sinsemilla failed to dull the pain. He didn't answer when his phone rang off the hook. When he finally lay down in bed, sleep wouldn't come. From the mists of yesteryear he remembered Marva's admonition that sometimes Anancy was too clever for his own good.

31

October-November 1976, Kingston

Two days after the downing of Cubana 455, gunshots raked the Cuban Embassy in Caracas. Matt Gallagher didn't have to ask who did it. Meanwhile CORU in Miami was claiming responsibility for the bombing of the airliner. A cable came in stating that the two Venezuelans, Ricardo and Lugo, were in custody in Trinidad. Matt hoped they wouldn't rat out Bambi, but the following week the Caracas police raided the properties of Posada and Orlando Bosch and placed both under arrest. In Bambi's office was found a hit list referencing Cuban embassies and business interests around Latin America, down to the make, color and license plates of cars belonging to Cuban ambassadors. Most incriminating was the listing of the flight schedule for Cubana 455. Bambi was in hot water. Behind bars, Orlando Bosch directed terrorist reprisals against the state of Venezuela to intimidate authorities into releasing him.

On October 15, one million people massed in Havana's Revolution Square as a furious Fidel Castro vented the nation's agony over the loss of life on Cubana 455. Who were these cowards who killed women and children? The whole nation wept as one. Castro pointed his finger at the CIA—at least one of the bombers, he claimed, had been on payroll. In fact all four suspects were chummy with the CIA. Castro would really have been incensed if he'd known that US intelligence had been aware an attack upon a Cuban airliner was imminent and hadn't warned the Cuban government.

It was only after the Letelier murder and Cubana 455 bombing that CIA director George H. W. Bush thought it proper to inform Congressman Ed Koch that he had since mid-July been targeted for assassination by Condor terrorists. Koch screamed for FBI protection but was given none. As president, Bush would grant Orlando Bosch asylum over the objections of his own Justice Department and pardon him for his monstrous crimes that even God Himself could not forgive. In a slick bit of symmetry, Florida Governor Jeb Bush would successfully lobby Attorney General John Ashcroft for early release of Dionisio "Pool of Blood" Suarez and Vergilio Paz, convicted murderers of Orlando Letelier. Matt Gallagher's buddy Bambi (Posada) would also find safe havens in the United States. In 1998 George H.W. Bush protected even Pinochet himself, calling attempts by a Spanish judge to bring criminal proceedings against the mass-murdering dictator "a travesty of justice."

212

At his desk in the embassy, Matt Gallagher drank coffee and read from a CIA document of the hundreds of assassination plots against Fidel Castro the agency had attempted or devised, including:

--The old exploding-cigar routine.

--The trusty poisoned-pen routine.

--The tricky magnificent-fake-seashell-rigged-with-explosives-and-placed-in-conspicuous-undersea-location-to-attract-the-scuba-diving-aficionado-Castro routine.

Fuck, thought Matt, *why doesn't somebody just pop the bastard?*

The sun sank beneath the western horizon as Jesse James with loving tenderness worked the wood. Witnessing the gradual emergence of a bare-breasted Nanny of the Maroons was a creative giving of birth that was highly pleasing. Legend had it that Nanny had fought off the Redcoats by taking their missiles into her crotch and firing them back. Nanny was an Obeah woman, her magical invincibility to British weapons akin to the invisibility of Sioux warriors in the time of the Ghost Dance. The Maroons were fierce warriors who fought their European foes to a standstill, Jamaica called the "Land of Look Behind" because scared-shitless British soldiers would ride two to a horse, one astride backwards to guard against attack from the rear. Soon Jesse James would sand Nanny to a high sheen and his woman would take her to the craft market and try to sell her. If only the tourists would come back... maybe someday when all this tribal warfare business was finished and done.

Earlier that day an embassy man had come calling, a black man asking questions about Mr. Matt. Say him name Freddy. Questions like had he "witnessed anything strange" or "gotten the feeling something wasn't quite right." He could have answered yes to both questions a thousand times over from what he'd seen in his lifetime so he couldn't figure what the fella was getting at. Nuff things strange in Jamaica. Nuff things not quite right. Starving children with swollen bellies plenty strange. Can't buy flour plenty not quite right. The embassy man, Mr. Freddy, said if "something come up" he should get in touch. *Wha' dat mean?* Something always a come up in Jamaica. Man seem like him dance around what really bother him.

Working on his piece in front of Chinaman's shop, Jesse James kept watch for the Gallagher kid, grateful the youngster hadn't ratted him out to his father. The radio was on and Jesse James whistled along whenever a reggae tune came on. For supper he had bun and cheese; like many Jamaicans he often went without so the children could eat, leaving himself only a few J for rum or herb. Sleep too he could do without, especially on those nights the gunshots sounded too close for comfort, and that was nearly every night.

Some kind of civic announcement came on the radio:

213

"...advised to use extreme caution when cooking and should not eat rice which has been purchased in the last week. To repeat, a recent shipment of rice has been contaminated with the insecticide parathion and..."

Jesse did not hear the rest of the bulletin as he dropped chisel and bare-breasted Nanny and in a flash was on his motorbike racing home. His wife had planned to buy rice that afternoon and cook rice 'n peas for supper.

He pushed his speed as fast as he could manage, flying through Crossroads and finally reaching the outskirts of Ackee Walk, not far from Tivoli Gardens. From there he zipped down a maze of alleys and paths until reaching his yard. This government tenement was a horseshoe-shaped concatenation of apartments connected by adjoining kitchens. Each had a small bedroom or two and a cramped living room where families fortunate enough to have a small black-and-white TV gathered around to watch American soap operas and local programs. The housing project was dangerously situated between rival JLP and PNP districts.

Jesse James flew into the yard, hollering "Pansy! Pansy!" from the seat of his bike. He raced past the breadfruit tree in the central courtyard and practically ran the bike in the open front door of an apartment on the far side. If anything happened to his girls, the Lord could go ahead and take him too.

"Pansy!" he cried, scrambling off the bike. "The rice, Pans, the rice!"

Suddenly his common-law wife appeared in the door, barefoot and serene, a big buxom woman with her head swathed in colorful cloth.

"Howard," she said, "what got yuh so het up?"

"Where the girls?"

"Over Nana house," Pansy Elliston's expression turning dead serious as she read the stark fear in her husband's face. "Wha' gwan Howie, tell me straight out."

"Radio say rice shipment contaminate with poison. Parathion. Say nah eat nuh rice come in last likkle while."

"Dear Lawd!" Pansy cried, clutching at her locks in hysterics. "Nana gwine feed them. Shoulda cook them food meself, Howard. Dear God forgive me."

"Go warn the neighbor-them. Me a go fe me girls."

"Pray them alive still, Howard. Pray them alive."

And Jesse James was on his bike and gone.

At Jamaica House Michael Manley held his regular meeting with the heads of the security forces. Violence was much reduced, they told him, thanks to the State of Emergency, though it remained at unacceptably high levels. They were adamant that "outside agitation" was at play. *Foreign influence.* It was old news and Manley's mind drifted. He was back in

Beverley's good graces and taking her out for dinner tonight—a gourmet buffet at one of the big hotels. Strange... he'd fired Cathy Gilchrist as Bev had demanded and not missed her while moping in Bev's doghouse. Now that he'd weathered that storm and was again The Man, thoughts of Cathy drifted into mind incessantly.

As his officers took their leave, Manley sat in quiet contemplation. Another shipment of grain contaminated. At the start of the year it had been flour—twenty dead in two separate incidents—and now rice. Parathion had been banned from Jamaica for many years. Now 168 tons of rice had to be destroyed—enough to feed every family in the country for weeks. Manley prayed nobody would die from the evening meal of rice 'n peas.

Was an unseen hand at work? Three incidents in less than a year could not be mere chance, especially regarding a banned substance. Manley took up a thick hardbound book from his desk and turned to a well-worn page earmarked with a crimped corner. He read once more—as if to convince himself the words were not from some science-fiction horror story—about principles of "economic warfare" through such underhanded means as the sabotage of major industries, blocking of critically needed imported goods and contamination of agricultural products.

The book was Philip Agee's 1975 "*Inside the Company: CIA Diary*," the former CIA case officer's shocking expose of the clandestine operations of the United States Central Intelligence Agency. While serving in several Latin American countries, Agee had become so appalled at the Agency's unscrupulous meddling in the affairs of sovereign nations that he turned apostate, giving up his career to write his bombshell book, publishing in England to skirt Agency attempts to silence him. Every time he sat down with the book Manley wanted to punch a hole in a brick wall. *Contamination of agricultural products!*

Agee described standard practices for "destabilizing" foreign governments—techniques like fouling the bearings of buses, dumping dirt in the gas tanks of government vehicles, blocking shipment of needed parts, poisoning the food supply. Fouling a large shipment of a staple like rice or sugar could be achieved rather easily through the use of contaminated sacks. The idea was to create economic upheaval in order to discredit the targeted government and speed its downfall. Make the economy "scream" loud enough and the people would rise up against their leaders, whom they would blame. Strategies of attack included propaganda, the infiltrating of labor unions, youth groups, student movements and other mass organizations and limiting the availability of basic goods through various means (including "legal" mechanisms like trade agreements, embargoes and sanctions). Agee's 600-page confessional detailed how the CIA subverted and sabotaged peaceful, freely-elected governments one after another while the United States professed to champion the spread of democracy around the world. The suffering of the people not an unfortunate collateral result but *a targeted goal.*

Consumed in disgust, Manley heaved the book across the room.

The 125-cc motorbike engine whining full bore, Jesse James raced through JLP and PNP territory alike without stopping for anything. He reached Barnes Gully and his mother-in-law's place, a small free-standing house with fenced yard, to find that everyone had already eaten dinner with rice 'n peas. Fortunately, Nana had used uncontaminated rice purchased the previous week and all were alive and well. The government had gotten word out so quickly that no one would die from the outbreak—lesson learned from the fatal flour contaminations at the start of the year.

After joyful squeezes, Jesse James told the girls to round up their things—their mother would be frantically awaiting news of their safety. Nana threw a fit at the idea of them riding on the motorcycle after dark, so she asked her neighbor who had a beat-up old car to drive them home. Jesse James was walking his bike out when he heard a dog barking from the yard across the way and spied two Jamaicans casting glances over their shoulders in suspicious manner. The bigger fellow looked like someone who lived in his tenement, a street tough named William something—wait a minute, it was him. *William the Conqueror.* He was starting up a Yamaha motorbike. The smaller one jumped on behind and they took off in a hurry.

Not knowing why, Jesse James followed the two to a seedy hotel at the end of a secluded street. Motorbikes and cars were parked out front and not clunkers either. Jesse James took cover behind a section of crumbling wall and watched as the two approached a unit at the far corner of the complex and were admitted by a man holding what looked like an automatic rifle. The curtains were drawn and Jesse James could not see what was going on inside.

A high-powered, late-model vehicle turned onto the street, looked like a big American car. Jesse James crouched low and watched. Three men came out of the car and as they moved into the light he could make out Matt Gallagher, Frank Lake and… *that black embassy man.* Street savvy held Jesse James quiet and still—trust no shadow after dark, even if it pays your salary. When it was safe, he walked his motorbike down the street and lit out in a hurry.

Inside the safe house, Matt, Frank and Freddy McGinnis met with Operation Werewolf personnel. Matt counted twelve men, though there could have been more in the back. Charles Darnell was still in police detention under the State of Emergency, but Garrett Anderson had been released and was now Operation Werewolf's ringleader; William the Conqueror and Pocket Thunder his top muscle.

216

Major Anderson was in the center of the room with the two rudeboys when the three American intelligence officers approached. William the C suddenly whirled and slammed a sheet of paper down on the table.

"Check it," he said.

It was the poster for the Smile Jamaica concert. Matt read aloud the words printed in big letters across its face: "'Bob Marley in association with the Cultural Section of the Prime Minister's office presents.' Smile Jamaica, is it?"

"Manley wan' wriggle up next to Bob Marley and steal the election," William the C said in great anger. "Craven muthah fuckah."

Matt ignored the rudeboy and spoke to Anderson.

"What's the move, Major?" he said.

Anderson's plan was a tried-and-true Jamaican standby—the roadblock. Pull the vehicle over, shooting breaks out and it's all over.

"Excellent," Matt said, but Freddy McGinnis saw wheels turning in the chief's eyes.

November 19, 1976, Kingston

The phone rang at the House of Dread and Island Record's in-house lawyer Diane Jobson picked up.

"Person-to-person collect call for Mr. Bob Marley from Miss Cindy Breakespeare," the operator said.

"Long distance for the Skipper," Jobson shouted down the hall. "London calling."

Bob, out front kicking the ball around with the guys, came running and picked up.

"Ites. Oy, Cin, wha'ppen man?"

"I won!" Breakespeare cried forty-six hundred miles away in the UK. "I won Miss World!"

"Yuh win, man?"

"Can you believe it? I'm so excited!"

"When yuh a come home?"

"I have to stay here a while on official duties. Cyan't wait to see you. Still cyan't believe it, likkle me from Jamaica. Great, don't?"

"Yeah man, is great fe true."

"See you soon. Love you."

"Cool, cool."

The new Miss World's romance with her wild-man Jamaican lover soon made torrid copy in the British tabloids, painting a false portrait of Bob as an irresponsible wastrel wantonly spilling his seed with every pretty girl that came along when in fact he was a tender and doting father to all his children and as a rule loving and respectful to their mothers. Not that he

217

gave a damn if some bloodclot newspaper editor had an opinion how many beautiful black pickneys he should sire.

In Kingston the *Smile Jamaica* single was out and playing on all the sound systems, even getting air time on the radio. Don Taylor flew to New York to hire a film crew to shoot the concert. Bob and Island Records were covering all expenses. The Wailers jammed nightly in the rehearsal room out back. Third World and several local acts had been lined up to perform and Bob tried to recruit Peter and Bunny to reunite for one night, but Peter wasn't about smiling, he wanted equal rights and justice, whereas Bunny simply felt the event was too political. He wasn't the only one. Tensions boiled to a fever pitch as a JLP motorcade was shot up and a PNP constituency office ransacked, blood spilling on both sides. The people cried out for peace and put their hopes in Smile Jamaica.

November 21, 1976

Montego Bay's Sam Sharpe Square was jam packed, people spilling around corners and down side streets. Bodies hung out windows and off balconies until hardly one more human torso could be crammed in anywhere. As darkness fell, reggae music blasted from a sound system on the back of a flatbed truck. The massive crowd was orderly and well-behaved despite the elbow-to-elbow squish-up.

From a second-floor balcony Scott looked down upon the throng, a mass of humanity such as he had never seen in all his born days.

"Must be a hundred thousand people here," he said.

"More," said Mr. Morrison. "Maybe half again as many."

That morning the Morrisons had closed the family jewelry shop for the day and picked Scott up for the long drive to Montego Bay. Marva promised a night to remember. Seaga had been on Michael Manley's back to call the elections and everyone was buzzing that tonight was the night. Marva's brother Troy still languishing in Gun Court lockup.

"Ninety thousand here in '72," Mr. Morrison went on. "Today at least fifty thousand more. I was there, I oughta know."

"This place is full of history," Marva said. "Used to be Charles Square, after the English king." She pointed down into the heart of the roiling, heaving square. "Sam Sharpe was hung down there. Led the 1831 slave rebellion and paid with his life."

"One of the Seven Heroes, isn't he?" Scott asked. "Baptist deacon?"

"They hung him anyway. Said 'I'd rather die on yon gallows than live a slave.'"

"Que cojones."

"Charles Square," Marva spat with great rancor. "What did King Charles ever do for Jamaicans other than keep us bound in slavery? Joshua renamed it Sam Sharpe Square to help black people feel proud of our heritage."

"Good man."

"That's why we're going to win."

"Manley shoots himself in the foot," said Mr. Morrison, who aligned himself with the rightwing of the PNP. "He said here in this square, coming back from Cuba last year drunk on visions of Communist Utopia, that if anybody wanted to get rich there were five flights a day to Miami. Lot of people took him at his word and left Jamaica taking their money with them, worsening the foreign exchange crisis."

"Look at all the people Joshua has taught to read," Marva retorted, "the houses he's built, roads, health clinics, farmers who have their own piece of land to work for the first time, the minimum wage, women's rights. Be fair, daddy."

"A story for you, young man," Mr. Morrison said. "A doctor wanted to leave Jamaica and take his money with him. He put a cast on his leg and made an anonymous phone call to the authorities saying a doctor traveling with a phony cast was trying to smuggle a large amount of cash out of country. He then went to the airport and bought a ticket for Miami. The police nabbed him and cracked open his cast, finding nothing of course and making the man miss his plane. He returned to the airport the next day with a brand new cast and waltzed unhindered onto a plane with $40,000 US stashed inside. The authorities were too embarrassed to stop him again. True story."

"You'd rather have Seaga in office?" Marva said.

"I'm not saying Manley is all bad," Marva's father said. "He has done many good things. But he is no Joshua and if he moves too far left he'll destroy the party. Opportunists like Seaga will win the day. In politics one must above all be a pragmatist."

"What about doing the right thing?" Marva countered. "Standing up for the weak and the poor? Ask them what they think of pragmatism as they suffer in their shit-hole."

Just then a tremendous wave of excitement rose up in the huge crowd as Michael Manley was spotted. He moved freely among the people, clasping hands, kissing babies, embracing grandmothers, pumping his fist in a triumphant gesture. The faces of the people glowed with love and affection. Manley's programs were improving their lives and they would fight to the death for him. If Michael wasn't Joshua to lead the way to the Promised Land he was the next best thing.

Manley, the last speaker of the evening, was called up to an earth-shaking ovation. The master orator worked his audience with PNP slogans. "Socialism is Love" and "We know where we're going." He spoke of shared struggle, achievements and mistakes and the long road ahead. His voice crackled and sizzled like a Bible-pounding evangelist, fists pumping the air and whipping up the masses. He brought out the Rod of Correction to a tremendous roar. Even Pop Morrison whooped and hollered. Scott was swept away with everyone else as he and Marva pogo-ed up and down in frenzied delirium.

In closing, invoking the vision of a brighter tomorrow, Manley announced to a thunderous cheer the date of the election—December 15, ten days after Smile Jamaica. Detractors would accuse him of piggybacking onto the concert to get political mileage out of Bob Marley, but between Seaga hollering for elections and the continuing violence, the sooner the elections were staged the better. Hopefully the bloodshed would diminish after the populace voiced its will.

In the morning Manley set out for Savanna-La-Mar, along the western coast of Westmoreland, where he was to visit the local constituency office to firm up support before the election. He was heading straight into an Operation Werewolf ambush.

Arnold Bertram and Finance Minister David Coore accompanied him in a government Jeep along with two police officers escorting on motorcycles. Manley drove. At Chicester, a dot on the road near the Hanover-Westmoreland Parish line, a roadblock had been set up and manned by a Security Forces squad commanded by Major Garrett Anderson. Manley got out to investigate as Bertram and Coore wandered off to stretch their legs.

Something struck him as odd—despite the queue of waiting cars, there were no vehicles emerging out the other side, the road ahead deserted for a good half-mile. He smelled trouble. Anderson stood with a dozen men holding rifles.

"What is the holdup, Major?" Manley demanded.

Cold hard faces stared back at him. The two motorcycle officers held back by their bikes. Michael was alone facing a dozen armed men whose leader had pointedly not acknowledged his greeting and who stood there scowling hostilely.

One of the motorcycle officers drew his sidearm but in the face of twelve rifles was at a loss. His colleague reached over to stay his arm and he holstered the weapon.

Now Michael was completely alone. The rifles lowered in his direction. He brought all his powers of concentration to bear as the men pointed their guns at his chest. The moment called for decisive action; weakness and hesitation could well be fatal.

He strode forcefully toward Anderson.

"Stand down, Major," he commanded. "I order you and your men to shoulder your weapons."

Anderson stood mute. His men looked to him for an order. The called-for action had seemed simple enough before. Just say "Fire!" and Manley would be dead. Now it loomed monumental and grave, akin to killing one's own father. Murdering the patriarch, leader of the nation, the tribal elder. Anderson stood frozen, beads of sweat breaking across his brow, an awful quaking in his gut.

Manley bristled with indignation at the failure to respond to his order. He changed tact and turned from Anderson toward the line of soldiers.

"Stand down, men!" he barked. "As your commander-in-chief I order you to lower your weapons."

The men glanced anxiously to Anderson for the order to shoot or stand down. Manley strode forward as if he would single-handedly wrestle their weapons away and administer beatings. Finally, a soldier lowered his rifle. Others seemed determined to act still, but a second shouldered his weapon, and another, and the moment had passed.

Manley and the others got back in the Jeep and sped off to Savannah-La-Mar and the meeting with the local party constituency.

32

March 1981, Santa Barbara

In his funk following the Tosh concert Scott missed a couple sessions with Dr. Mitchell and Phil dropped by on the pretense of making a buy. He didn't attempt any midnight head-shrinking, just sat and smoked and listened to tunes with the kid, hoping the presence of another human being was therapeutic somehow, as Scott didn't seem himself at all. Phil said he'd enjoyed the concert and hadn't realized Scott had fumbled the words and that in any case it was no big deal, the show had clearly been a great success. Zack stopped by and said basically the same thing. As did Suzette on the phone from LA, adding that there wasn't anything going on between her and Reggie—or her and Zack for that matter—and that he shouldn't be so paranoid. He should laugh it off, believe in himself and come back stronger next time. She knew he could do it and if he wanted he could call her. Even Reggie called to check on him.

Before he left, Phil Mitchell said he hoped Scott would come to the office and talk things out. They were making good progress and he should see it through. It'd be a shame to do all this work, come all this way and then quit with the prize so close at hand.

I'm tired of talking, said Scott, increasingly filled with a sense of dread that things had grown out of control and were heading toward disaster. But after a couple weeks he got back on the bike and rode over.

Phil Mitchell was lining up a long putt on the carpet as Scott entered the office.

"Right with you," Mitchell said, hovering over his stroke, the plastic cup-hole beckoning like golfer's Valhalla. His grip was unsteady on the club shaft, the DTs coming on, and he pulled the dimpled ball wide of the cup and off the green entirely.

"Nicklaus dodges a bullet," Scott quipped, though he was not in a jovial mood. He boggled that a putt could be missed so badly.

"I'll skin that damn Golden Bear yet," Mitchell said, foregoing the ritual handshake to hide his trembling hands. "Come sit."

Scott doffed his tam and flung his locks as they sat. They caught up on each other's lives, Mitchell sharing that he and Aunt Sylvia had gone to the movies and subsequently done a weekend retreat together. Yoga and meditation in the woods with a bearded guru.

"Separate sleeping bags, I hasten to add," Phil winked, but in truth he was ambivalent about the relationship. Sylvia was gentle and giving but didn't float his boat, erotically speaking. She couldn't hold a candle to the spectacular Karen, age and gravity working insidious effects on the body beautiful. Even worse, her kind knowing eyes seemed to see through him in his hollowness. Phil was sure she'd sniffed out his every weakness. He clung to old crutches to see him through.

Had Scott called Suzette?

No.

"There's the phone," Phil said, finding comfort in his prescribed role of doctor/healer.

"What... call her right now?"

"No time like the present."

"Gotta do this my own way, Doc."

"Why not go for the gusto?" Mitchell said, clasping his hands behind his head as if to wax poetic a moment. "Full speed ahead and damn the torpedoes."

"If I don't get my shit together I'll fuck things up."

"Which can be a great learning experience."

"Yeah, like a racehorse breaking its leg."

"A lion cub taking down its first antelope."

"It's all about getting over that first hurdle. Believing in yourself somehow."

"All there is, man, is hurdles. If you're waiting for smooth sailing it's not coming and it'd bore you to death anyway."

"Better cut down on the herb, Doc. You're tripping."

"I hear Marley's in Germany at a cancer clinic."

"Oh yeah? I heard he's chillin' in Shashamane."

"What's that?"

"A Rasta community of Jamaican expats in Ethiopia. Property Haile Selassie I set aside for repatriation for Africans of the Diaspora. Bob went there to catch a little R 'n R in the Fatherland."

"George said doctors confirmed the cancer and that it was actually a stroke that day in Central Park."

"George tell you about the Pittsburgh show two days later?"

"No."

"Brilliant. Awesome. Awesomely brilliant. Sound like a stroke?"

"The tour was cancelled, wasn't it?"

"Maybe Bob needs a rest. Maybe it wasn't even Bob. Could've been Carly or Family Man or anybody else. Nobody's in better shape than the Tuff Gong. Skip'll be just fine."

"Wasn't Bob baptized into the Ethiopian Orthodox Church?"

"Rastas have a strong link to the Orthodox Church. He didn't renounce his faith."

"But why would he pick now to get baptized? Because he's sick?"

"How do you know it wasn't something he'd been meaning to do for a long time? Jesus, Doc, you never let up, do you. Killer bees could take a lesson from you."

"You feel like I'm attacking you."

"Swarming would be the word. To tell the truth I don't have a clue what you're doing. Not a fucking clue."

"Why didn't you check for Bob at the Bowl shows?"

"Where we going with this, Doc?" Scott folded his arms across his chest. "We've passed the point of diminishing returns. I'm tired of coming in and bleating like a whiny loser. Bashing our heads against the wall for nothing. Don't push a guy over the edge."

"Let's try something, shall we?" said Mitchell.

"Here we go again," Scott rolled his eyes.

"I'll say a word and you respond with whatever springs to mind."

"Play your little game."

The word association test was originally devised by Carl Jung to plumb for unconscious complexes. Unusually slow or quick responses, facial and bodily reactions, and bizarre verbal associations hinted at unresolved conflicts and buried traumatic vestiges. Mitchell hoped merely to breach the kid's defensive walls and get him talking. Get him off the skunk hole.

"*Bread*," Mitchell gave the first word.

"Water," Scot replied.

"*Jamaica.*"

"Smile."

"*Sex.*"

"Geez...."

223

"Whatever comes to mind."

"Lot of words come to mind."

"First one that pops up."

"Fuck," he sighed, at a loss, then saw the irony of his utterance and tittered "heh-heh."

"*Bob.*"

"Awesome. Incredible. Dreadlocks Lion. Mag--"

"--One word is enough," Mitchell cut him off. "First word that comes to mind."

"Sorry, Doc."

"*Invincible.*"

"Immortal."

"*Gun.*"

"M14."

"*Knife.*"

"Kill."

"*CIA.*"

"Mother-fucker. That's one word."

"*Father.*"

"Filthy-lying-cunt-whore. That's one long word. Oops."

"*Marva.*"

"Marvelous, magnificent, Madonna, Michelangelo miracle, marriage. That's a lot of words. Sorry, I'll do better."

"You and she were talking marriage?"

"Good question," Scott said, stroking his jaw

"We'll come back to that. *Afraid.*"

"Wait… you said something. One of your words, what was it?"

"Invincible?"

"No."

"Gun? CIA?"

"Knife… it was knife."

"Yes?"

"I'm seeing something. It's… oh no. Oh dear Jah. Troy. Ah geez, no."

"Troy?"

"Marva's brother. They stabbed him in Gun Court. Killed him. Son of a bitch."

"Tell me everything that comes to mind. Hold nothing back."

"I rode over to Marva's, people were swarming over the porch and yard. It seemed like a party at first but expressions were solemn. People crying and carrying on… Marva runs up and sobs in my arms like a baby."

"Go on."

"It was a wake for Troy. I did what I could to console her and went back a couple days later. It was Third Night...."

Three days after Troy Morrison was killed Scott rode over to Marva's and again found the place astir with people, the family preparing food and attending to guests. Marva in a long black dress passed with a plate of fruit.

"Scotty, soon come, hear?" She delivered the fruit to a table across the room and returned.

"Hi, honey." She smacked him a kiss.

"Still got a lot of company, I see," Scott said, relieved to find Marva calmer and more composed than she had been the other night.

"It's tradition. Everybody paying their respects to Troy."

The Morrison house was currently a "dead yard." In Jamaican religious belief, at the time of death the body went to the grave, the spirit or soul flew straightaway to God, but the ghost hung around in a kind of limbo. Since African days certain rites had been performed to help the ghost or "duppy" make the journey to the spirit world. The word was a corruption of "door peep," the invisible presence peeping in through cracks and keyholes. For nine nights before burial family and friends gathered at the dead yard, the home of the deceased, to support the bereaved and help the dearly departed fly to the realm beyond. (The duration of the rite oddly reminiscent of the nine-day mourning period following the passing of a Pope.) Food and drink were served, there was storytelling, dancing and singing, dominoes and other games. Over-proof white rum flowed freely. It was more a period of merrymaking than mourning, a celebration that the loved one was "gwan a better place." Friends and relatives came from miles around and no one waited upon an invitation.

Possessions of the deceased were often placed in the coffin for familiarity and jonnycakes—"journey cakes"—for nourishment on the journey home. If truth be told, of equal concern was assuring that the lingering duppy would not create all manner of havoc for the living. Precautions had to be observed, the details of which tended to vary somewhat by local custom. In preparing the body for burial, the corpse typically had to be washed with great care by two men working head to foot at precisely the same pace... pockets in the death suit had to be cut out or sewn up lest the ghost return with a cache of stones to sling—duppies known for their uncanny accuracy... all buttons had to be cut off and many other steps taken. It was crucial that no tears fell on the body or the duppy would haunt you. Urgent remedies would then have to be invoked, like planting pigeon peas on the grave to "tie down" the roving malign energy. A footloose duppy could be manipulated to harm people by a practitioner of Obeah.

225

As Troy's death had been violent, Mrs. Morrison sewed into her son's death suit a ratchet knife and sent his ghost on a mission of revenge by whispering in the deceased's ear "Go do your work." Forget throwing stones. Take this ratchet and get the bastard who done this terrible thing to yuh, my son. If more than one, get all of them. *Gwan sweep out the yard.*

"Better let you tend to your ghosts," Scott said. "I mean guests."

"I'm glad you're here," Marva said. "There's going to be singing later. It's Third Night. The duppy rises up and roams around."

"The duppy—that's the ghost, right?"

"Yes."

"They sing to it?"

"Sankeys, hymns. It's tradition. Sometimes sing on the fortieth night too. They say the duppy can wander forty days and forty nights, like in the Bible. I'll fix you a plate."

About nine o'clock, thinking he would make a polite exit, Scott found Marva to say goodnight.

"Guess I'd better mosey on—"

"Hush. Never say you are leaving or the duppy will follow you home."

"Holy shit."

"If that happens you have to write an X on the ground as fast as you can."

"An X?"

"Like Latin number ten. Duppy can only count to nine. He'll get confused."

"What if he takes off his socks and shoes?"

"You're making fun of us."

"It's a little strange to me, that's all. Don't be angry."

"These are our traditional beliefs. I didn't sit down and dream this up."

"I know, I know. I'm sorry."

"Come Saturday night," she said. "It's Nine Night, very special. Big feast, singing and dancing all night."

"Got it!" Scott cried. "The duppy can only count to nine because there's only nine night fe dead yard."

Marva smiled and Scott breathed more easily. "I'll ask momma if you can stay here," she said. "Maybe you could sleep in Troy's room."

"Cool... I think." Sleeping in a haunted house—in the ghost's old room, at that.

Marva walked Scott out to his bike.

"Don't talk to anyone you meet on the road after dark," she said. "Might be a duppy."

He didn't believe in ghosts but riding home a whistle or sudden screech of tires sent a shiver down the back of his neck such as he had never known.

Scott's voice trailed off and he lapsed into a brooding quietness as the clock ticked toward the top of the hour.

"Are you all right?" Dr. Mitchell asked.

"Tired, Doc," Scott sighed deeply. "Tired of the whole thing."

"You've recovered a lot of material. You're winded, that's all."

"I think we're about done here, man. Just want to get on with my life. You think Jamaicans have the luxury of going to a shrink?"

"Did you go to Marva's for the wake?"

"Let's cut our losses, Doc. Going any further could ruin everything. End up a catastrophe. I'm teetering on the brink here. Bad mother-fucker feeling about the whole thing. Mother-fucker, that's one word."

Time was nearly up and Mitchell thought not to argue the point. But as he showed his patient to the door, Scott lingered.

"Something was holding me back," he said. "About going backstage to see Bob."

"At the Bowl shows."

"Couldn't face him."

"Why?"

"I felt... uh... ashamed or something."

"Why should you feel ashamed?"

"I don't know."

"Let's talk more next week. We're really close. We'll get this worked out."

Bob Marley was not in Ethiopia catching R 'n R in the Fatherland as Scott had wanted to believe. That was a cover story released to the press by Rita to protect Bob's privacy. George was right: Marley was at Issels' clinic for last-gasp cancer patients in Germany.

After collapsing into Skill Cole's arms as they jogged in Central Park that September 1980 morning, Bob was helped by Skill and Pee Wee, Bob's personal physician Dr. Fraser, back to his room at the Essex House hotel. Bob's body had "frozen up" and he couldn't walk. Over the next couple hours Bob's faculties slowly returned and he was able to walk again. The next morning Dr. Fraser took Marley to a neurologist. Examination revealed a malignancy in Bob's brain. A large, cancerous, extremely deadly tumor. The melanoma which had been discovered in 1977 and which doctors had warned constituted a grave threat to Bob's health had metastasized throughout his body. The neurologist said that Bob had suffered a stroke in Central Park and had only weeks to live. Two or three weeks at most.

The *Uprising* Tour had just begun in Boston the week before. Plans were in the works also for a grand tour with Stevie Wonder, Grammy winner for Best Album three of the last four years. These were exciting times, Bob reaching new heights bringing his music and message to Brazil, New Zealand, Zimbabwe and beginning to break through to his black bredren in North America, black radio stations finally giving air time. If last year's tour had drawn crowds of 100,000, there was no arena on earth which the Wailers wouldn't sell out and have an overflow beating down the gates. And now this worst of all possible news.

Marley flew to Pittsburgh with Skill and Pee Wee the Tuesday after his collapse in Central Park. A devastated Rita was waiting to read the riot act—why hadn't the tour been stopped so her husband could get medical care? Who were these cocaine snorters who only saw the dollars that would be lost? Bloodsucking hangers-on there may have been, but everybody in the regular entourage loved Bob dearly. Most would have laid down his or her own life to save him. Bob had always called the shots and in the face of tragedy the tendency was to defer to Skipper's wishes. If Bob wanted to play on, so be it—Wailers would stand by him all the way. And so on to Pittsburgh's Stanley Theatre and another awesome show, complete with two encores and Bob's soul-wrenching rendition of *Redemption Song*, which tore the hearts out of everybody.

Rita was furious. Lover and baby mother who had become more like a spiritual sister to Bob, she had always watched out for him—washing out his underpants every night in the days he only had one pair, ironing his clothes before shows, chasing unwanted women from his room, swallowing her pride and taking in his children by other women and loving them as her own. She immediately contacted Bob's mom and with Mother B and Skill Cole siding in, the tour was cancelled after the Pittsburgh show.

The next day Bob flew to Miami and checked in to Cedars of Lebanon hospital, where he'd had the operation on his foot three years before. Doctors there sent him straight to Sloan-Kettering Cancer Center in New York. Medical evaluation confirmed the brain tumor, with the additional findings of cancerous growths in his lungs and stomach. Again the Tuff Gong was given only weeks to live. Radiation therapy was begun immediately.

The next day, as a local radio station broke the news that Marley was a patient at Sloan-Kettering, Marley left the hospital to safeguard his privacy and checked in to the Wellington Hotel, continuing his treatment as an outpatient. Bob felt strong enough to go out and watch 38-year-old Muhammad Ali's futile "comeback" fight against Larry Holmes on closed-circuit and Skill took him out to play soccer on a Sunday, but Skip could do little more than bunt the ball a few minutes before having to retire.

Bob suffered another small stroke and was put on chemotherapy, which caused his locks to fall out. On November 4, at the urging of his mother, Bob was baptized in the Ethiopian Orthodox Church. The ceremony took place in Bob's room at the Wellington, conducted by Abuna Yesehaq, Archbishop of the Ethiopian Orthodox Church in the Western Hemisphere. Bob was christened Berhane Selassie, "Light of the Holy Trinity."

Danny Sims and Rita wanted Bob to go to the clinic in Mexico where Steve McQueen was undergoing treatment. Then Pee Wee and Skill found out about Issels' clinic. Mexico was warm where Germany was cold and damp—but on November 7, McQueen died and the decision was made. Bob, accompanied by Skill and Pee Wee, departed with all haste for Bad Wiessee on Lake Tegernsee in predominantly Catholic Upper Bavaria. The Catholic Pope the ultimate symbol and manifestation of Babylon.

Upper Bavaria is the German state of Munich, Nuremberg, Bayreuth (with its summer Wagner festival), heavily-bombed Wurzburg, and Dachau. It is one of the most picturesque regions of Europe in the foothills of the Alps near the borders of Switzerland, Austria, and the former Czechoslovakia. Fifty kilometers south of Munich, at 2300 feet elevation, is Bad Wiessee, a spa resort blessed with healing springs but stained by a dark history. In 1934, in the purge known as the Night of the Long Knives, Nazis stormed the Hanselbauer Hotel here and routed the rival Brownshirts of the SA (Sturmabteilung), executing many including SA leader Ernest Rohm. Josef Issels was in fact a former Nazi and member of the SS. He would later claim to have petitioned to leave the party upon being ordered not to treat Jews.

Arriving at Bad Wiessee on November 9, Bob Marley took heart. Issels, who'd survived a Russian prison camp after the war, radiated confidence and conviction. Believing that a healthy body could not contract cancer, Issels aimed to restore health by purifying the immune system through natural methods like organic foods and clean living. Other methods, including blood transfusions, hyperthermia—"heat" therapy using intense beams of ultraviolet light—and administration of the experimental drug THX had earned Issels the designation of full-fledged quack by the medical establishment.

Against all odds, Bob rallied. His weight was down and his appetite poor, but he took walks of up to one hour on mountain trails and kicked the soccer ball around in the gym. His mother and Dianne Jobson flew in to offer support. Rita jetted back and forth from Jamaica bringing favorite foods from home, which had to be smuggled past the kitchen staff. Dianne helped him conduct business via phone to Jamaica, London and Nassau. Cindy Breakespeare sensed it was not her time and entrusted Bob to the care of his family. His birthday party and the company of old friends buoyed him. He was already well past his allotted two or three weeks to live. His spirits were up.

Would Jah save the Rastaman after all?

33

End of November 1976, Kingston

Edward Seaga was at it again. All along, the crux of his campaign to become Jamaica's new prime minister had been his relentless castigation of Michael Manley as a communist and a bumbling idiot who was running the country's economics into the ground. Seaga styled himself a financial wizard who understood these matters far better than Manley and claimed only he could steer Jamaica's ship away from ruinous calamity to the distant shores of prosperity. In some instances he had shown remarkable insight, even prescience anticipating the government's wheeling-and-dealings. He promised his followers that if he were elected "money would fall from the sky like showers and jingle in your pockets"—from which statement the most ruthless of the Jamaican gangs, the Shower Posse of Tivoli Gardens, took its name.

Now came Seaga's most outrageous claim—that the Manley administration was negotiating loans from the IMF which would stipulate a massive forty percent devaluation of the Jamaican dollar, allow unemployment to rise and put a cap on government spending, striking a severe blow against the social programs that were the very backbone of the PNP's drive to improve the lives of ordinary Jamaicans.

The PNP leftwing nervously shrugged off Seaga's lunatic ravings. Michael Manley, the people's champion, suddenly renouncing everything he stood for to be reborn a Nixonian capitalist? Somebody must have fixed Seaga's business. Still, he had been uncannily accurate of late—some were convinced he had spies inside Manley's administration—and a word of reassurance was sought. The job fell to Bev Manley.

She brought it up over early morning coffee and peanut porridge in the breakfast room at Jamaica House.

"Mike," she said, stirring rich Jamaican dairy milk into her cup of brew, "these rumors about the IMF."

"Rumors, that's exactly what they are," Manley said, looking up from his morning newspaper.

"Because it would ruin everything we've worked for."

"It won't happen, I promise you."

"I'm reading this book by Cheryl Payer called *The Debt Trap*. Countries that follow an IMF program, she says, almost always end up worse off, having to cut vital social programs just to service the interest on the loans. She calls it a bottomless pit… you pay and pay and pay but the debt never goes away. It's a trap."

"I'm not going to let Jamaica fall in any bottomless pit."

Pleased, Bev leaned over and kissed her husband. Joshua was still chipping away at Babylon's walls. But Manley didn't have a clue how he would live up to his promise.

Jesse James was leaving his yard to tail Scott to school when he noticed several unruly types congregating outside William the C's flat. There'd been a lot of traffic down that way recently and by the looks of it not church-going types getting together to slap dominoes and watch the Reggae Boyz on the telly.

Suddenly two rudeboys tore out of the yard on a motorbike, issuing a stream of profanity all down the street. At the corner the rider on back tossed something in the gutter. After a discrete few minutes Jesse James rode over and stopped to check his bike as if there were some mechanical problem. A wadded-up sheet of paper lay in the street. When he was sure no one was watching he picked up the paper, stuffed it in his pocket and sped off.

Three blocks down the road he stopped for a red light and examined the wadded paper. It was a poster for the Smile Jamaica concert. Nothing sinister here.

He had to hurry now or he would miss the kid—maintaining the ruse for Mr. Matt's sake. The two had come to be on friendly terms, stopping and chatting patois when no one was watching. Scott was curious how Jesse James got his name and Jesse asked about the various countries the kid had lived and how his father lost his eye.

Jesse James followed the Gallagher youth to Sunridge High and returned to his yard, where he worked on a new sculpture in a planned "National Heroes" series. He remembered the Smile Jamaica poster in his pocket and took it out to inspect. Why would that guy just sling it in the gutter like a piece of trash? Jesse James pressed out the wrinkles and tacked the sheet up on the wall. His girls dearly wanted to go to the concert to see the great Bob Marley and he planned to take them.

The new piece, ironwood about fifty percent larger than a man's head, was to be shaped into the image of George William Gordon, hung alongside Paul Bogle in the Morant Bay uprising despite being part white. As Jesse James chipped away with chisel and hammer the riddle of the poster returned again and again to mind. If those rudies were JLP and thought Marley was throwing in with Manley, they'd be vexed, plenty vexed. He remembered that big Cuban Mr. Matt met with that day at the Cinnamon Lounge and the passing woman who'd called him an "ass."

In the shock of sudden clarity the hammer slipped from Jesse James' hand and dropped on his toe. It wasn't *ass* that the woman had uttered.

It was *assassin*.

Jesse James shuddered. Was the American Embassy in the murder business? He glanced at the Smile Jamaica poster and read aloud the words printed across the top: "Bob Marley in association with the Cultural Section of the Prime Minister's office presents--"

And he got it. Somebody thought Bob Marley was in cahoots with the PNP and boosting Manley for re-election. Somebody was mad enough about it to kill one of them—*or both.* At the Smile Jamaica concert by the looks of it.

Should he tell someone? Tell who? The black man from the embassy? Why should he trust him? Was he thinking insane thoughts? All this over a crumpled poster and a Cuban coming out of a bar. What if he was wrong? *What if he was right?* He admired Bob Marley and Michael Manley seemed sincere in trying to help the Jamaican people—he sure wouldn't want to see either of them killed. He had to say something. But what if he opened his mouth to the wrong guy?

Those closest to Bob Marley fussed and fretted. Blunt warnings to abort Smile Jamaica *or else* continued to come in over the phone. Marcia Griffiths of the I-Three freaked so bad she got on a plane and flew to Miami. Judy Mowatt had another vision:

Rooster and three chicken inna yard... someone take potshot at rooster and hit one a dem chicken and bloody innards spill onna de ground.

A cock and three hens... damn if that didn't seem just a little too much like Bob and the I-Three. Bob brushed off all concerns—*show haffi go on.*

And then, from a different direction altogether, tragedy struck.

After going through the motions of tailing the white *bwoy* to school for morning classes, Jesse James went back to his yard and walked over to the flat across the way that had seen so much traffic lately.

"Oy," he hailed. "Hello the house."

A moment later William the C walked around the side, barefoot and cranky from being woken up.

"Who make ruckus in me yard?" he said. "Wha' yuh want, boy?"

"I-man can work."

"Nuh work here."

"Please, suh, long time nuh job come me way and my daughter-them hungry every day."

"Gwan with yuh."

"Me beg fe me likkle girl-them can eat. Me do anything, anything."

"Nuh work me have fe beggar-man."

"I-man work hard, seen?"

"Yuh deef, man? Gwan 'fore me lick yuh head."

Jesse James got down on one knee.

"Me begging, man, yuh nah see it?"

William the Conqueror gave Jesse James a good sizing up. For an older fellow, he was spry and gutsy as hell.

"Can shoot gun, old timer?"

"I-man can do that."

"Ever kill a man?"

"Plenty man me a kill," Jesse James lied.

"What beer yuh drink?"

"Me drink rum."

"Say there nuh rum. What beer yuh drink?"

"Heineken."

"Can kill big man?"

"Big man can dead same as likkle man."

"*Big, big* man me mean… famous man."

"Sometime famous man need fe dead."

"Come back inna de morning."

"Thank you, my brother."

"Hey."

"Yeah?"

"Them need fe dead, believe it."

Jesse James walked back and got on his bike. *Big famous man—* who could that be but Marley or Manley if not the two of them? Sure looked like mistuh Matt had his hand in it too. Maybe that was what the black embassy man was talking about.

Next morning, Jesse James walked over to William the C's flat. He hadn't slept well… gunshots last night. Close by too.

"Oy," he hollered.

Two minutes passed and he hollered again.

"Oy. Yuh say come back inna morning."

Jesse James wandered around the side of the flat.

"Anyone there? Hello?"

There was a window high up on the wall with no curtains. Jesse James edged over and stood on tiptoes to peer inside. It was a bedroom, a slovenly 10' x 10' space crammed with the artifacts of ghetto existence, clothing strewn everywhere, bottles of Heinie, a plastic cup with a cigarette butt floating in a half-inch of rum… and sure enough, there on the rickety two-boards-of-a-bed was the fucking guy sprawled out on the sheets, dead to the world.

Jesse James tapped on the window.

"Mister. Mister."

The man didn't move. He was really out of it. Bottle of rum by the bed.

Jesse James shifted to get a better look—and in the next instant staggered backwards onto the seat of his pants.

The man was dead fe real.

William the C lay staring up at the ceiling, a bright red bullet hole in the middle of his forehead. His conquering days behind him.

Jesse James skulked back to his yard, grabbed some supplies and headed for the hills like a Maroon dodging Redcoats. He would really have gone high up if he'd known that across town, William the C's compatriot-in-arms Pocket Thunder also lay dead in his bed, his woman alongside, bullet holes in both their heads.

With these two out of the way, Matt Gallagher ordered Al Capone and Wild Bill Hickok to get their goon squad ready. He lavished them with guns, money and cocaine. Not about to go through a cut-out, he skirted Agency regulations and personally handed Al Capone $2000 in US greenbacks under the table, with a promise of $2000 more when the job was done. Marley and Manley, a package deal. Wipe both scumbags off the face of the earth.

Fuck Operation Werewolf. They'd had their chance and blown it. That couldn't be allowed to happen again. Time to go law of the jungle, let the fur fly and the blood run and may the best man win, and that sure as hell wasn't going to be anybody other than Matt Gallagher.

When word of the murder of the rudeboys and woman got around, Freddy McGinnis was certain the chief was working a rogue operation against Manley and, he suspected, Bob Marley as well. He could read it in Gallagher's eyes. McGinnis, to whom Bob Marley had become a folk hero, was desperate to stop any action against the reggae star and was now against eliminating the prime minister as well. What was Michael Manley doing besides trying to take care of his people? What on God's earth was wrong with that? What were they doing in Jamaica in the first place? Frank Lake had come around to a similar position on Marley but still felt Manley had to go in order to prevent the spread of communism—though he had to admit farmer cooperatives and a minimum wage didn't seem quite on a par with Marx and Lenin and Russian ICBMs. Not quite in a league with gulags and re-education camps. For a moment it flashed on Lake that it was all a big lie, this facile labeling of actions to improve people's lives as something evil—an appeal to fear to keep the American populace in line like sheep. He quickly brushed the thought out of mind.

Lake dug up Jesse James' 201 file to get his particulars and McGinnis promptly went off to find him, figuring he had until the Smile Jamaica concert to stop the twin assassinations. He dropped by James' common-law-wife's place in Ackee Walk—just across from where one of the rudeboys was murdered—but the woman didn't know where he was, or if she did wasn't telling.

Starting Monday of the week of the concert an armed PNP "vigilante group" posted a round-the-clock guard at the House of Dread. The "Echo Squad" patrolled the grounds in teams with automatic rifles on hair trigger and put a halt to the usual nonstop flow of humanity in and out of the place. Unauthorized persons were turned away at the gate. A gang of JLP gunmen who had been extorting money from Bob to cover a gambling debt of Skill Cole's was sent packing after a tense standoff that threatened to explode into a second OK Corral.

Matt Gallagher issued strict orders to his son to steer clear of Hope Road and avoid large gatherings. Elections were coming up, more violence could be expected and Scott was to be home before dark when the State of Emergency curfew kicked in. But with his father gone every evening, Scott took his chances with the cops and popped by the House of Dread for a few minutes early Monday evening on his way home from visiting Marva at the dead yard. The presence of armed guards manning the gate gave him cause for alarm.

"What's going on?" he called out.

"Gwan with yuh," a hulking guard scowled, rattling his rifle.

"I'm a friend of Bob Marley." Scott could hear Wailers jamming from the rehearsal room out back. "Hear them there?"

"Galang bwoy 'fore me lose me temper."

The man's forbidding scowl made it clear Scott wasn't going to get in without Bob himself coming to the gate and that being out here after dark with these militia goons wasn't a particularly good idea. Smile Jamaica was not without an element of danger, it seemed. He worried about Bob and the crew.

34

April 1981, Santa Barbara

As week to week Scott and Dr. Mitchell progressed inexorably toward the ultimate conclusion of his time in Jamaica, Scott had grown increasingly uneasy about what was to come. Everything seemed to be boiling to an explosive, catastrophic head, birds singing outside his window at night, a black moth fluttering into his room—harbingers of death at every turn. Now an altogether disgusting memory had raised its ugly head. He showed up for session burdened with an overwhelming sense of impending doom.

"Here under protest," Scott said as he entered and sat. "If something happens it's on your head."

"We'll exercise all due professional diligence," Mitchell said.

"I feel so much better."

"This is all going to work out. We're getting down to the nitty gritty here, Smile Jamaica and the end of your time in Jamaica. We must be close, very close."

"Someone spit in my face."

"What?" Mitchell recoiled.

"Someone spit in my fucking face."

"When was this? In Jamaica?"

"Where else would it be?"

"You don't remember who it was?"

"Nope."

"So we come to that big weekend. Friday Nine Night, Saturday Troy's funeral, the big concert on Sunday."

"Oh, boy," Scott flushed hot, heaving at the chest and wrenching his palms.

"Are you all right? We're just talking."

"Devil and Daniel Webster were just talking too," Scott springing up to pace.

"Start with what you remember. Did you go to school that Friday?"

Scott crossed his arms at his chest and squeezed his shoulders. He couldn't hold it in any longer. Doc M and Aunt Sylvia were right, he had to get it out or he was going to blow. He wandered in chaotic circles about the office, grabbing the practice putter from the corner.

"Yeah, I went to school."

"Wouldn't you like to sit down?" Mitchell asked, eying the golf club in patient's hand.

"No."

"Were kids at school talking about the concert?" Phil asked, following patient with his eyes as he paced about, cuffing the putter behind his neck with his wrists.

"Boy, were they," Scott sighed and words began to flow. "Everybody was excited. Henry, Marva and I made plans to hook up at Heroes Park early on Sunday... at the Simon Bolivar statue."

"Ah."

"After school that Friday I stopped by Hope Road. The guys are out bumping the ball. Bob waves me in the gate...."

Scott hopped in the circle and booted the ball around with Bob and the crew, everybody doing their little tricks, bouncing the *pelota* off body parts like it was attached by a string. It was quiet around the place thanks to the Echo Squad scaring everybody off.

Marley and the guys had started the day with a jog out at Bull Bay beach, barefoot and bare-chested like natural men. Looking out over the still waters of early morn a black man like Bob couldn't help but visualize the wooden ships carrying the ancestors across the Middle Passage from West Africa, the name-places reflecting European commoditization of a continent and her people: Gold Coast, Pepper Coast, Ivory Coast, *Slave Coast*. You could almost hear the creaking of the caravels bobbing on the swells, the clanging of shackles, the rustling of swallowed-up souls. The voiceless shrieking of duppies.

Walking along the shore after their run, Bob told his spars about an eerie dream he'd had that night.

"I-man in pure gunshot," Bob said. "*Bam. Bam. Bam.* Bullet lick everywhere and nah catch me. Dream say 'nah run' and me wake up."

Rita too was having bad dreams. Marcia Griffiths had fled the island in fear. Judy Mowatt had awoken that morning to discover three of her chickens dead.

The omens were not auspicious.

"I left Hope Road early to get cleaned up for Nine Night," Scott told Dr. Mitchell as he bumped about the office, too nervous to sit, the putter resting on his shoulder like an on-deck batter's war club. "Marva's dad asked my dad's permission and the Big Cheese said okay. I was going to stay in Troy's room. Ground Zero in a real haunted house. What kid wouldn't dig that? The ultimate freakazoid. I was psyched to the max. Maddy fed me mackerel run down and gungo peas and I went over to Marva's before curfew... about seven, I guess. She was beautiful beyond words... she was wearing a purple dress...."

Wearing his best slacks and shirt, Scott rode in to the dead yard to a lively, milling throng. Dominos going hot, children laughing and running about scuffing up their Sunday finery, people carrying on and having a good time. Dancers doing the traditional *dinki*. On the veranda a big table was laid out with a white tablecloth and Jamaican delicacies like fry fish and bammy, which had to remain untouched until midnight in case the duppy was hungry. Marva was stunning in a purple dress revealing an arresting extent of cleavage that drew admiring looks even from the women. The ladies didn't cloak themselves like grannies at these affairs, no suh, Jamaican daughtahs popped style every opportunity and then some. Purple, white and black appropriate colors for mourning.

About eight o'clock prayers were said in Troy's bedroom, which had been left undisturbed and with a light on since his death. The professional sankey singer arrived, a big man named Abraham with a voice like a black Burl Ives. He was kept replenished with one hundred proof white rum at all times. Following tradition, Abraham called out the lyrics ("tracking") so everybody could join in. Some hymns Scott vaguely knew, such as *Rock of Ages*, but others like *Roll, Jordan, Roll* were unfamiliar. Marva said the singing would carry on until daylight, with extra oomph put into it around midnight, when the duppy was thought to pass through the yard.

The taxi plied the coastal road east out of Kingston to Bull Bay and beyond another fifteen miles to Morant Bay in the far southeastern corner of the island. Freddy McGinnis got out and paid the driver. Earlier that evening he had dropped by Jesse James' yard to plead with his woman for help finding him. When he'd said that Bob Marley's life was in danger, Pansy had hurried next door to her neighbor who had a phone and returned ten minutes later to send him off to Morant Bay. Jesse James would be waiting for him there, she said, by the statue of Paul Bogle.

McGinnis had read about Bogle, son of a freed slave, a Baptist deacon and leader of the 1865 Morant Bay Rebellion. Following emancipation, poll taxes prevented blacks from voting and plantation owners hoped to restart slavery. A petition was sent to Queen Victoria asking for Crown land to farm, as cultivable acreage was scarce in hilly Jamaica. The queen replied in her wisdom that the aggrieved should work harder. When black protesters were murdered, rebellion broke out and a few whites were killed. A wholesale slaughter of blacks ensued and many, including Bogle and William Gordon, a free coloured with white blood in him who would also be named one of the Seven Heroes, were strung up.

The statue, another Edna Manley work, was in front of the Morant Bay courthouse near where the hangings had occurred. The small bronze had caused a tremendous stir when it was installed—the first public statue in Jamaica of a black man.

McGinnis waited in the dark until a sudden voice startled him out of a year's growth.

"Wha' yuh want?" the voice demanded. "Nah turn around. Look straight ahead. Why yuh here?"

"Jesse James?"

"Start talking, embassy man."

"I'm afraid something bad might happen to Bob Marley."

"Why come fe me?"

238

"Maybe you know something."

"Maybe *yuh* know something. Yuh and one-eye man."

"I think he is going to kill Marley."

"Him yuh friend."

"He's going alone on this. And I wouldn't call him a friend."

"What about Manley?"

"Manley's in jeopardy too. How about we have a beer and talk about it?"

"Rum."

"Rum it is."

Final tune-ups for Smile Jamaica started early that night at the House of Dread. A drama group Rita was involved with was planning to perform *Brashana O* at the annual Boxing Day winter pantomime at Ward Theatre and she would have to leave to attend rehearsal around nine o'clock. Wailers convened in the converted slave quarters out back. Everybody was there—with the notable exception of Marcia Griffiths—even the Zap Pow horns: Glen DaCosta on tenor sax, David Madden on trumpet, and Vin Gordon, trombone. A new guitarist was on hand, Donald Kinsey, an American blues-rocker who had played with Albert King and a trio called White Lightning. On keyboards with Tyrone Downie was lanky Earl "Wyah" Lindo, a former Wailer back in the fold after a stint with Taj Mahal. Chinna Smith came in as second guitar and Neville Garrick and Gilly helped out on harmony vocals. Kinsey and Lindo were freshly in Jamaica after backing Peter Tosh in concert in Boston just days before.

Bob pushed the band hard. After touring all summer they were already sharp, but Skip was a stickler and this one was for the people. Fearing the worst, Judy Mowatt slunk to the door between songs and peered into the night, every rustling a potential danger. Garrick dashed to the house to retrieve the herb stash and found it seriously lacking. Up-Sweet, the crew's favorite ganja man, was due to stop by with new stock any minute. Up-Sweet always had the best Sinsemilla.

"Maybe the guard send Up-Sweet away, Skip," Garrick fretted.

"Gwan tell them bwoy let him inna the yard," Marley said.

Seeco Patterson didn't want Neville to approach the guards alone and tagged along. Coming around the side of the house they saw to their surprise that the gate was unguarded and the Echo Squad nowhere to be seen. The two went back and informed Marley, who was relieved the patrolling militants were gone—too much gunman in Kingston as it was. His dream of the previous night flashed into mind... *pure gunshot.* It was just past 8:30.

At the US Embassy, Gallagher sat alone at his desk. Everything had been taken care of—the Al Capone hit squad armed, paid, given basic

239

training and corrupted by cocaine. The Hope Road surveillance site shut down. The Echo Squad bought off and dispersed. Rumors had been spread that gangsters were out to get Marley over a gambling debt incurred by Skill Cole—the perfect cover story, given that Cole had fled the country and toughs had in the past weeks been coming by Hope Road daily to extort money from Marley, whom as Cole's best friend they held responsible.

Matt was pleased. One year in country and things were mounting toward a rousing success. He occupied himself browsing through Castro assassination documents. Many CIA schemes for dealing with the Cuban leader were bizarre—like putting itching powder in his shoes. Matt's favorite was the booby-trapped seashell. His imagination conjured fanciful plots for taking care of the Rastaman: A soccer ball inflated with sarin nerve gas. High-voltage strings on his guitar. A viper nestled into those gorgon locks. What fun. If the current plan failed, creative schemes might be resorted to. Something, anything....

Scott ceased his restless pacing across the rug in Dr. Mitchell's office and stared motionless into space.

"Are you all right?" Mitchell asked.

Scott tucked the head of Phil's putter under his chin and remained silent.

"How long did you stay at the wake?"

"A while," he said, finally sitting.

"Who spit on you?"

"Not getting any more on that. Uh...."

"Yes?"

"The hunchback. He was there at the dead yard. Quasimodo with his bones and fetish objects. I'm seeing him now, yes...."

At the dead yard Abraham the sankey singer took a long swig of rum and sang *Roll, Jordan, Roll* at the top of his lungs. Suddenly a wave of excitement crashed over the yard as a stoop-shouldered old fellow with a lion-headed walking cane and an aura of immense authority passed through. The "Four-eyed" was here, a mystic who saw through the fogs of mundane existence to the world beyond—the realm of duppies. The graybeard hunchback was a Myal man.

From the West African roots of Jamaican spiritualism two branches had emerged, one malign and the other benevolent. Obeah represented the black arts, Myal the good—angels of darkness vs. angels of light (though perhaps it wasn't quite so clean-cut as that). Bob Marley's maternal grandfather, Omeriah Malcolm, had been a Myal man skilled in methods of natural healing. In cases of violent deaths like Troy's, a Myal man was often

240

called in to perform a rite rather like an exorcism to allow the deceased a peaceful transit to the spirit world.

The Myal man, a magnificent fellow with all manner of beads, shells and other doodads strung around his neck, went to the top of the yard, opened a burlap sack and spread sand and ashes on the ground. Stepping out of his sandals, he sat cross-legged and with a short stick drew a circle in the sandy ash and inscribed within the circle a square. The square he divided with intersecting lines into four quadrants. From his sack he took chicken bones, a bundle of twigs, hair, cat ears, dog teeth, parrot beaks and various other fetish items and cast them into the four quadrants of the square as he chanted and hummed.

Marva told Scott that the duppy would come through the yard at midnight.

"Everybody tries to catch it," she said. "If it wasn't so spooky it'd be hilarious, grown men and women running about grasping at the air, lunging and sprawling in their fancy clothes like they were wrestling a greased pig. Just when someone shouts that he's got it and proudly shows off the bundle of nothing in his hands, someone else points off in a different direction hollering 'See him there!' This goes on until the Myal man determines that the duppy is caught. Then there's the problem of tying it down."

"You have to tie it down?"

"Yes or it will keep wandering. You have to put it in a small box and bury it with the coffin or tie it to a cotton tree."

"How do you tie a ghost to a tree?"

"Bury it under the tree. Then we'll sweep Troy's room and turn his mattress and bed against opposite walls so the duppy won't recognize the place and stay around to haunt it. "

"Good thinking."

A slim young woman danced nude before a wolfpack of wild-eyed men in the dark recesses of the little bar in the off-the-beaten-path town of Morant Bay, so brimful with Jamaican history and folklore. In a corner nook Freddy McGinnis sat with Jesse James and ordered him a fresh shot of Appleton rum.

"You say you heard shots the night William the Conqueror was killed?" McGinnis asked.

"Hear shots every night," Jesse James said, turning from the bawdy scene in the shadows. In his youth he'd have been back there howling with the hounds but as father of two girls he didn't approve of such goings-on.

"Know someone named Thunda?" McGinnis asked.

"Yeah."

"Bullet turned his brain into Swiss cheese just like William the C. His woman too."

Jesse James chugged his fresh shot of rum like it surely would be his last.

"Something going on, fe sure," he said, his eyes darting nervously to the corners of the room, as if he feared he were being watched.

"Looks like the move will be at Smile Jamaica."

"So me figure," Jesse James said, unable to resist a glance back at the naked child thrown so casually to the wolves by the winds of fate.

"So it wasn't an Obeah man," Mitchell said, sensing a turning point. "It was a Myal man. A *good* witchdoctor, not evil. You were all worked up over nothing. There is no curse, never was."

"We don't know anything for sure," Scott retorted. "Don't go taking bows quite yet."

"Did you spend the night in Troy's bedroom?"

"Don't remember."

The phone rang and Phil picked up.

"Yes, Jazz. That's fine. No. I'll—" Mitchell stopped midsentence. Sitting across from him, Scott was staring at the phone and turning white.

Mitchell swiftly ended the conversation and turned to Scott. "Are you all right?"

"The phone," he whispered.

"Yes?"

"It rang. At Marva's. Oh God. Oh dear Jah Jah. Need to stop."

"Talk to me. Who was on the phone?"

The golf club fell from Scott's hand as he collapsed onto Dr. Mitchell's couch. He collected his stash from his jeans pocket and began to roll a joint, planting his elbows into his sides to steady his trembling hands.

"Scott—"

"In dire need of a spliff here, Doc. Wanna throw me out, fine."

"Do as you like but keep talking. Who was on the phone?"

"Death... everywhere I look is death."

"What do you mean?" Mitchell set his lighter out on the desk.

"Can't breathe." Scott took the lighter, torched his spliff and sucked down massive hits.

"Scott, what do you mean everywhere is--"

"Rasta nah deal with that!" Scott snapped. "Rasta deal wit' life!"

"Then let's go for it. No more running from it. Let it come, Rastaman."

"Bloodclot."

"Keep talking, friend. It's just me and you. Who was on the goddamn phone?"

242

"It was Marva…."

At the dead yard the Myal man was in a trance and chanting in tongues, holding all in spellbound captivity. Chills ran down Scott's flank in sudden icy torrents. This little hunchbacked man was like the conduit for all cosmic forces in the universe, as if an epic battle between mythic entities was to be fought in his very person. Scott felt himself caught up in it all, such that whatever cataclysm were to come to pass would surely smite him as well as the others. He was in this as much as they were.

Suddenly the phone rang, like a message from the Other Side. Everybody stared at the infernal contraption with its ominous chiming as time seemed to stand still. After many rings the spell broke and Marva rose to answer the phone as Scott bit into a jonnycake and looked around at folks enjoying themselves in the midst of death. There seemed something in that to ponder but he couldn't quite put his finger on it.

Suddenly there came shouts of exclamation and shock. Marva rushed to Scott with a look of horror on her face.

"Bob Marley got shot!" she cried.

It was fifteen minutes past ten.

One and a half hours earlier…

Around 8:45, the veil of night having fallen at the House of Dread and rehearsal going well, Bob called for a break. The main instrument players ran through the bridge to *Jah Live* and Bob went to check on Judy, pregnant with Skill's baby and looking green at the gills. Skill still hiding out in Africa.

"Feel all right, Jude?" Bob inquired, looking after his buddy's woman.

"Yeah man, me fine."

"Gwan home and get some rest. Keep yuh structure healthy fe the baby."

"Yuh always know best, Bob."

Bob asked Neville Garrick to drive Judy home. Garrick cringed at missing out on Up-Sweet's fresh marijuana, but as a relative newcomer he was low man on the totem pole and Skip's word was law, and now Judy was running to the bathroom to vomit. Meanwhile Rita collected her things and summoned Shanty and Senior, two likkle boys from the neighborhood who'd ridden in with her from Bull Bay.

Bob went to the tiny kitchen just inside the back door of the house to eat a grapefruit.

At the Kingston Sheraton, Chris Blackwell met with Jeff Walker, head of publicity for Island Records, Perry Henzell (of *The Harder They*

243

Come fame) and David Silver, director of the American film crew Don Taylor had hired to record Smile Jamaica on celluloid. They waited for Don Taylor.

Taylor had just returned from Miami picking up a royalty check for Bob. A profligate sort given to high-stakes gambling and whiskey, Taylor unwound with a few hands and curried goat dinner at the House of Chen, a Kingston gaming establishment. Around 8:00 he drove over to the Sheraton, but Blackwell had already left, leaving word he would rendezvous with Taylor at Hope Road.

Blackwell had gone to Lee Perry's Black Ark studio in Washington Gardens to listen to a song Scratch had written for Bob titled *"Dreadlocks in Moonlight."* Blackwell liked Perry's rendition of the tune and suggested he release it himself on Island Records. Chris waited while Scratch mixed a demo tape. The delay may have saved Blackwell's life.

Around 8:45 Don Taylor left the Sheraton for Hope Road. En route, two white Datsun compacts driving with their lights off fell in behind him. Inside were Al Capone, Wild Bill Hickok and a crew of five men, a couple of whom by age were more properly called boys. All were armed to the teeth with M16s and everything else.

At Hope Road, Neville Garrick and Judy Mowatt drove out the unattended front gate in Bob's BMW heading for Bull Bay. An instant later—mere seconds—Don Taylor turned into the compound and parked under the front alcove. He could hear the instrument players rehearsing the bridge to *Jah Live* out back. Taylor went inside the house to show Bob the $90,000 royalty check he'd fetched from Miami. Meanwhile the two white Datsuns that had tailed Taylor pulled into the yard and the seven youth piled out in a hurry. Al Capone and Wild Bill Hickok, both armed with M16s, took up positions on the Hope Road side of the property as the other five surrounded the house. Rita came around to her VW Beetle and loaded Shanty and Senior into the backseat for the drive home to Bull Bay. Inserting the key in the ignition, she observed unknown males wielding guns creeping toward the house. Rita fired up the Bug to make a run for it.

In the small kitchen at the rear of the main house, Bob was peeling his grapefruit and Donald Kinsey standing nearby as Don Taylor walked in.

"Oy, Bob," Taylor called.

"Don Taylor. Yuh back."

"Got the check. Say, that grapefruit looks juicy."

Bob peeled off a section of grapefruit for Taylor. Suddenly there came a popping like a string of firecrackers going off outside the house. *Pop! Pop! Pop! Pop!*

"Who the bloodclot set off cracker in me yard?" Marley vexed. Firecrackers not an unusual occurrence during Christmas season.

Outside, the Capone gang opened up on the house and rehearsal room out back like it was D-Day at Omaha Beach. Hearing the shooting just as she was starting the VW, Rita turned to see a youth slinking around to the kitchen area where Bob was. The sound of the engine turning over drew the youth's attention and he squeezed off a volley with an automatic rifle.

"Duck, Mummy, duck!" Shanty and Senior cried, hugging the floor as a flurry of bullets blew out the rear window. Rita ducked and stepped on the gas, bullets riddling the car like Bonnie and Clyde's death scene. As the VW squealed toward the front gate and the safety of the street, Rita felt a heavy stream running down her head to her neck.

I'm dead, she thought. *Shot in the head. This is how I die.*

One of the white Datsuns had parked sideways in front of the gate, blocking the exit. With nowhere to go, Rita pulled the emergency brake and rested her head on the steering wheel, agonizing for Bob's safety and waiting to die. The shooter ran up, saw Rita hunched over the wheel with blood streaming down her neck and the two unmoving small bodies on the floor in the back. Rita held perfectly still.

"Everybody dead!" the gunman shouted.

At the front door another hooligan poked in and blasted hot lead into the interior of the house. Tyrone Downie's girlfriend, taking cover behind the door, saw that he was a kid about sixteen. She held her breath and froze as bullets ricocheted around the room.

In the rear kitchen, as Don Taylor was coming forward to receive a slice of grapefruit, Bob noticed a rifle jutting in the back door and pointing straight at him.

Brrrap-a-tat-tat. The gun exploded in a burst of fire. Hot rounds sprayed the kitchen, chewing gaping holes in the walls. Bob remembered his dream—*Nah run*—and took no evasive action other than turning sideways, as if to make a narrower target. In the same instant, Don Taylor crossed in front of Bob and five bullets tore into DT's groin and lower back. Spewing blood, Taylor collapsed onto Marley, who cried "Selassie I Jah Rastafari!" Taylor lost consciousness and fell to the floor. Sirens began to wail, neighbors turned on their lights and the shooters ran for the getaway vehicles.

Wild Bill Hickok hustled over to the bullet-shredded Beetle for a last look. Bodies slumped motionless inside. Wild Bill reached in the driver's side window and put his gun to Rita's head. She felt the steel against her skull, felt the trembling hand vibrating down the barrel. She held perfectly still.

"Gwan now!" Al Capone shouted and Wild Bill eased his finger off the trigger. He ran for the car and the two Datsuns squealed into the night. As fast as it had started, the blitzkrieg was over.

245

As quiet settled in the wake of chaos, Rita dared to lift her head—was this what it was like to be dead? Shot in the head. Would Jah appear in his resplendent robes, the King of Kings? Blood was streaming down her face and neck but Rita was conscious. It seemed her dreadlocks had saved her life. Alive—for how long?

She turned and found the two pickneys in the backseat miraculously unhurt, hugging the floor and frozen in fear.

Rita ran for Bob. Rounding the house to the rear door, she gasped in horror—the scene was painted in a death mask of red, blood everywhere, Don Taylor lying morbidly still on the floor and Bob sitting there with his clothes soaked crimson.

"Robby!" she screamed. "Oh Jah!"

"Rita," Bob said. "Yuh head bloody."

"There blood all over yuh, man."

"Me all right. Don Taylor dead or something."

Bob had been shot but not seriously wounded. A ricocheting bullet had creased his chest and lodged in his left forearm. It was Don Taylor's blood that soaked his clothing. The five bullets that had hit Taylor almost surely would have struck Marley if DT had reached for that grapefruit an instant later.

Others began to emerge from hiding. Bob's friend Lewis Griffith was gut-shot and in serious condition. None of the Rastas wanted to touch the "deader" Taylor so Bob lifted DT up himself and with the assistance of a police officer freshly on the scene got him out to a vehicle. A woozy Rita got in a car with Diane Jobson at the wheel. Bob and Griffith were loaded into vehicles and the caravan of the wounded drove with police escort to University Hospital, out at UWI in Mona. They were lucky in one sense—had they still been living in Trench Town they would have been taken to the downtown hospital, where security was lax and gunmen were known to storm in and shoot up the place. Bob's own mother had once been refused admission to University Hospital.

Bob and Rita had both survived automatic weapons fire at almost point blank range. They saw the hand of Jah.

The phone rang at the embassy and Matt grabbed for it.

"Gallagher."

"Marley dead!" a highly agitated voice shouted. "I-man kill Marley DEAD DEAD DEAD!"

"I told you not to call here." It was Al Capone, coked out of his mind, calling from a noisy bar.

"The money. Want I money."

A call came in on the other line. It was Frank Lake.

"Marley has been shot," Lake said. "Got the radio on?"

"Is he dead?" Matt switched on the radio.

"They took him to University Hospital."

"Wait, here it is. Hold on."

The JBC news bulletin, spoken by a male announcer:

"Entertainer and reggae star Bob Marley, Rita Marley and the manager of the Wailers Don Taylor are patients in University Hospital after receiving gunshot wounds at Marley's home at 56 Hope Road tonight."

"Sonuvabitch is alive," Matt snorted, grabbing the other line to Al Capone.

"You there, asshole? Get in there and finish the job or it'll be you they're sending flowers."

Returning to Kingston from Morant Bay, McGinnis heard the announcement on the taxi's radio.

"Hear that?" the driver exclaimed. "Bob Marley shot."

"Ah, fuck," McGinnis said, turning to Jesse James in the back seat, the Jamaican equally crushed by the news.

Arriving at University Hospital, Marley and Taylor were carried in on stretchers. The bullet which had grazed Bob's chest and chipped his sternum had lodged deep inside his forearm just below the elbow. Taylor had lost a large amount of blood and was drifting in and out of consciousness at death's door. Rita lay in a ward with a bullet embedded under her scalp but not penetrated through to her brain—her dreadlocks truly had saved her life.

Michael Manley heard about the shooting and he and Beverley raced to the hospital. Bob was sitting up on a bench in the Emergency Area as they arrived. Immensely relieved Bob was okay both hugged him warmly, the prime minister wondering in anguish if he was partly to blame for calling the elections so soon after the concert. Manley immediately assigned a JDF security squad to Marley. Don Taylor urgently needed a blood transfusion but the hospital's blood bank was critically low and the only person holding a key was away at a Christmas party. The shortages Manley decried were real. Welcome to the Third World, under siege.

Marva's words so stunned Scott that he couldn't move. *Bob Marley got shot...* what did that mean? Everything about him seemed to move in slow motion, blurred faces contorting in horror and looking to one another to make sense of it. But when the TV clicked on and the bulletin about the shooting announced that Bob, Rita and Don Taylor had been shot and taken to University Hospital, Scott burst out the door like he'd been blasted out of a cannon.

"Scott wait!" Marva cried. "It's not safe." But he was already on his bike and pumping hard. He didn't know exactly where University Hospital was, but the UWI campus was easy to find and the hospital had to be right there. Once he got close he was able to follow the torrent of traffic swelling the road.

Reaching the hospital, Scott found the scene a-swarm with police. He jumped off on the fly as his bike careened into a row of croton. Two cops with weapons drawn cut him off at the door and patted him down. There in the waiting room was Bob sitting like Buddha in blood-soaked clothes.

"Bob!" he cried.

"Oy, Scotty."

"You all right, Skip?"

"Jah protect I and I."

"Rita okay?"

"She be all right. Don Taylor nah know Rasta and him have tougher time of it. Selassie-I watch over we. Ever living."

"You're a bloody mess. Who would do something like this?"

The white coats called Bob in for surgery to stitch up his wounds.

"Time fe see doctor," Bob said. "Gwan home, Scotty."

"I'm waiting right here."

"No, man. Neville Garrick there drive yuh home. Street nah safe after dark."

"I'll come by tomorrow."

"Hope Road dangerous right now. Maybe the whole of we stay another place. Gwan now."

Bob followed the nurse into surgery. Scott watched until Gong disappeared from sight. He nodded at Neville Garrick but the stunned Garrick was lost in his mind somewhere. Scott retrieved his bike from the bushes and rode home, peeled off his clothes and went to bed, only to stare up at the dark ceiling, his mind racing. Why had his father been so concerned about something happening this weekend?

He heard the car as it pulled into the drive and a couple moments later the knock on his bedroom door. The door opened ajar.

"Awake?" Matt poked his head in.

"Dad?" Scott pretended to rouse from sleep.

"Bad news."

"What happened?" Scott bolted upright, thinking his father knew something he didn't.

"Your Rasta friend got shot. He's in the hospital."

"He's okay, right?"

"You already knew."

"It was on the radio."

"You went to the hospital, you little twerp."

"My friend gets shot and I'm supposed to sit at home twiddling my thumbs?"

"What did you hear about Marley?"

"Why the sudden interest?"

"He's your friend."

"Where you been tonight, dad?"

"At the embassy, what do you think?"

"So late on a Friday night? Did you know something was going to happen?"

"Something is always happening. Why are you giving me the third degree?"

With that Matt slipped out, closing the door behind him.

"Seems like you knew something!" Scott shouted through the walls.

For different reasons, father and son slept fitfully that night. For Bob Marley sleep came hardly at all. After his injuries were stitched and bandaged and Rita tended to—surgery to remove the bullet beneath her scalp having to wait until the swelling subsided—Marley was quietly removed to Chris Blackwell's estate at Strawberry Hill in coffee country 3000 feet above the city. Manley's security forces stood guard backed by machete-wielding Rastas perched in trees like militant guardian owls. Bewildered that any Jamaican would take up arms against him, who walked freely through any ghetto and turned no sufferah away, Marley smoked spliff after spliff. Still peace of mind eluded him.

Slumped in misery on Mitchell's couch, Scott cradled his head in his hands. He clenched his jaw and winced as if in great pain, like he were reliving the past all over again. As if the bullets that tore into Bob Marley and his friends were piercing his own flesh.

"Are you all right?" Dr. Mitchell asked.

"I knew things were coming hard, but sonuvabitch."

"But this is all a matter of history. Even I seem to remember something about Marley getting shot. How could you not know?"

"That's it," Scott said, leaping to his feet, the ring of finality in his voice. "I'm done. Calling it right here."

"Slow down, man. We're making excellent progress."

"I'm burnt, man. Flamed out. Fed up with the whole thing. Just want to live my life. Too many dark clouds hanging over."

"Bob didn't die. He's okay, right?"

"Been a slice of 'dise, Doc, but I'm done. Maybe we have come a long ways like you say but the risk is too great. The face of catastrophe is staring at me here."

"You said you'd stay if I smoked with you."

"My ass is on the line. You sit there with nothing to lose."

"We're so close. Almost to the finish line."

"Why is this so important to you?"

"Because it's not important to you." Mitchell threw up his hands. "That's not true. Because I want to help you. Want to have that accomplishment."

"Ah. It's not about me, it's about you."

"It's both."

"Thank you."

"So we can go on?"

"No."

"I took risks, smoked with you. I... shit."

"Take care, amigo," Scott reaching across the desk to offer his hand. "Come by and smoke spliff any time you want. No midnight head-shrinking though."

"Let's talk it out," Mitchell pleaded, ignoring the proffered hand. The kid waved a goodbye.

"Adios, muchacho. *Vaya con Dios.*"

"You're making a mistake."

"Don't beg, Doc. Doesn't become you." Scott reached the door and had his hand on the doorknob.

"I'll make you a deal," Mitchell blurted.

"Make it quick."

"I'll give you my car."

"What?"

"The Beamer."

"Have you lost it, man?"

"Stay and we'll finish it, long as it takes. Marathon session to the bitter end, pull out all the stops and hash it through."

"You want to give me your Beamer."

"We'll order out and live on pizza and smoothies."

"You'd have to order out for your booze and drugs too."

"I'll go cold turkey."

"Can't give me your car, Doc, be serious."

"I'll sell it to you for a song. Damn thing leaks oil anyway. Five hundred dollars."

"Come on."

"Three hundred. Three hundred for a classic 1972 BMW 2002 tii. You'll have a Beamer like Bob like you always wanted."

"Get a grip, man."

"A hundred bucks. Twenty-nine ninety-five."

"Earl Scheib'll paint it for that."

"I'll throw in the paint job."

250

"BMWs aren't allowed in Alcatraz last I checked. If I go into trance and hatchet murder you or something."

"So we have a deal?"

"Jesus H. Christ, Doc. You're like gangrene or something."

"Come sit down."

"Some of us work for a living."

Phil tossed his car keys and Scott snatched them out of the air.

"Come to my place tonight and we'll grind it out."

"What's this?"

"The Porsche. A loaner. Not giving you the damn thing. Jazz'll give you directions. It's settled."

Scott stared at the jiggling keys in his hand like they held a clue to this bizarre turn of events. He felt like he'd walked into a trap somehow.

"See you tonight," Phil said. "Don't trash my car or I'm giving you up to the Obeah man."

35

The Porsche roared up San Marcos Pass in early evening darkness. Since leaving Dr. Mitchell's office that morning, Scott had driven to work at the bike shop, but business was slow and he was allowed the afternoon off. He got a wild hair to bomb down to Los Angeles to show Suzette and was halfway down 101 before he came to his senses. If it took a Porsche to woo her, it wasn't worth it.

He found Doc M's place without difficulty. As he rolled up the driveway, Mitchell came out to greet him.

"Missing on the third cylinder," Scott said, tossing him the keys.

"Really?" Mitchell scanning for dents and scratches.

"I'm messing with you, man," Scott grinned, but his bravado was thin and false.

Phil led him in through the garage, where they stopped to ogle the prize BMW.

"There she is," Mitchell said. "Nineteen seventy-two 2002 tii. Best year. Kugelfisher fuel-injected two-liter engine, four on the floor Borg-Warner full synchromesh transmission, independent suspension front and rear. Leaks a little oil."

Scott circumambulated the German sports sedan, running his fingers languidly along its classic lines, the gun-metal gray chassis primed for a bitchin' paint job. They went inside and Mitchell poured two glasses of apple juice as Scott checked the place out.

"Nice place," he said. "Hot tub and everything."

"Let's get started." Phil gave a glass of juice to Scott and ushered him into the living room to the couch he passed out on every night. Phil took the easy chair opposite.

251

"Friday night," Phil began. "The shooting at Hope Road. Bob and Rita have been wounded and taken to University Hospital. Remember?"

"First things first, Doc. A little spliff."

"Just a little. I don't want you drifting off."

"One hit each, okay?"Scott said, producing a joint. He lit it and took his usual rapid-fire tokes until Mitchell wrestled the cigarette away from him.

"Enough," Phil said. "Deal's a deal." He took a small hit.

"Friday you went to the hospital to see Bob. Now it's Saturday morning, the day before Smile Jamaica. What's happening?"

Scott stared into the swirling mists of December, 1976 and fear raised its ugly head.

"More herb," he cried, grasping for the joint, but Mitchell held on firmly.

"It was the day of Troy's funeral, right?" Phil said.

"Think I made a big mistake, Doc. Keep the damn car."

"Focus on the funeral. Did you go?"

"I was there."

"Tell me about it. Was it morning, afternoon?"

"Jamaican funerals never middle of the day. It was early in the morning."

"Okay."

"I should go, really."

"You're doing fine. What was the funeral like?"

"There were rituals. Pouring rum into the grave… throwing dirt back between your legs so the duppy won't follow you home."

"Yes."

"The coffin had to be lifted three times before starting out from the funeral parlor. Old Ashanti ritual. Announces to the earth goddess that a new spirit is coming to join the ancestors. Asase, the earth goddess. I should go home, Doc, really, I'm telling you. Feeling queasy in my stomach."

"Old African rituals, yes yes."

"A hot daughtah came forward crying her eyes out and holding a baby. Said it was Troy's son. Nobody saw that coming. Baby was passed three times over the coffin to protect it from the duppy. Girlfriend was probably wearing red underwear to prevent El Ghost-o from copulating with her. Least that's what Marva said."

"And after that?"

"Everybody's talking about Smile Jamaica. Is it going to happen? Will the Tuff Gong come out of the hospital and play?"

At Strawberry Hill, Bob Marley powwowed with the Rasta elders. Marley dearly wanted to do the concert but not to the point of committing

252

suicide. Up on stage he'd be a sitting duck. Reasoning with the brethren all day amid gathering clouds of ganja decided nothing.

Good news came in. Don Taylor was alive. The key to the blood bank had been located and life-saving transfusions administered. Taylor was stabilized but one of the five bullets was lodged dangerously near his spine. An operation could leave him paralyzed for life. He would need to seek treatment in the United States.

With the days winding down before the elections, the Manleys hit the campaign trail hard. An Evelyn Wood speed-reader, Michael took along Phil Agee's *Inside the Company* for spare moments. Agee—who happened to be in Jamaica that Saturday evening to deliver a speech about his experience as a CIA agent in Mexico, Ecuador, and Uruguay—painted a disturbing portrait of US economic policy vis-à-vis Latin America. The pathway out of poverty for the poor countries of the South, it was promised, was to be found in "open and free trade" and unregulated foreign investment. In fact the policy and its programs did a great job helping one country in particular—the United States. Even JFK's much-ballyhooed Alliance for Progress had the same effect: In the decade of the 1960s, private foreign investment, mainly American, input $5.5 billion to the region—*and took out $20 billion.* To protect profits like that the United States would gladly prop up dictators and put down the revolutionaries, conveniently branded communists, socialists, terrorists. The CIA was the enforcer, "the secret police of American capitalism" in service to the many US companies operating in the region and their shareholders. The old colonial system of slavery had not died but metamorphosed into free-market economics that continued the rip-off better than ever. But then Manley didn't need to read Agee to know that. He wondered if in his democratic socialism he hadn't bitten off more than he could chew.

"What happened after the funeral?" Dr. Mitchell asked, still holding the joint, which had gone out.

"I went home. Wasn't supposed to go out that weekend, but no way was I missing the concert. I lay low Saturday night so Big Daddy could think he was the Man. All part of the dance."

"Okay."

"I taught Maddy to play gin rummy and she taught me to make ackee and saltfish, the national dish. It's called saltfish but you soak it all night to get the salt out. Be careful, Maddy said, ackee is poisonous...."

Maddy took the boy out back to the ackee tree and showed him which fruit to pick. Ackee had come to Jamaica aboard slave ships from

West Africa and that man again, Captain Bligh, subsequently delivered specimens to Kew Gardens in London.

"Only ripe ackee can eat," Maddy said sternly, "and nah look at the color. Ripe fruit pop open by him lonesome, see it there?"

She plucked a red fruit about the size of a pomegranate from the tree. It had split down the side.

"Don't never pry ackee fruit open, hear me now?"

"Got it," said Scott. "Pop, not pry."

"Otherwise gwine dead 'fore morning. Need tomato, onion, chili, thyme, but most important is Scotch Bonnet pepper. Haffi do it right. Ackee 'n saltfish Jamaica national dish. Harry Belafonte sing 'bout it. Him Jamaican on him momma side, yunno. Live Yard when him likkle boy."

After their delightful dinner—ackee cooked up like scrambled eggs and went great with rice 'n peas, calaloo and of course saltfish—Scott showed Maddy the ins and outs of gin rummy. He won every hand but in Maddy's defense the TV was tuned to her favorite American soap, *The Bold and The Beautiful.*

The YWCA auditorium on Arnold Road was packed to the rafters for Philip Agee's talk. After nine years with the CIA in Latin America, Agee quit the Agency in 1969 to write his insider's expose. He was hosted tonight by the Jamaican Human Rights Council. Among the audience was one of Frank Lake's men frantically jotting notes. The *Gleaner* that day had reported that a flour shortage threatened 6,000 workers with layoffs.

Handsome with a thick thatch of black hair, Agee, 45, did not speak about his years in Ecuador, Uruguay, Mexico. He spoke about Jamaica. His claim that the CIA was staging a destabilization program against the Manley government threw the crowd into an uproar. He laid out methods—labor actions, strikes, propaganda, economic sabotage. Outraged gasps greeted his contention that guns and cocaine were being smuggled into Jamaica in a covert war against the Manley administration. Agee's *J'accuse* pointed fingers at the North American press, US State Department and US-dominated international banks as well. All played vital roles, Agee said. And he was just warming up.

At the embassy the phone rang and Matt picked up.

"Gallagher."

"Matt, Frank. Are you sitting down? This asshole Agee really dropped a bomb. The cunt spilled the beans about our operations down here. In front of a whole fucking auditorium."

"Faggot cocksucker."

"There's worse."

254

"Worse? What could possibly be worse? Man's a traitor to his country. I'll kill the sonuvabitch. Swear to God I'll kill him."

"Can we stop now?" Scott asked, reaching for the joint on the coffee table.

"We're sailing along here," Phil said, grabbing the spliff before Scott could reach it.

"Just a little hit, Doc, come on. Give me some of that shit you take. That Vicodin opium shit."

"It'll be all right. Did anything happen while you were playing rummy with Maddy?"

"Can't breathe," Scott said, tugging at the collar of his T-shirt. "Feel like I'm taking my dying breath."

"Let's deal with Saturday night. You're playing gin with Maddy."

"I went to Dickhead's room to call Marva so Maddy could watch TV. It was a big room, real big...."

Scott closed the door behind him and glanced around. He'd never been in his father's room alone before. It was much larger than his with a king-size bed, dresser, walk-in closet, desk with chair, TV and stand, an easy chair with nightstand and phone. Atop the dresser was a small black-and-white photo from Vietnam, dad with the guys—this from the days he had both eyes.

Overcome with curiosity, he peeked in the walk-in closet. Shirts and slacks and a couple suits hung on hangers. A US Army Rangers dress uniform was under wrap. In one corner was his father's M16, in the other a filing cabinet, locked. He didn't see the M14 sniper rifle anywhere.

Closing the closet he plopped in the easy chair and called Marva. They talked for hours, cooing lover's songs.

"Thought there were two rifles," Mitchell said. "M16 and an M14."

"Well, there was only the M16 that night," Scott snapped. "Please, Doc, just one little hit?"

"We're making excellent progress."

"I'm calling off the deal and going home. Not joking."

"Keep the faith. We come to Sunday, December 5th, 1976. The day of the big concert."

"Smile Jamaica."

"We're almost there, friend. Keep pushing. What do you see?"

"I'm supposed to meet Marva and Henry at Heroes Park, five o'clock. By the Simon Bolivar statue. I left the house early, about four. Walking down on foot. Nobody knows if Smile Jamaica is happening or not. Something to tell Marva... something important...."

255

At Strawberry Hill, Tony Spaulding, PNP Minister of Housing, urged Marley to play Smile Jamaica, which was scheduled to go on as a tribute to him whether he showed or not. Not playing would be letting the terrorists win, Spaulding said. But Bob wasn't one to be bullied or intimidated. Roberta Flack flew in for the concert and was driven up to the hideaway. Her presence buoyed Marley, as did news that Don Taylor was off the critical list. Chris Blackwell chartered a medical jet and Taylor was evacuated to Miami to have the bullet at his spine surgically removed. Within days Taylor would be up and walking, though one of the bullets had to be left permanently in his left thigh. Miraculously, no one would die from the Friday night shooting.

At University Hospital, a groggy Rita Marley was desperate to know what was going on. When Judy Mowatt came to visit, Rita staggered to her feet with her head swathed in bandages and the two drove up to Strawberry Hill in all haste. Rita begged Bob not to play the concert, which wasn't going to be much of a show without him. Except for Third World the other acts were not of superstar status. The American film crew showed up at Strawberry Hill and loaned a high-performance walkie-talkie to Bob before going back to Kingston to set up in case things somehow came together.

As the film crew arrived at Heroes Circle, Bob got on the walkie-talkie to Cat Coore, Third World's brilliant guitarist and Bob's good friend, who was setting up for Third World to play. By now it was four o'clock in the afternoon.

"How things look, Cat?"

"Is crazy here me a tell yuh, Skip. Must be fifty thousand people... never see anything like it me whole life."

"Better make concert after the election," Rita cautioned. "Let things cool down."

"Nah safe now," Judy said.

Marley took his spliff and went outside to walk alone around the property, losing himself in the magnificent surroundings and spectacular views, Blue Mountains to the north, the St. Andrew Plain and sparkling blue Caribbean to the south. Aromatic herb filling his lungs, Jah's splendorous creation blessing his eyes, the Gong felt all human separateness melt away. One Love.

Departing the house for Heroes Park Circle, Scott found himself caught up in a sea of humanity streaming from every direction. The trek to the Circle he figured at a bit less than an hour, which should put him there in plenty of time to meet Marva and Henry at 5:00 as planned. He carried the photo of Bob and him in his pocket as always. The air crackled with excitement as folks bounded along in a spirit of unity and coming together. There hadn't been anything like this since the Independence celebrations of 1962. Smile Jamaica had transcended ordinary human experience and become mythic: It was as if Bob having taken a bullet for the people made them all part of a great religious drama requiring the enactment of sacred rites of consecration that honored their hero for his sacrifice, fulfillment of the rites requiring nothing more—and nothing less—than Dionysian, orgiastic enthrallment in the evening's music.Their very enjoyment would be their Holy Communion. The Smile Jamaica concert had become the Jamaican equivalent of the Eleusinian Mysteries of ancient Greece, without the secrecy, and those who opened their hearts to Bob's message of One Love would be transformed forever. The very real element of danger only knit the people together more closely still, and caused them to laugh and joke in nervous exaltation as they flowed along the streets of Kingston to the holy altar.

Scott hoped Marva would arrive before Henry so they might have a few moments alone and he could whisper sweet words in her ear. Words he'd never told anyone before. Words of endearment rising from the deepest part of his being. He knew now that they were meant to be together forever as surely as fish were meant to swim and birds to fly. Their love was ordained in the stars, like the intrigues and romances of the Roman pantheon. She was the long lost missing half, soul mate and anima. Completion and fulfillment. Miss Marva Morrison of Kingston, Jamaica. The One.

He arrived at Heroes Park to find it already swamped with people. National Heroes Park Circle was a large grassy oval with its main axis running north and south just east of Orange Street; the northern end had been the site of the colonial racetrack whereas the extreme southern section was devoted to the Monument to the Heroes, shrines to all seven of Jamaica's national heroes. Towards the north end was a large grassy space where a stage had been erected and around this were the crowds assembled. Down by the Monument was the Simon Bolivar statue, where Scott waited for Henry and Marva.

Henry was first to appear, emerging from a crowd and walking fast toward Scott. Strange, his face seemed to be contorted in anger, his gait and posture sending the same signal. Something must have happened.

"Oy, Henry," Scott waved. "Over here."

Henry strode forward without waving back, his eyes locked in a cold bellicose stare. Something was wrong, all right.

"Henry?" Scott cried, worried that something had happened to Bob.

Henry's demeanor grew fiercer and more combative with each step.

"What is it man?"

Henry now stood before him mute and trembling in rage. Scott opened his mouth to speak when Henry hocked loudly and spat as hard as he could in Scott's face.

"What the fuck was that?" Scott staggered backward.

"White scum. Come near me I'll kill you."

"What in the name of Jah is going on? Henry, please."

Henry receded into the milling thousands and disappeared. Scott waited anxiously for Marva's arrival, needing her more than ever.

Shaking violently and gasping for breath, Scott lunged forward on Dr. Mitchell's couch and put his head between his knees as if he were going to vomit.

"Suffocating," he blathered, grabbing at his throat. "Can't breathe."

"Take it easy, man," Phil said.

"Dying, gotta stop, gotta stop."

"All right, one more hit of herb."

Scott's arm shot out like lightning and retrieved the unfinished marijuana cigarette on the coffee table. In two seconds he had it re-lit and was sucking hard.

"Enough," Mitchell snatched it away. "So it was Henry that spit on you."

"My best friend. Oh God."

"Go on. You're doing well."

"Feels like the end of the world."

"Breathe, man. Did Marva ever show up?"

"It's getting dark," Scott took a deep shuddering breath. "She's not showing up. I'm waiting at Heroes Circle like a fool with his world tumbling down around him…."

It was well past the time Marva should have shown up. Scott paced around the icon of Simon Bolivar in confused bewilderment at Henry's cruel assault. By now it was well past sundown and on the far side of the green expanse of Heroes Park klieg lights were turning on, down where all the people were gathered. He scanned the four corners for sign of Marva. Where was she, dammit?

At the northern end of the oval, across the street from the stage at a distance of some two hundred yards, stood an abandoned warehouse. On the second floor of the warehouse, at a window looking out over the park, a lone warrior scanned with binoculars. He checked his weapon, a Vietnam-era M14 with high-powered scope. Sniper rifle superb. He loaded, aimed toward the stage and sighted in, careful not to extend the barrel out the open window. Want something done, do it your goddamn self.

Passing anonymously through the crowd was Freddy McGinnis, also carrying binoculars and a .38 shoulder-holstered under his jacket. He scanned the outer perimeter of the park for sniper positions, glassed the roofs and balconies and windows of nearby buildings. What would he do if he did sight a sniper? Shoot him? What if it was Gallagher himself? McGinnis sensed he was out there all right, a deranged lone wolf on the prowl, driven half mad by blind patriotic fervor and whatever personal demons made his mind as singularly focused as his eyesight. If it came down to it, could he shoot the miserable sonuvabitch? Could he kill his chief?

Working their way through the crowd as well were Jesse James and five of his grownup cousins holding machetes down their pants leg or discretely at their sides and watching for trouble. Jesse James' girls were safe in the company of several adult males deep in the middle of the crowd, waiting for Bob Marley.

At Strawberry Hill, Marley checked in with Cat at Heroes Circle via walkie-talkie.

"Wha' gwan, Cat?"

"Place jam-pack, Skip," replied Coore, son of PNP minister David Coore. "Mus' be eighty thousand an' dem still a come. Third World gwine play now. Make we test the water."

Coore grabbed his guitar and Third World took the stage to open Smile Jamaica. The concert was being broadcast live on Jamaican radio and everybody at Strawberry Hill heard the cheers. There was a short tribute to Bob and Rita and the crowd went crazy. The people's outpouring of love touched Bob.

"Get everybody to Heroes Circle," he shouted, as Third World started up with *Satta Massagana*. But there was a problem. All the band had been located except Family Man. Cyan't play reggae without your bass man.

Cat Coore rang back after their set.

"Everything cool, Skip," Coore said.

"Cyan't find Fams," Marley said.

"I-man play bass fe yuh," said Coore, who as a youth had received classical training in strings and been considered a child prodigy on cello.

"Me a come. Wailers a go play."

The Tuff Gong was ushered into the backseat of a red Volvo with the commissioner of police. Surrounded by a squad of police cars, the Volvo headed down the mountain. Rita and Judy followed in a VW driven by Pee Wee Fraser. As the caravan raced at high speed toward Kingston, lights flashing and sirens wailing, the Commish opened his attaché case and assembled a machinegun. Over the walkie-talkie Bob heard the announcement that he would play. The ensuing roar of the crowd filled him with love for his people and a burning desire to win the peace.

The entourage rounded a bend and ran smack into a massive JLP rally, rattling jumpy nerves. Rita feared they would all be killed but instead of potshots and firebombs came cheering and chants of "Bob Mar-lay, Bob Mar-lay." Proving if it needed proving once again that Bob Marley transcended politics and tribal divisions.

In his hunter's blind in the warehouse across from Heroes Circle, Matt Gallagher scanned the huge gathering with the binoculars. Something caught his eye and curled his lip in silent rage. There in his circular field of view was Freddy McGinnis snooping around like Sherlock Holmes. Matt knew instantly what McGinnis was up to and what he was going to do about it. He kissed his teeth in contempt and shook his head, for he had come to like McGinnis, in an adversarial sort of way, a protégé to take under his wing and mold into a respectable case officer—and by the looks of it he had figured things out. Matt took a kind of bittersweet pride in that, but it wasn't going to get McGinnis off the hook. The biggest test of all he'd failed—unswerving loyalty to the home team.

From the outer fringe of the crowd, McGinnis pondered the best location for a sniper with scope. A window on the second floor of an old building across the street seemed ideal, but checking through the binoculars didn't reveal anything suspicious.

Setting down his own binoculars, Gallagher found McGinnis in the scope of the M14. He was a moving target and people bobbed in front of him but any second there would be a clear shot. With all the noise and hubbub no one would hear the crack of the bullet; the man would fall and those few who saw the blood oozing from his chest would be ignored by the masses. Matt circled his index finger around the trigger but realized in sober reflection he couldn't jeopardize his prime targets. Cocksucker would have to wait his turn.

A siren *whooped* loud close by. Gallagher took up the glasses and there was the Rastaman stepping out of a red Volvo. The crowd, now 80,000 strong—an incredible 3% of the entire island—erupted into a tumultuous cheer. Bob made it! *Man rise offa 'im deathbed fe play fe yuh, people!*

Pacing impatiently at the Simon Bolivar statue, Scott heard the roar and saw the flashing lights. Where the hell was Marva? She would just have to find him—he couldn't wait any longer. He began wending his way through the milling mass of humanity toward the action. Another huge roar sounded as Marley was hoisted up on stage.

Gallagher sighted in his rifle on his dreadlocked target. Illumination was poor and clouds of ganja smoke swirled in the air. Friends and fans congregated on stage to shield Marley with their bodies. For anyone other than a top marksman, it would be a difficult shot. Matt knew there would come an opening and he would squeeze one off. One would be enough and the Rastaman would be history.

Up on stage, Cat Coore greeted Bob warmly. Standing by were Carly, Tyrone, Wyah, Seeco, Don Kinsey, guitarist Chinna Smith and two of the three Zap Pow horn players, Glen DaCosta on tenor sax and David Madden on trumpet. The famous Georgie, fire-tender of legend George Robinson was there with Rasta drummers pounding away on the akete skins. The atmosphere sizzled with tension but a sense of community prevailed, a coming together like Bob always preached in his songs.

Watching with his binoculars, Matt Gallagher blinked and thanked his lucky stars. Coming into his field of view was Prime Minister Manley, jumping up on stage to embrace Marley to another great roar from the assembly. Gallagher quickly set aside the binoculars and sighted in the M14. Damn, he might be able to pop the both of them right now and go have cocktails.

"Bless you, Skipper," Manley hailed the reggae star. "You all right?"

Gallagher had them both in his sights. Two quick kill shots, that's all it would take.

"Good fe go, Joshua," Marley greeted the prime minister.

"Hit me with it," Manley said, as Gallagher squeezed back on the trigger, slowly, gently, don't jerk, like an arrow flying from the bow of its own mind. The Zen-like beauty of the hunt, primal necessity of the kill.

At the last instant Manley moved out of view before Gallagher could fire. Matt adjusted and followed as the prime minister hustled off stage and climbed atop a VW van where his wife and daughter were spread out on a blanket in plain sight. He was a sitting duck and could be taken at any time. *Was the man an idiot?* Marley would have to be the first shot, then quickly swing over and plink the Commie asshole Manley. With luck, the traitor McGinnis as well. But Marley was bobbing and moving as people congregated around him. Gallagher had to wait. An opening would come and he'd be ready.

Bob Marley stepped up to the mic and peered out over the vast congregation. He uttered no complaint about his pain nor spoke in anger about his attackers. No call for vengeance issued from his lips.

"When me decide to play this concert two anna half months ago," he simply said, "dem say there no politics. Me only play fe love of the people."

The crowd echoed his affection with a tremendous cheer. Someone ran up with Bob's guitar, but with his left arm wrapped in bandages—the bullet still lodged below his elbow, where it would stay the rest of his life— Marley couldn't play. Wailers would perform one song, he said and started in on *War*. The crowd roared and the love fest was underway. Skipper threw everything he had into it, venting the emotions of the last three days, whipping his locks and dancing with abandon. Carly's sticks rocked the beat,

Cat kicked it on bass, Chinna and Kinsey came in on guitar as Tyrone and Wyah tickled the keyboards. Another great roar erupted as Rita was lifted up on stage in her hospital robe, her bandaged head swathed in an Ethiopian headdress. Judy was right behind in a psychedelic orange maternity dress, looking beatific and big as a house.

Working his way through the throng was Scott Gallagher, still fifty meters from the stage. His intent was to get close up front but bodies were packed like sardines and he had to get down on hands and knees and crawl the last part. Getting kicked, stomped and cursed all the way.

The Wailers segued into *No More Trouble*. Were ever lyrics more appropriate? The place was sizzling, raucous, absolutely on fire, Judy and Rita trilling like angels as they backed Bob's vocals. Family Man finally showed and joined in. Thriving on his people's adoration, Bob let go of any thought of getting off quickly. Wailers were pushing on through.

By this time, Freddy McGinnis was letting down his guard. Seemed like if something were going to happen it would have gone down by now. It was only getting darker and smokier and in any case the music was so damn infectious he couldn't resist moving and grooving with everybody else. An alluring Jamaican woman dancing alone to the reggae beat caught his eye and he thought to throw a move at the *irie daughtah*. As the Wailers rolled on with *Get Up Stand Up*, he was just another fan among the adoring multitude.

"God oh Jah oh Jah!" Scott cried, bursting to his feet.

"Easy," said Phil, but Scott was drenched in sweat and completely out of sorts.

"That's it," he cried. "I'm done."

"What are you seeing, man?"

"Forget it. Give me a ride home." Scott edged toward the door.

"Wait—"

"Wait, shit. I'll walk home if I have to. Everything is dark, man. It's swallowing me up."

"What's the worst that could happen?" Phil said, getting to his feet and cutting Scott off at the door.

"Get out of my way, Doc. Don't make me hit you."

"You already lived through it once, man. You survived. Let's smoke a little ganj and talk it out."

"Forget you and your Babylon psycho-babble. You can shove that piece of twat Beamer too."

"You know what? You're right. Just fuck it. Fuck the whole thing. What's the worst that could happen? Death? Fuck it. We all gotta die sometime. If it's the end of the world we'll find a better one or go down in flames together. Come on."

262

Phil took Scott by the arm but the kid yanked it away.

"Fuck off!" he cursed.

"We get through this together or go out together. You want to be alone now? Wanna go home to your duppies? Come with me."

Phil grabbed his keys and this time Scott didn't resist. Phil led him into the garage, turned on the light and closed the door to the house behind them.

"Get in," Mitchell said, opening the passenger side door of the BMW and nudging Scott in. Phil dashed to close the outside garage door before getting in the driver's seat and starting 'er up.

"What are you doing?" Scott said as Phil locked his door and reached over to secure the passenger side. "Why'd you close the door?"

"Say it with me," Phil said. "Fuck it. F-U-C-K-I-T, fuck it. Just fuck the mother-fucker."

"You're losing it man. There's no air in here."

"What happened at Smile Jamaica?"

"Can't see it."

Mitchell revved the engine, sending a gray plume of exhaust into the closed space. "Think, man. What happened? Did Marva ever make it?"

"Not seeing her."

"What song is Bob singing?"

"Uh... *Baldhead.* Finishing *Crazy Baldhead.*"

"Where are you?"

Scott swallowed hard. "Crawling to the front on my hands and knees."

"Spill your guts, man. Let's get this poison out of you."

"Crazy baldhead," Scott muttered, glancing out the rear view window at the gathering cloud of exhaust....

Slithering snake-like beneath foot-stomping revelers, Scott reached the stage and wrestled to his feet to the displeasured grunts of those who had staked out positions hours ago. Boogying shoulder-to-shoulder and elbow-to-elbow with his fellow worshippers in these modern Mysteries he tried to catch Skip's attention to show he was present in full loving support. He pushed to the edge of the stage, hoping to slap Bob some skin and send those damn baldheads packing.

"Skipper!" he shouted. "Oy, Skip. Give thanks and praises, man."

Skip didn't look over. Scott had the strange thought that he was avoiding eye contact. Probably to concentrate on the music, he reassured himself.

Like Freddy McGinnis, the people surrounding Bob on stage began to relax their guard. Just a little. But it was enough. Gallagher sighted in the M14, easing the rifle's barrel just slightly out the window. The shot would

263

come quickly now. Marley, Manley, and with luck that asshole turncoat McGinnis, fucking Benedict Arnold prick.

The Wailers pushed forward with *Positive Vibration* and *Smile Jamaica*. For McGinnis, something touched a chord deep inside, whether it was the lyrics, the jubilant revelry of the crowd or just the pleasure of dancing with the fetching Jamaican woman that had caught his eye. Whatever it was made him think of Addie Mae back in the Birmingham of his childhood. In a flash he relived the whole history of his relationship with her, from going to the library in second grade to research their favorite animal to the horrific manner of her early and tragic death. He had known Addie Mae as a trusting and innocent girl but it seemed now he could see something forbidding in her eyes, some dark cloud roiling up from the depths of her being. A message... a warning.

Bidding him be careful.

Don't let your guard down, Frederick Douglas.

McGinnis quickly spun and looked to that suspicious window across the street. Was that a glint of light? He hoisted the glasses for a look. It was dark and he couldn't make out much... was that a rifle with scope?

McGinnis drew his .38 and—too far to shoot—pushed his way as fast as he could through the masses, women screaming, men shouting and clearing out of the way. It was slow going and a few people including one woman got bowled over. As he reached shooting range on the outer fringe of the crowd, and seeing the glint that looked like a rifle still there—an M14, he thought—he planted his feet wide, grasped the .38 in two hands and fired six shots at the window.

Within seconds he was taken to the ground by several burly Jamaicans. The .38 was wrestled away and a severe beating administered despite his protestations that there had been a shooter in the window across the street. A violent argument broke out until it was resolved that he had shot *away* from the crowd, giving his story an air of plausibility; no one, however, came forward claiming to have seen a shooter in the window. A flurry of panic ruffled the rear section of the crowd but dissipated before it reached the front area by the stage, like a harmless wave lapping at the shore. Most folks never knew it happened.

Scott was desperate to get Skip's attention, having been ignored by him moments before and trashed by his best friend before that. Wailers were in to *Rat Race* and as Marley sang that Rasta didn't work for the CIA, their eyes finally met and Marley let loose his wickedest screwface. Scott staggered backwards as if hit by a cannon blast. What in God's name was going on?

Two hours earlier at Strawberry Hill, Tyrone Downie was sitting with Marley and glancing over the newspaper when he came across the account of the shooting at Hope Road.

"'No suspects have been identified by the police,'" he read. "Big fucking surprise."

His eyes drifted across the page to a small notice inserted just before the edition had gone to press.

"What's this? Oy Skip, what the name of that white bwoy that come around?"

"Wha' say, Jump?"

"White bwoy name Gallagher, nah so?"

"Yeah man, Gallagher."

"Remember say him daddy work at the embassy? Listen here. 'Former CIA agent Philip Agee claimed before a packed YWCA auditorium that he believes the United States is involved in a destabilization program against the government of Michael Manley. Agee named eleven persons at the US Embassy he claimed are working undercover for the CIA, including Station Chief Matt Gallagher.'"

"Say that there?" Marley asked.

"Check it fe yuhself."

Bob spun the paper around. As he read, his eyes burned with rage. Jamaicans killing their brothers was bad enough but foreigners coming in to run amok was intolerable. He'd taken the white bwoy into the good graces of his heart and treated him like a younger brother and here him fuckin' baldhead CIA daddy a come mash down the town.

Bludgeoned by the naked rage in Bob's eyes, Scott reassured himself there had to be some mistake. Bob must have been looking at someone else or thinking something known only to him. Surely his imagination was getting the best of him.

"Yes, Skipper," he called again. "Truth!"

Marley danced, lashing the air with his locks. The denim sleeve of his left forearm was soaked with blood oozing from the bullet wound.

"Irie ites!" Scott kept at it. "Chant down Babylon, Rasta."

For a brief instant Marley looked right at Scott and again flushed screwface. Scott gasped as if gut shot. Was the whole world going crazy? He tumbled into the crowd, seeking anonymity. Reality had been turned upside-down, those who'd loved him yesterday hating him today. The Wailers played eight more songs, a ninety-minute set, Scott cooking in his juices the whole time, paralyzed with the thought that Bob, like Henry, had mysteriously turned against him.

The Wailers wrapped up with *So Jah Seh* as Marley opened his shirt and tapped his sleeve to show his bandaged wounds. Scott made one final attempt to put his world back together. He pushed forward to the front and tried to gain the stage. He was blocked by Tyrone Downie.

"Fuck off and die, white bwoy," Downie said.

"I don't understand," Scott cried. "What did I do?"

Bob bid the crowd goodnight, mimicking the fast draw of an Old West gunslinger before laughing and running off stage. The crowd, wary of violence breaking out, dispersed in record time. Scott wandered around in drunken circles as the great tide of humanity flowed back into the sea of night. Eighty thousand people vanished within minutes. Scott fell to his knees on the grass and sobbed. This was more than he could bear. Someone was carrying away a rifle, looked like an M14. The photo of Bob and him fell from his shirt pocket but gazing upon it only made the pain worse. Like a caged bird finding its freedom it fluttered away. He clutched at the turf as if to yank soothing balm up by the roots. If a chasm in the earth had opened at his feet he would have let it swallow him whole. His mind conjured images of Marva to ease the pain. He had to declare his love for her and receive hers in return. Scrambling to his feet he ran for her, his last hope in this world.

Hard and fast he ran, convulsing in spasms of horror and confusion. People walking home from the concert studied him oddly as he flew by, some tossing flippant remarks. It seemed the world had turned harsh and impersonal again. He ran and didn't stop for anything.

Reaching Marva's yard he vaulted the back fence and crept to her window, a beckoning portal to life resurrected.

"Marva!" he cried too loudly to be secretive. He tapped frantically on the windowpane, lifted the window and was boosting himself inside when the light flickered on.

Marva saw him and shrieked. "Nooooooo!"

"It's me, hun," he said. "Not a duppy."

"GET OUT!" she screamed, the same hatred on her face he'd seen with Bob and Henry.

"Marva, don't do this to me I beg of you! I love you and you love me. We're meant for each other."

"GET AWAY FROM ME!" Marva hollered to wake the dead. She sobbed hysterically and lights came on, followed by the sound of hurried footsteps. Scott ran for the fence, vaulted over and took off. Marva's weeping following him home like a demon curse.

"Jah Jah, oh God." Scott hunched between his knees, banging his head against the 2002tii's glove compartment. Moaning and gasping for breath.

"I'm gonna die," he cried and coughed from the gathering fumes.

Phil jolted the kid's shoulder.

"Stay focused or we're both going down," he said. "Gotta keep working here. Not much time. What did you do?"

"I don't care any more."

"It was a misunderstanding, man. They blamed you for the sins of your father."

"It's over."

"That's it then? We go out together in this godforsaken four-wheeled coffin? Two losers crying their way to the grave? It wasn't your fault, man. Fuck it. Just fuck it. What did you do after that? There's no time, dude, do you understand, you have to do it now."

"Do it now," Scott droned in semi-stupor.

"RIGHT FUCKING NOW," Phil shouted, and coughed from the fumes.

"Went home," Scott said, gathering energy from a wellspring of buried anger. "Went home to see the bastard... see for myself...."

Reaching his yard, Scott let himself in. No one was home. He paced agonized circles on the living room floor before collapsing into a chair and burying his head in his hands. After an anguished eternity, he picked his head up and saw on the table in front of him a newspaper. In a small column on the right-hand side of the front page he read the awful truth. Jamaica was drowning in blood and misery and the United States was sticking in the shiv. No wonder Henry and Bob and Marva hated him and his father and anybody remotely connected to the CIA.

But maybe Agee had it wrong. Could an outsider really know what was going on? He ran to his father's room and tried the filing cabinet in the closet, locked as he'd found it before. The desk also locked. Nothing on the floor. Nothing in the dresser drawers. He smashed down his fists in frustration. He noticed the M16 in the closet but not the other rifle, the M14 sniper rifle. Was that it in the park?

His attention was drawn to the jade Buddha atop the dresser. He fingered the smooth surface of the sculpture, tipped it on end and felt beneath.

Something was taped to the bottom.

A key.

Scott ripped the key free and dashed to the filing cabinet. He tried the lock—it fit. Each of the drawers was filled with files and documents. The entire bottom drawer was marked *Chile*. In the middle drawer were files labeled *Argentina*, *Bolivia* and *Venezuela*.

The top drawer was labeled *Jamaica* and was full of files. A folder tabbed *Operation Werewolf* caught his eyes. Inside he found lists of men and materiel—dynamite, guns, ammunition. He rifled through the file and saw more names, dates, places. All the pages were photocopies of original documents. He pulled out another file labeled *Michael Manley* and saw behind it a folder labeled *Bob Marley*. As if unearthing a sacred treasure, he lifted the Marley file out of the drawer and opened it.

And there it was. Names, descriptions, times, dates, everything. Bob Marley, Rita Marley, all the Wailers, Chris Blackwell, Don Taylor, others. Numerous photographs were included—some showing him with Marley.

Another page was headed *"Surveillance post -- 56 Hope Road."* On several following pages was a chronological listing of persons under headings *Arriving* or *Departing*, with dates, times of day and notes. His own name was entered many times corresponding to days and times he knew he'd been at the House of Dread.

It was true. Everything the renegade CIA man had said was the stinking rotten truth.

A car pulled into the driveway. The monster was home. He entered the house mopping blood from his ear. When the bullets had come zinging through the window at his perch above Heroes Circle, he'd fallen to the floor, rolled and scrambled out the door, leaving the M14 behind. One of McGinnis' shots had nicked his left ear.

He hadn't given up that easily. With blood streaming down his face, he raced past the mob wrestling with Freddy McGinnis and drew his .45, pushing aside those who didn't scurry out of the way fast enough. When he reached shooting range he stopped and planted, and as people in front of him hit the ground he grasped the .45 with two hands and had a bead on Marley when the blunt face of Jesse James' machete slapped down on his thumbs with great force. Gallagher knocked Jesse James to the ground with an elbow to the jaw and managed to escape through the crowd.

Jesse James lay unmoving on the ground. His girls saw him and screamed. They had already witnessed their older brother get shot dead in the street and now was their father to be taken as well? Finally he stirred with nothing worse to show than a bad headache.

"YOU LIED!" Scott screamed as his father entered holding a bloodied rag to the side of his face. The back of his hands was deeply bruised where Jesse James' machete had slapped him. "You said you didn't work for the CIA!"

"What are you yelling about?" Matt said. "I suppose you read this Agee bullshit."

Scott slapped the Werewolf file down on the table.

"Bullshit? Here's bullshit."

"Little punk, you got in my files? These were under lock and key."

"Operation Werewolf, dad? Dynamite, guns, surveillance post at Hope Road? Lying sack of shit."

"You want to do this now? All right then. High time you knew what your father does for a living. Yes, I work for the CIA in service to my country."

Scott covered his ears and made incoherent noises to block out the horror of his father's words.

Gallagher pulled Scott's hands from his ears.

"Shut up and listen," Matt said. "It had to be done. It's vital to the security of the nation. If it wasn't me it'd be someone else. Start packing. We're leaving."

"What do you mean, leaving?"

"We're going back to the States."

"Why? For how long?"

"We're out of here."

"I'm not going anywhere with you, you Nazi prick."

"Watch your filthy mouth. Our flight leaves tomorrow morning."

"TOMORROW? No fucking way." He had to patch things up with Bob and Marva and Henry. If he left now, those wounds would never heal.

"I'm going to bed," Matt said. "We leave here at oh nine hundred."

Every cell in Scott's body burned with rage. Unbearable agony ravaged every pore, lasering through his skin to the core of his being. His dearest friends in the world hated his guts. Because of his father. If only they could see that he wasn't Matt Gallagher. He hated the CIA too. And Station Chief Matt Gallagher.

Matt went into his room, leaving Scott to deal with it and hopefully come out the other side as a man. Scott reeled to his room and collapsed sobbing on his bed. Catastrophic pain seared his insides in an incendiary mass of anguish and wrath that blocked out the sun and expunged joy from the world. This evil bolus had to be vented before it consumed everything in its path. Suffering metamorphosing into an overwhelming motivation to act.

An ancient atavistic instinct seized control. He stood, muscles tense, hormones flushing into his bloodstream, an upright bipedal hunter-warrior with superhuman strength. The most fearsome killing machine evolution had yet achieved.

It was dark and deathly still. With riveted, mindless focus he stepped in measured paces to the living room and let himself out the sliding glass door to the backyard. Crossing to the tool shed, he groped about for the gardener's machete.

Steel blade secured, he turned back for the house, his footfall heavy and unrepentant. At the sliding glass door he slowed, the muscles in his neck popping like steel cords, lips curled, canines bared, attention narrowed to pinprick awareness, sharp as the tip of a sword.

He entered the house. Walking slowly now, compelled by a force so deep inside it seemed alien. The pounding of his heartbeat lost in the unbearable noise in his skull.

At the door to his father's room he paused. In a fleeting microsecond the faces of Henry, Bob and Marva flashed and coalesced into a composite, a human chimera colored with features of his mother as his ravished mind sought reasons in the unreasonable, redemption in the irredeemable.

His hand grasped the doorknob. It turned freely and the door opened ajar.

Listen in. The sound of his father's breathing. Regular, slightly aspirated, as if in mild snoring. Enter cautiously. Walk lightly on the bare wooden floor. Was there a creak in the boards? Easy. Must not wake him. Sneakers might squeak. Moving without effort, machinelike. Knowing without thinking. Dark except for ambient light—moonlight?—filtering in through the curtains. Closer. Closer. Right hand firmly gripping the machete's throbbing phallic handle. The weapon's power of life and death flowing up his hand to the primitive reptile brain deep inside his skull. The killing center.

Standing over his father now. At his head. The man lying on his back, eye patch removed, eyes closed—they *looked* closed in the dim illumination, or was one eye open, and was it the good eye? The low snoring like the whine of an alleycat. The head enormous like that of Holofernes, severed by Judith... the barrel chest bulging beneath the thin white sheet. A Cyclopean monster. Pollution upon the civilized world. Abomination. This body needed to be destroyed for the benefit of all. Good victorious over Evil.

The machete raised overhead as if by itself. The buzzing inner pandemonium all-consuming, blotting out the world until there was nothing else, neither the breath of the wind nor the silent chatter of stars. The awful godforsaken din and its imminent blessed cessation the Yin and Yang of existence, the Antipodes, heaven and hell, earth and sky, to be united in the splitting of the foul melon. Was that one open eye watching him like some Poe demon?

STRIKE!

With immense speed and power the naked blade descended from on high like a guillotine toward the wicked head. Like an avenging raptor swooping to crush vermin. The executioner's axe. In a frozen mote of time moonlight diffracted off sharpened steel onto an eye, that ugly fiendish eye, open and watchful, a black cat in the window of the soul.

Fast as a coiled rattlesnake a muscular arm shot up and caught Scott at the wrist, blocking the downward thrust. The naked man beneath the sheet rolled to the side, forcing Scott's arm down and his body off balance, whereupon he sprang to his feet and threw the boy to the floor, twisting his

270

wrist until he cried out in pain and dropped the machete. In one motion Matt picked his son up and secured him in a headlock. As Scott kicked and twisted, Matt applied more pressure and the boy went limp. Matt carried him to the bathroom, threw him in the shower and turned the cold water full blast. Scott spit and punched at the drenching stream.

"Cool off, you degenerate," Matt shouted. "You want to kill your own father? Fuck you. I'm through with you, hear me? Worthless sack of shit. This is the way you repay me for bringing you into the world and raising you to be a man? You'll never be a man, scumwad."

Matt grabbed a handful of neckties from his bedroom drawer and wrestled Scott to his room. He threw him on the bed and secured his feet and hands to the bed posts.

"Filthy lying cunt-whore!" Scott cursed. "Filthy lying cunt-whore!"

Matt grabbed his son by the throat. "Shut up if you don't want to get gagged."

Scott went limp and Matt released his grip, whereupon Scott resumed kicking and shouting.

"Have it your way," Matt sighed, stuffing a tie in Scott's mouth and looping another around the back of his head. Scott struggled in vain.

"Fuss all you want," Matt said, "maybe by morning you'll be a human being again."

"Thank God you didn't kill him," Phil said, switching off the motor. "Let's get the hell out of here." Pulling his shirt collar over his nose and mouth, Mitchell reached over and opened the passenger side door and pushed the kid out.

Scott fell limp and silent to the cement floor. Panic stricken at the thought he'd killed him, Phil raced around and dragged him in the house, closing the door to the garage behind. The kid wasn't moving. Phil threw open the sliding glass door to the deck and ran out the front to hoist the garage door to ventilate the toxic fumes before racing back inside.

He found his young patient standing wide-eyed and dazed, holding the practice putter like a bludgeon.

"Are you okay?" Mitchell asked, freezing in his tracks.

Scott said nothing and shuffled forward Zombie-like. Mitchell backed away slowly, like they taught if you were confronted by a bear, for the kid seemed at an animal level of consciousness, acting on instinct. Possessed, an automaton.

He raised the putter high over his head and Phil dove for cover.

"Filthy lying cunt-whore!" Scott yelled at the top of his lungs and slammed the putter down full force on the sofa.

He hit it again. And again. And again. Yelling the same profane oath over and over again at the top of his lungs. *Filthy lying cunt-whore.*

Hoisting the club overhead and slamming it down with a violent thwack of iron on leather. Whipping the shaft like Judith's sword, as hard as he could. Grimacing, grunting. Tearing up that sofa with all his might. The whole room seeming to shudder and throb. Phil flinched and watched silently. A kid's psyche was worth more than a couch any day. Better that than his head. Maybe that couch needed to die anyway; he'd spent far too many nights on it in his own little self-absorbed world. Scott whaled on that helpless lump of furniture exactly one hundred times. When he was finished the golf club fell from his hands and he passed out on the battered couch. Mitchell spread a blanket over him and went to the bedroom to sleep in his own bed for the first time in a long while.

36

Joint in hand, Phil stood barefoot on the deck 'neath starry skies. Down the mesquite-and-chaparral-covered coastal slopes his eyesight ran to tree-lined streets of the city and beyond to tiny hobby-horse vessels bobbing in the harbor, and further still to moonlit waters of the coastal Pacific, the Channel Islands rising on the horizon like the spine of a sea dragon, the peaks of a submerged lost continent. The marijuana took him away to hidden realms of mind. What would his father say? His son clinging to his woman long after she'd gone. No father would approve of that. Hardly the stuff of war heroes. He was as messed up as the kid had ever been. Paranoid, self-destructive, cowardly.

Suddenly he went faint and grabbed the railing to avoid collapsing in a sprawl. What was this inner necessity? What was being asked of him? On impulse, he cranked up the hot tub. After all this time. What was this strange fear of water? While the redwood spa heated he stared out over the ocean. He wouldn't be going swimming out there any time soon but he sure as hell could take a soak in the goddamn tub. He and Karen had enjoyed sitting naked under the stars, glass of wine in hand. All this time and he hadn't been in. Just contemplating it sent his pulse up and scattered butterflies in his stomach. A dim awareness: His anxiety was an infinitesimal shred of the terror his father must have felt on that awful Pacific December morn.

When the water was hot, he slipped off his robe and stepped in. When Karen was around they would go anywhere together, do anything, take long swims in the sea, dive with sharks in the Caribbean, snorkel among giant tortoises in Costa Rica. Anything, as long as she was there. Her presence dispelling all fears.

Memories of his mother came to mind. She hadn't coped well after his father's death. He saw her face frozen in a mask of suffering, taut with insatiable longing, her eyes worlds distant when she tucked him in at night. Aching coldness in her voice.

Easing down into the water, something exploded inside him and he was seized with absolute panic. He lunged for the safety of the wooden siding, fell short and splashed headfirst into the water. Desperately he clawed for a handhold, choking on the murky hot water. It was like drowning. Heart pounding in his ears. So familiar this feeling. So primal a sensation. Hands on his shoulders, soft hands, the most beautiful tender hands that ever could be, the water warm in this small tub of terror. His mother's Della Robbia white marble face unmoved by emotion, unheeding of his cries as she ministered to him, eyes ever averted, directed off to the side, at her hands, the ceiling, anywhere but at him. What color were they, those beloved frozen eyes? What was she saying and why was her voice so sterile, her tone so accusative? What were her hands doing, those soft and tender monster hands, as they pushed his head under the water, holding him down until it seemed he would suffocate, then pushing him down again and again and again as he squirmed in impotent rage, sobbing-gasping-choking on the water, a hair's breadth from drowning... his mother finally wrapping him in a towel and carrying him bawling and traumatized to his bed, lungs burning, her barren eyes cursing him to Hell for having the same face as her dear man lost beneath the sea.

Phil clutched the edge of the hot tub and hung on. Holding on he was safe, but something told him safe was not the thing right now. It was time for boldness and confrontation and being a rebel. Just fuck it. Inhaling deeply and filling his lungs with oxygen, he submerged back into the stinging water until his head was under. Holding until he couldn't last another second he quickly stood up, bursting through the surface and sucking at the cool night air, gasping for breath and life anew.

He repeated the action many times before stepping free from the catacombs of frozen time and showering off the chlorine.

37

December 6, 1976—Exile from Jamaica

Matt and Scott Gallagher made their Air Jamaica flight to Miami the next morning. Scott had gone limp and Matt had had to bundle him into the car and march him onto the plane. Numb with hate, he wouldn't look at his father or speak to him. They flew first class, but as soon as the seat belt sign flickered off Scott fled his seat. The entire flight he paced the aisles or stood in the back, drawn deeply within, not eating, not smiling at the fetching stewardesses, obsessed with thoughts of revenge, the faces of Bob and Marva and Henry seared into his psyche. He agonized for Bob's safety with gunmen on the Rock trying to kill him.

But Marley wasn't on the Rock. Shortly after dawn that morning, he'd been hustled in the company of Neville Garrick aboard a private jet chartered by Chris Blackwell and flown to Nassau, Bahamas, where

273

Blackwell had a home and the West Indies headquarters of Island Records was located. The Tuff Gong, like Scott Gallagher, was in exile from Jamaica.

Touching down in Miami, Scott flipped out. As he and his father deplaned to wait out a three-hour layover before their flight to Washington, the restraints in his psyche burst. He broke away and raced through the terminal screaming at the top of his lungs, knocking into people and bringing security chasing after him with guns drawn. He ran madly about until as the cops closed in he rammed into a heavy duty plate glass window. The window didn't break but his head did, necessitating a short stay in hospital. His wounds weren't terribly severe but upon his release he had—for psychological more than physical reasons—forgotten much of what had happened in Jamaica and virtually all the painful events surrounding Smile Jamaica. Matt immediately put him on a flight to Los Angeles to live with his Aunt Sylvia in Santa Barbara.

He never heard from his father again.

With the CIA chief of station and several other outed case officers fleeing Jamaica, Operation Werewolf was left on shaky footing. An election eve hit on Michael Manley involving busting gunmen out of lockup in the Kingston jail and storming Jamaica House fizzled out and the next day Manley swept to victory by the greatest margin in Jamaican history, capturing 56.8% of the vote as the PNP won 47 of 60 seats in parliament. Despite the CIA's massive destabilization campaign and outright attempts at assassination, Manley had prevailed in a big way. Hope was born anew. Four more years for Michael's social programs to work their magic. And with Jimmy Carter coming in to office as the American president there seemed a real chance Manley's New International Economic Order would push through and in one fell swoop set the Third World on the path to a better future.

But like an angry pit bull the CIA just keeps coming. Even as Gallagher and the others were fleeing the island the new chief of station and case officers were flying in. The destabilization program was soon back in full swing—more psy-ops, more anti-Manley propaganda, more goon squads, graffiti-painters, strikes and shortages, more mayhem and murder. More making the economy scream and the people suffer.

The police never managed to track down the Hope Road shooters, but all indications are that they met with swift justice at the hands of dreads faithful to Marley. By gun and by machete, they paid the ultimate price for their folly. One reportedly hung himself and another was said to go insane and stagger off never to be seen again. Those at the top who planned the action would never be held accountable.

In the Bahamas, Bob Marley holed up and licked his wounds. Despite the triumph of Smile Jamaica, the Rastaman was sorely distressed that any Jamaican would take up arms against him and his family in the sanctuary of his own home. Rita and the kids and most of the Wailers gathered round and their love helped lift his spirits. Cindy flew in from London and discretely situated herself on nearby Paradise Island. Under balmy Caribbean skies their romance blazed hotter than an assassin's bullets.

Green grass springing beneath her bare feet, Beverley Manley walked in the community garden behind Jamaica House, pulling weeds and pruning branches in the morning cool. Michael was off jogging around the reservoir and she was glad for the moments alone. With the elections two weeks gone she could finally breathe again. The lush grounds at Jamaica House were a blessing but it was no place to raise a family. Soon they would move into a private residence on Washington Drive. But Bev's dream of a cozy nest in which to raise a family was due for a rude awakening.

Lost in her pruning, Bev didn't notice her husband striding intently across the grounds until he was upon her.

"Bev," Manley said abruptly, still in his jogging outfit.

"Mike, how was your run?"

"I need to talk to you."

"Of course. Let me just clip this last—"

"*Now,* Bev. It's extremely important."

"What is it, Michael?"

"Put the shears down."

"The shears?"

"Put them down."

Bev studied the tool dumbfounded a second before setting it gently on the ground.

"There we are, shears down," Bev's heart beating fast at the gravity in her husband's voice. Something was wrong, terribly wrong.

"I..." Manley began, paused, cleared his throat and looked down at his shoes. "I..."

"Out with it man."

"Meet me in my office. Ten minutes." Manley turned and strode away as urgently as he'd approached.

Bev ran up the back stairs, washed her trembling hands and donned clean clothes. What else could it be but another affair? It sounded like this time he'd gone off the deep end and fallen in love with the little whore.

She found Michael in his office sitting with his back to the door, still clad in his sweaty trunks and T-shirt.

"Mike?" She knocked lightly.

"Come in and close the door," he said without turning around.

Bev did as instructed and came around to sit across from her husband. She dabbed a tear at her eye, expecting life-shattering news.

"Bev, I need your loyalty now more than ever before. Can I count on you?"

"I don't know what you are asking."

"This is not easy for me."

"It's a woman, isn't it?"

"There is no woman," Manley shook no.

"Then what?"

"An agreement with the IMF is pending."

"The IMF? How can that be? You promised that... you... oh my God."

"Bev—"

"Lies! It was all a bunch of lies."

"Honey, I had no choice, the country is next to bankrupt. We are sinking into financial quicksand."

"You dare do this without coming to us on the leftwing? No secret negotiations, you said. 'Jamaica will never sell her soul to the IMF.' So Seaga was right all along."

"Seaga is a pestilence upon the land."

"Forty percent devaluation of the Jamaican dollar? Strict caps on spending?"

"That's the way it works if you want to borrow the money."

"At what price the money? For forty pieces of silver we sell our soul? Our programs are working. They are making a difference in people's lives, I see it everywhere I travel around Jamaica."

"Our programs arc working but the crisis of foreign exchange is dragging us into a morass from which there is no escape. We'll have to close the schools and lay off every industrial worker."

"*We?* It's *you. We* didn't go to the IMF—*you did.*"

"Listen to me. There is no capital to buy penicillin or rice or flour. People will starve to death. I'm talking weeks, not months. Days even."

"You said you'd fight. 'We are not for sale' shouted to the rafters. You *promised.*"

"My God, Bev, do you think if there were any other way?"

"I cannot sit here and listen to this any longer." Bev jumped up and stormed out.

Manley slumped into the big overstuffed chair, sinking so low it seemed he was a child sitting on the throne of his father.

Anxious to get back to making music after weeks of lollygagging around the beach, Bob and the Wailers left their tropical Eden for the cold climes of England. Cindy returned to London as well and the fires of young love flamed on. The band took a flat in Chelsea and worked at Island Record's Basing Street studio, Bob keeping a bachelor pad for himself in Earl's Court where he could entertain his beauty queen. The band was strengthened with the addition of blues-rock guitarist Junior Marvin, filling the gap left by the short-tenured Don Kinsey (who'd fled the island shortly after Smile Jamaica). Long and lean and sexy, Marvin added an element of showmanship onstage, sliding to his knees and blasting with his axe like it was a reggae Tommy gun. The Wailers were back in business. With Cindy as his muse, Bob's creative genius flourished, giving birth to tender paeans to love like *Waiting In Vain* and *Turn Your Lights Down Low* as well as militant scorchers like *The Heathen* and *Guiltiness,* all on the masterful *Exodus* album, a work of such incendiary brilliance that to listen to it once could change your life forever and which catapulted Bob Marley's star into the musical heavens alongside the greatest of the great in any genre, Sinatra, Armstrong, Dylan, Davis, Hendrix. *Exodus* would be judged by *Time* Magazine as the greatest album of the 20th Century and the *One Love* track chosen as the Millennium Anthem by the BBC, a song for the ages. It was during this period of exile in England that the Crown Prince of Ethiopia, Asfa Wossen, gave Bob the ring of the deceased Emperor Haile Selassie I and Cindy Breakespeare conceived a child by him, a boy who would be born with a good measure of his father's immense talent and who would be named Damian—aka Junior Gong.

After the 1976 elections the shooting and killing in Jamaica decreased as expected for a while but the tribal war between JLP and PNP was soon raging once more. Fidel Castro's state visit to Jamaica in 1977 added fuel to the fire. As the police cracked down with heavy manners, Claudie Massop and Bucky Marshall, according to legend, found themselves sharing a jail cell. Expected to end up killing each other, they conceived the idea of a truce. Why should ghetto brethren a fuss 'n fight when all it did was prop up the fat cats in office?

Word was sent through the grapevine to the leader of the Twelve Tribes, Prophet Gad, to contact Bob Marley about returning to Jamaica to perform at a Peace Concert that would bring the warring factions together. Marley agreed to meet Massop from the JLP and Marshall and Red Tony Welch, representing the PNP, on neutral ground in London. Massop guaranteed safety for Bob and his family in Jamaica, which Marley took as confirmation that it had been hoodlums friendly to the JLP that had tried to kill him.

Marley agreed to do the show and the One Love Peace Concert was announced for April 22, 1978—the twelfth anniversary of Haile Selassie's three-day visit to Jamaica in 1966. Bob was overjoyed to be home in Jamaica after a year-and-a-half absence. People by the thousands took to the

277

streets in celebration of his return, dancing and singing and drumming in wild Nyabinghi abandon. The airport was thronged with a multitude surpassed only by that attending the arrival of Haile Selassie I in 1966. Skill Cole came home from Africa. The venue for the concert was the National Stadium, the talent fabulous: Dennis Brown, Culture, Mighty Diamonds, Ras Michael and the Sons of Negus, Jacob Miller and Inner Circle, Big Youth, Beres Hammond and Peter Tosh playing with Word Sound and Power featuring Sly and Robbie. Perhaps the finest lineup in reggae history. Michael Manley, Edward Seaga and Mick Jagger were in the second row behind a phalanx of journalists as Tosh lit up a spliff and berated the police and government for a good half hour. (Months later Peter would be beaten to within an inch of his life in police custody.)

Wailers came on to top the bill around midnight before a large, ecstatic crowd. After a magnificent set Marley called Manley and Seaga up on stage. Manley came reluctantly, but as lightning flashed and thunder cracked in a clear night sky, Bob clutched their hands and held them overhead in a symbol of peace and national unity.

"Love and prosperity be with us all," Marley said in benediction to the masses. "Jah Rastafari."

The Tough Gong's gesture was heartfelt and noble but the truce was short lived. This was Cold War politics. This was destabilization and defeating socialism. The CIA wasn't singing Kumbaya and raising hands in symbolic unity. The streets of Kingston once again ran red with blood. Claudie Massop was gunned down in a police ambush after—it was rumored—he'd called Edward Seaga a warlord to his face. Bucky Marshall was shot to death at a Brooklyn nightclub and the two ghetto dons who'd overcome bitter enmity and gang rivalry to stage the historic Peace Concert—cooperating far more than the two political parties ever had—were erased from the scene.

On the 1978 *Kaya* Tour, Bob was presented the Third World Peace Medal by the African delegations to the United Nations in honor of his fight for equal rights and justice. The former rudeboy from Trench Town now recognized as one of the world's great humanitarians, though few outside Jamaica knew the full extent of his giving. Michael Manley the same year was awarded a United Nations special award for his efforts against apartheid and in 1979 the Joliot Curie Medal of the World Peace Council. At home in Jamaica, his efforts were less widely cheered as increasing violence and CIA subversion took horrible tolls.

Late in 1978 Bob Marley finally made pilgrimage to Africa, journeying to the Ethiopian fatherland. He hooked up there with Allan Cole, who was coaching the Ethiopian Airlines soccer team. In Addis Ababa, Marley attended a rally in support of the Rhodesian liberation movement led by Joshua Nkomo and Robert Mugabe against the racist white government.

Bob began writing the anti-colonial anthem *Zimbabwe,* which would become the spiritual center of the album considered by many to be his masterpiece, better even than *Rastaman* and the exalted *Exodus.* The album was *Survival.*

The following year Zimbabwe won independence and Robert Mugabe was elected the new nation's first black leader. Bob Marley and the Wailers were invited to perform at the Independence Ceremony on April 17, 1980. Bob underwrote the trip out of pocket to the tune of a quarter million dollars, flying in crew, professional PA system, even the stage. Prince Charles was on hand to oversee the lowering of the Union Jack in Rufaro Stadium in Salisbury, soon to become the new capital of Harare. "Ladies and gentlemen, Bob Marley and the Wailers" echoing over the PA system were very possibly the first official words spoken in the new state of Zimbabwe. Legions of freedom fighters, finding themselves outside the locked gates looking in, hand-grenaded the fence and flooded in as police fired tear gas, sending the Wailers running for cover. Half an hour later they resumed playing before ecstatic, newly liberated Africans. For Bob Marley it was the pinnacle of a career that was a nonstop highlight reel.

Some weeks after returning from Zimbabwe the Wailers began the *Uprising* Tour, selling out stadiums with crowds up to 100,000. In Milan Bob pulled an audience bigger by tens of thousands than had come out for the Pope the week before. After the tour, as Bob prepared to go home to Jamaica, a warning from the CIA was relayed to him through former manager Danny Sims. New elections were coming up and the violence in Kingston was spiking to horrendous levels, casualties far surpassing the already horrific numbers from the previous election year of 1976 as guns and cocaine continued to flood onto the island. A PNP member of parliament was gunned down in cold blood by police as walkie-talkies picked him up pleading for his life: "I am Roy McGann the Minister, don't shoot!" Five young people in the PNP Youth Organization, hardly more than children who had built their own clubhouse with scraps of zinc, calling it the "Socialist Joint," were machine-gunned to death in their beds in retaliation for PNP gunmen shooting up a JLP dance. The murder count would hit close to 900. It was Manley vs Seaga II and the CIA was not about to lose the second round of a fight this big. Marley was warned not to return to Jamaica or the '76 shoot-out at Hope Road would "look like a fucking skirmish." Marley took it to heart and stayed away. He never returned to Jamaica as long as he lived.

The lawlessness sank to new depths of depravity in a grisly crime in May 1980. A fire at the Eventide Home for the Aged on Slipe Road in Kingston killed 153 senior citizens under highly suspicious circumstances: phone lines cut, residues of petroleum-jelly explosives—not available in

Jamaica—and various other signs of arson found among the ashes. *Evidence of foreign influence.*

When in early 1977 Beverley Manley informed her PNP colleagues of her husband's intention to go the IMF route, the leftwing fought back. Prime Minister Manley received their grievances and ordered an exhaustive review of alternatives to taking IMF money. The best minds in the country came up with a set of proposals, but the crisis of foreign exchange couldn't be swept away with the magic of the slate board. His hands tied, Manley signed on to three major agreements with the IMF in the period 1977-79, with increasingly stringent terms. By 1979 Jamaica had become the largest per capita recipient of IMF funds in the world. The debt trap was sprung. Under an IMF regimen, the misery index grew ever worse. Unemployment, which Manley had early on made significant strides in reducing, rose sharply to 28%. Hateful graffiti scribblings of *IMF* came to mean *Is Manley Fault.* Manley would later describe having to go to the IMF as "unadulterated agony," claiming it set Jamaica back fifty years.

Jamaicans couldn't take it any longer. In the October 1980 elections, Edward Seaga was elected prime minister by a landslide. Taking office at the beginning of the Ronald Reagan era, Seaga opened his arms wide to American capitalism and was the first foreign head of state received by the new president. Aid and investment flooded in, Jamaica becoming the second highest per capita recipient of US aid in the world, after Israel. The island was primed to become a regional showcase of the wonders of capitalism. Over his eight years in office Seaga would sign on to six major agreements with the IMF and four with the World Bank—under much more favorable terms than those forced upon Manley—as Jamaica became the largest per capita debtor to both institutions.

This wondrous Caribbean Utopia was not to be. Beverley Manley's worst fears came to pass as the suffering of the Jamaican people rose to appalling new levels of wretchedness. In accordance with structural adjustment stipulations imposed by the IMF and World Bank, Seaga cut subsidies for basic food staples, abolished many of Manley's progressive programs and raised taxes, Jamaica becoming after Guyana the most heavily taxed non-communist nation in the region. By 1989, Seaga's policies had reduced the number of jobs by some 30%. Jamaicans flooded the embassies for visas to escape the misery and seek work in the US and UK. A long downward slide had begun as the nation's debt rose from $1.8 billion US at the end of the Manley era to $4 billion in 1988 to $6 billion in 2009 (in foreign debt alone, $13 billion total debt) as Jamaica became the most heavily indebted nation on earth on a per capita basis. Servicing the debt robbed crucially needed funds from health, education and other social programs, with no end in sight; by 2009, fifty-eight cents of every government dollar would go to paying down the loans (which never seemed to go away). If the Jamaican economy were a prizefighter he would be sitting on the stool bruised and battered, barely able to stagger to his feet and fight on on guts alone, the matter of his defeat long settled. Even Seaga became fed up and turned away from the bloodsucking IMF. Meanwhile the Jamaican dollar underwent repeated devaluations that would see a long continuous decline. Roughly at parity with the US dollar in 1976—actually, about 10% *stronger*—by 2012 its Jamaican counterpart would sink to $1 US = $87 J (making a $12,000 car in 1976 money cost more than $1,000,000 in 2012 currency). With Reagan in the White House, Manley's New International Economic Order—already weakened by Jimmy Carter's disappointing lack of support—was dead and buried. Free trade zones established under Reagan's Caribbean Basin Initiative brought sweatshops in which materials shipped in from the United States were assembled for re-shipment back to the US—cheap goods for the American people stitched together by Jamaicans working under dehumanizing conditions for wages barely adequate for bus fare and lunch money, the multinational corporations typically paying little or no local taxes for many years. Americans wore their smart Tommy Hilfiger and Brooks Brothers fashions in ignorant bliss. Jamaican agriculture was virtually destroyed as cheap, heavily-subsidized produce marked "USA" flooded in under the "free trade" banner which prohibited protection of Jamaican farmers through subsidy or tariff. Farms and dairies built up over decades of backbreaking work were ruined within a few short years, driven out of business, their half-starved cattle sold off for hamburger meat. Fresh milk a thing of the past, the children drank powdered milk from vast surpluses dumped by the US.

Finding an ally in Seaga, Reagan pushed hard on eradication of ganja. Cocaine flooded in to fill the void. Crack devastated the lives of countless Jamaican youth. Turning to drugs instead of the politicians as a source of income, the Kingston gangs raged out of control. When Seaga declared war on them, many rankings fled to New York and Miami, where the Shower Posse became a scourge, gaining a reputation as perhaps the most violent gang in the nation. The influx of guns, crack and cocaine wreaked havoc on (mostly black) communities now in the First World as well as the Third. Evil begets evil: The violence the CIA had enflamed in Kingston leapt like wildfire back to the United States—the suffering, as always, borne largely by the huddled masses in the cities.

Many of Michael Manley's reforms would benefit Jamaicans into the future. Early childhood deaths remained low, an outcome directly attributable to Manley's efforts—including his welcoming of Cuban doctors and nurses to the island; the infant mortality rate had decreased by almost two-thirds over the course of his two terms. Untold numbers of new mothers, many of whom were JLP partisans and blindly hated Manley, owed their children's lives to him and his programs. Had the international economic program he championed been achieved he might literally have changed the world.

In the end, then, the CIA achieved its aims, with Manley defeated and Marley in exile (again). Ultimate victory had taken four years longer than planned, but had never really been in doubt. The Agency simply wasn't going away and would not give up until it had won. Manley's great experiment was over, democratic socialism in ruins, the dream of lifting Jamaicans out of poverty and building a vibrant, viable society destroyed. Michael Manley himself was left a humbled if not broken man, alienated from and eventually divorced by Beverley, reviled by many of his fellow citizens rather than revered as the great hero he could have been had not his every step been slandered, subverted, sabotaged. Years later, when she came to understand the impossible situation Michael had been in—for he had kept most of it inside, even from her—Bev forgave, but it was too late to save the relationship. Manley married again, to his fifth wife but would succumb to prostate cancer at an age earlier perhaps than might have been, at 72 in 1996. His tomb would be located in Heroes Park *outside* the Shrine of Monuments rather than within in the company of the seven giants. Jamaica left to languish in Third World squalor as far into the future as the eye could see.

38
End of April, 1981, Santa Barbara

Emotionally drained, Scott pulled back into himself. He felt purged but raw and vulnerable and wrestled with enormous guilt for having attempted to kill his father. He devoted himself to quiet reflection, study of his psychology textbook and soaking up the professor's Tuesday night lectures. He didn't answer his phone or call anyone. Phil Mitchell dropped by and they smoked spliff but didn't get into heavy discussion, other than Phil opining that if Marley were the man Scott had been portraying all along, he would soon have gotten over his pique and not held any grudge against him. Within a matter of days he would have ceased blaming him for the sins of his father. Scott should have gone backstage to see Bob at his local concerts. It would have been all right. Marva, now that would be a tougher row to hoe. Too many shattered dreams there, Phil said. Better let it alone and move forward.

At Bad Wiessee, Bob Marley rested and followed Dr. Issels' regimen. A sharp unrelenting pain in his bowel required an operation, which helped greatly. You see a problem, you deal with it. The Big C was daunting but the Tough Gong was hanging in there, trusting in Jah Jah to see him through. There was so much to live for, a tour with Stevie Wonder in the works, Brazil, Japan, New Zealand, the whole world to conquer. Nobody loved life more than Bob Marley. He had recently been awarded the Jamaican Order of Merit by new Prime Minister Edward Seaga, Ziggy collecting the honor in his stead. Gong was cheered but the fight before him remained tough.

39

May, 1981, Kingston, Bad Wiessee, Santa Barbara and the World

The morning broke fair and mild over the West Indies. At Bull Bay east of Kingston, songbirds chirped in the trees, children played at childish games, a lazy rooster crowed hours behind schedule. At her home not far from the Rasta camp, Judy Mowatt sipped bush tea and nursed her infant child. The seed she had carried in her belly these nine months had been born healthy and beautiful, praise Jah.

She thought of Bob far away in Germany and her heart ached for him. His presence was strong in her across these many miles, the two mystics communing in unseen ways. He was less Bob to her now than he was Joseph the Prophet. A strong sense of peace settled over her... Jah would watch over her dear friend. The ways of the Lord were beyond comprehension, let Jah Jah will be done.

Suddenly, from a clear blue sky, a bolt of lightning flashed down from the heavens and slanted in through the window of Judy's house. Everyone saw it. As if directed by a higher force, the sizzling blaze flew straight at a framed picture on the mantel and radiated upon it for the longest time, like the exaggerated electrical display in a mad scientist's laboratory. The bolt knocked the picture to the floor and struck deep emotions in Judy Mowatt's heart.

It was a photograph of Bob.

One week earlier...

In Bad Wiessee, the tea leaves were painfully clear. Bob was getting weaker and weaker, his weight down to 70 pounds. Dr. Issels told him there was nothing more he could do for him. Bob called Rita in Jamaica and told her to bring the children and meet him in Miami. His mother too. It was time to go home.

On Sunday, May 10, Bob arrived in Miami en route to Jamaica and was readmitted to Cedars of Lebanon Hospital. His family gathered round and Bob spoke as a father to sons Ziggy and Steven, leaving them with words he hoped would keep them on the path of righteousness and ease the inevitable sufferings of a sometimes harsh world. Leaving the children behind was torture, but Marley took comfort in their health and wellbeing and knew Jah would watch over his flock. A great sense of peace settled upon him.

On the morning of Monday the 11th Rita went for carrot juice and when she came back Bob's eyes were closed.

"It's over," the doctors said.

Rita began chattering hysterically about Bob going "straight to the foot of the Father," as 600 miles to the south lightning flashed through the window of Judy Mowatt's home in Bull Bay.

Bob was with Jah. Joseph of the Twelve Tribes of Israel, Berhane Selassie the Light of the Holy Trinity, Tuff Gong, Skipper, Mr. Music, Voice of the Third World, the *likkle bwoy* from Nine Mile with the piercing stare who read palms, ghetto rudeboy become King of Reggae, humanitarian extraordinaire and one of the world's great champions of freedom and human rights, Robert Nesta Marley, O.M., had passed to his eternal reward.

Bob's body was flown home and lay in state in the National Arena for two days, his Gibson Les Paul in one arm, Bible in the other, the ring of Haile Selassie I on his finger. Rita had saved his dreadlocks, which radiation therapy had caused to fall off, and she'd laid them too in the coffin. At a state funeral, new Prime Minister Edward Seaga delivered the eulogy and Manley, now opposition leader, spoke as well. The Wailers backed by the I-Three played Bob's songs and a new generation of Marleys calling themselves the Melody Makers—Ziggy, Stephen, Sharon, Cedella—sang. So did Bob's mother, Cedella Booker. Tyrone Downie, overwhelmed with sadness, couldn't bring himself to attend.

After the funeral the coffin was loaded on a flatbed truck and the cortege set out for Bob's final resting place at Nine Mile in the lush hills of St. Ann where he was born. All of Jamaica it seemed lined the seventy-five-mile route to bid a last goodbye to this great hero. Nobody had ever seen anything like it. Young and old, teachers and schoolchildren in their uniforms, businessmen, laborers, Rastas, folks from all walks and stages of life stood as one to honor the man who had strove so mightily to bring them together. Sadness there was, but revelry and dancing as well, and music. Always, *always* music. When it hits you feel no pain.

"Sing," Bob had said to a broken-hearted Rita in those last minutes, when she despaired of facing the world without him. How could she go on with such a gaping hole in her heart?

"Sing, Rita," Bob said, "and everything be all right."

She did. And it was.

Three times zones to the west of Kingston, the hills of the Santa Barbara Riviera basked in the warm midday sun. Phil Mitchell sat out on the deck and read over a psychiatric report he had written on a patient. It was too sunny to read and Phil went inside to fetch sunglasses. As he was heading back the phone rang.

"Hello."

"Dr. Mitchell? This George at Black Star Liner."

"Yes, George?"

"Yuh hear the news, suh? Bob Marley die."

"Ah, shit. Just today?"

"Yes suh, at the hospital in Miami. Heading home fe Jamaica and never make it."

"That's a shame. I appreciate your calling."

Phil slipped his sunglasses on and went back out on the deck, his mind occupied with Marley's passing. What effect would this have upon Scott, who'd worked through so much raw psychic material lately? Would it find him defenseless and vulnerable? If Marley getting sick had hit him so hard, what would Marley dying do? Phil thought he better go look in on his patient. He got in the Porsche and headed down the hill, hoping his efforts with the kid until now would see him through, and that his own life's work was not in vain.

He punched the buttons on the radio for anything on Marley's passing. Mainstream AM radio had nothing, but switching to FM Phil thought he heard Jamaican patois being spoken and tuned in, catching the tail end of an interview.

"Listen fe the inner voice," the gravel-throated speaker said and Phil's intuition told him it was Marley. "The voice speak truth."

"That was Bob Marley," the DJ came on, "speaking in what may well be his last recorded interview. Today, Monday, May 11, in Miami, Florida, Bob Marley, the soul rebel, is dead."

Phil sensed an authenticity in Marley's voice, a simple honesty that rang like a bell. A deeper understanding of Scott Gallagher's enthrallment with the reggae star dawned. As the DJ spun *Soul Rebel*, Marley's words echoed in his ears.

Listen fe the inner voice. The voice speak truth.

Stan White had said much the same in different words—that healing came from the gut rather than the head, from a wisdom beyond rational thought. Like Jung's "healing power of the unconscious." Had he done enough to enable the kid to accept Marley's special qualities as projections of his own buried potentials and take Bob "back inside," reintegrating these lost elements of his personality? Or had he merely stoked the fires of the kid's rage and left him unable to cope, vulnerable to catastrophe?

Phil gritted his teeth and pressed hard on the gas. He hoped that Scott hadn't yet heard, that he could deliver the bad news himself and cushion the shock.

Scott was lying on the couch reading his psychology textbook when he had an urge to listen to FM. The instant he switched the radio on the news of Marley's death aired. His world went blank. Listening in stunned

285

silence to the tributes and memorials, he saw nothing except the handsome face of Robert Nesta Marley hovering before him like a disembodied god. He sank into the couch, crushed by fate, pain rising in every corner of his body. As if the cancer that had slowly been eating at him was surging into the final throes. A fatalistic calm settled over him as he imagined his bodily processes moving into their final catabolic phase, blood pressure plunging, cellular metabolism slowing, heart pumping less and less. As in Obeah and Voodoo, the mind could override autonomic physiological processes and shut them down. It wouldn't be long now. He was ready. Pain faded into numb oblivion as black crows flew up from the dying vapors of his mind, the life force seeping from his pores, he could feel it draining away. And if there really were an afterlife he would make Bob understand the truth and he would be forgiven.

Memories rushed to mind, of Bob and Marva and sweet Jamaica, beyond to the days in South America, Argentina, Chile, Victor with his guitar, the bombers flying over, soldiers with their guns, dead bodies in the streets. Further back still and there she was—his mother, her hair glistening like a black gold corona around the dazzling sun of her smile, eternal and undying, the pole star in his psychological heavens. He felt again the softness of her hands, the sweetness of her kiss, the soothing warmth of her breast. Then there was the strange box in which she lay still and cold, eyes closed forever, the sun turning ashen gray in the daytime sky. He gasped aloud and imagined Bob laid out in an awful box like that. He longed for parting words from Bob, some last precious wisdom that would push him up from despair or pull him across to the other side. Yet he knew that Bob had held nothing back, he'd laid it out there for all to see and there was nothing more to say. He'd come all this way only to learn what he'd known from the beginning.

There came the rumble of a car rolling up the driveway. Scott knew instinctively it was Dr. M checking on him. He'd heard the news and worried his patient might freak out. Didn't trust him to make it through. Scotty the Unable. Treated like a helpless child once again. Scotty the Defeated. Couldn't make it on his own. Scotty the Weak.

It pissed him off.

Out in the Porsche, parked behind the BMW 2002 which had formerly been his, Phil Mitchell pondered the wisdom of intervening in the kid's affairs. A therapist wasn't supposed to do that. The whole point was to get patient to sort things out on his own. Stand on his own two feet. If he went in and said he'd come to buy weed Scott would sniff it out. He'd see through it. Long term it might cause more harm than good. Phil stayed in the car and wondered if the kid had heard him drive in. Maybe he'd just back out quietly and leave. He sat and sought the wisdom of the balance.

He heard fumbling at the gate and stepped out of the car just as Scott came out.

"Hey, Doc," Scott said sadly.

"Hey. Guess you heard."

"How can Bob Marley die?" Scott plopped on the hood of the Beamer, wrapped his arms around his shins and rested his head forlornly on his knees. "It's like the moon falling from the sky."

"You all right?"

Scott shook "no" and buried his head into his knees.

"Wanna talk?"

"God it hurts," he sniffled and quickly caught himself, sucking up the emotion.

"It's okay to cry," Mitchell said. "They lied to us when we were kids."

"I can't believe he's gone."

"You can let it out."

Scott buried his head deeper into the crevice of his knees. He felt Mitchell's hand gently on his shoulder and raised his head, specks of teardrops at the corner of his eyes.

"We should keep on with the work until you consolidate your gains," Mitchell said. "You've come a long way, but…."

"It's okay, Doc," Scott said, brushing back the tears. He slid down from the BMW to face the man who had become so much of what his father should have been.

"This is going to hurt a long time," he said choking back the trembling in his voice, "but I'll be all right. Know why?"

"Why?"

"I don't hate anymore."

"Your father?"

"My father, the CIA, the system… maybe even myself. Change has to come, things are messed up for sure but hate's not going to win the day. It just hit me what I'm doing to myself. Hate rots you inside out."

"Like cancer."

"Yeah."

"Rasta deal with life."

"Yes I. Must deal with it as it comes."

"Bob's great lesson to us all."

"They say he never gave up no matter how bad the pain got. As much as he yearned to be with Selassie I the father he fought to his dying breath to stay with us. The gift is just too precious, this life we are blessed with."

"Boy, isn't that the truth."

"There's a little bit of wisdom in everybody, Doc. You believe that?"

"Absolutely."

"Maybe he finally got through to me. That little voice of wisdom."

"I'd say so."

"Wanna go for a run?"

"Now?"

"I'm afraid if I sit down the demons will creep back in. Gotta run it out. Consolidate those gains."

"I don't have sneakers."

"We'll barefoot on the beach."

"Let's do it."

Scott went in and put on his trunks and they drove to East Beach. Scott took off running and Mitch in slacks and shirt kept up a few minutes until Scott, supercharged with emotion, put it into overdrive and left him far behind. Phil fell back into a steady walking gait and watched as the kid became a stick figure halfway to the horizon—and suddenly fell hard to the sand, as if shot.

"Scott!" Mitchell yelled at the top of his lungs, though the kid was too far down the beach to hear. The voice of wisdom had come too late, it appeared. Failure, again, failure for both of them. Phil ran as fast as he could. All this work for naught.

When he finally reached his young patient, Phil found him lying on the sand doubled over in a fetal curl and sobbing in great shuddering paroxysms of guilt and pain and loss. Phil sat quietly and did not intrude as rivers of emotion gushed out and after many minutes the convulsions finally abated.

Without speaking they stood and hugged tight, as if instinctively knowing only human contact was appropriate at this moment.

"Thanks for helping me, Doc," Scott whispered.

"Thank *you*," Mitchell replied.

They walked to the car and on the way home stopped off for pizza and beer.

40

Summer 1981, Santa Barbara

"Yo, Dread."

Scott looked up from the flat tire he was repairing to see what the shop manager wanted.

"Take your break if you like," Terry the manager said.

"Almost finished here," Scott hollered, stuffing the patched inner tube back into the tire and the tire back onto the rim. The UCSB bike shop encouraged bike owners to do their own repairs under the watchful eyes of skilled employees, but Scott had gone ahead and done the work on this one. The bicyclist wasn't the handy type. Cute as they come too. Green eyes and flaming red hair to put Rita Hayworth to shame.

"Like your dreads," the young coed cooed coyly.

"Oh, thanks." Scott filled the tire with air.

"How long you been growing them?"

"Going on five years."

"Letting 'em grow?"

"Maybe. Then again I might just up and cut them. Don't want to get too stereotyped."

"I think they're cute."

"There we are," Scott said, holding the bike upright for the fetching lass.

"Thanks a lot," she said. "Do I pay you?"

"You can take care of it inside."

"Well, thanks again."

"So what's your name?"

"Bridget."

"Do you like reggae, Bridget?"

"I *love* reggae," she said.

In these days Scott experienced within himself an awakening of curiosity to know more about himself and the world. He wanted to study psychology and literature and economics and philosophy. History, definitely history, America, the Indians, slavery. The struggle of the Jews and Palestinians. Colonialism, capitalism, empire, the miseries and intrigues of Africa. The Greeks and Romans and the mythologies of native peoples for the ancient wisdom they preserved. Anancy and his stories. This thing called democracy. His mind filled with questions. Had Columbus brought development to the New World or only suffering? Were the CIA's dealings in Jamaica typical? What had happened in Argentina and Chile? Had fate been kind to Victor in Santiago? Every country he and his father had lived (beyond the few months in Venezuela) had been disrupted by a military coup during the time they were there. Another coup in Bolivia just last year, the "Cocaine Coup" they were calling it. It wasn't enough simply to have an opinion, you had to dig up the cold hard facts to get at the truth. Zack said that if he really wanted to get a handle on the *shit-stem* and understand what was going on in the world—beyond the moral wisdom he'd found in Bob— he should start with Howard Zinn's *A People's History of the United States* and Noam Chomsky's *Manufacturing Consent* and take it from there.

With the flood of returning memories, Scott remembered that Bob had renounced his BMW as being too much a symbol of Babylon materialism, a bad example to the youth in a poor country, and bought a

Jeep. He thus gave the keys to the 2002tii back to Phil Mitchell and told him if he didn't want it he should donate it to charity. Marva's phone number in Kingston flashed into mind, as did Henry's. He wrestled with calling them or getting on a plane and flying down there. Was Marva married now? Was she happy and well? Could the past be rectified? He knew he would go back some day. He would always sing, whether or not he became a big star or made a career of it. Then there was Suzette to think about and Bridget and all the other fish in the sea. The idea of enrolling in UCSB and studying psychology full-time appealed to him… maybe even going on to graduate school and becoming a psychologist like Dr. M. If nothing else to unravel further the incredible mystery of himself.

There was the matter of his father. He could be hiding behind a bush watching him right now or off in Timbuktu somewhere. Might be dead and buried. In any case, he had to find out. And if Big Matt was alive—Scott sensed he was—he would have to face up to him, stand tall before the one-eyed bastard and have it out with him. With words, not machetes.

The crossroads lay before him, stretching to unknown reaches, calling forth, beckoning. Knowing not which step to take, he was eager to journey forward into the mystery. Deal with life, yunno?

ONE LOVE -- THE BEGINNING

Agee, Philip. *Inside the Company: CIA Diary.* Bantam Books, 1975.

Black, Stephanie. *LIFE AND DEBT* (dvd), 1999.

Bordowitz, Hank (ed.). *Every Little Thing Gonna Be Alright: The Bob Marley Reader.* Da Capo Press, 2004.

Davis, Stephen. *Bob Marley—Conquering Lion of Reggae.* Plexus, 2011.

Dinges, John. *The Condor Years: How Pinochet and His Allies Brought Terrorism to Three Continents.* New Press, 2005

Dinges, John and S. Landau. *Assassination on Embassy Row.* Pantheon, 1980.

Gill, Lesley. *The School of the Americas: Military Training and Political Violence in the Americas.* Duke University Press, 2004.

Gunst, Laurie, *Born Fi Dead: A Journey through the Jamaican Posse Underworld.* Holt, 1995.

Jaffe, Lee (and R. Steffens). *One Love: Life with Bob Marley and the Wailers.* Norton, 2003.

Kaufman, Michael. *Jamaica Under Manley: Dilemmas of Socialism and Democracy.* Lawrence Hill, 1986.

Kinzer, Stephen. *Blood of Brothers: Life and War in Nicaragua.* David Rockefeller Center for Latin American Studies, Harvard University, 2007.

Landau, Saul. *"The Coup Lacked Professionalism."* Counterpunch, Jan. 11-13, 2003.

Manley, Beverley. *The Manley Memoirs.* Ian Randle, 2008.

Manley, Michael. *Jamaica: Struggle in the Periphery.* Littlehampton Book Services, 1982.

Manley, Rachel. *Drumblair: Memories of a Jamaican Childhood.* Key Porter Books, 2009.

Marley, Rita, with Hettie Jones. *No Woman No Cry: My Life with Bob Marley.* Hyperion, 2004.

Panton, David. *Jamaica's Michael Manley: The Great Transformation (1972-1992).* Kingston Publishers, 1993.

Steffens, Roger and L. J. Pierson. *Bob Marley and the Wailers: the Definitive Discography.* Rounder Books, 2005.

Taylor, Don. *Marley and Me: The Real Bob Marley Story.* Barricade Books, 1995.

Utley, Harold. *USMC Small Arms Manual*, 1935.

Volkman, Ernest and J. Cummings. "Murder As Usual." *Penthouse Magazine*, December 1977.

Webb, Gary. *Dark Alliance: The CIA, the Contras and the Crack Cocaine Explosion.* Seven Stories Press, 1999.

Notes

On some few occasions minor liberties were taken with the historical record in order to further the storyline of the novel. The fatal shooting of two Jamaican police guards described on pp. 35-36 actually took place outside the Cross Roads branch of the US Embassy. Secondly, Philip Agee's talk at the YWCA in Kingston—and the report of a flour shortage that threatened layoffs—in fact occurred on September 12, 1976 (p. 254). Agee's remarks are embellished here without significantly altering their substantive implications. Luis Posada Carriles is a known terrorist but his participation in the July 1976 bombings in Kingston is not proven. There is some controversy over whether Manley or Marley conceived the idea of the Smile Jamaica concert. Involvement of the CIA in the December 3, 1976 incident at Bob Marley's home seems likely if less than certain; there is no indication that the non-musical events at Smile Jamaica happened as depicted here. Can fiction be truer than the literal truth?

See David's Facebook author page or website (under construction) for "Dave's Faves" hotta than fyah reggae tunes, trips to Jamaica (music, work/helping, fitness, culture and more) and other fun stuff. On a personal note, David needs accommodations in pleasant surroundings to continue writing and is thus seeking a patron with space to offer. Post on his Facebook page: www.facebook.com/StirItUpCIAJamaica
Or email him at: stiritupBob@gmail.com

52043758R00164

Made in the USA
San Bernardino, CA
10 August 2017